KILLER DANCE

LOUISIANA SECRETS   BOOK THREE

PATTI CORBELLO ARCHER

Copyright

Introduction

Welcome to *Killer Dance* – book three in my Louisiana Secrets series.

You will find extraordinary characters and incredible relationships. Attraction and passion. Mystery and suspense. Depth. Intrigue. Great interaction. And action and thrills.

But most importantly, you will enjoy another wild love story dripping with sex appeal and desire.

And the story begins…

Patti Corbello Archer

Louisiana Pronunciations:

Atakapa (Uh-tak-uh-pah)

Calcasieu (Kal-Kuh-Shoo)

Atchafalaya (Uh-Cha-Fuh-Lai-Uh)

Crawfish Etouffee (Kraw-fish) (Ay-too-fay)

KILLER DANCE

Chapter 1

West Fork - Calcasieu River

Lake Charles, Louisiana

Ominous clouds crawled like fingers across the northeastern sky as Raven ran along the river. Thunder growled in the distance. Breathless, she stopped, glancing behind her. Lightning branched through the clouds. An unmistakable warning. Brushing hair out of her face, she turned and raced to outrun the storm.

In minutes, she neared a small bayou that snaked away from the river, weaving inland. And that's when she saw them. Dropping to her knees, she crawled silently through brush and weeds till the riverbank was only a few feet away. She peeked. Then slowly aimed the camera at a family of alligators she had been watching for a couple of days.

The mother was massive. Brooding. Lethally protective as her young swam nearby. And at only a few months old, Raven had already witnessed the viciousness of her babies' needle teeth at catching small prey.

With a quick glance to the southwest, Raven smiled. She'd made it just in time. The sunset was in place. Wispy clouds inlaid with shades of gold, orange, pink and purple danced across the sky. Fanciful. And perfect. Dusk and a storm. Beauty and the beast. She had waited all day for these intriguing shots.

Focusing her camera not far from the mouth of the bayou, she snapped pictures from various angles. Some shots showed the gators framed in the growing storm. Viciousness evident. Other shots showed them through the glorious colors of dusk. Just baby gators at play.

But before long, louder rumbles warned of the approaching storm. Looking up to check the weather, movement caught Raven's eye. A raccoon neared the river's edge. Gentle. Furry. Such a cute little bandit. He dipped black gloved hands in the river for a cool taste. Raven grimaced. Oh, no. And in the next second momma gator exploded from the wet darkness and snatched him.

Then the storm winds hit. Driving winds. Loud. Impressive. Leaves and branches blew through the air. Trees swayed in a wild dance. Raven stood to run for cover and locked eyes with a man on the other side of the bayou.

He stood in the trees as his long hair whipped in the wind. A brief premonition of danger caused chills to race across her skin. She touched the gun on her hip. But with another flurry of wind, her hair blinded her. Swiping it away, she looked again.

He had vanished. Heart pounding, she glanced around, then spun and looked behind her. Nothing but the storm.

Locking her camera away, she jogged to the trail. Lightning struck. The loud boom vibrated the ground hard. She screamed in reflex and ran. One, because of the strange man somewhere in the woods. And two, because of the natural lightning rods all around her. Trees as far as the eye could see.

She was wet by the time she found cover under a high bluff overlooking the river. The front winds had passed but it was pouring rain. Perching on an old stump, she texted home so they wouldn't worry.

***

Raven: Storm caught me. Sheltering under a bluff. Be home soon.
Callie: Stay hidden. Crazy lightning. Take pictures on sunny days.
Raven: What fun is that?

***

Smiling at Callie's remark, Raven put her phone away. Weather concerns were common since her one-time nature photography hobby had turned into a side business as an author. Which meant she was used to taking chances to get the perfect shot. Unusual ones. Exciting. Weather included.

And that thought reminded her of the man. She glanced down the riverbank. No movement. Hopefully he was long gone. Dismissing the odd encounter, she stared across the river through the rain…

Moving to Louisiana a few months ago had been necessary. She had sold everything but her car and personal belongings. Loaded up. And took off with her almost three-year-old son, Lance. And it had been the right thing. No. The only thing she could do.

She needed to start over. Be safe. Try to put it behind her. Besides, she knew she wouldn't ever live in that house again. Too many reminders. And there were too many well-meaning expressions of sorrow from neighbors and people she knew. She was not going to live like that...not raise her son burdened with a past no one would let go.

And the day she drove away, she'd never forget the relief at seeing Minnesota fade in the rearview mirror. It was finally over.

Interrupting her thoughts, the rain stopped as suddenly as it started. She looked up. Clouds were breaking to the east. Clear weather was coming. So was night.

Climbing back to the trail, she jogged home.

About ten minutes later, she ran out of the woods. Winded, she slowed to a walk and glanced around her new place. It was a sweet four acres along the river where the road ended, and the river continued. Gorgeous land. Secluded. The type of place she had dreamed about.

And it was right across the river from over 1,000 acres of Sam Houston Jones State Park. Originally named for the Texas folk hero who traveled these parts, it was now named to honor the state's 46th governor. But this part of the park was uninhabited. Natural. The trails, public park, cabins, camping, and picnic areas were further downriver.

She headed to the house, positioned uphill, safe from the dangers of flooding. Initially, she had intended to build a home. But then heard of an old Acadian home being auctioned in Lafayette, a city eastbound on Interstate 10 halfway to Baton Rouge. And intrigued, she'd bought it at first sight and had it moved. She restored what she could and updated the rest. It was a fabulous home full of character.

The house was white. Two-stories. Almost four-thousand square feet. Porches on all four sides. The wood was mostly tongue and groove oak in the floors, walls, and even ceilings. The rest was cypress. Some as columns and some as beams for ceiling bracing. There were six bedrooms. A large kitchen and den. Tons of windows with storm shutters and an amazing giant attic that was large enough to be a third floor.

Reaching the porch, Raven shucked her boots and turned them upside down on the rack to dry. Callie, Lance's nannie, opened the door. Lovely with olive skin, green eyes, brown layered hair, and all the right curves – she did not look forty-nine years old.

Lance ran out and launched himself into Raven's arms. Shocked, he said, "Momma! You're wet!"

"I got caught in the rain."

"Did you play in it?"

Laughing, she said, "You could say that."

"Nannie wouldn't let me."

"I know, baby. She's the boss." She winked at Callie as she headed inside, and said, "Just not my boss."

Callie said, "Yeah, but you need a boss."

Grinning, Raven patted dry with a towel then ran upstairs to shower, calling out, "I won't be long!"

***

Entering her bedroom suite, Raven removed her belt, pulling the 9MM pistol and 10-inch hunting knife out to dry. Then peeled herself out of soaked jeans, socks, and a tank top. Turning on the shower she caught a glimpse of herself in the mirror. She paused and stared at the scars, hating the reminders that she couldn't leave behind in Minnesota.

Then stepping in the shower, she let the water drain the image away.

Several minutes later, she was dressed in her favorite jeans. Ones that had so many holes they were barely pants, and a workout shirt. Then dried her long red hair absentmindedly. Her mind returning to the past.

Her life hadn't started out complicated, it had been amazing. Beautiful. Her father was a missionary with strong Irish heritage. Her mother was a nurse – with Native American heritage. A unique combination that had made growing up exciting by learning the best of both worlds.

And by the time she graduated college, she was a registered nurse like her mom - and a newlywed. Her husband, Beau, was a geologist. Half Sioux. A big man with an even bigger heart. And life was perfect.

For a while.

But in less than a year she became a widow at only twenty-three years old. And buried her husband before their son was even born. And as if that wasn't enough, a few months later life exploded. With deceit. Betrayal. And a living nightmare.

Her scars proved it.

But in time, prison doors had shut all that behind her and she could breathe again. Then her parents returned to the mission field. And after serious consideration she made plans to seek her future where some of her ancestors had begun. In Louisiana. She was an Atakapa descendant. The earliest Native Americans in southwest Louisiana.

Because of songs and stories her ancestors passed along, she had learned of her famous grandfather, Wolf, and his close friends, Pirate Jean Lafitte, and Sam Houston. But it was the national news last year that revealed Gabrielle to her – descendant of Lafitte – and gave her a link to her own ancestor.

And a place to start over.

After showing up in Louisiana this past July during a holiday weekend, she gained an instant family with Gabrielle, her husband, and their friends and relatives. They were amazing people. Safe. Impressive. Brave. Sincerely kind. And as thrilled as she was at the beauty of destiny after over two hundred years.

And only one day later, the call came from Brazil about Adam—

A knock on the door interrupted her thoughts.

Callie opened the door a crack, and said, "Hey—"

But Lance pushed through and ran in excitedly. "Come eat, Momma! Nannie fixed spaghetti! I'm starving…hurry…"

Laughter faded as they headed downstairs.

Steel from next door was sampling the spaghetti sauce when they reached the kitchen. Good-looking in his mid-fifties. Tough and muscular. Short gray hair. Gray eyes. A stubble beard.

He grinned and said, "I couldn't help myself."

Callie said, "Go ahead. At least your smile indicates it must be edible."

"Your food is always delicious."

"You're just hungry. I'm a passable cook. But Lexi, now that girl can cook." Glancing at Raven fixing Lance's plate, she said, "When does Lexi start?"

Raven said, "In two days. She's anxious to treat us to generational Cajun recipes she learned helping her grandmother cook. And gumbo is the first recipe on my list!"

Callie said, "Amen to that! Even the smell of gumbo is amazing."

After dinner, Lance watched cartoons and played with his dog while the adults drank coffee and relaxed around the table.

Pretty sure of Steele's reaction, Raven said, "I just wanted to mention that as the storm hit, I saw a man across the bayou. It seemed like he was watching me. Then he disappeared. Figured I would mention it in case the dogs' fuss when you make your rounds."

Steel frowned as he stood. Concerned. He said, "Did he threaten you?"

"No. Shocked me though. I mean, the storm was hitting, and he was watching. It was a bit creepy. Then he disappeared."

Callie said, "That's a lot creepy, Raven."

Steel said, "What was he doing?"

"Just standing in the trees near the trail."

"What did he look like?"

"Long hair and a beard. Kind of tall. I couldn't see facial features. It was just a quick glance through whipping wind."

"Did you notice weapons?"

"No."

"Have you told Adam?"

"I will. Haven't had time yet."

He nodded, heading for the door, and said, "I'm going to take a four-wheeler ride with the dogs and make sure he's not hanging around. Thanks for dinner...and your company ladies."

Their goodnights faded as he left.

Callie said, "Adam won't like that there was a man in the woods. Or that you haven't told him."

"I know. But the guy vanished. I didn't want him to get ten speeding tickets on the way home for someone who isn't there."

"True."

"Besides, he's not my guardian."

Laughing, Callie said, "You're kidding, right? He would turn into a raging lion if harm came near you. Just because you think you can hold back love doesn't mean you have. Droves of hot cherubs have driven arrows into both of you."

Raven gave her the look, and said, "Says the one who Steel pants after."

"Steel is hot." Callie fanned herself. "And I'm closer to acknowledging my interest."

"Interest is a pitiful definition, and you know it. You are into him. And Steel wants all things you. You are sexy. Fun. Beautiful. And Lance needs an uncle."

Laughing, Callie said, "You, my dear, are hilarious. *You* are the definition of sexy."

Lance called from the back of the sofa dividing the room, "Momma, what's sexy?"

Groaning, Raven hugged him and said, "It's a grown-up game."

Jumping on the sofa, he said, "Can I play the sexy game when I grow up? Does Adam play it?"

Callie laughed at the look on Raven's face.

Raven thought...oh yeah. Adam played the game. Way too well.

Then her phone rang.

***

Glancing at the caller, she smiled, walking on the front porch, and said, "Hey, Adam. How's your trip?"

"Did you really take pictures out in the woods during a storm?"

"No. It was before the storm. Then I had to wait it out. I didn't see you drive up. Are you back?"

"You're splitting hairs, beautiful. And no, I wish I was home. You wouldn't be in the woods alone in bad weather."

"What's a little water?"

"Don't forget lightning. Strange men – which we will discuss later. Did you miss me?"

"And if I say yes?"

"Then I'll wake you up when I get home."

Watching Steel ride near the tree line on the four-wheeler, she said, "What time will you get in?"

"Late. Close to midnight. Will you wait up for me?"

"Maybe. I guess you'll know when you get here."

***

Putting the phone down, she smiled – with a sigh.

Adam. The unexpected element to her new life was as hot as a raging bonfire. He was Gabrielle's brother-in-law. And the youngest of three brothers – Dakota and Sean were older and both FBI.

Now, it was obvious all three brothers were born with an amazing dose of Native American heritage that showed up in one generation. But Adam...he got that something extra. A sugared charisma. Oozing sex appeal. And a wild masculine focus that made trying to hold him at arm's length as useless as trying to stop the tide. He was coming in.

7

But when they'd first met a few months ago it had been as his nurse. He'd been in a wheelchair. Drugged. Fresh from a terrible accident in the mountains and jungles of Brazil on a mission trip. And he quickly wanted more than nursing. Then more than friendship. Then more than kissing. He wanted her.

And making a total alpha move, he bought twenty acres of land surrounding hers along the river. So, next door, his place was in the final stages of construction. And until his home was complete, he lived with them – which made it a very heated complication.

***

Long before midnight, Raven walked downhill to the wharf. Two of Adam's dogs followed her. Adam bought them first, for security, and second, for his new business, Quest Search & Rescue. One was a bloodhound named Hercules and the other a German shepherd named Atlas. The third was an Australian shepherd named Simba - Lance's guardian dog. They were all super intelligent and meant business.

As the dogs checked out the area around her, Raven settled in a double swing. Since they lived at the end of the road far from any neighbors, it was private. Peaceful. But of course, potentially vulnerable, which was Adam's main concern. But the beauty was undeniable.

Smiling up into the Louisiana sky, the storm had cleared as quickly as it came. Now stars blanketed the heavens, and the only sounds were nature. The lapping of the river against the bank. Owls. Hawks screeching. Crickets. Occasional splashes in the river as fish, reptiles, or mammals hunted for food or drink. And the gentle rustle of wind in the trees. In the far distance, she heard an outboard motor. Someone night fishing perhaps.

She loved sitting on the wharf. They all did. It was multilevel with a mini kitchen. Lights. Swings. Table and chairs. Firepit. A Tahoe sport boat was housed in dry dock one and Adam's new Diamondback airboat for Quest was housed in dry dock two.

Her phone dinged. A text.

***

Adam: Are you up?
Raven: I'm on the wharf with the dogs.
Adam: I like that you waited up for me.
Raven: You're lucky.
Adam: You missed me.

8

Raven: A little.

Adam: A lot.

Raven: You aren't supposed to text and drive.

Headlights flashed down the road.

Adam: I'm almost home.

Raven: I see you.

Adam: You are about to do more than see me.

***

Tingles raced from her stomach to every nerve ending. Adam wreaked havoc on her senses purposely. Day by day he revealed the hungry intimacy burning in him – breaking through her defenses deeper and deeper. But it wasn't a surprise. She had always known it would come to this. How could it not?

Chapter 2

Adam saw the dogs prancing around his truck as he rolled to a stop next to the wharf. He killed the engine. But his focus was on Raven as she walked to the edge of the deck and waited for him.

She was the most gorgeous woman he'd ever seen. Silky red hair hanging down her back. Heart-shaped face. Almost black almond-shaped eyes. Fair skin. And full lips that kicked up on one corner when she smiled. Like now. The fire and mystery in her eyes teased him. She was secretive. Private. And the sensual way she moved wrenched his gut. The ache for her worsened every day.

Raven watched as Adam touched the dogs as he headed toward her. The look of him made her groan inwardly. Always did. Tall. Dark. Wildly handsome with long black hair. Wearing tight jeans, boots, and a snug gold pullover. His hard lean body, powerful. Sexy. And the look on his face confirmed he had more than missed her.

He stepped on the deck and wrapped his arms around her. Body to body. He sighed at the feel of her against him and ran his hands over her back. Her arms. Shoulders. Under her hair to her neck. And smelled her. Nuzzled her neck. Felt the power of their voiceless hello enflame them.

Raven held him. Arms around his waist. Sliding up his back. Face against his chest. He was firm. Strong. His scent filled her. And her protective walls quickly crumbled as he handled her. Caressed her. Wooed her without a word.

Then he tilted her face and kissed her. Groaning as her hot sweetness set him on fire. He deepened the kiss, holding her face to his as passion danced between them.

Breathless moments later, he kissed her neck, her ear, and whispered, "I missed you."

A breathless giggle. "I can tell."

He touched her cheek. Her lips. And watched her eyes reveal what her mouth wouldn't say - aware that her emotional walls would be locked back in place soon. Hiding. Or thinking she was. But he knew.

Tucking her against him, he said, "Come sit with me. Talk to me. Tell me all your secrets and I'll tell you mine."

It worked. She laughed even though she knew what he was doing.

She said, "I doubt that you have secrets, Mr. Communicator. You, who address anything and everything."

He chuckled as they settled in the swing, and angled, to talk face to face.

She said, "Tell me about your trip. Your parents, Sean, and Samantha."

"Dad's arm is much better. The surgery and physical therapy will get him back in shape in no time. He's upset at himself for climbing the ladder. Mom too. It scared her half to death. Sean's able to go back and forth from Quantico to check on him. Samantha helps on the weekend. And Dad told me to tell you that none of his nurses looked like you."

Smiling, she said, "I told you I would go."

"I know. But everyone knew you needed to be here. If his injury had been severe, yes. But I'm glad it wasn't. I well remember you taking excellent care of me. There was nothing like leaving the jungle in agony and waking up at Dakota's house with you leaning over me – wanting me."

"Adam! You were my patient! I would never—"

"You saw me naked. Gave me a bath."

She hit him on the arm and said, "Nurses don't think of patients like that! You were in terrible shape—"

Chuckling, he said, "Easy Raven…I'm just picking. You were the epitome of excellent nursing care." He lifted his right leg and said, "The bite scars look atrocious, but my foot and leg work like they did before the accident. However, I won't be modeling this leg for the camera anytime soon."

"Did they ever send you a picture of the Anaconda that attacked you?"

"Not yet. The medical mission group will be back in the states soon, then send me some. I still hate that snake."

"I understand completely. You know, you never told me how you got involved in missions with two brothers in the FBI."

"Why don't we save that discussion for another time. It's a long story. Besides, I have a question for you."

"No surprise there."

"Why didn't you tell me about the man in the woods today?"

"I intended to. Steel beat me to it."

"Why didn't you call me right away?"

"Several reasons. You weren't here. You would be concerned and drive too fast. I only saw the guy once. And I don't answer to you."

He watched her and thought about what she said. There was a whole lot of information in those few sharp comments. She had drawn the line and watched him. He saw the flash ignite in her gaze. Temper. Temper. She usually hid it well. But going head-to-head with her wasn't how he wanted to handle it tonight.

Raven fought her temper. Ugh. She hated it when he treated her like she was weak – like she needed someone in charge of her. She was in charge. She had to be. She knew what it was like to fight to live. But he didn't know any of that. Not yet. He knew something had happened, but that was all.

Adam pulled his phone and chose a song on his playlist. A soulful love song played softly in the night air.

He stood and said, "Come dance with me. It's beautiful tonight and we rarely get time alone."

She felt her defensiveness ease off as he watched her. Intense…but crazy sexy.

Taking his hand, she said, "We need to have a talk soon about where you've learned all this strategy you use on me. I thought Dakota and Sean were the FBI profilers."

Holding her head against his chest, he said, "We'll do that. And at the same time, we can talk about what you're hiding from me."

She looked across the river as his words faded away. The dread of telling him what happened two and a half years ago, or 30 months, or 910 days – however you counted the time.

She closed her eyes as he held her. Tight. Safe. Possessive. But gentle. She knew he loved her. He didn't hide it. And he knew she loved him. His eyes told her that. His lips too. She realized she was quickly losing control…if she ever really had it at all.

After several dances, they headed to the house. And even though it was late, they shared a quick Coke and talked about deadlines for the next couple of days. It was a busy week with his new business.

Adam said, "I need to get an early start in the morning – I have a ton of things to catch up on, and the contractor will be at my place at seven. Then I have errands to run preparing for the Quest grand opening this weekend. So, in between those meetings, are you free to check out the bayou and show me where you saw the man? We can't have a threat lurking out there."

"We can head out there anytime you need to. I can work around you. At some point tomorrow I need to photograph a fox family I saw up in the hills. I've got an editor deadline to meet on my next book. Other than that, I'm free for whatever you need."

"Raven, is it possible you caught the guy in some of the pictures you took today?"

"What a great thought. I'll check first thing in the morning."

"Hopefully you'll see something. And I'll message Dakota to come meet us. We'll take the dogs out to track the guy."

"The FBI?"

"Might as well. If Dakota was your brother, wouldn't you get him to help you look?"

She nodded. Point taken.

He smiled and said, "Come on. It's late. Let me walk you to your room."

Puzzled, she said, "Why?"

The look he gave her told her. He pulled her close, and said, "Because I'm yours. Because I want you to get used to me near your bed. I want in it, Raven."

His directness slammed her. Passion first, as tingles shot up her body. And irritation because he intended to shock her - and put a stop to her delays. He didn't always show his alpha side, but there it was. She needed to think - and turning away, she silently headed up the stairs.

He followed with a smile. No. More. Delays.

Raven checked in Lance's room. He was sound asleep with Simba in bed with him. Simba wagged his tail at seeing Adam and got a quick hello rub.

Then they walked to her open bedroom door. Unsettled, she refused to look in her room. Just thinking about the bed behind her made it grow enormous in her mind. And for more reasons than her secrets. The anticipation made her squirm.

Adam saw the heat she fought. And the something else he didn't know yet. He lowered his lips to hers, determined to blow this door open between them as beautifully as he could. His breath brushed her lips. His tongue touched them. Raven's mouth opened.

Breath mingling, he said, "I'll get the marriage license this week. It expires in thirty days. But we'll sign it long before it expires…won't we?"

"But…there are so many things you don't—"

He kissed her.

13

She put a hand on his chest and pushed back. "Wait a minute…you haven't even asked me to marry you yet."

"I'm here. I've always been here. Ready. Waiting. Wanting. I've been asking – for months."

"I'll…think about it."

His grin flashed, then he kissed and backed her into the room. When she felt the bed behind her, she stopped. Her eyes met his.

He said, "I love you, Raven. Marry me quick."

And with a sexy glance, he was out the door.

***

Before dawn, Adam was drinking coffee, checking his phone, and watching the news when Steel arrived at the house from his barn apartment. Callie pulled sausage biscuits out of the oven. Raven came downstairs with Simba on her heels and let him outside.

Adam stuck a finger in her jean pocket as she passed by - and tugged teasingly. She faced him and mouthed *maybe*, then headed to the coffee pot. He smiled watching her walk away. She was going to make him work for a yes, although they both knew it would be.

But at some point, they had a lot of talking to do. She still refused to talk about her past, which told him it was huge. All he knew was what she told Dakota and Sean when they questioned her the day she arrived. Why had she left everyone and everything she knew and moved with a child to start over? Was she running?

She had agreed, sort of. She said she left Minnesota because of something. And that something was in prison for life. No parole. And no longer a problem.

KPLC's local weather station came back on, and Adam said, "Head's up everyone. They said earlier there's bad weather coming."

They listened to the meteorologist. A late season tropical system that went ashore south of Brownsville, Texas, popped back out in the Gulf of Mexico and developed into Tropical Storm Mason overnight. It was expected to make landfall again around Sabine Pass - the Texas and Louisiana border - tomorrow afternoon or evening. A storm surge, wind gusts up to 70 miles per hour, and heavy rain could impact southwest Louisiana. The only good news was that a coming cool front would quickly sweep it eastward.

Turning the sound down, Adam said, "I thought we were out of hurricane season."

14

The only Louisianian in the room, Steel said, "November storms happen. Not often, but they do. This storm won't have time to strengthen which makes it good for us."

Raven said, "I have a hurricane preparedness list. I'll check it and see if we need anything from town."

Nodding, Adam said, "I'll make sure Dakota and Gabrielle know too. We need to be ready to ride it out by noon tomorrow in case it speeds up."

His phone rang. Answering, he waved at Raven and headed out the door with Steel. The contractor had arrived.

***

Driving across the yard to his place, Adam was pleased at how well the house, business, and barn had turned out. He had chosen the rustic barn-style buildings so they didn't distract from the beauty of the land. The house looked like a fancy barn. Barndominium they called it. Two-story. Stained a rich caramel hue. Large windows complete with storm shutters. A huge double barn door entrance under a tall front porch.

Walking inside, he stepped into an open room. Massive. Tall, exposed ceilings with beams that held hanging lights and ceiling fans. The main seating area was in the middle. An L-shaped staircase led to the bedroom loft. The kitchen was underneath the loft with a long island that sat ten, including a commercial flat grill behind it, much like a hibachi setup. A fireplace, television, and den seating were at the east end of the room. A hall led to three guest bedrooms. An office was on the west end, surrounded by low decorative panels that you could see through. It hinted at privacy but overlooked everything.

The contractor called out from upstairs, "Come on up, Adam. Check it out. We are putting the finishing touches and need to know if you want any changes."

Joining him, Adam whistled at the transformation since he'd left two weeks ago. The master suite was simple and fabulous. Two walls were glass panels with views of the woods, corral, and part of the river. A skylight above. The bed was on a carved wooden base built into the floor, painted white.

The master bath had an open shower with multiple waterfall showerheads and a floor that looked like white sand. A double vanity held jeweled turquoise sink bowls. A jacuzzi filled the corner by the window.

Adam said, "Ben, this is perfect. Exactly what I had in mind. What's not finished? This looks ready."

They walked out of the master suite down the hall to three smaller bed and bath suites that were more traditional. Obviously for children.

Ben said, "The guys are finishing the closets and light fixtures in here and need to finish the shelving in the kitchen pantry and washroom. I think Steel found a few things we need to finish in the other buildings. His barn apartment is complete."

"Great news. When do you think the house will be move-in ready?"

"I'd say, upstairs by next Monday afternoon. And downstairs by day after tomorrow."

Adam said, "That's what I needed to hear! I'm holding the grand opening for Quest Search & Rescue this Saturday. All I need is downstairs. Oh - about the storm tomorrow, can the guys close all the shutters when they leave today – and make sure they don't leave anything outside to fly around?"

"We'll get it locked down tight for you. Everything is built up to hurricane code so your place will be fine. And Raven's was updated as well."

Adam headed downstairs and saw his brother pull up. Special Agent Dakota Nash. And there was no doubting they were brothers. Same olive skin, dark eyes, and long black hair. They met at the door with a powerful handshake and grins.

Dakota said, "Welcome home. Thanks for staying longer after dad's surgery. I know mom was thrilled."

"She was – and dad's doing good. Sean checks on them often. Besides, I had extra help here with Steel, the contractor, and Raven handling things. But you have a very pregnant wife."

"That I do! In fact, Gabrielle will come by later. But let me look around… Man, your place is great. I love the open space. And that snack bar and grill - I'm ready for steak already."

"You're always ready for steak."

"Hence my comment."

Chuckling, they headed upstairs to the master suite.

Dakota checked out the glass walls and said, "This bedroom is spectacular. Gabrielle is going to make me remodel when she sees this."

Adam chuckled. She probably would.

Dakota walked in the bathroom and whistled. "Where did you get the idea for all this?"

"I've traveled. Paid attention. And noted great features in places I stayed. I kept a list. You see the results."

"Obviously, you mean business for this bedroom. When do you plan to get Raven in here?"

"It won't be long."

"Be specific."

"That's the only answer you're getting."

Dakota looked at Adam thoughtfully, and said, "We're already in November. I bet you a grand you'll get married in December."

Adam smiled. Dakota would lose that bet. He planned to be Raven's husband by Thanksgiving. Next week.

Dakota said, "So, give me the spill about the man Raven saw in the woods."

Heading downstairs, Adam said, "Let's go to her house and I'll fill you in. We're hoping she caught him on camera. Did you hear about the storm…"

***

Across the yard, Raven ran upstairs to her studio. She had taken way too long looking at the hurricane prep information and knew Adam would be home before long to search the woods.

She did a happy dance entering her newly finished studio/office. Half of the room was set up as her photography office. And many of her favorite images were displayed on two walls in various sizes. Animals, fish, insects, birds, and scenery. Interesting images of people's faces showing emotion or curiosity. Native Americans. And lots of pictures of Lance.

One corner was set up as a play area for him with toys in a basket under a blue table. The opposite corner was her desk. And her computer had three large monitors – two of which hung on the wall. A long-padded bookshelf followed under the windows as a seat. And the other half of the room was simply a wall of mirrors and a bistro table behind the door.

Sitting at her desk, she removed the memory card from the camera and loaded it into the computer. Small images popped up on her desk monitor. Making them larger, she scrolled through them looking for the man she had seen. It took her a while since she had taken dozens of pictures.

It wasn't until the sky began to darken with the coming storm that she noticed the man. Looking at the continuous line of images that followed, it looked like he pulled up in a canoe down the trail and walked toward the bayou. Then turned into the woods. She figured he must have noticed her when the wind hit – probably blowing her red hair like a beacon. He stopped and watched her. No expression. No movement. And that was the end of the pictures. She enlarged the best view of his face and left it on the screen as she hurried to dress for a hike.

After braiding her hair, she slipped on hiking boots, and a black tank workout shirt. She hooked her holster and hunting knife. Then grabbing her camera, she jogged downstairs.

Lance had just shoved the last bite of pancake in his mouth when he saw her. He waved his empty fork and smiled as syrup dripped on his chin.

Talking with his mouth full, he mumbled, "Momma, Nannie fixed me pancakes."

"I see that!" Raven said.

She gave him a hug and he responded with a sticky kiss. She licked the syrup off her lip as Adam walked in.

He checked her out with a sexy smile and touched the skin exposed by her short shirt. He pulled her belt loop making their hips touch.

Dakota walked in behind him and said, "Hey, Raven. Wow. You better walk behind Adam, or he won't see anything but you."

Raven grinned at them. Always heckling. Typical brothers.

Dakota ruffled Lance's hair and smiled at Callie.

Raven said, "I found the guy in my photo shoot. I left the pics on my office monitor for you to see."

They followed her upstairs.

She showed them the consecutive pictures of the guy's movements and they studied the closeup of his face.

Adam said, "I don't see any change of expression. He just stopped moving. That could be not wanting to be seen or…"

Dakota said, "Interest."

Raven said, "Ugh. Not want I wanted to hear. Whose property is he on, Adam? I don't know the boundary line."

"Mine. My property continues another acre or more down the river."

Dakota said, "Do you know who lives beyond that?"

"Further down I've seen a big house on piers. An old one. But it's a good distance from the river and blends in. Like someone who doesn't want company. Ever."

Raven said, "Maybe it's him I saw."

Dakota said, "Maybe. But if it isn't him, he might want to know someone's roaming the area too."

Adam said, "And if it isn't the neighbor, we'll get Sean to run his picture and find out who he is."

Raven said, "You can get him to do that at Quantico?"

Adam smiled as Dakota said, "Oh yeah. We can do that."

They headed outside ready to hike. Adam whistled for the dogs.

Less than thirty minutes later, Adam and Dakota followed Raven across the log that served as a bridge over the bayou, to where the man had stood. They saw footprints and the dogs picked up his scent easily enough. Neither rain nor wind would wash that away. The only thing was…the trail didn't go far. The dogs stopped a short way down the riverbank. Landing scars were visible on the roots but that was it.

Adam said, "Why don't we head down to the neighbor's place and find out if he's the mystery guy or knows of him."

Dakota said, "Let's go."

Raven said, "Wait. Adam, I have a couple of spots around here to get pictures. I'm armed and have my phone. Rather than me follow you around, why don't I get the pictures I need before the tropical storm messes with my scenes. I'll hide and text if I notice anyone."

Adam climbed to the top of a nearby hill and looked around. He didn't see anyone. And the dogs weren't alerting at all.

He said, "Just pay attention to what's around you, ok? We should be back this way in less than an hour. Where are you headed?"

She pointed south and said, "There are wild pigs in a marsh less than thirty minutes away. And a fox family before that. I'll be near there. Message if you find anything. Don't call though. And I'll be careful."

Giving her a quick kiss, he said, "You better be…we have plans."

Pushing him to follow Dakota, she teased, "Maybe…"

***

The guys followed the dogs on the trail. They covered quite a bit of ground and noticed a lot of footprints. This was certainly a common walking area for someone, or a lot of someone's. Adam glanced south where Raven had hiked. He realized she seemed confident being armed, but he'd never seen her shoot. That suddenly bothered him a great deal. He should know her skills. He started jogging toward the neighbor's place.

Raven was pleased with her hike. She had found a beehive deep in an old oak tree branch that was cracked. She photographed the bees flying in and out of the massive branch covered with moss and ivy. The only sounds around her were the bees in front of her and the birds in the trees.

When she finished there, she headed through the woods toward the hills with tall grass. That's where she hoped to find the fox kits playing outside the den. It was an unusually late season for babies, but she was grateful for the opportunity to catch them in action.

Pausing to check the wind direction so they wouldn't catch her scent, she neared the edge of the tree line. She lowered in the grass and crawled slowly into the field. After a few minutes, she stopped and peeked to see if she could see anything. Nothing.

She waited several minutes, then heard them. And about fifty feet away, a tiny fox kit leapt in the air like he had bounced on a trampoline. She smiled. Now she knew where to go.

Her phone vibrated with a text.

***

Adam: Where are you?

Raven: I found the fox kits. Crawling closer now. Everything is quiet.

Adam: Ok. Keep in touch. And listen for trouble.

Raven: Yes, Sir.

Adam: Cute.

Raven: I thought so.

***

Raven peeked over the grass again and saw momma fox. She ducked and crawled closer. Then stopped and listened. All was quiet. Then she peeked again, continuing the process several more times until she reached a burnt tree.

Lightning had obviously struck the pine tree. And the top third of it had cracked and fallen at an angle – still leaning against the tree. She crawled to the base of it and stood next to the trunk. Now she had a clear line of sight.

Positioning herself, Raven snapped pictures. The three kits were adorable. They played like all baby animals as they rolled, fought, bit, jumped, and explored. Momma fox laid close. Ears alert. Listening.

A few minutes later, momma fox jumped to her feet and yapped sharply. All four darted into a hillside den near the base of a pine tree. Raven listened, unsure why they bolted. She didn't hear anything. She didn't see anything either. She waited. Listening.

Eventually, she heard grunting noises and looked around. Was that—

A man's voice scared her as he yelled, "Climb the tree! Hurry!"

And wild pigs burst out of the tall grass. They charged Raven in a fury. She screamed and fought to climb the slick part of the broken tree. The pigs scrambled underneath her, ramming, and gouging with their tusks what she was hanging on to. She slid down a bit. If they knocked the broken tree over...

A man ran through the tall grass, yelling at the pigs, and pulled a gun. The tree jerked under her as the pigs rammed it again. Raven screamed. She was going to fall. The man fired and one pig dropped to the ground.

Disbelieving, Raven watched the pigs charge the man. He stood steady, aimed, and fired. Another pig dropped. Then in shock, Raven saw the man toss the gun and pull a knife.

***

A good distance away, Adam and Dakota heard a man yell and Raven scream. They unleashed the dogs and ran towards the fading sound. And then they heard her scream again followed by two gunshots.

***

Raven knew the pigs would maim or kill the man with only a knife to defend himself. She dropped to the ground, pulling her pistol as she ran toward the fight.

The man brandished his knife against the two charging pigs and watched the red-haired woman run toward him with a gun.

He darted to the side so she could shoot. She stopped, aimed, and fired. One pig nose-dived into the ground. The last pig attacked him. It ripped into his leg with the tusks. Falling, he yelled and stabbed the pig as it shook his leg and stomped him. But the animal just squealed in rage and ripped his leg again. He screamed.

Raven knelt on one knee, aimed, and shot the pig standing over the man, once. Twice. Three times. The pig collapsed on him, blood everywhere.

She heard barking, then Adam's yell behind her as she ran to the man. She hit her knees beside him, yelling, "Hurry, Adam! Hurry!"

Adam reached them and lifted the dead pig off the guy. The smell was atrocious and the blood alarming. The man moaned and tried to sit up as Adam knelt on the other side of him.

Raven laid a hand on the man's chest, and said, "Lay still, please! I'm a nurse. I need to check your wounds," and hurriedly scanned his body. It was hard to find wounds on the man with the mixed animal and human blood, so she looked for exposed skin.

Dakota reached them, taking in the scene, and called 911.

Raven found blood pooling under the man's calf and said, "I need a tourniquet."

Adam handed her his shirt and a strap.

Raven told the guy, "I'm sorry. Take a deep breath - this is going to hurt. I've got to stop the bleeding."

He nodded and growled as she wrapped the two gashes tight. His eyes rolled and he was out. She checked his pulse. Steady. She pulled open his shirt and didn't see any other open wounds. They rolled him to his side to check his back. Nothing on his upper body but a few tattoos. Some scrapes. Bruising. Nothing else was apparently serious. The danger was blood loss.

Adam knew they needed help getting him out of the woods, so he called Steel.

***

Steel answered, "Hey, Adam."

"I've got an injured man in the woods and 911 on the way to the house. I need you to drive into the woods to us. Follow the old trail we found to the southwest. When it ends start blowing your horn. We'll find you. Bring blankets. Sheets. Towels. Water. And hurry."

"Anyone else hurt?"

"No."

"I'm coming."

Dakota took off through the woods in the direction Adam pointed.

***

Finally, there was quiet in the bloody grass.

Grateful that it wasn't Raven on the ground, Adam met her gaze over the unconscious man and asked, "Are you hurt?"

"I'm not. I'm just covered in soot. But I would have been if not for him."

"Is this the guy you saw yesterday?"

"I'm pretty sure it is."

"Where did he come from? What happened?"

"I was taking pictures by the burnt tree, and something spooked the fox. I heard grunting in the field grass but couldn't see anything. I was trying to figure out what it was when he yelled to climb the tree.

"I did, but the burnt bark was slippery. And the pigs kept attacking the tree to knock me off. He came running and shot one pig. The other three charged him. He shot another one. Then he threw his gun and drew his knife. I have no idea why he tossed the gun."

The man interrupted hoarsely, "My gun jammed."

Raven said, "I'm so sorry you were hurt. Thank you for helping me. We've got first responders on the way."

He grimaced and moaned at a new wave of burning pain.

Adam said, "What's your name?"

They barely heard, "Hunter," and his eyes closed again.

***

Dakota followed the sounds of the horn and found Steel in the truck. Grabbing supplies, they headed back at a quick pace.

Steel said, "How far?"

"About ten minutes. Did you tell Callie to watch for the ambulance?"

"Yeah. They'll be ready for us."

***

The dogs barked as Dakota and Steel neared Adam.

Raven and Adam wrapped Hunter's leg in towels. Then the guys moved him to a makeshift stretcher made of blankets. Raven gathered up Hunter's gun, knife, and her camera.

The stretcher was efficient but made traveling slower as they headed back to the truck. They tried not to jostle Hunter. He woke once but didn't stay awake long.

23

When they reached the truck, Raven and Adam climbed in the back. Dakota and Steel lowered Hunter's legs to rest on Adam and put his head in Raven's lap. It would be bumpy – and an unpleasant ride home if he woke up again.

***

They saw the flashing lights long before they exited the woods and stopped at the ambulance. They got him out of the back and onto a stretcher. He was pale from pain and blood loss. The paramedics checked his vitals and set up an intravenous line. And finally gave him a pain killer.

Dakota joined Gabrielle who had just arrived. And Callie held Lance who was fascinated with the flashing lights and commotion. Even a few passing boats on the river stopped to watch the activity up the hill.

Two deputies looked at the victim's face. It was hard to recognize anything with long matted hair and a beard splattered in blood.

The oldest deputy said to Adam, "I don't recognize him. Does he have identification?"

"I didn't check. His name is Hunter."

"Ok. We'll meet up with him at the hospital to fill out the report. Good job taking care of him."

Adam said, "That's what we do."

"What do you mean?"

"We are Quest Search & Rescue. Our grand opening is this weekend. Come if you can. And hopefully, not because there is another injury."

The ambulance took off, sirens screaming.

Chapter 3

After the first responders left, Raven smiled at Gabrielle. Beautiful with dark hair, amber eyes – and very pregnant.

Raven said, "How are you feeling?"

"Like a whale. But forget me. What about you? You were the one attacked. That was crazy."

"It was unexpected. I was watching for a strange man, not a herd of furious pigs. Much less, both."

Adam joined them, pointing across the yard at the barn, and said, "Raven. See that blue can on the top rail of the fence?"

"Sure."

"Do me a favor and shoot it off."

Laughing, she said, "Really? You decide to check out my shooting skills after the fact?"

"Come on, shoot, and let me see for myself."

Grinning, Callie covered Lance's ears. Raven shot once. The can flew off the fence. Shot again and the can jumped in the air. Shot the third time and the can disappeared in the brush. Cocky, she blew the end of the barrel and holstered her gun.

Impressed, he said, "Ok. You're all that. Now what about the knife?"

Callie headed inside with Lance.

Raven backed away from Adam, and pulling her blade, dropped into fighting stance. Legs apart. Arms spread. She brandished the knife, eyes locked on his. And Adam knew without a shadow of a doubt that Raven could fight. He nodded.

She sheathed her knife and joined them.

He said, "We do need that talk, don't we, beautiful?"

"We do."

Callie and Lance stepped back outside.

Lance hollered, "Mommy, was it a mean pig that hurt that man?"

25

"Yes, baby, but he won't hurt anyone ever again."
Adam high-fived Dakota, and said, "Not with momma shooting!"

Laughter faded as they headed inside for an update on Tropical Storm Mason.

The meteorologist predicted a five-to-six-foot storm surge in southwest Louisiana. Or higher if the tide was in. That would seriously threaten low lying homes, residents, and businesses near the intercoastal waterway, lakes, rivers, swamps, and bayous. Evacuation was underway in those areas already.

They were all grateful the surge wouldn't breach the hills their homes were built on.

Adam said, "The storm hits tomorrow around six p.m. if it stays on the same course. We need to prepare for wind and rain. Power outages. And flooding of the wharf and road. Steel, we'll need to haul boats and furniture to the barn. And the contractors are going to close all the storm shutters for us. Dakota, what about your place? We can come help."

"I'm good." Dakota said. "I'll just close the shutters and bring the boats uphill. Gabrielle's dad is going to give me a hand. But shouldn't we move your horses to his ranch? He's over an hour inland with a partially brick barn."

"Good idea."

"We'll come get your horses. Don't worry about it. You have two homes to see about, and a stranger."

A few minutes later, Dakota and Gabrielle headed home to the east side of Moss Bluff, along the main river where they lived.

Adam and Raven grabbed a quick shower and took off to Lake Charles to check on the victim at the hospital.

***

Steel followed Callie into the house. Lance ran upstairs with the dog. Cleaning up the kitchen counter, Callie didn't notice Steel behind her until she stepped back into him.

She said, "Oh! I'm sorry—"

And his arms slid around her. Caressing her. This was no accident. Callie looked at the stove in front of her thinking only of the hands holding her. And the body against hers. She'd known this was coming.

He kissed the side of her neck. His lips warm. No. They were hot. Open. His tongue touched her neck. She closed her eyes at the sensation spreading through her.

He whispered, "Turn around, Callie."

"Lance...is upstairs."

"Exactly."

Turning her to face him, he lowered his lips and said, "It's time..."

He kissed her. And in seconds, his passion. His hunger. And the touch of his body consumed her. Callie grabbed his shirt, not hearing the sounds she made. But he did.

All Callie knew was that the reality of kissing him was so much better than the dream.

And their relationship changed. In the blink of an eye. No...with one kiss. And touch. Seasoned with several months of waiting.

And then as only a child can do, Lance asked curiously, "What are you doing to my Nannie?"

Callie stepped away covering her smile. Steel grappled for an appropriate answer for a not yet three-year-old.

He lied, and said, "My lip hurt."

"Does it feel better now?"

Steel glanced at Callie. He winked and said, "It sure does."

Lance offered, "Momma helps Adam's lip too. Mine doesn't hurt."

Steel struggled not to laugh, and looking at Callie said, "I'm going to leave this with you and head down to the wharf. I need to start unloading the dock...and burn off some of this...heat."

Callie said softly, "Take care of that lip."

He laughed all the way out the door.

***

Adam stopped down the road not far from the house. Raven looked up from the hurricane shopping list as he unbuckled and leaned over. His lips covered hers for a long, passionate kiss as his hand slipped behind her neck, holding her there. The hurricane list dropped unnoticed to the floor as she reached for him.

He groaned and said, "Baby, I want time with you. I need time with you. We have no privacy."

"I know—"

27

"We could take a boat ride and hide down one of the cuts off the river. Or drive into the woods. Better yet, take a horse ride – on one horse. Or, better still, just marry me, Raven, and let me light you up."

Fire shot through her at his words. Almost uncontrollable. And she climbed across the console into his lap. Wildly kissing, they played with fire.

He burned. Painful now. Holding her face, he said, "Raven, tell me you love me…"

"I love you."

He smiled and kissed her. She'd finally said it. He said, "Tell me you'll marry me soon."

Without answering, she kissed him, then climbed back in her seat. He waited.

Giving him a hot look, she said, "Maybe."

He got out and walked to the water, waiting for the passion to ease. When he got back in the truck, he glanced at her. Still simmering.

She shrugged and said, "At least you know I love you."

He touched her lips and said, "Don't make me drag you to the altar."

***

A few miles down the road, Adam's phone rang. His cousin.

He answered, "Hey, Piper. Mom said you would be calling. Are you really moving to Louisiana?"

"I am. Lake Charles in fact."

"Are you serious?"

"Come on, Adam. You can't be that shocked. Louisiana wooed you, Dakota, and Sean down there. And they're already married. How close are you to tying the knot?"

Glancing at Raven, he said, "I'm holding both ends of the rope."

Laughing, she said, "Can you at least wait till I get there?"

"It depends on when you're coming."

"Friday. I want to be there for the grand opening this weekend."

"Terrific! Do you want to stay with us?"

"No, but thanks. I leased a flat in Lake Charles – one that Sean told me he stayed in. Besides, all of you live by the river and swamps with alligators and things that bite. Oh. Sorry. Didn't mean to remind you of the Anaconda."

"No problem. In fact, Raven was attacked by wild pigs today and saved by a strange man in the woods."

"Well, were in the world were you, hot stuff?"

"Dakota and I were looking for him."

28

"Obviously, you missed him. Was he that slick?"

"It appears so. We're heading to the hospital now to check on him. He's going to need quite a few stitches. And I have questions for him."

"I bet you do. Is Raven alright?"

"She's perfect."

Understanding his meaning, she said, "You have it so bad, cuz. But anyway, I need to run. I'll give you a call when I hit town."

"You got it. See in a couple of days."

***

Raven said, "Did I hear you right? Piper is really moving to Louisiana?"

"She'll be in the Lake Charles FBI office. I never expected she'd leave the east coast for here."

"It is a surprise. She's fabulous and I really like her. Though tell me, why is she single?"

"Not sure. Work focus, maybe. She's private. Skilled. And tough."

"She's going to thrill some Louisiana men."

"Heat them up more than likely."

Grinning, she glanced out the window as Adam pulled off the interstate following hospital signs through town. They were almost there.

***

They checked in at the ER desk. Adam and Raven followed a nurse down the emergency corridor to treatment room ten.

Opening the door, the nurse said, "He's—" and stopped abruptly, gasping.

All three of them could see the bloody, but empty hospital bed. Bloody clothes on the floor. And a stripped male nurse tied and gagged on the floor.

The two deputies from earlier walked up behind them, and said, "How's the patient?"

Glancing at a stunned Raven, Adam said, "Missing."

The commotion was immediate. More cops. Detectives. Forensic techs. And treatment for the new victim. After cops had finished taking Adam and Raven's statements, detectives and a forensic team followed them home. Their place now contained evidence of a criminal.

***

Raven showed detectives her photographs of Hunter, then emailed the links to the department.

Detective Rex Callaway, who was intense and athletic, and looked like he should be on a SWAT team, said, "Age is hard to determine from these pictures. After meeting him face to face and seeing him in action, how old do you think he was, Raven?"

"Thirty at the most with bright blue eyes."

Callaway said, "Adam. What can you add?"

"He was in good shape. Not so much a gym bod, but more outdoorsman. Active. Strong. Like me actually – but shorter."

Handsome Detective Maverick Patterson, who looked like he would be at home on a movie set, said, "Why was he on your land?"

"Good question. And one we wanted an answer for. Both times he was seen, he was by Raven."

"That's alarming. Did you notice any identifying marks like tattoos?"

Raven said, "Yes. A few Indian designs."

"Indian as in Native American?"

"Yes. I'm part Sioux and Atakapa."

Glancing at her red hair and fair skin, he said, "How many generations back?"

Adam chuckled and said, "Don't let her appearance fool you. She's all warrior."

Callaway said, "I see Native American in you, Adam. Easily."

Adam said, "Yeah. Sioux. My mother's a quarter. And wait till you see my brothers. We have our own tribe."

A few minutes later, they headed downstairs. Adam pulled the box with Hunter's gun and knife out of his closet and handed them to Callaway. Who promptly handed them off to forensics.

Adam said, "I guess you're going to want to check out the attack area in the woods. Want to ride a four-wheeler or walk?"

He pointed to the machines Steel left by the porch for them.

Looking at his suit and shoes, Patterson said, "Let's ride."

***

Rolling to a stop beside the bloody area where the pig battle had been fought, the detectives made notes as forensics took evidence.

Raven pointed northwest toward the bayou and said, "He came from that direction."

They followed a somewhat visible trail of smashed weeds, then followed footprints through the woods all the way to the bayou. A canoe was pulled on the bank. Nothing was inside except two paddles.

Adam said, "I don't know where he was held up when we crossed the mouth of the bayou. The dogs didn't even alert. Maybe he was downriver watching us."

The detectives studied the area.

Patterson pointed across the river and said, "Is that state park land?"

Raven said, "Yes. Follow the river right and it takes you to the public park area. The land across is uninhabited as far as we know. I've never seen anyone over there. Just fishermen on the river. And every type of watersport machine you can imagine."

Patterson called the Calcasieu Parish Sheriff's Department Marine Division to come pick up the canoe. Callaway called the ranger at the park. And Adam called Steel to bring the Tahoe boat. They were going across.

Steel reached them first and Adam and Raven boarded. Park Ranger Dubois showed up next and they filled him in on the issue at hand. Patterson stayed behind to wait on the sheriff's boat, while the rest rode across.

They rode along the bank from both directions looking for evidence of a boat landing on park land. It wasn't long before Adam and Raven called out to the others. They had found the slide marks where they presumed Hunter drug the boat in and out of the river. The ranger tied off, then he and the detective disembarked – making Adam and Raven stay aboard the Tahoe until the area was cleared.

***

Curious, Raven said, "Adam, how is it you are so knowledgeable about crime and evidence procedure? You know the right questions to ask. Comments to make. Even the way you process is professional."

"I have a Criminal Justice degree. I planned to follow Dakota and Sean into the FBI. But I—"

And the sheriff's department boat roared around the bend interrupting them. They pulled up to the bayou by Patterson and loaded the canoe.

Dakota wasn't far behind them and pulled up next to Adam and Raven on the park side of the river. They bobbed in the water waiting for permission to go ashore.

Adam said, "We need to talk about Hunter. We know he couldn't have been a random visitor. Once, maybe. Not twice. And certainly not after violently escaping the hospital. He was up to something."

Dakota said, "He was watching Raven."

Raven said, "Wait a minute. He saved me and got hurt in the process. What type of creep does that?"

Adam locked gazes with Dakota. The answer could be worse than the question.

Thankfully, Ranger Dubois called out, "All clear. Come on ashore."

Once on land, it was easy to see the drag trail of the boat. It went into the woods about fifty feet. They didn't find any trash. No clothes. No food. Very neat – too neat. No evidence.

Callaway said, "It looks like he just stored the boat here when he wasn't using it. How far to the park, Ranger?"

"Quite a way to the nearest trail. Then over a mile to the closest cabin. A little further to where the camping begins."

Dakota said, "What about unoccupied vehicles for a long period of time when the park is open."

***

The Ranger radioed, "Hey, Brad. Is that black F-250 pickup with the Montana plates still in the park?"

"Nope. Someone dropped off a guy and he took off about an hour ago. Why?"

"Call me if the truck comes back in the park. Do not confront him. Do you know anything about the driver?"

"He needs a bath and a haircut. Not much of a talker. He was limping today. Too much hiking I guess."

"Name?"

"No reason to ask."

"License plate number?"

"Nope."

"Anything at all come to your mind about him or the truck?"

"His canoe was missing. Oh. The word raven was scrawled on the back window."

***

Raven gasped, and Adam drew her into his arms – locking gazes with Dakota. This was personal.

Callaway called dispatch, "Put out a BOLO on a black F-250 pickup with Montana plates with the word raven on the back glass. Possible weapons. The driver has long dark hair and beard. Twenties or Thirties. Right leg calf injury. Wanted for questioning on an attempted kidnapping, assault, and theft. He left Sam Houston Jones State Park an hour ago."

Chapter 4

The clanking of metal keys was loud at the end of cell block G in Montana State Prison. Inmate 356782 opened his eyes and glanced back over his left shoulder. The guard he called Cash tossed a burner phone on the bunk and rubbed his fingers together, then moved on. He would come back later for payment. An outside text cost plenty.

Rolling over, the inmate pulled the phone in the shadows. Tapped the screen. A text popped up.

***

I found her.

***

Chapter 5

By that afternoon, Tropical Storm Mason was roaring and swirling across the Gulf of Mexico bearing down on southwest Louisiana. Which meant, get ready. Now.

At the barn, Dakota loaded Adam's horses in the trailer and headed north to his in-laws' horse ranch for safer boarding.

Adam and Steel finished moving the remaining items off the wharf into the equipment barn. Furniture. Portable kitchen. Tahoe. And airboat since the road and wharf would be underwater in less than twenty-four hours.

Heading back to the house to check with Raven on the storm supply list, Adam groaned as he stepped in the kitchen. The aroma of chicken and sausage gumbo filled the room. His stomach growled.

Callie laughed.

Steel walked in behind him, sniffing in appreciation. He said, "I didn't know you could make gumbo, Callie. You've been holding out on us."

"I wish! Lexi talked me through it over video chat. She felt sorry for us knowing we'd be cooped up during the storm without Cajun food. That is a chef sin in her eyes."

Adam said, "Then Lexi needs a raise before she even starts."

Lance ran in the kitchen, arms up, for Adam to hold him. Picking him up, Adam said, "What are you doing, little man?"

"Guess what? I saw Nannie help Steel's mouth."

Callie smiled and stirred the gumbo. Steel chuckled. They were busted.

Adam fought to hide a smile, and said "Was it hurt?"

"Yeah. Like when Momma helped you. I told them mine doesn't hurt."

Adam chuckled and said, "It's going to be a long, long time before yours hurts. Now tell me, where's Momma?"

"In her office. She wants the music to fix her. Can you help her?"

Setting Lance down, he said, "I hope so, little man. I'll go check."

Callie said, "Hang on a second, Adam. I have an idea. Steel, would you mind bringing Lance and me to the store to get supplies for the storm? Then we can give Adam and Raven a little privacy. She must need it if she told Lance that."

Steel said, "Sure! Let's go. I'm ready when you are."

Adam said, "Thanks, Callie. Steel. I appreciate that."

As they drove away, Adam locked the doors and headed upstairs.

***

Dressed in black leggings, a crop top, and barefoot, Raven shut the studio door. She needed to dance. Needed the release it always gave her. And it had been so, so long since she'd been able to really let go and get lost in it.

Since…that night.

She stretched and warmed up, then hitting play on *Fallin'* by Alicia Keys, she faced the wall of mirrors, posed, and closed her eyes.

Letting go…

***

Adam heard the music begin and tapped on Raven's door. She didn't answer, but that didn't surprise him since the music was loud. He loved the song she was playing and cracked the door open to see if she was at her desk. No. He stepped inside and looked behind the door.

And stopped breathing.

Raven's red hair was loose. Wild. Whipping around her as she undulated and spun her body to the music like she was part of each word…each note. Sensual moves to a sexy, hot rhythm poured out of her. Passionate. Flaming. Free.

He groaned, feeling the impact as her fire was clearly exposed in all its beauty. His muscles flexed in response to the call she made as she touched her body. Teasing a partner, she didn't even know was watching. Then time disappeared as he watched her get wilder as she crawled, jumped, and arched – offering everything. Then spun to land in a straddle as the last word faded.

Raven's chest heaved from exertion. Breathless. She opened her eyes and saw Adam. His wildness was barely restrained, and his gaze was hungry. So was hers.

36

He started toward her, and she stood, then ran. She leapt. Catching her, Adam groaned as her legs wrapped around him, holding tight. And he couldn't kiss her deep enough. Get close enough. Or touch her enough as she ran her hands through his hair and burned with him. The taste of wildfire.

Voice ragged with passion, Adam said, "I imagined ballet when you mentioned dance."

She laughed. Sexy. Throaty. And he kissed her again.

Several sweaty minutes later, she slid down.

He said, "I don't need a cold shower. I need an ice bath. And a wedding."

Turning her to face the mirror, he kissed her neck and said, "Look at us. Do you see what I see?"

She met his gaze. Of course, she did. And felt every bit of it too.

He saw it in her eyes, and said, "Say it, baby."

"Marry me, Adam."

Lowering his lips, he said "I thought you'd never ask."

A minute later, she said, "You knew I would."

"I did, but I didn't know when. So, how does a Thanksgiving wedding sound? Can you plan something in nine days? Or tomorrow if you prefer. I would be thrilled with tomorrow. You pick."

"I can plan a private wedding in nine days. But just so you know, my body prefers tomorrow."

He kissed her again. It was going to be nine hard days. Literally.

***

After dinner, Adam lit the firepit and went for the mail. Heading back inside, he saw Steel helping Callie with the dishes.

Tossing mail on the table, he said, "Raven still bathing Lance?"

Callie said, "Yeah. Go on up. But prepare to get wet."

Adam chuckled when he reached the second floor. Water was even in the hall.

Raven heard him, and said, "Help!"

Lance and the dog were in the tub and Raven was as wet as they were. He laughed as they splashed even more water on Raven.

She said, "Please wipe my face."

Adam grabbed a dry rag, wiped her face, then kissed her. He said, "Are they ready to be dried off?"

"Yes. Would you dry the dog while I tend to Lance?"

"Sure," and in short order, he was wet too.

Finally, boy and dog ran downstairs.

Adam said, "How about sitting around the fire pit for a while? Everything will be wet after tomorrow's storm."

"A fire sounds perfect. Let me change."

"I can help you."

"But then we'd have a fire in the house."

"You're right. I'll take my massive fire outside to sit around the tiny fire."

She giggled as he sighed dramatically and jogged downstairs.

Before long, everyone was seated around the fire, sipping hot chocolate. It was a beautiful night ahead of the storm. The dogs lounged around the fire too. Lance in the middle of them.

Raven glanced at Adam and said, "How long will it take forensics to check Hunter's DNA and fingerprints?"

"A day or two. I'm not sure if the storm will hold them up. But honestly, he wasn't concerned about leaving prints behind. He might not even be in the system."

"Which leaves us with nothing."

"Not really. They'll trace the gun. And look for the truck. His DNA may have a lead but that takes a while."

"They presume he's heading north?"

"I think so."

"But I don't know anyone in Montana."

"That you know of. With social media, work contacts, and past relationships, people move and don't always update their current location."

She thought of Zack. But he was locked away in Minnesota – a long way from Montana.

Adam said, "Can you think of anyone that would have intense emotions about you? Good or bad."

She turned and stared at the fire. They all knew that was a yes.

Callie stood, and said, "Hey Raven, we'll bring Lance inside and watch a movie or something. You have a lot to talk about and it's been a heck of a day."

Raven said softly, "Thanks, Callie."

Adam noticed the look that passed between the women.

Callie said, "Anytime. You know that. Take all the time you need."

***

Raven watched them head inside, then glanced at Adam. He decided to ease the tension and patted his lap. She gave him a tiny smile. He wiggled his eyebrows. She laughed and he pulled her over.

Snuggled together watching the fire, he said, "Let's talk. You go first."

"Finish your story. Why did you walk away from your degree…and your path to the FBI?"

"It took a while for me to realize I didn't want to spend my life focusing on criminals and trying to outthink them. I'm trained - even good at it. But I want the flip side of that profession. I want to spend my life touching people. Helping them. Letting them know someone cares. That's why you're a nurse, right? And why you took such amazing care of me. And even why you saved Hunter today."

"No wonder I love you."

He kissed her. Then said, "Once I grasped the depth of the career struggle I faced, I started going on mission trips. Working it out. Letting my faith lead me. My church sponsored my minister's license, so I had authority for weddings, funerals, hospital visits – that type of thing as I traveled. And in Brazil, I found my answer. Quest Search & Rescue was born."

"That's inspiring, Adam. It really is. So many people don't listen to the promptings of their heart and spirit. What else did you discover?"

"You mean besides wanting to be your husband and the father of our children – including Lance, our firstborn?"

Turning to him, she said, "The things you say…that's…beautiful. But yes, even beyond that."

He said, "Political public service. A place to listen to the people and make the laws. Fight for them."

Shocked, she said, "Are you talking about the presidency?"

Chuckling, he said, "Can we start with running for mayor of Lake Charles in a few years?"

Abruptly standing, she paced in front of the fire and said, "Adam, you need a better woman than me. Someone that hasn't been the wife of another man. A virgin. Sweet and innocent. Without a past filled with…with…so much that you don't even know yet. I'm just not pure enough for the good in you."

And with that, he'd never loved her more. He joined her, wrapping her in his arms, and said, "Your words prove you wrong, Raven. They are the epitome of purity. Now, walk with me. Tell me about Beau."

She blinked at his quick switch of subject. Especially that subject. She said, "Why?"

39

"Because I want to recognize him in Lance. Because I want to know what memories and qualities of him you want to see continue in his son. Because I want to know the man you chose."

Raven closed her eyes and said, "You are such an extraordinary man, Adam. What an unbelievably precious thing to think…much less say."

He led her toward his house, and said, "Tell me about him."

She paused as her mind returned to college. Way before the ugly, and then said, "We met my sophomore year in college. He was handsome. Intense, but fun. Smart, and about to graduate with a geology degree. A man of integrity. Thoughtful. And kind."

Smiling to herself, she said, "In many ways we were so different. I was working on my nursing degree and performing in dance competitions. A life filled with people and action. But Beau literally studied the Earth, camped with family and friends, and spent leisure time learning the wisdom and warrior skills from our Sioux heritage." She smiled. "He trained me well."

"He certainly did."

A few steps later she said, "We married near the end of my senior year and Lance was on the way not long after that. We had a good marriage. Loving. And worked great together building a home. A future.

"But then he began to have issues with me continuing dance competitions. Something worried him. Of course, being pregnant, I was about to have to sit out anyway, but he wanted me to stop competing right away. Permanently."

Glancing towards the river, she said, "After the shock passed, I got it. I had a male partner and we spent long hours in practice. And it wasn't only that - Beau felt I might not be safe for some reason."

Adam clearly understood Beau's point after seeing the sensuality of her dance. Unlocking his porch door and flipping on the lights, he said, "So what did you decide to do?"

Stepping inside, Raven gasped, and said, "Adam, your place is gorgeous! I can't believe all they've added since I've been here. It's so…you. Wild. Earthy. Exciting. I'm really impressed."

He bowed with a grin and said, "Thank you. I like that. Just wait till you see upstairs. But I'll show you that later – they aren't quite through. Now…back to your story. What did you decide about dance? Were you able to give it up for him?"

Nodding yes, she said, "I finished the competition we were already committed to, then quit. It was hard stepping away from it, but I had always known I wasn't going to pursue a dancing career."

"You loved Beau."

Expecting a quick affirmative, her sudden frown surprised him.

Shrugging like she was confused, she said, "I…always thought I did."

"What do you mean? Why question it now?"

"Because." She paused. "I didn't burn for him the way I burn for you. I can taste the love for you on my tongue. And, I know now, that I never gave him, what I know I will give you."

His fire was fast and hot as he groaned, kissing her, sliding hands down her thighs, backing her toward the kitchen island. Then lifting her on the counter, he pressed in.

Cupping her face, he said, "Raven, you didn't keep anything from Beau. Love isn't always the same. It isn't a formula. It's chemistry and there are a lot of combinations. What we have is amazing. Powerful. And we both know it's going to light us up. Hot, and often…"

They kissed passionately, lips and bodies connecting. With want. Anticipation.

Then breathless, she said, "But Adam…you need to know…there's so much I haven't said—"

His phone rang. He growled, and said, "Ignore it. Keep talking."

"I didn't bring my phone. What if it's about Lance?"

Groaning, he kissed her quickly, then checked the caller. Callie.

***

Hitting speaker, he handed her the phone, Raven said, "Is everything alright?"

"Lance is fine. He's sound asleep. It's…Raven, it's something else. You might want to come home."

"What is it? You're scaring me."

Adam tugged her toward the door, and said, "We're on our way, Callie. Be right there. Steel with you?"

Steel said, "I'm right here."

"We're on our way."

***

They rode the four-wheeler across the driveway that connected their properties and headed inside. Callie was at the table, contents from a large manilla envelope spread out.

Locking eyes with Raven, she said, "I thought it was junk mail. No return address and it was addressed to the household. But…"

41

Raven's gaze dropped to a large picture unfolded on top of the stack and walked closer. Her mind raced back to the past at supersonic speed. To…Zack. She looked at the beautiful picture of them after winning their last dance competition.

He had been holding her in the air in a barely-there black glitter costume. Their laughing faces were thrilled. And the picture screamed intimacy with one of his hands on her bare thigh, the other cupping her rib cage as he held her against him. She closed her eyes. It had been hard work. A terrific professional victory. But how had she not seen what was so obvious to her now.

Adam scanned the gorgeous picture of Raven in the arms of a blonde man, then focused on the article titled, *Deadly Dancer Trial.*

Raven smoothed the picture, then answered a question no one asked, "We met as freshmen in college at a dance audition. A competition group was looking for new talent and liked the way Zack and I looked together. They signed us up as partners.

"By the end of the day, we were friends. Before long, he was one of my best friends. I admired him. Trusted him. Confided in him. Trained with him. And we had a cool group that we hung out with.

"But things changed when we were sophomores. He wanted to take me out – just us. So, we went out twice. But…I couldn't get into a romantic zone with him. He was like the brother I never had. And I guess when he realized it wasn't going to happen between us, he backed off.

"We never discussed it, and I was glad. I couldn't imagine what he needed me for anyway. He was handsome and had women all over him. I never thought of it again. And barely a month later, I met Beau. We were an instant couple. And Zack and I continued competing."

Tired of looking at the picture, she pulled it off the table and let it flutter to the floor behind her. She looked at three white envelopes labeled uncreatively one, two, and three.

Adam checked the original package, and said, "Raven, there's no postmark. It wasn't mailed. We need gloves on. Let's take a little precaution in case they end up being evidence."

In a minute, gloved, Raven opened the first envelope and pulled out a handful of closeup snapshots of her. Zoomed in personal pics. Intimate. With obvious sexual focus as she exercised, sweated, strained, wiped down. Put on lipstick. Brushed her hair. Laughed. Licked ice-cream. Laid in the grass as she studied at school. Wet…in bikinis at pools, rivers, camping.

Glancing at Adam's concerned face, she said, "I've been watched, and photographed for years. How could I not know?"

"You probably know them. It could have been Zack."

"Surely someone else would have noticed him, or anyone else doing it – and said something to me. And these didn't come out at the trial."

"Everyone is aiming phones at everyone these days. There is no privacy anymore. No one would think a thing because they're busy taking pictures and videos themselves."

"Why am I getting them now?"

"I don't know, baby. But we'll find out. Do you want to check the next pack?"

The next envelope contained pictures of the woods. No people. Just a campfire. Trails. A cliff. Raven gasped and laid them on the table shuffling them.

Adam said, "What is it?"

Voice tight, she said, "Beau. He camped all the time…had a favorite spot. Let me see…" Then starting with the campfire, she lined the pictures up, ending with the cliff.

She glanced at Callie and said, "Is this what I think it is?"

Callie, Beau's aunt, nodded. A tear dripped down her face.

Raven swiveled and ran outside…across the yard…the scream welling up faster than she could run. Sliding to a stop she looked into the night sky and screamed. Adam had followed, knowing something was crazy wrong. But her sudden stop – and scream - hit him like a sledgehammer, drenching him in goosebumps. Then she struggled to breathe. Hyperventilating.

Stepping in front of her, he formed a cup with his hands over her mouth, and said, "Easy Raven. Think about something else. Relax. Just breathe, baby. Loosen your muscles."

Grabbing hold of his hands, she tried not to panic - her lungs burning from lack of air. He pulled her in his arms. Rubbed her back. Calming her down. She began to gasp. Tiny ones. Getting bigger. He soothed her. Whispered in the dark until she could take deep breaths. Softly, he kissed the top of her head.

She said into his chest, "Adam. Those pictures…the trail…the cliff…was where Beau fell. That's how he died on the camping trip. Why would someone send me those?"

Adam frowned, looking back at the house as warning bells went off inside him. Why indeed. His comforting tone belied his thoughts as he said, "We'll find out. Was Beau alone on the trip?"

"No. He always brought others. Teaching them about the land."

"Ok. Who all went on the trip?"

Stepping back as she wiped tears off her face, she said, "His cousin, a couple from the dance troupe, and Zack brought a friend of his from back home. Oh, and my dad. Beau had finally talked him into going. I was supposed to be there, but the doctor wouldn't let me. It was too far from a hospital since I was seven months pregnant."

Adam didn't like the thoughts lining up in his mind. He said, "Do they know why he fell?"

"The investigation concluded it was an accident. They found evidence he was scraping near the edge of the cliff for a sample. His work kit was nearby. No one saw or heard anything but his yell as he fell."

Adam nodded, and they headed across the yard. He glanced around. The darkness reminded him of secrets. They needed answers. His gut was shouting *warning* at the top of its lungs.

***

Back inside, Raven headed to Callie and hugged her, then said, "That was shocking. I'm sorry for the scream."

"No apologies, honey. That was a horrible thing for someone to do."

Steel said, "Adam, do you think Hunter left it?"

"It seems likely." Then picking up the last envelope, Adam said, "Why don't I open the last one, Raven?"

She nodded.

Adam could feel something hard as he opened it. He pulled out a folded brown paper and an arrowhead necklace fell out. Raven moaned when it clattered on the table. But Adam's eyes were glued to the three words on the paper. *Beau didn't fall.*

With that ringing through his brain, he watched Raven pick up the necklace. Her confusion quickly gave way to alarm.

Holding up the necklace, she said, "Beau never took this off. Yet they couldn't find it when they searched around his body. How is it that I'm holding it?"

Hating to, but having to, Adam showed her the note. Saw the blow of truth hit her. And she fainted. He caught her, carrying her to the sofa as Callie ran for a wet rag.

Raven woke as Adam touched the cold rag to her face. With sorrow filled eyes, she sat up and said, "Someone pushed him. It was bad enough that he fell. Now this…who are they? Where are they? Why did they do it? And why tell me now? To brag?"

He didn't tell her what he thought. Not yet. This pandora's box seemed like a distraction somehow. A deadly one. But he'd find out.

As they headed back to gather up the evidence, he said, "We'll get the answers, Raven. We'll catch them. And they'll pay for all of it. I promise."

***

As Raven headed upstairs, Adam called Dakota.

Dakota said, "Hey. You ready for the storm tomorrow?"

"Tropical, yes. But it seems we have a different storm already here."

"Besides Hunter?"

"Yes."

"Tell me."

"We received an anonymous packet in the mailbox today. No postmark. And it's all about Minnesota. About a trial involving Raven - and three envelopes of secrets. And they all mean trouble."

"I hear you loud and clear. I'm on my way. Give me an hour."

***

After telling Steel and Callie that Dakota was on his way, Adam headed upstairs to check on Raven.

Thoughts ran through his mind with each step. Obviously, Beau had been right. Raven hadn't been safe dancing. Had he seen something? And had he known he was in danger too? But there was also the fact that Zack had been in her inner circle. So, this had been a deep betrayal, leaving emotional scars and trust issues. No wonder Raven had been private. Hesitant. Secretive. Inner scars were vicious.

***

Raven looked out the window in her bedroom. Still. Silent. Knowing it was past time to tell Adam. His FBI family would get the trial info immediately. Then they would delve into Beau's death. She leaned her head against the glass and sighed. It was suddenly raining Minnesota misery in Louisiana. Why wouldn't Minnesota ever go away?

She heard Adam's footsteps.

45

Adam saw her at the window. Slipping arms around her, he said, "Come lay with me."

Leaning back with her on moss green floral shams, he said, "Dakota will be here in a little while."

She nodded against his chest, then said, "There's so much to tell you. I don't know where to start. And it's all ugly, Adam. I don't even want it in your head. It even tastes bad to say it."

"Raven, there's nothing in your life that I don't want to know. You need me to know. Why don't you start with what the jury decided, and we'll go backward?"

Glad for a place to begin that wasn't emotional, she said, "Zack was found guilty of first-degree rape, attempted kidnapping, attempted murder, and assault with a deadly weapon. All the other charges are minor compared to those."

He clenched his jaw at the pain exploding in him at what Zack had done to her. Groaning, he squeezed her, wishing he could take it away, and said, "Raven…baby…that's horrible. I'm sorry seems so meaningless. Shallow. I would rather just kill him."

She needed the love rush she got at his seemingly vicious words – and slipped her arms around his neck. There was nothing like knowing someone loved you. Cared about your every breath. And wanted to protect you. Defend you. Be your hero.

After a few moments she leaned back to look at him. Seeing the pain and rage in his eyes, she said, "How much do you want to know?"

"All of it. Anything. Everything."

"Ok. But remember this was a trauma, Adam. A crime. It's not who I am – it's just where I've been. Like your trauma in Brazil. Our life, what we feel together is more powerful than any memory I've got. Tell me you get that. I'm not a victim. I *was* a victim. Anything else is just a reminder."

He kissed her lips. Her cheeks. Nuzzled her face – and understood her request. She needed him to listen to her story. That's all. It wasn't fixable.

Nodding, he said, "I hear you, baby. I'm listening."

She sat up, cross legged, next to him but not touching. She needed a little space.

Beginning, she said, "Lance was an infant. Not quite six months old and the joy of my life. Beau had been gone for almost eight months by then and though I was still grieving, I was trying to find my new normal.

"I worked shiftwork at the hospital and Callie took care of Lance. We had lots of friends. Activities. Family. Church. And rarely did a day pass that someone didn't stop by the house with food, a hug, a movie, a joke, or an invitation.

"So, it wasn't unusual that one Sunday afternoon, the dance team dropped by to visit and encouraged me to return to competition. They had been on me about it, and it was getting harder to say no now that I wasn't pregnant. And Beau...

"Well, anyway, the excitement of dance seemed like a beautiful light at the end of a long dark tunnel. So, I finally agreed to meet them at the studio the next night. Callie came and got Lance, and I went to practice for the first time in almost a year. I was thrilled but a little rusty. Practicing in the living room wasn't the same as a studio.

"But anyway...after we warmed up, Zack and I worked on a couple of routines that we had danced before, since I didn't know the new stuff. And I'll be honest. It was a little awkward. It had been a long time since my body had been handled. Zack was attentive, working with me like we had before, giving me time to warm up. Eventually, we got into a good rhythm and things felt like they used to. For a little while.

"But after looking around me. In the mirror. And at the others. It wasn't normal anymore. I was different. I wasn't eighteen. I was a widow. A mother. A grieving wife. And I didn't want my body to be touched. And I knew dance competition was over for me.

"I apologized to Zack, but I knew he was upset."

Raven slid off the bed and paused, getting ready for the next part. Adam followed her off the bed and leaned against the wall. He waited, gut clenched. This was it.

She said, "I took a quick shower after I got home. Zack was leaning against the bathroom wall as I stepped out. I screamed, grabbing a towel. My mind raced for answers to questions blowing up in my brain. I was drowning in vulnerability knowing he had chosen this moment for that very reason.

"Smiling, he took the towel from me, backing me into the shower. He explained how much he loved me. How he had tried to do things my way. Waited as long as he could. Done everything humanly possible to get me to love him. And what thanks did he get after all these years? I quit on him. No more dancing. So now we were going to do things his way, and as soon as Lance got home, we were leaving.

47

"And though I heard him, my mind struggled to grasp everything he said. I think it was the fear for Lance that finally broke through the shock, and I panicked. Fought. Screamed and busted his lip. Cut his cheek. And he got…turned on. Not surprising since I was naked. And he unzipped his pants. But I shoved him. We busted through the shower glass, falling on the floor. I slipped in blood and glass as I scrambled over him - and ran to the kitchen.

He raged and followed. I heard his shirt ripping and glass crunching under his shoes. I barely got the snack bar between us. But the look on his face told me it wasn't for long – he was totally out of control. He jumped across the bar, picked me up and slammed me on the counter near the stove. It knocked me out.

"When I came too, he was raping me. I reached behind me for something. Anything. And felt the knife block. I ended up pulling a steak knife and sliced him across the chest twice and he backed away. Then he grabbed a knife.

"As I tried to get away, he hit me in the face. I landed on the floor, dazed, my jaw on fire. He sat on my stomach and carved a Z across my chest. All the while explaining that I was his. Always had been. Always would be."

Walking to the window, she looked outside seeing nothing but the past, and said, "Then he dropped the knife and began to rape me again. And while he was distracted, I grabbed his knife and stabbed him in the neck."

Turning to look at Adam, she said, "I learned later that Callie and Lance reached us first. Neighbors were screaming and pointing at the house. Cop cars with sirens and flashing lights were coming down the road. Terrified, she had raced in and found us. Her and Lance were both screaming when someone got them out of there."

Adam said, "Raven…"

She said, "Blood was everywhere. But I didn't kill him. A hair closer and the knife would have severed his artery. I didn't see him again till court almost a year ago. He never said a word in his own defense. Just watched me as the court drama played out.

"My broken jaw had long healed by that time. My chest too – the tenderness gradually fading. But the worst part of the cuts…"

She started unbuttoning her shirt as she watched him. "I didn't get to hold Lance for a long, long time. That's why I haven't had plastic surgery. Because I can't hold him if I do. So, this…remains…"

Her shirt slid to the floor. She pulled off the sports bra she always wore. And pain tightened Adam's throat like he was locked in a vise. Raven's breasts were amazingly beautiful. Full. Perfect. But around them was a massive Z

48

scar. A jagged line across the top. Diagonal through the middle. And the final line across the bottom.

Adam had her in his arms before she said another word. Her feet left the floor, arms tight around his neck.

He said, "I'm so sorry. So, so sorry, Raven. But scars…baby…we both have them. Even God has scars. You are beautiful to me. Your breasts. Your body. Gorgeous. And I can barely see the scars. Honestly. I just see you."

He felt her sob, but it was silent. Her tears dripped. She whispered, "Are you always perfect?"

"Just when I'm with you."

And he kissed her. Soft as a whisper. His wet cheek brushing hers. Tears mingling.

A few moments later he said, "Where is Zack?"

"Minnesota Correctional Facility – Faribault. But he won't get out. No parole."

"He's dead if he does. And I'll get Dakota to confirm he's there. Often."

Car lights flashed through the front window.

He said, "Dakota's here…but I need to do something first."

And trailing his lips along the whole Z scar, he marked her with his touch. Then said, "He was wrong, Raven. You're mine. You always will be."

Chapter 6

The man known as Hunter was making great time. He'd already cut his hair, popped out the blue contacts, and shaved his beard. He'd dumped the black truck with Montana plates at a rest area before he left Louisiana. Then stole a white Toyota at a gas station while someone ran inside to pay. He'd left that car north of Houston, then nabbed a dented silver pickup outside of Dallas just after dark.

Now he was cruising the backroads of northern Oklahoma in an old black Jeep. Grimacing, he popped a few more pain pills he'd snatched off the nurse at the hospital. He sure hadn't planned to take a hit from the wild pig for the woman. Or for her to save him. But unexpected things happen. His job had been to find Raven. Not connect. But the pigs altered the plan.

He glanced at the clock. Almost midnight. He'd have to hide and catch a few Z's before dawn because he still had eighteen long hours to drive. This party was just beginning.

Chapter 7

Back on the river, it was close to nine p.m. by the time Adam and Dakota set up the research office in Raven's studio. Sean was live on video feed from his home in Quantico working with them.

Raven's wall monitors were filled with scanned images of the items from the mailbox. And the wall of mirrors worked perfectly as evidence boards. Folding chairs and tables sat in front of them as a work area. The printer Dakota brought with him was spitting out paper nonstop.

Gabrielle, forced to stay off her feet by Dakota, helped sort paperwork at the tables. Raven looked closely at the pictures and notes taped to the mirrors.

***

They heard Sean's phone ring over the video feed.

Sean hit speaker so they could hear, and said, "Hey Jackson. Thanks for the quick response. Is Zack still in the Minnesota Correctional Facility?"

Everyone turned to watch and listen.

Jackson said, "No, actually. His family has money and influence. They got him moved to Montana State Prison, closer to them. They live in Idaho.

"When?"

"Two months ago."

"Did you make sure he was there at last head count?"

"Yep. He was cozy in his bunk an hour ago."

"Would you do a daily check for me?"

"Sure."

"I owe you."

"Doubt that. I still owe you for half a dozen things. Forget it."

***

After Sean ended the call, Adam said, "That Zack's in prison is a relief, except that Hunter's black truck had Montana plates. And to me, Montana plus Montana equals no coincidence. Zack's up to something."

Dakota said, "Or someone wants us to think he is. I think we have plenty to begin a formal investigation."

Sean said, "I agree. I'll contact the director in the morning. In the meantime, we'll get a head start going through the trial docs, as well as Beau's accident investigation. We need to know everything Raven knows - yesterday."

Adam said, "I'd like to have local Detectives Callaway and Patterson in the loop because of their investigation on Hunter. And you know Piper will be here before the weekend. She called me today to tell me she's assigned to Lake Charles."

Dakota said, "She let me know. And told me to stay off her turf without her permission."

Sean said, "I got that call too. She knows us well, obviously. We better tell her before she gets here so she's ready to hit the ground running."

Then glancing at Raven as she ran her fingers over the edge of one of the pictures she was studying, Sean said, "Raven…"

She turned to face the monitor.

He said, "We'll need you to tell us about Beau and Zack. You know more than you know you do. We need profiles of them as they relate to you. The dynamics of their personalities and the relationships that existed. And I'm sorry. It won't leave much room for your privacy. We need everything. Are you ready for that?"

"Who's ready for that? I'll just do it." She sighed. "I keep trying to put Minnesota behind me, but it won't stay there. It makes me nervous for Lance."

Adam joined her at the pictures and said, "What are you looking at?"

She pointed to the right corner of a cliff picture, and said, "I see a mark here, but I can't read it. A few pictures have the same marks."

Using the scanned copies, Dakota zoomed in, and said, "It looks like we need to check all the pictures."

Watching the big screen, Raven said, "Is that an R?"

Adam said, "It certainly is."

Dakota began to zoom in on the edges of all the pictures. They waited, writing down each letter he found. In the end, they had found fourteen letters. M, T, E, N, I, N, E, O, V, R, A, N, D, O.

Sean said, "Hang on. Let me plug them into a decoder. It'll be faster."

Five minutes later, Sean held up a list of words and phrases the fourteen letters formed. He had circled one phrase. *I'm not done, Raven.*

Raven threw up her hands and said, "Not done with what? Beau was killed. Zack's in prison. It seems done to me. Or is this just mental torture? Could Zack have sent this picture packet just to find a way to continue his sick dream? Or is someone else talking to me? Hunter?"

Adam said, "Zack absolutely could have had it sent here. But there could be other variables. Other players. Like Hunter. Zack can't do it alone."

Dakota said, "We need to go through the trial evidence. Pictures. Videos. And Beau's info. Then we'll be ready to get with you, Raven."

Sean said, "On that note, Raven, please check your personal videos or pictures that include Zack. Especially in the time preceding Beau's death. Including dance practice. Zack might have hidden his feelings in competition, but not otherwise. Gather what you can. We may notice something you don't. Gabrielle can help you."

Adam slipped his arm around her and said, "And can you get us names and pictures of the campers that went with Beau on that trip?"

She nodded solemnly.

He kissed her forehead, and said, "I'm right here if you need more help."

Gabrielle said, "I'm game, Raven. Ready whenever you are. We can work on the porch, in your bedroom, on the wharf, or wherever. We can bring coffee or wine."

Dakota said, "No wine for you."

Raven winked and said, "What about a margarita?"

They all needed the laughter that followed.

Adam's phone rang. Detective Callaway.

***

Adam answered, "Hey, Detective. Any news?"

"Yes. Louisiana State Troopers found Hunter's black truck in Louisiana just before the Texas border. It's a stolen vehicle. A drunk left it outside an Oklahoma City nightclub a week ago and it got swiped. The plates were stolen off a different truck two weeks ago in Montana.

"So that leaves us tracking a specific string of vehicle thefts heading back north. We presume to Montana. No one fitting Hunter's description has been seen. He doesn't keep a vehicle long, and he's traveling fast.

"Oh. One last thing, his fingerprints are not in the database, and it'll take a few days for DNA results. But hopefully he won't return to Louisiana. Ever."

Adam said, "Agreed. But more is going on. Someone left a threatening packet to Raven in our mailbox about her past in Minnesota. So, my brothers and another family member, all FBI, will be handling an investigation. We plan to keep you and Patterson in the loop."

"I hate to hear about trouble for Raven. Someone's going to get shot messing with y'all.

"A better definition is dead."

"That happens when people get stupid. Ok, then. Batten down the hatches for the storm and we'll see you after the river goes down. I'll fill Patterson in.

***

After the call, Dakota said, "Hunter's good at what he does. There is no way this is the first time he's done this work. He's prepared. Shifty."

Sean said, "Agreed. And I think he'll be back. I find it hard to believe this was just a mailbox run. But if he's driving back and forth to Montana, it'll be days before he's back – especially in winter. That gives us more time to figure out what he wants and why."

Adam said, "That doesn't make me feel any better."

"Me either. But at least it lets us know there's another plan out there."

***

Downstairs, Callie, and Steel watched the late weather update on the storm that would hit tomorrow. The dogs were laid out in front of the television. Their ears twitched every time they heard Adam's voice upstairs. Steel looked behind him toward the kitchen. Callie stood nearby. Solemn. Nervous. She hadn't relaxed since opening the mail earlier.

He had an idea, and said, "Callie, can you help me with something?"

"Sure. You want some coffee or a snack?"

Rubbing his neck and shoulder, he said, "No, I must have pulled a muscle working out last night. It's been catching on me all day. Would you please—"

Stepping behind him, she said, "Sure. Show me where it hurts."

Watching him touch both sides of his neck and shoulders, Callie said, "Got it," and leaning over the low-back sofa, she began to knead and soothe his warm skin.

Steel hid a smile and groaned at her touch. Especially, since his mind took him where he preferred to go with her.

Callie felt guilty. She hadn't noticed Steel hurting today with all that had been going on. He was always physical, and she took his impressive strength for granted. And she certainly admired his body. Well, more than admired.

She glanced down at his bulging chest, flat stomach, and... She forced her gaze back to the television. He worked hard to keep in shape - even offered her to work out in his private gym with him. But while she believed his offer was sincere, he was also sincerely interested in way more than that. They both were. But today's kiss was just the beginning. There were things he didn't know that were important to her. Even at their age.

Steel rolled his neck sideways as she slid her hands up and down his neck, across his shoulders, dipping down his chest and back. And before long, he smiled...pretty sure she had forgotten about the weather. The change in her touch told him that.

Drawing her around to sit by him, he kissed her palm and said, "I like you touching me, Callie."

She felt the impact of his lips and words. Then anger flared. "You played me."

"Not in the way you mean. I did it for you. You've been tense. You needed to relax."

"So, I get to massage you because I am the one tense? Shouldn't it be the other way around?"

"My thoughts exactly," he said, and laying down on the sofa, pulled her on top of him.

Amazed at the hot intimacy of his move, she pushed back, looking down at him.

He drew her close, holding her face against his chest, and said, "Relax, Callie...let me..." and his large hands caressed her back. Her waist. Her arms and shoulders...wanting to roam lower.

Callie listened to his heartbeat. Felt the strength of his hands covering her. And stilled – loving it. But she refused to think of their intimate position. Liar, she told herself. How could she not think about it? He felt so good. His hands roamed lower.

She said, "Easy, Steel. Don't you dare massage anything else."

He raised her chin, his hot gaze on hers - his thoughts clear.

She said, "Don't even think about it. You lied to me."

"Not really. I was thinking of both of us. My body does hurt. Just lower."

Her eyes widened in shock. Mouth agape at his directness. She said, "I can't believe you said that. That was—"

Pulling her closer, he said softly, "Hot...I know. See what you do to me?" And he kissed her.

Callie felt his hunger and the pit of her stomach exploded in desire. He heard the sound in her throat and pulled her tight, making sure she didn't miss anything, and felt everything. Then he shifted, and they were on their sides, belly to belly, his leg draped over hers. Holding her there. Their breath mingled and Callie thought of the others upstairs.

She said, "Steel..."

"Callie..."

"I'm not—"

"You are."

From the staircase, Raven said, "I'll say she is," and her and Gabrielle giggled as they startled the entwined couple.

Callie moaned, sitting up, mortified at being caught. Again. And said, "There is no privacy anywhere. It's embarrassing. I'm not sixteen."

Raven said, "No truer words have ever been spoken. A hill on the river full of singles and no place to make out."

Steel chuckled as he stood, offering Callie his hand. She frogged him on the leg and he laughed.

Raven said, "Oh guys, thank you. We needed that chuckle. Don't be embarrassed, Callie. But it really was steamy. The dogs are sweating."

Gabrielle laughed so hard she had to sit on the stairs, holding her belly, trying not to wet herself. Steel whistled for the dogs to follow and headed outside laughing. Adam and Dakota jogged downstairs to see what was going on. But Callie's pink face and Steel's laughter told the tale.

***

After the women went to bed, Adam gave Dakota and Sean Raven's firsthand account of Zack's attack. Minus the personal sharing between them. It was critical that they heard about it since valuable details always got left out of the formal statement in the file. After trauma, pain, fear, and shock, so many things distracted and interfered with a victim's thought processes.

But later, the victim might recall or say something that impacts everything. So, with fresh input on her story, they compared it to the original, and were processing their findings.

Adam said, "Zack was more emotional during the attack than the formal statement indicated. Almost like he was the one betrayed. Desperate. Not simply a predator."

Dakota said, "I agree. He didn't go there with the intention of killing her."

"No." Sean said. "He went to claim her. Rape her - though he didn't consider it that. And then take her and Lance."

Adam said, "Until she pulled the knife. That changed everything. He hadn't realized the momma terror he caused. She intended to kill him to protect her son. He went from friend to enemy in the blink of an eye."

Dakota said, "He couldn't see beyond his delusion."

Adam said, "Did you see the look on his face in court? That's not hate. It's anger. Betrayal. Hunger. And love…as warped as that is."

Sean said, "All those years touching her…waiting his turn…he was primed to blow."

Nodding, Dakota said, "Which takes us back to Beau's death and the note in the package. Zack or someone else could have killed him."

Adam said, "Easily. Why didn't law enforcement investigate? They took accidental death at face value. That doesn't make any sense."

Dakota said, "Even the statements from the guests on the trip were more exclamations of shock instead of direct answers on their location when it happened."

Sean said, "The murderer – and we can safely call it that at this point - could have been someone on the trip. Or it could have been someone waiting in the woods for him to show up. Beau didn't exactly make it hard for someone to find his favorite camping spots."

"No." Adam said. "Maybe because he didn't consider himself a target. Though he was concerned Raven might be if she continued dancing."

Dakota said, "I wonder why. She's stunningly gorgeous. But 95% of men wouldn't harm her for it. Is her dancing powerful enough to make someone cross the line from fantasy desire to criminal desire?"

Adam said, "I think so. Especially in Zack's frame of mind at the time. I've only seen Raven dance once and she didn't even know I was watching. She's professionally amazing and sensually enflaming without even trying. And Zack was trained to handle her - and still lost control.

"In fact, looking at the facts now, I'm shocked he waited eight months to make his move after Beau was killed - unless he didn't think she was approachable. Which makes sense that when she told him she quit dancing with him for good - he snapped. He'd waited too long."

Sean said, "So, he's in prison wanting what he still doesn't have. Her."

"Exactly." Dakota said. "Either he plans a prison break or finding someone to do what he can't."

Adam said, "Which brings us to Hunter. The missing link."

Sean said. "I doubt Hunter is his name."

Dakota said, "Nope. Just his occupation."

***

Down the hall, Callie was fading off to sleep when her phone dinged with a text. Expecting Raven, she tapped the screen. It was Steel.

Steel: Feel like talking?
Callie: What do you want to talk about?
Steel: Us.
Callie: Define us.
No response.
Callie: Steel?

She heard a light knock on her door. She gasped. No, he didn't. Climbing out of bed she walked to the door and stood there. Her text dinged.

Steel: Open the door, Callie.

She opened it. In the hall light, the silver in his hair glistened. He was dressed in jeans and an unbuttoned shirt. She could see muscles rising from his stomach to his chest.

She raised her eyes to his and whispered, "Steel...what are you doing?"

"Trying to talk to you alone."

She glanced down the hall where Adam and Dakota were, and said, "But—
"

"Come with me."

Then he pushed her bedroom door open and flipped the light on. And winking, he led her to the bathroom at the end of the hall and shut the door.

She smiled, feeling like a teenager.

He said, "You do what you have to with the FBI down the hall."

She giggled.

His eyes roamed her tousled hair, full lips, green eyes, and perfect curves in pajama shorts and a tank top. No bra.

He groaned and said, "Callie, I've never seen you look more beautiful. You're hot."

She whispered, "Have you looked in the mirror, Steel?"

Holding her face, he said, "I'm going to kiss you. Hold you. And talk to you. I did not come here for sex. You'll know when I do."

And he kissed her. Hot. Demanding. Then groaned as she met him with the same. Her hands slid up his stomach and chest to wrap around his neck. He sat her on the counter...finally, alone with her. He pressed in - making a definite point – as he pulled her closer.

A few minutes later, breathing heavy, Callie said, "Steel..."

"I know..."

"I'm sweating."

He kissed her, and said, "Me too. But I'm ready for round two."

Teasing, she said, "How many rounds does it take to reach the knock-out round?"

Pulling her against him, he said directly, "I'm already there, Callie. Been there a while. Just so we're clear."

The look on his face. The feel of him. The words he spoke, laid it out there. All of it settled deep inside her. She touched her stomach with the impact. Boom. No more beating around the bush.

He leaned against the wall across from her, and said, "Three months. We've seen each other every day as we live and work on this hill. Attraction. Flirting. Sexual tension. All that brings us to this moment. But I've been ready since I met you. I want to know what you're ready for. So, tell me. Ask me questions. Give me something. Please. I'm burning up."

She liked his honesty. She nodded and said, "I already know what kind of man you are, Steel, or we wouldn't be at this place. So, no character questions are necessary. But I can tell you I like the way you carry yourself. Your strength and integrity. Your confidence. Directness. Your smile. The look in your eyes. The tension in your body when you're wanting what you can't have yet."

He took a step closer, and said, "Ok. Let's do love talk then. I'm into the way you express yourself. Sassy. Loving. You like to touch. Your body is more sensual when I'm around. And your eyes are teasing. When you look at me, I know what you're thinking."

"You can't know that."

He stepped closer. "You look at my muscles. My body. And wonder how powerful I am in bed."

Her cheeks went bright pink.

He smiled.

She said, "A thought doesn't make it real."

Cupping her face, he kissed her softly and said, "But it will be."

Teasing him, she said, "Ah. You think so? When?"

"When you marry me," and he took advantage of her gasp and claimed her lips.

Moments later, he said, "Say yes. Please, Callie. I don't care if it's fast. I'm not a young man. I don't have time to be slow."

Slipping arms around his neck, she said. "It's been yes."

Groaning, he said, "For how long?"

"Since I started thinking about you in bed."

"I knew it."

"Yeah. Well, you're hot...and..."

"I love you, Callie. You have no idea how much."

"I do, Steel. I love you."

He kissed her, and said, "I want to make love to you over, and over, and over till your legs won't hold you up, and my lips capture your screams."

He saw shock hit her first. She blinked, then groaned. He scooped her off the counter, kissing her.

She said, "Steel...I felt that."

"I know, baby."

"I still feel it."

He groaned and said, "Easy with the words, Callie. I'm feeling them too."

"What if...I have something to say that might shock you?"

"I don't shock easy. Go ahead."

"I've never had sex, Steel. Ever."

His gaze locked on hers as it registered.

She said, "I know I'm kind of old to be a virgin—"

He kissed her. Soft. Wild. Gentle. Hard. Filled with desire...and totally shocked.

***

Raven couldn't sleep. It was three a.m., and the house was quiet. She heard rain. Not the outer bands of the tropical storm, just rain. And her mind wouldn't leave her alone. She tossed. Turned. Then got up and stared out the window. Rain ran down the glass.

Questions tormented her. Thoughts. Memories. Everything spun like she stood inside a tornado watching a horror movie. Beau thrown off a cliff. The rape. Pain. Screams. Scars. Fear. Now Hunter. And danger lurking again. Watching.

Tears slipped down her face as she thought of Adam. She needed him. Wanted him. Loved him. Ached to have memories with him. She didn't want to wait to make love to him. What if someone took her and she never got to be with him? She needed her last memory of making love to be with him. She wanted the look on his face. His kiss. His body. Her warrior. With his passion roaring in her like the coming storm.

She couldn't breathe and headed downstairs in the dark. The dogs looked at her, tails wagging. She knew she was panicking and didn't know what to do. Maybe the rain would wash the fear away.

She opened the door. Walked across the porch, down the steps, into the dark rain.

Adam heard the dog whoof at his door and jumped out of bed. When he opened his bedroom door, he saw the back door wide open. And the rain. Then he saw Raven in the yard, facing the darkness.

He ran.

And could hear her moaning as he reached her. Not wanting to startle her, he slipped his arms around her and said, "Baby, what's wrong?"

She turned, her tears mixing with rain and touched his bare chest, watching the rain drench him. He was so beautiful wearing nothing but jeans and love. She couldn't imagine never…

And she moaned again.

He said, "Talk to me, Raven. Let me help you."

"I'm so scared. And I ache. What if I never get to know you? The rape was the last time… And then Hunter got so close. What if someone takes me before we make love—"

And groaning, he picked her up, kissing her as he carried her across the yard to his place. Neither of them paid attention to the rain. Passion covered them and love lit the way. Wet. Wild. Burning. They barely made it to the porch.

Her clothes blew away in the wind. He kicked his wet jeans aside. Then tried to key in his security code while holding onto his wildcat. Just once. And then he didn't care that they were outside in the rain. He covered her scream with his kiss and took her where she wanted to go.

And again, on the other side of the door.

And then upstairs on the bed she hadn't even seen yet.

Much later, Adam smiled as Raven fell asleep in his arms with a satisfied flush. Safe. Entwined with him and their new memories. Fear long gone. Replaced. And suddenly the word love seemed way too small for what they had just experienced. He'd never forget as she cried out to him for what only he could give her. Him.

But now came the hard part. Their agreement. To not make love again till they married. Nine hard days just became harder. Beautifully harder because they would be like two electric wires. Sparking. Sizzling. Arcing.

But he wouldn't have it any other way. No one could take from her what they shared. Ever.

He woke before dawn and the rain had stopped. They laughed as he slipped on cold wet jeans, then wrapped her in a sleeping bag he had found in the utility room. Then he carried her home.

Chapter 8

Kip checked in at the Montana State Prison visitor center early Tuesday morning. He cracked a joke as usual for the stone-faced guards trying not to grin.

"Come on, man." Kip said. "This place is drab. Live a little. Laugh a lot. Hump a lot. My motto."

The guards let a smile slip and shook their heads. Kip was always cool. A young biker. Jeans. Leather. Tats. Spiky hair. Earrings.

The guard said, "Shut up, Kip. This is prison. Fun's against the rules."

"Tell'em to stuff it, boss."

With a warning look from the guard, Kip held up his hands, and said, "Ok. I quit. Oh, wait. One more thing. Check out my new old-man tat. I saw one on an old sailor last week."

He pointed at a cartoon tattoo of two mating pigs titled *Makin' Bacon*, and said, "Tell me you don't like bacon."

They pushed him through for a pat down.

Satisfied as usual, Kip made it through the process and headed to the table to wait. He found that charm was much more effective in getting what he wanted - and a lot less work. Glancing around, about half of the tables were already occupied with inmates and guests. Then keys rattled on the back wall, and the metal door opened. He saluted Zack as he headed across the room in his orange jumpsuit.

Zack sat.

Kip smiled and leaned forward, arms in front of him on the table, and said, "Great taste in clothes, man. I'm jealous. Do you have a hard time choosing what to wear every morning?"

"Shove it. There's probably one with your name on it somewhere in here."

Kip laughed.

Then careful, because ears were always listening, Zack said, "You look like you've been touring on your bike again."

Kip said, "Yep," and laid his hand on his left forearm, one finger touching a Louisiana tattoo, and said, "You got that right. Found me the hottest woman around. Fire hair and a body that makes you do all kind of illegal things."

Zack got the message and nodded. That was the truth. He said, "Did you have any trouble on the trip?"

"Yeah. Took a whiz in the bushes and ran into some wild hogs with tusks long as daggers. Kind of exciting protecting my chick though."

A frown crossed Zack's brow and he said, "She hurt?"

"Nope. Hero that I am, saved her, and took the jabs myself. Ended up doing a vanishing act from the doc later. A real adventure."

Zack nodded and said, "You deserve a reward for that."

"Was hoping that would be the case. So…tell me…when's the next snowstorm? It was hot where I was."

Zack said, "I heard a nasty cold front will arrive in the early morning hours. Lots of white. Lots of wind. Lots of cold. I hope you've got something besides a motorcycle to ride."

"Oh yeah. All set up. I hate to be cold."

"Cold is alright. There are worse things. Where are you headed now?"

"I've got some shopping before the storm. Want a steak?"

Zack said, "Save it for me. Appreciate you stopping by."

Kip stood and said, "No problem. What's a brother for?"

***

Back in Louisiana, Dakota watched Adam pour a cup of coffee and add two heaping spoons of sugar the next morning as the news came on. He raised his eyebrows without a word. Adam never used sugar. Then Raven came down the stairs meeting Adam's quick glance at her. She smiled and Dakota knew they didn't see anyone else in the room. And wasn't surprised. He'd shut the door last night as they disappeared in the rain.

Adam met Raven at the base of the stairs. Pulling her face to his, they kissed, ignoring everyone. Remembering everything. Explaining nothing.

Lance headed for his momma to get in on the fun, but Steel quickly intercepted him and brought him to Callie. And they smiled, remembering their hot kisses last night. Dakota and Gabrielle locked gazes. He touched his heart. She smiled, touching hers, and her belly. Love was alive and well on the river this morning.

After their kiss, Adam hugged Raven and whispered, "I love you."

She whispered, "And you did, baby…very, very, well."

He kissed her again. Hard and fast.

Dakota cleared his throat and said, "Helloooo. Does anyone plan to watch the weather report or just make out this morning?"

Steel said, "I vote for make out," and everyone laughed, breaking the intimate spell in the room.

And as the commercial ended, the meteorologist explained that the outer bands of Tropical Storm Mason were due to reach southwest Louisiana by noon. It was nine a.m. now. They had three hours before heavier wind and rain hit. And then the storm surge would push ashore close to six causing all waterways to swell and overflow their banks.

***

Gabrielle's phone rang. She answered, "Hi, Mom!"

She listened and said, "I don't know let me check. Hey Gabrielle, mom insists on you letting Lance stay at the ranch with them, so the girls have someone to play with while everyone is cooped up with the weather. She promises that if she can handle dad's shenanigans, she can handle three toddlers – and maybe even get more sleep."

They laughed at the comment. Jimmy, a retired army captain, planned romantic ambushes frequently. They were almost newlyweds themselves - with twin girls less than a year old.

Raven said, "I don't want to put her to any trouble."

Gabrielle tapped the speaker as Serena said, "It's no trouble. You have your hands full, honey. Let us help. Please."

Callie said, "Raven, maybe I should go with Lance to help."

Serena said, "I love you for offering, Callie, but I know they need you there with all the research, hungry men, a storm, and two homes. I'm good. Blaze is home for a few days before they transfer him to a new army base. I promise. We will be fine. We have a fortress here and two army men."

Raven said, "Thank you, Serena. Really. I appreciate it."

"Our pleasure. Jimmy and Blaze are leaving now to get Lance. They're bringing all the dogs so let him bring his."

Gabrielle said, "Thanks, Mom. I love you."

"I love you! And take care of my grandbaby you're carrying around."

***

The next hour was a flurry of activity pulling all the vehicles in garages. Hauling yard furniture to the barn. Gathering dog food to keep at Raven's. Loading flashlights with fresh batteries. Ice-chests with drinks. And thawing and preparing meat for three big men and three women. One very pregnant.

Raven decided to check her medical supplies and make sure she was equipped in case Gabrielle went into labor or they had a medical emergency.

***

She texted Adam: Would you bring my Quest medical kit when you are done?

Adam: Why? What's wrong?

Raven: I'm a nurse. There's a storm. A flooding river. And a very pregnant Gabrielle. Just being prepared.

Adam: I don't know how to deliver a baby.

Raven: I do.

Adam: Thank God. Anything else?

Raven: Did you find my clothes yet?

Adam couldn't stop laughing long enough to text a response.

Raven: Adam?

Adam: That question was unexpected. I was laughing.

Raven: It's not your panties in the woods.

Adam laughed again.

Raven: I know you're laughing.

Adam: I love intimacy with you. I did not expect humor. I love this.

Raven: So now you want text sex?

Adam: I'm certainly thinking about it now that you've mentioned it. How about you?

Raven: I'd rather have what you gave me last night.

No answer.

Raven: Adam?

She heard the truck and laughed. He slid to a stop in the mud, and in seconds shoved open the back door. His eyes found hers - and they were as hot as lava. She screamed and ran upstairs, startling Callie and Gabrielle. She didn't get far.

Pressing Raven against the wall, Adam said, "Get your purse. We're leaving."

"Where are we going? What about—"

66

"Walk to the truck or I'm carrying you."

"You're so alpha, Adam. It's hot…"

"Get in the truck, wildcat. I'm sweating."

"I bet I know where we're going."

"Then hurry up. It'll be a miracle if I can wait thirty minutes much less eight more days."

***

In record time, Adam opened the door to the Clerk of Court, and kissed Raven as they walked in. The staff inside clapped and whispered, stunned at the gorgeous man and woman.

An older woman walked to the counter and said, "Welcome. You realize that steam followed you in?"

Adam laughed as he handed over their identification, and said, "That's been happening a lot lately. We think a marriage license will help us with that."

Checking their paperwork, she looked over the top of her glasses at Adam and said, "You're a minister?"

One the female clerks in the back said, "Holy cow. My preacher doesn't look like that."

Two male clerks looked at Raven, and said, "And our preacher's wife doesn't look like her either."

After more laughter and a legitimate license, they left. It was storming.

On the way home, Adam said, "The license is burning a hole in my pocket."

With a smile, Raven said, "It isn't in your pocket."

"It's a metaphor."

"Ah. I see."

He said, "Do you want to see more?"

She laughed and said, "What about the agreement we made?"

He said, "You started this hot game. That wasn't in the agreement."

"I love games."

"I see that."

Using his words, she said, "You want to see more?"

"I dare you."

She slid her hands under her shirt and cupped her breasts. He ran off the road. She screamed, then laughed.

Then his phone rang.

He growled, took a deep breath, and glanced at her - trying not to stop the truck and give her what she was asking for. His phone was still ringing.

She said, "Are you going to answer your phone?"

It quit ringing. And started again.

He picked up his phone. It was Angel calling from New Orleans. A close friend.

***

Raven gasped, as Adam answered bluntly, "What."

Angel cracked up and said, "Man, what is wrong with you? Did I call at a bad time?"

"It could have been better."

"Oh man, this is hilarious. You're never rude. It's got to be Raven."

"No. Yes. Well, it's the eight-day wait until we get married."

Angel couldn't talk. He just laughed.

Adam said, "Sorry, Angel. You just caught me in the moment."

"I have never heard you frustrated. That was awesome. I'm impressed. I thought you were perfect. Now I feel better knowing you are just a man like the rest of us."

"I'm going to hang up on you."

Trying not to laugh, Angel said, "No. Wait. I'm sorry. I just wanted to check in with you on the coming storm and make sure y'all are ok. I know it's a wee baby storm but still."

Sighing, Adam said, "It's ok. I was just letting out a little steam since you know what it's like to wait for a wedding. And yes, we're ready for the storm. Dakota and Gabrielle will be there too."

"Why? What's up?"

"So much has happened in a couple of days. Can I call you this evening while we watch the river rise?"

"Call me. And congratulations on your engagement."

***

Mid-afternoon Adam, Dakota and Steel stood outside in rain ponchos watching the river.

Adam said, "How high has the river gotten around here?"

Steel said, "A park ranger told me earlier today he'd seen it get halfway up the hill."

Adam whistled, and said, "That's a lot of water."

68

Dakota said, "I'm just glad there's a hill."

Chuckling, Steel said, "Along with floods, there will be snakes, gators, and animals looking for high ground. Wind gusts. And flying debris. You shouldn't roam around outside even though you have your own RN."

Adam said, "She had me get her medical kit out of the office in case we need it. Especially since we'll be flooded in. Gabrielle only has a few weeks left so she wants to be prepared."

Dakota said, "I appreciate that. But don't talk about it. I refuse that scenario."

"I get that. But at least you know Raven knows how to deliver a baby. That should help."

"Well, it doesn't. So, don't say it again."

Steel grinned and changed the subject. He said, "Back to the river…you'll be shocked at how intimidating the river looks swollen with all sorts of debris. No telling what we will find along the road after the water goes down."

Adam said, "I imagine. How long will the surge last?"

"Here by us, if rainfall isn't heavy, it'll recede fast if it doesn't connect with the incoming tide. But once the water goes down, it'll dry quick enough. By Saturday for Quest's grand opening, you won't even know it flooded."

"That's good news. What about Cameron Parish along the gulf? How will they fair?"

"They'll flood and everything will be inundated with salt water. They'll lose animal stock that can't get out. It won't be pretty but at least this isn't a catastrophic storm. They'll be back to normal soon. At least around New Orleans, that's what I've learned."

A big wind gust showered the men with a barrage of leaves and small branches. They jogged back to the house.

As they dried off in the kitchen, they watched Raven showing Callie and Gabrielle some simple dance moves.

Gabrielle got tired and sat down. She said, "I have no stamina. I'm a wimp. I used to run for an hour and barely sweat."

Kissing her forehead, Dakota said, "Honey, you weren't carrying a watermelon while you ran."

Raven and Callie gasped in shock. Adam looked at Dakota. Incredulous. He did not just say that. Steel disappeared down the hall.

Gabrielle frowned at Dakota, and said, "Are you telling me I look like a watermelon?"

Dakota realized his sweet attempt at encouragement failed miserably. Dangerously. He had lost his mind. He knelt beside the chair and said, "That is not what I meant, Cat."

"You can't prove that FBI man. And don't call me Cat right now. It's inappropriate to butter me up with a nickname while I'm pissed off."

He tried to touch her, and she shoved his hand away. "Don't touch me."

"Gabrielle—"

Gabrielle looked at Raven and said, "Hand me my throwing knives, please."

Raven said, "He didn't mean—"

"Just hand me the knives and don't try to help him. He can run."

Dakota said, "I'm sorry. I would cut my own throat before hurting you."

Gabrielle said, "But why? Let me do it for you."

Callie backed down the hall, not quite sure what was going on. Raven was totally lost at how to handle this. She didn't know this side of Gabrielle at all. She wondered if maybe Jean Lafitte's genes…

Adam laughed from where he sat on the stairs and said, "Go ahead, Raven. Let her show you what she's got. Dakota earned it."

Raven handed Gabrielle her leather pouch, looking apologetically at Dakota, and then to Adam for help. Adam joined her as Gabrielle unwrapped the tiny sharp knives and picked one up, brandishing it at Dakota.

Dakota said, "What do you want?"

"Stand up."

"You do want more children, right?"

Raven felt Adam's silent laugh. But she didn't see anything funny yet.

Dakota stood before his gorgeous, very pregnant wife with a razor-sharp dagger in her hand.

She said, "Take off your shirt."

He unbuttoned it. Dropped it. Gabrielle's amber cat eyes met his and she nicked his stomach. A tiny drop of blood appeared. He didn't flinch. She smiled and stood. He put his hands behind his head and watched her. He liked her wild like this. She slid the blade over his lips. His neck. Down his chest. And in a flash, she slung the knife - piercing dead-center a star carved in the fireplace mantel.

Dakota scooped her up for a kiss.

Raven looked at Adam in awe. He winked. Then she glanced behind her, and Callie was doing a fist pump. And Steel watched from the hall. Impressed to see Lafitte's granddaughter in action at last.

The observing couples headed upstairs to give them privacy.

***

Dakota said, "I didn't mean it like it sounded, Gabrielle."

"I know that."

"Then why—"

"Because I needed a reminder of who's behind this belly. Who'll always be behind your babies."

"Did you have to draw blood?"

"It defeats the purpose if I don't."

He laughed. She was killer hot. It was just who she was.

***

Later, while everyone watched the storm come closer to shore on TV, Callie heated the leftover gumbo. It was always better after a day or two.

Steel followed the smell into the kitchen and said, "That smells amazing. I can smell the taste. I love that about Cajun food."

Callie said, "I know. Isn't that crazy? I can't wait for Lexi to get here tomorrow to teach me more recipes. Or whenever the river goes down, I guess. Have you checked outside lately?"

"We'll step outside after the news."

"Is it safe? It's noisy out there."

"It'll get noisier. But we should be fine for a few minutes. We're a decent distance from the trees and flying debris."

Nodding, she turned to stir the pot.

Steel glanced at the others watching the weather. He moved behind Callie and snuggled. Then kissed her neck. And distracted, she dropped the large metal spoon in the pot. It clanged loudly.

Dakota called from the den, "Steel, you better not make her scorch the gumbo."

Everyone laughed while Callie fished the spoon out of the pot.

Then the news ended, and the men started dressing in rain gear again. Raven frowned. Things were beginning to slam against the shutter covered windows and the dogs were getting restless.

Steel said, "It'll pass after a few hours, Raven. Just think, only in Louisiana can you get a tropical storm one day and have Thanksgiving a few days later."

She smiled even though she didn't want to, and Adam kissed her.

71

He said, "We won't be long. I promise. We're ready for gumbo."

***

The force of the wind caught the front door, slamming it against the wall as Adam opened it. Everything was flying horizontally. Rain and small debris. Ducking his face, he led the way on the front porch staying close to the wall. He scooted toward the fireplace that provided a small wind break. Dakota and Steel followed suit. The porch was littered with branches and leaves, but the shutters were holding firm.

Wiping rain off his face, Adam saw two snakes up ahead. He looked down at his feet. No snakes. Then the dogs began to bark inside. Adam shielded his face looking through the rain.

Steel yelled at the same time a young buck ran on the porch and slammed into the shutters between Adam and Dakota. Scrambling, the deer tripped Adam and he fell with the terrified animal.

Adam protected his face. The buck trampled him a bit, then jumped up, leapt off the porch and disappeared into the storm.

Adam slipped in mud, water, and forest debris, and finally got to his feet. Touching his bloody lip, he glanced at Dakota and Steel. They laughed.

Adam yelled, "Welcome to Louisiana!"

And for the next several minutes they watched the river swell. And ducked from missile branches. The road vanished. The wharf was underwater. And the wind and rain were wild. Tropical Storm Mason was here.

Chapter 9

A few miles from the prison, Kip backed a white moving truck into the barn. Then shut the doors and got busy. Gone was the cool biker dude. The tattoos were washed down the drain. Some had been temp tats and the others he drew – like the Louisiana one and the pigs.

Now he was dressed like a cowboy. Weathered jeans. Boots. Flannel shirt and thick jacket. Stubble beard. Black hair and green eyes. A cowboy hat hung on the back of a chair.

Two duffle bags sat packed with polar snow wear. Pure white. Headlamps. Heated mitts and boots. Two waterproof backpacks carried pistols with silencers. Plenty of ammo. Knives. Tasers. Radios. Twist ties. Maps. Burner phones. An insulated box held a pint of blood. And next to that was a first aid kit, camping gear, food, and energy drinks.

He got a text.

***

Two a.m.
Lead me in.

***

Kip filled the gas tank. Tucked his Glock in his waistband and bundled up. He grabbed one of the duffle bags and a backpack and started the snowmobile. He took off across the abandoned farmland.

Chapter 10

After darting through a flurry of wind, rain, and debris from the storm, Adam slammed the front door shut behind Dakota. Callie hurriedly gathered their wet things while Raven handed them towels. And sighed. Adam was bleeding in several places. Without a word, she went for her medical kit.

Joining them in the kitchen, Raven looked at Adam. Soaking wet. His face bloody. Hoof marks all over him. And he was covered in mud and leaves while laughing like he'd been on vacation.

She caught his eye and wiggled her medical kit. "My turn," she said, and led the way to the bathroom.

She pointed in the mirror, and he checked out his wounds. She shook her head at the boy in the man.

He said, "Are you planning to fix me up?"

"I am. Why don't you take off your shirt and have a seat."

He peeled off the wet shirt, wincing, and tossed it in the tub. Then closed the toilet lid and sat. She cleaned his face. Noted the injuries. Checked his scalp.

He said, "I'm fine. I just tangled with a deer on the porch. I hadn't expected that bonus."

Dryly, she said, "Men." Then checked his chest, arms, and back.

He smiled at her barely concealed irritation and slid his hands down her thighs. "Baby, I'm fine."

She handed him a few wet rags and said, "I know. Wipe your chest and arms for me. Do not touch your back though."

He wiped, frowning as she threaded a needle.

She said, "You have a small slice in your shoulder. I'll need to clean and stitch it. It will hurt – and you earned it, hot stuff."

He laughed. "It's just a guy thing."

"I am well aware. I've nursed many guy things. Now, drop your pants for me. You have blood on your legs."

74

Smiling, he stood and said, "I thought you'd never ask," and dropped his pants, stepping out of them totally naked.

Meeting his gaze, she said, "What is it with men and no underwear?"

All he knew was that he didn't care about injuries. He wanted something else. But he was filthy. She knew and tried to hide a grin as she checked his legs and tried to ignore what was becoming blatantly obvious.

Struggling to stay focused, she turned to her medical kit and said, "Your legs are fine other than a few impressive bruises and a couple of cuts and scrapes. Do you have any groin injuries?"

Their eyes locked. No answer was necessary.

He slid a finger down her zipper and said, "You have two seconds to go or you're not leaving."

She walked to the door. Glancing back, she said, "I need to stitch your back after you shower. I'll be waiting with the needle. It's a nurse thing."

***

They were in the middle of enjoying Callie's gumbo when Sean texted:

Director Washington approved three lines of investigation for the task force. Find out what links Beau's death, Zack, and Hunter. Video chat at 10:30 tonight.

So around nine p.m. everyone but Adam headed upstairs to work on the investigation. Adam finally called Angel back.

***

Angel answered with a laugh, and said, "Are you in a better mood?"

"Yeah. Sorry about that. I had just run off the road."

"Should I ask why?"

"No. Now listen, I'm going to give you the bulleted version of what's going on."

"Shoot."

"An FBI investigation is underway that involves Raven's past. A strange man showed up in the woods near Raven on Sunday, and again yesterday. Except yesterday, he got injured in an accident and later disappeared from the hospital. We think he is also the one that left a package in our mailbox threatening Raven."

Angel said, "Man, I get it. Jade and I are there. Just say the word. You know that."

"Thanks. I do. But we are just gathering info right now. We'll discuss this Friday night when you and Jade arrive. And what do you think about Raven and I following you back to New Orleans after the grand opening? It will do Raven good to get away for a day or two. Maybe we can help with the case you told us about and clear her mind from all this."

"It's a plan. Whatever you want."

***

After the call, Adam thought about something Angel had said earlier today. Engagement. And smiling, he slipped on a rain poncho and headed out in the light rain to his house. He could do something about that tonight.

***

Raven was rubbing her neck reviewing dance videos when Adam texted her.

> Adam: Come meet me.
> Raven: Where?
> Adam: Downstairs in my room.
> Raven: Do you need something?
> Adam: You. And hurry.

Intrigued, Raven headed downstairs. Steel and Callie were watching a movie. She waved and went down the hall. Adam was waiting and pulled her in his arms, shutting the door. He kissed her. His hands caressing.

He said, "I have something for you."

"I see that...and like it."

Smiling, he said, "In addition to me."

"I don't need anything but you."

Kissing her again, he drew her to the bed. Pulling her on his lap he said, "Now, close your eyes."

Expecting a romantic game, she gasped when he slid a ring on her finger. Her heart ached at the beauty of the moment. She wrapped her arms around his neck, and said, "I love it, Adam. I love it."

Smiling, he said, "But you haven't seen it yet."

"I don't care. It's perfect."

He squeezed her and said, "It was my grandmother's engagement ring. She gave it to me as a gift for my bride. And while I can buy anything you want; this ring reminds me of you. Look..."

She glanced at her hand and gasped. "Oh, Adam..."

She touched the ring. It was a princess cut diamond solitaire. A big one. Surrounded by red stones. It sparkled. Vibrant. Like elegant fire. The band was a double row of diamonds. The ring was beyond fabulous.

She said, "It's unbelievably gorgeous. Are those rubies?"

"Actually, they're red diamonds. Very rare. Priceless, like you. And they match your hair."

"I've never, ever, heard of red diamonds." She kissed him. "And only you would notice they match my hair."

He winked. "I'm good at what I do."

She kissed him. "Yes, you are... It looks fragile. How careful do I need to be?"

"It's built like Fort Knox. She washed dishes with it. Bathed us. Worked in her flower beds. Golfed. Rode horses. It's perfect for a warrior like you."

Leaning against him as she looked at it, she said, "I really love it. But...what do you mean by priceless? Or do I want to know?"

"Don't ask. It's yours. Show it off and enjoy being engaged, for a few days anyway. And that brings me to something else I wanted to talk about. I think I should move into your room. I'll never sleep worrying about you. We have a lot going on and the thought of finding you outside—"

"I'm not going to argue. It was terrifying...but it ended up—"

And their lips met, remembering how they ended up.

He said, "We also have decisions to make regarding our homes. We'll do whatever you want. You know money isn't a problem, right?"

"I gathered as much from what I've heard." She said with a grin, "Is it clean money?"

He laughed. "Yes. It's Inheritance. Investments. Income."

"That's a lot of I's. I have some of those in my tiny portfolio, but probably lowercase I's.

He laughed again.

Adam touched her face, and said, "I like to see you be yourself. No secrets. Wild. Playful. Free to love me. And...I know we won't have time for a big honeymoon right now—"

"I disagree. Big is not a problem."

He felt the burn. And pulling her with him on the bed, he rolled on top of her, then said, "We both know waiting for the wedding will be hard. So, tell me now…do you want a hot game…or the real thing?"

"I shouldn't tease—"

"Tease me. I plan on making you squirm every chance I get. In fact," he kissed her neck, "I'm thinking about buying an island for us to have a place to burn."

Surely, she didn't hear him right. "You're kidding."

"No. What do you think?"

"I love the water. It sounds fabulous! But, Adam, it's hard to find bikini tops that hide my scars."

He should have thought of that. "It'll just be us on the island. You can wear anything you want. Or nothing at all. I vote for nothing."

She smiled, grateful, he could disregard scars that were literally the initial of another man. "I see you have a lot of naked in mind."

"I love you, Raven. I have a lot of everything in mind with you."

Someone knocked on the door.

Dakota said, "Hey, Sean and Piper are on video chat ready for the meeting."

Following Dakota upstairs, Adam motioned Steel and Callie to join them. He had an announcement to make.

***

Once in the office, Raven, Gabrielle, and Callie sat at the table. Dakota, Adam, and Steel stood behind them.

Sean's video feed was on the left wall monitor. Handsome as always with shoulder length black wavy hair, he was dressed casually in jeans and a navy-blue FBI shirt. He smiled when Adam and Raven walked in.

Piper's video feed was on the right wall monitor. She was knockout beautiful with long brown hair the color of shiny melted chocolate, and sexy blue eyes seasoned with mega attitude. And tonight, she still had on a fine black suit even though it was late. She waited impatiently for everyone to get settled.

Grinning, Adam said, "Hey, Piper. Beautiful as ever. Though you look like you're ready to eat a criminal or someone's pet tiger."

Delighted, she laughed, looking like Miss America at an interview.

Steel said, "Holy cow," and everyone laughed.

Piper, still smiling, slid right into interview mode, and said, "Who might you be, big guy? And which branch of the military did you serve?"

"Call me Steel. I'm retired army."

She continued, "And what's up with that possessive hand you've got on Callie?"

"She's taken."

Piper smiled. "A man of few words. Handsome hunk too." Then glancing at Callie, she said, "Hi there, Callie. You look happy and beautiful. Does he have anything to do with that?"

Callie smiled. "Hi Piper. You bet he does."

Steel said, "You know, Piper, my first impression was wrong. I do see a Nash family resemblance now. I let the lack of Native American looks fool me. My bad."

Laughing, she said, "I like you, Steel."

He smiled. "I like you too, Piper. And what's this I hear you are single? I need to find you a Louisiana man."

"Well, don't, or I'll shoot you. I don't know if I like Cajun seasoning yet."

Chuckling, Sean said, "Enough. This will never end. We have work to do."

Piper said, "Who put you in charge?"

"Director Washington did. You aren't in Lake Charles yet and Dakota is on leave. Did you notice Gabrielle's belly?"

"A ridiculous comment. I can see."

Still laughing, Gabrielle gasped, and said, "You are going to send me into labor with laughing. Stop! Please! This is Raven's house - talk to her and let me breathe."

Piper and Raven smiled at each other.

Raven said, "Hi, Piper. I love your suit."

"Hey, gorgeous. I love your hair. You've got to promise me, if you have a little girl with red hair that you will name her Flame and make me her godmother."

Raven smiled at Adam. He said, "And on that note, it's my turn to make an announcement. Raven and I are engaged."

Cheers echoed around the room.

Adam continued, "But a short one! We are aiming to get married next week – Thanksgiving Day."

After congratulations and hugs, Adam pointed to Sean. "You've got the floor."

His smile fading to seriousness, Sean said, "We do have some updates, Raven. We'll start with a few new facts, then move on to analysis, ending with strategy. You ready?"

She nodded.

"To begin, we have reviewed the pictures and videos you've sent us so far. The conclusion is simple. Zack didn't lie. We think he's been in love with you for years. Now obviously, time, frustration, or any number of other factors warped it for him to attack you - but there it is.

"And I said all that to say, we agree with the code we found on the pictures. This with Zack, is not over. It may never be, considering the steps he's possibly taken with Hunter."

Raven didn't say anything. Just let the words *this is not over* flutter through her like leaves falling on the ground. Her stomach churned. Muscles tight. No. No. No.

Her silence revealed the impact. But Sean continued, "Next, we checked into why Beau's death was closed so quickly as an accident. It turns out that the investigator who gathered all the evidence was killed two days later under suspicious circumstances. And Beau's case was bungled when someone with no experience, or interest, got it on their desk."

Raven closed her eyes. It was getting worse. Beau and the ranger were killed. And she wondered for a fleeting second if two deaths made someone a serial killer.

Piper said, "Raven, everyone that was on the camping trip with Beau has been cleared in our investigation. Except Zack of course, and his friend from back home. And no one on the trip seems to have a picture of that friend or much information about the guy. He just kind of faded into the background for everyone, which happens, but is unusual. Can you shed any light on him?"

"I don't know much. I was supposed to meet him on that trip. And Zack didn't talk about him all that much. He lived out of state and moved around."

"What facts do you remember hearing about him?"

"Seems like his name started with a C or a K. And he was supposed to be smart. Funny. Oh, and a ladies' man. Women liked him."

"Do you know how Zack knew him?"

"Zack's an only child with a small extended family. But they're wealthy and socialize. They know everyone. And it seems like Zack said something about connecting with him just before he graduated high school, and they clicked. He claimed they were blood brothers or something along that line."

"Did you think it was odd you didn't meet him all those years in college?"

She shrugged. "Not really. I mean, Zack had his life. I had mine – especially once Beau and I got together. But we connected all the time through dance, school, and friends. I didn't think about his family unless he brought it up."

Piper said, "Ok. That helps." She flipped a page and looked up. "Now, can you tell us about you and Zack? Define your relationship, as best you can, before the attack."

Raven felt the knot in her throat as feelings warred on which would win. She got up and walked around. The others watched and waited for the details that meant everything.

Fighting the vulnerability, Raven met Adam's eyes. She would talk to him. "We became fast friends when we met as new dance partners. He was awesome. So much fun. A close friend in our groups. We shared secrets. Laughed. Had classes together. Chatted about anything and everything. I mean, think about college…your friends are everything."

She stopped as her eyes filled with tears. "I trusted him, Adam. I loved him as a great friend. And as a dance partner he was fabulous. A wonderful dancer. Professional. Considerate. Impressive. Supportive. We…were good together…but not…"

Adam wiped a tear off her cheek. He understood her pain. The betrayal. It must have been traumatic.

Piper said, "Raven, we're going to get into more personal questions. Ok? Nothing extremely invasive if I can help it."

Raven glanced at her and nodded.

"Adult competition dancing appears highly sensual." Piper said. "Not that I'm judging – just trying to learn what his frame of mind might have been. I mean, routines are meant to be an expression of passion and love. Right?"

Raven agreed, "Yes. But the routines were performances. We acted like the emotions were real. There were crowds of people watching. We were in costume. Makeup. We were meant to be a beautiful and enticing portrayal to all – including us. Until the song stopped. It was like a scene in the movies. We won awards. It wasn't real…"

She looked at Adam. So very sad, and whispered, "To me…"

Adam said, "Raven—"

She stopped him and said, "No. I should have considered the physical aspect for Zack. Especially since he tried to make it personal. But since I wasn't looking for that in dance, I disregarded his interest. I totally missed that it became a problem as I continued to dance with him.

81

"And it wasn't just that I was his dance partner. I was his friend. I should have noticed the things I missed. I saw the pictures you looked at. His hidden pain. Frustration. I'm ashamed I didn't have enough awareness to look at the man touching me. And hurting because of it."

Adam said, "We can't help who we love, Raven. You or him. But he changed. He lied by deception and lived an illusion. He wasn't the friend you thought you danced with. He was a monster in the making."

"I get that, Adam. I'm not saying it's my fault. I'm saying I was a selfish friend. I'm saying I knew other couples dated and should have paid attention. Switched partners. I mean, his hands were all over me and I didn't think about his feelings. I just danced. I know now, that's what Beau saw. And he died over it. Didn't he?"

Dakota interrupted, and said, "Listen to me, Raven. Every sexual assault victim on the planet has done what you are doing. Even as profilers we try to think like the bad guy – to find reasons – and learn how and where it all went wrong. But only to catch him. The truth is, Zack crossed the line. He chose to let it become the monster he fed. That's on him. Everyone gets rejected. You grieve and move on. That's what healthy people do."

He paused, glancing at Adam with a warning first, and said, "And while we think back on all the what if's…you need to know that all of this tells us one thing."

She knew she didn't want to know, and whispered, "What?"

"We think he's going to come for you again."

Raven stared at Dakota. No. He did not say that.

Adam saw the shock and slipped an arm around her. "Raven—"

She looked at Adam and said, "No. That's not possible."

Adam rubbed her back, and said, "You are right. Not tonight. Because at bed check in Montana State Prison an hour ago, Zack was in his bunk. So, it's not tonight. We have time to prepare."

Raven's mind scrambled for the right hole to put all the pegs in. Focus. Focus. Focus. She said, "What about Hunter?"

Sean said, "We're pretty sure he's the guy Zack brought on the camping trip. The friend."

Piper said, "We're digging into their past. We'll find out who he is."

Raven said, "So what's Hunter's role in all this?"

Adam said, "It sounds like a partner. Family? Friend? I don't know. But someone to help Zack get what he wants."

"Why would he do that?"

Sean said, "Something happened to form a link with them. Two needs met. Hunter's getting something valuable he wants."

"Ok," Raven said. "But you're talking about Zack escaping and becoming a fugitive. Fugitives rarely make it. They're on the news. Tracked by all law enforcement. Caught or killed. Why choose a dead end?"

Everyone evaded the terrifying answer.

Sean said, "We're working on that."

Raven walked across the room as they quietly watched her unwind and shake loose her rigid muscles.

After a moment, she said, "I need some time to listen to my screaming instincts. I need to think. I can't handle any more tonight."

She glanced at Adam and said, "Meet me on the porch in fifteen minutes, please? I need to be alone."

Following her downstairs, Adam watched her step outside. He sent the dogs out with her. Sitting in front of the fireplace, he watched her pace on the porch. Light rain from the tropical storm fading away.

But now a new storm was coming. A Cat 5. A killer storm named Zack and Hunter. Adam felt the rage, and the roar, building inside of him for the two men about to walk into his lion's den.

Chapter 11

Deer Lodge, Montana

The snowstorm started just after midnight in Deer Lodge, Montana. A small town of less than three thousand people nestled in a valley about three and a half miles from Montana State Prison. It was dark. Quiet. And frigid, with low visibility.

At one a.m., a white moving truck pulled over on Golf Course Road not far from the airport. Lights from the runway were a welcome beacon. The driver glanced around the cab of the truck. It was strategically normal. Food wrappers tossed around. A flashlight. A map. Real estate papers showing a house rental next town over. Cash and change scattered on the console. A couple of coats. One for snow. One cozy, warm, and well worn. A cowboy hat hung on a hook on the back wall. A phone was charging. And a lot of pictures of half-naked women were taped to the dash. Everything looked like a traveling cowboy always ready for a new half-naked filly.

Sliding up his sleeve, Kip glanced at his iPhone watch, and tapped an app. A GPS signal flashed right where it was supposed to be. All was well. He set the truck mirrors to see behind the truck and settled back to wait.

***

Inside cell block G, Inmate 356782 rolled off the bunk to the floor. He screamed like a crazy man. And after long, painful moments chaos erupted as he was dragged by two guards to the infirmary since he couldn't stand. The smallest guard radioed ahead, hollering for the doctor and cussing, trying not to get vomit on his boots. The cell block behind them went berserk and guards came running, passing them in the hall.

The inmate was barely conscious when the guards reached the exit to the outdoor walkway that led to the infirmary. Grabbing jackets for themselves, the guards keyed in the code and headed into the white night of swirling snow. They carried the inmate by his arms and ankles, hurrying to reach the other door.

A female nurse and male orderly met them at the entrance to the infirmary with a stretcher. The guards slung the unconscious inmate on the stretcher and locked his right wrist to the rail with handcuffs. They hadn't rolled two feet down the hall, when he woke and started screaming, rolling back and forth, completely out of control with pain. They shoved the stretcher faster and jogged. A few minutes later, they wheeled him into the emergency clinic.

The nurse said, "Listen! We have a problem. Dr. Powell left before midnight to get home before the storm hit. Dr. Williams was supposed to be on the way, but he's late. We don't have a doctor here."

***

The veteran guard, Troy, radioed the front gate and said, "Has doc arrived?"

"Nope. Haven't seen him. And if he's out in this, no one can see him now. He better have a dozen blankets in his Jeep or he's going to be a doc popsicle come morning."

***

The inmate screamed grabbing his right side, gagging.

The nurse touched his forehead and said, "Look at me. When did the pain start in your right abdomen?"

He gasped, "Hours...ago."

"I need to test your side. Hold on to the rail. It's going to hurt but I'm trying to help you."

Gently, she pressed the area over the appendix and let go. He screamed and tried to roll in a ball yanking on the handcuffs. She checked him for fever. He was hot but shivering.

She said, "He needs a hospital. If the appendix ruptures—"

Trace said, "Forget it. No ambulance can make it here tonight."

"What about someone taking him in a vehicle outfitted for this type of weather? Town isn't far. It's the only chance he's got."

Troy called his captain, who called the warden.

A scowling Captain Rollins shoved open the emergency doors five minutes later, immediately taking in the scene. The inmate was in bad shape. Screaming. Jerking. Crying. Begging.

Rollins contemplated the situation. The inmate was a medium security prisoner. A lifer over a woman. And so far, a model prisoner - with a wealthy family who could cause a lot of trouble if they let him die. The warden said save him. He intended to obey.

Rollins tossed the youngest guard his keys and said, "Taylor, go get my Hummer and cover the back seat with plastic. I don't want him vomiting everywhere. Got it?"

Taylor headed to the ambulance bay doors, keyed in the code, and disappeared outside.

Troy said, "I can ride in the back with the prisoner, Sir."

"No, go back to cell block G. They're maniacs tonight and about to get themselves into trouble. Taylor can ride in the back with him."

"Without a cage?"

"If you think the bus can make it in this weather, help yourself and I'll go back to bed."

"Sorry, Sir."

"Then get back to G."

In ten minutes, the inmate was loaded in the back seat of the Hummer dressed in a guard's parka. Then handcuffed to the guard's wrist. He wasn't going anywhere. Before they had even left the prison walls the prisoner passed out.

Security cleared them and unlocked the gate. Captain Rollins turned on a massive amber light bar above his Hummer, and like a Moon rover, headed slowly out of the prison. Rollins glanced at the odometer and made a mental note of the distance to the turnoff. Anyone driving in snowstorms better depend on more than just visual. He glanced at the compass mounted on his dash and headed north northeast. Town was only three and a half miles away and he knew the distance for each turn.

It took a while before he made it to the first turn. Right. He glanced in the rearview mirror. Zack's gaze met his. Then Zack leaned forward and had dry heaves as he pulled the shiv out of his sock. Then was jerked back as Taylor pulled on the handcuffs.

Without hesitation, Zack stabbed Taylor twice in the neck and once in the heart for good measure. He died before reaching for his gun. Rollins skidded off the road trying to reach for his gun. Zack put the guard's gun to his neck.

Rollins said, "I've got to make it look real. I need to get off a shot like we're fighting. One out the ceiling and one through the door should do it."

Zack said, "Help yourself."

Rollins shot once through the roof, and another out the passenger door, then said, "The doc's Jeep is up ahead. All your gear is in the backseat. He's dead in the front. Now where's the rest of my million?"

Zack said, "You'll find cash in the canoe in your garage. Now, it's up to you to keep cool and not get caught spending money you shouldn't have."

"My problem, not yours."

"Don't say I didn't warn you. Now what injuries do you want? You pick. You asked for it."

Rollins reached for the door handle and said, "Left forearm to keep me from getting out."

Zack rotated the gun and shot him.

Rollins yelled, blood spraying, and growled in pain. He pointed to his right calf and said, "Hurry! Hurts like—"

Zack shot him again.

He screamed as blood filled his boot. He pointed to his temple and said, "Graze me and get out of here."

Zack said, "You want that money bad. My pleasure."

He put the gun barrel angled close to Rollins' head and pulled the trigger. The bullet gouged a path across his head and left a neat bloody hole in the top of the door. Rollins' head dropped. Blood dripped. Lights out.

Grabbing all the weapons, wallets, and phones, Zack headed to the doc's car. He pulled on the white snow suit, heated boots, gloves, and grabbed the backpack. Turning off their phones, he threw them. Then taking out his compass watch and putting on a headlamp, he followed the course. He had an invisible mile to hike.

Thirty minutes later, Zack reached the coordinates at a grove of trees and uncovered the snowmobile. Letting it warm up a bit, he texted Kip: *Coming home.*

***

Kip got out of the truck and walked to the back. Unlocking the bar, he raised the door and slid out the loading ramps. Inside the truck, he made sure the thick wall of mattresses would stop anything. Then he just watched for yellow lights.

***

Zack checked the tracker. He was close to Kip. He flipped the amber lights on bright and smiled as the matching lights on the truck's loading ramp came on. Lining up with the lights, he drove right into the back of the truck. In minutes the truck disappeared into a world of white.

Chapter 12

Quantico, Virginia

At six a.m. in Quantico, Virginia, Sean's phone rang. Looking at the caller, Sean knew why he had called. Zack.

He answered with a question, "When?"

Jackson said, "Around four hours ago through the infirmary. Two dead and one in ICU. He faked severe appendicitis during a whiteout snowstorm. The warden told the captain to save him, so the captain attempted to drive him to the local hospital. Zack stabbed the guard. Shot the captain. And possibly the doctor they found on the highway.

"So, he's gone. And no tracks since snow covered everything. FBI and U.S. Marshals are all over the place. Deer Lodge and Montana State Prison will be on the news before long."

"I'm on my way."

"Meet you in Montana."

Sean texted Dakota, Piper, and Adam three words: Video in ten.

***

On the river in Louisiana, the text did its job. Adam, Raven, and Dakota jumped out of bed, ran hands through their hair, splashed water on their faces, and headed to the studio office. Sean and Piper's video calls appeared.

***

Without preamble, Sean said, "Zack escaped from prison a few hours ago in the middle of a snowstorm. He killed a guard, maybe a doctor, and the captain of the guards is in ICU. Then he vanished. U.S. Marshals, FBI, and local law enforcement are trying to pick up his trail.

I'm leaving now to join them so I will provide first-hand information as we get it. I know you will prepare on your end. And Raven...*we will find him.*"

Raven didn't respond. Her mind was screaming.

Dakota said, "His craziness is going to get him killed."

Adam said, "And I'm the one that's going to kill him if he comes here."

Piper said, "I second that. So, guys, this means I'm on my way to Lake Charles. I'll call when I get there."

Adam said, "Got it. Just make sure you don't try to drive once you get here, Piper. The road could still be underwater in places.

"No problem. I'll get a helicopter. It's not like they can tell me no."

Sean said, "Ok everyone. I've got to sign off and catch a plane. I'll be in touch."

***

After Sean and Piper left the call, Dakota said, "We'll work on our plan here and connect with local authorities. Raven, prepare yourself. And I know it's hard, but this will be all over the national news before long. The reporters will dig into Zack's history and the trial. Everyone will want a piece of your nightmare."

Raven said, "As if Minnesota knowing my business wasn't bad enough."

After finally making it upstairs to join them, Gabrielle heard her and said, "Girl. I can go there with you from personal experience."

Adam said, "Hang on. That gives me an idea. What if we go to the media first? Put our slant on it and use it to help her instead of harassing her."

Dakota said, "Ok. Go ahead. I like that."

Raven said, "Then it becomes my story instead of his."

Adam said, "Yes."

Dakota said, "Great move, Adam. You'll have everyone watching for strangers and taking care of one of their own."

Gabrielle said, "Then why don't we tell them who Raven really is? Her local ancestors. Go to the museum. Do an interview. Show why she came home to Louisiana to be safe."

Adam smiled as Raven looked at him in wonder.

She said, "How did you just turn all this around? And tell me again why you didn't become an agent? I'm seeing agent in front of me."

He kissed her.

***

After breakfast, they sat around the table discussing strategy.

Raven explained, "He ambushed me in the shower in Minnesota. And…I have this gut feeling he'll go that route again. Not so much the shower, but the ambush. He wanted me to be shocked and vulnerable. Why wouldn't he want that edge again?"

Dakota said, "I get that it won't likely be a snatch and grab off the street. That makes sense. So, you are thinking he'll come here to the house? Or when you are away from here? You know him best. What you think means everything."

She got up and walked around. Thinking. "My house. My safe place. Where I sleep. Live. Love. Because he still wants what he can't have. The intimacy with me. Like he's a part of my life."

"What are your safe spots here?" Dakota asked. "And what concerns you?"

"I want Callie to take Lance somewhere and keep him safe. Away from me until Zack and Hunter are found. Though I don't think Zack would physically harm him. But Hunter might. And both would use him. I know it."

Adam said, "Then that's what we'll do. And hopefully this will be over in a few days. A week at the most. They will find him. You won't be away from Lance for long."

Gabrielle had an idea and texted her mom. Yes, was the swift reply. Gabrielle said, "Raven, sweetie, my parents offered Callie and Lance to stay at the ranch. You know they'll be safe, and they won't be far. And Lance won't even know anything is wrong since he's already there. It'll be like a vacation for him to play with the twins."

Callie's fear rose remembering Raven's previous injuries. She said, "Raven, of course I'll go join Lance. But you— I can't—"

Raven's hand closed over Callie's. "I know, Callie. I know. But I can't have him or you anywhere around me. Not again. I need to know that you have him. And we'll have a plan for Zack this time – we'll be prepared. It won't be like last time."

"But why can't you go somewhere? Hide?"

"Because I can't do this a third time. Or live looking over my shoulder scared to let Lance out to play. I'd rather stand and fight. Draw him here. He's coming anyway."

"But if they catch him and send him back to prison, he could break out again. How will it be over?"

"He'll never make it back to prison." Dakota said. "He'll be dead."

And that comment was just perfect for all of them.

Steel said, "After the water recedes, Callie, I'll take you to the ranch. And you know we won't leave Raven alone."

Dakota said, "Alright. One concern down. What else do you need, Raven?"

"Last time I had to run for a weapon. My knife and gun were in my bedroom, and I certainly wasn't running there. So, I want a few weapons around the house."

"Understandable. No problem. But there will be others around you with weapons. Like you said, it won't be the same."

She said, "Yeah. In the perfect scenario. But life happens. And Zack will be watching for an opening to slip in. Or force an opening. I will have a stronger chance of surviving if you prepare me to defend myself. Make me feel ready. That's what I need. I don't want to be afraid every time the door opens."

Adam said, "Then we'll do whatever it takes. We'll gather weapons and hide them when Piper gets here. She will be your shadow anyway. She'll probably push me out of the way...or try."

Remembering something, he got up and said, "Hang on. I'll be right back."

He returned with a case. Keying in a security code, it opened. A drone. He set it on the table. It was pale gray with clear compartments. And it was small. Only about eight by eight inches. But there were quite a few attachments including a camera and a bar of lights.

Raven said, "That's amazing. When did you get that?"

"When I was in Virginia helping dad. Sean trained me. I'm decent at flying it but nothing like him. And the best part is, Sean can access and control it from wherever he is."

Dakota said, "Very cool. It looks quite a bit different than his others."

"This is a residential model he is working on. Deceptively tough with great features. First off, it's solar and self-charging. And it activates and follows commands by voice, phone app, or control panel. Right now, I am the only one here that can command it."

He demonstrated by saying, "Eagle One," and the drone powered up.

***

In an FBI jet above Illinois, Sean's phone beeped. He checked. Eagle One was live. Good. Adam was showing the others. You never know if he might need to be hands on in Louisiana. But for now, he would be landing in Montana in less than an hour. They just got word of fugitive activity near Warm Springs.

***

Back in Raven's kitchen, a green light blinked once on the drone.

Adam explained, "Feature one is camera and video. When it's powered up, it's auto recording and listening. It also notifies Sean. And of course, there is no privacy after that point. If fact, let's go ahead and turn it off. Eagle One off.

"Now, feature two. It is loaded with GPS trackers and glue. The command is *track*. It blows a GPS tracker on whatever is in front of it – up to about six feet. See the yellow dot in front? That's it. You use it like any tracker to find someone or something; like a car, animal, someone lost, or any type of security concern.

"Feature three is for thermal scans. That's a heat seeking mode - but only Sean can direct it at that point.

"Feature four. A video camera cable. Now, say the drone gets knocked over or damaged. Or maybe we want it to look outside or under a door. The video camera cable will extend and follow instructions.

"And the last, feature five. It will be a weapon in the future. It's not active yet considering the residential aspect. See the red dot? That's the ammo launcher. And that's all I am aware of. But no telling what functions Sean has hidden in there."

Dakota said, "Where's mine?"

Adam laughed. "Sean said to tell you Christmas is around the corner."

"Why did you get yours now?"

"Maybe he likes me better."

Steel choked on coffee, laughing.

***

Once Raven's concerns were addressed, Adam, Dakota, and Steel opened all the storm shutters and spent a couple of hours cleaning the porch and yard from the storm. Everything smelled wet. Muddy. Woodsy.

A few small trees were down, tons of branches, leaves, and even totally random things blew in from somewhere. A clothes basket sat in the middle of the yard. A doll was caught in the tree. Christmas decorations were scattered in the woods. And the wharf was still underwater. Other than that, the houses, barns, and equipment were fine.

Adam measured the water on the road. Less than two feet deep.

He said, "It's going down quicker than I thought. Which is great. Piper texted that she hopes to be at the airport by four o'clock unless remnants of the tropical storm interfere with flights heading south."

Dakota said, "I hope not. She wants to check everything out. The property. River. Maps. Town. She's a stickler for facts. No detail is too small. I know she's going to burn the case investigators at the FBI because we don't have anything on Hunter yet. And she needs to meet detectives Callaway and Patterson as soon as possible. She loves to knock the locals off balance with her looks – then take over."

Steel chuckled and said, "She is a looker. It's a shame she's single."

Adam said, "Wild animals are gorgeous too."

"I get that, but they still find a mate."

"But the female still chooses, and Piper hasn't found her alpha yet. She will."

Dakota said, "I think he's here in Louisiana. What about Patterson? He's a pretty one. Smart too. Great instincts."

Adam said, "I was thinking that myself. I can't wait to see her knocked off balance."

***

Inside the house, Callie took three vintage cups off a hanging rack and set them on the counter. Pouring fresh Community coffee, she said, "Raven, have you thought about a wedding dress? I know all this is going on, but Thanksgiving is next week."

"I brought mom's wedding dress with me."

Callie smiled and poured praline flavored creamer into the cups, then got a toothpick.

Watching, Gabrielle said, "You are the sweetest, Callie. Are you making a design in our coffee?"

"Well, that was the plan, but at the moment the heart I attempted looks like a deformed squash."

Joining her, all three women laughed. And then they couldn't stop. Raven slid to the floor, laughing uncontrollably. Gabrielle tried not to pee on herself as she tight walked to the bathroom. And Callie joined Raven on the floor, wiping tears.

It took several seconds for the humor to fade.

Raven said, "Oh, Callie. I needed that. That was great. Feel free to do that anytime."

The stomping of boots on the porch let them know the men were coming in.

When Adam stepped through the door, he heard giggles. All three men stared at Raven and Callie on the floor. The women laughed at their expressions. Then they heard Gabrielle laughing as she came out of the bathroom.

Dakota said, "What's so funny?"

Raven pointed at the coffee cups on the counter. Adam reached the cups first. He didn't see anything funny and glanced at Dakota.

Dakota smelled the coffee and said, "Have y'all been drinking?"

Steel laughed as all three women lost it again.

Gabrielle finally collapsed in a kitchen chair and said, "Really. It was funny. Callie tried to make us a flavored art coffee with a heart. But..." She laughed. "It looked...like a squash..." and kept laughing.

The men laughed with the women. Glad for even a moment that their fear was pushed aside.

***

In Montana, Special Agent Sean Nash sat in an unmarked FBI van and watched the video feed following a truck.

So far, video in town had recorded a white moving truck passing a bank at two-forty-five a.m. headed south on Main Street from the direction of the prison. It matched the escape time. You could barely make out the snow-fuzzy image of the driver in a cowboy hat. No passengers. No other vehicles on the road.

At three a.m. the truck was picked up on the security camera at the Montana Department of Transportation still heading south. And the image was still fuzzy with snow. And no passengers.

An Interstate 90 camera caught the truck when it merged onto the interstate at three-ten a.m. A better picture. The driver was a white man. Short hair. No cowboy hat. No passengers.

Fifteen minutes later at the intersection of Interstate 90, and Race Track Road, a camera caught the truck. The image was fuzzier but now showed two passengers.

And ten minutes later at the intersection of Galen Road, the camera clearly showed two men. The driver with short hair and a jacket. The passenger, taller than the driver, with long hair, a cowboy hat and jacket. And for the next three cameras in Warm Springs, the image was the same.

Then finally in Opportunity, Montana, an hour after the first sighting, the truck took Stewart Street exit to a side road and headed back north toward the lake.

The findings at the lake became a crime scene twenty minutes later. Sean was on his way there.

***

The Director texted Sean updates: Captain Rollins woke up in ICU.
The U.S. Marshals are questioning him.
The warden is being questioned at the police station.
And autopsies are underway on the doctor and guard.
***

Sean called Dakota as he got on the interstate.

Dakota hit speaker and said, "We're listening, Sean."

"A white moving truck that showed up on video in town not far from the prison crashed at Warm Springs, Montana during the night. That is a small community twenty miles south of Montana State Prison. The truck broke through the rail and was found submerged in a lake with a busted windshield and windows. So far - no bodies. But preliminary evidence indicates there was a lot of blood in the cab along with multiple bullet holes in the doors.

"In the back of the moving truck they found two snowmobiles. We presume this was Zack. Possibly Hunter. We are checking cameras in all directions and monitoring complaints of stolen vehicles.

"But the good news is, there is a 50/50 chance Zack, and the driver are dead. However, the challenge is searching for bodies in the water, snow, and ice. And along with that, this is a wilderness area. Obviously, a body would be considered quick food for any animal.

"But divers are in the water and dogs are in the woods. Dead or alive, we'll find them. The problem is the next snowstorm hits in two days."

96

Dakota said, "Have they broadcast yet?"

"A news bulletin is about to go out warning about a fugitive. But I know Louisiana agencies won't suspect the connection. Let Lake Charles know. And I called Piper and left her a message.

"And Raven?"

"I'm here."

"Hang in there. The whole country will be on the lookout for them in five minutes. And better yet, hopefully, we'll find their bodies, and then this is over permanently."

***

Adam hurriedly texted Detective Callaway and Patterson to watch the fugitive news from Montana. Raven turned on the television. The Breaking News Bulletin interrupted the current programming on KPLC. Zack's mug shot filled the screen as the announcer said,

"The FBI and the U.S. Marshals Service have joined together in a manhunt for a prison break overnight from Montana State Prison. Be on the lookout for fugitive Zack Dawton. He is twenty-eight years old, six foot one, two hundred pounds, with blonde hair and green eyes. He has a large chest scar.

"Zack escaped during a snowstorm killing a guard, possibly a physician, and shooting the captain of the guards three times. It is believed he is traveling with a male accomplice. A crashed truck was found in Warm Springs, Montana, submerged in a lake. No bodies have been found. He is considered armed and dangerous. Do not approach him.

"He was imprisoned for the aggravated rape and attempted kidnapping of a young widow and her infant son in the highly publicized Deadly Dancer Trial in Minnesota. He is also wanted in questioning for the death of two other victims.

"Stay alert. It is possible he is heading south if he is still alive. Contact your local law enforcement, the FBI, or the U.S. Marshals Service with any information or tips. Thank you."

***

Adam took the remote from Raven's hand and hit mute. She stared at the screen, all the words from the broadcast still ringing in her ears.

He said, "Raven—"

She said, "I know it sounds terrible to hope he's dead, but I do. I can't deny it. I almost killed him myself. How many people has he hurt or killed? Besides me, there's Beau. The ranger on his case. The guard and the doctor. He shot the captain. Who else?"

Adam's phone rang. Detective Patterson.

***

Adam answered, "Patterson, you're on speaker."

"I looked up the trial. He's coming for Raven, isn't he?"

"Yes. The FBI's already on the case. There is a lot you don't know that you need to know."

"Once the road is passable, Callaway and I will be there. Raven?"

"Hi, Detective."

"I'm sorry."

"Me too. I hate to draw someone like that to Louisiana. I thought I was getting away to start over."

"You didn't do anything. But he's going to die here. If he doesn't die before he gets here. Dakota — you there?"

"I'm here. And my cousin will be here later today as the new Lake Charles FBI agent. And my other brother, Sean, is already on the case in Montana."

"What? Adam, how come you aren't FBI?"

Shocking everyone but Raven, Adam said, "I want to be the mayor."

"Ah. Well, there's that."

***

Late afternoon Piper called Adam. "I'm here." And referring to one of her favorite movie lines, she said, "And this is a baby airport. Where's it's mommy?"

Laughing, he answered, "Houston."

"Funny guy. Is the river down?"

"Yeah. The water's down. And listen, two Lake Charles detectives that are working on the accomplice case plan to head our way. I asked them to pick you up when you arrived. That way all of you can catch up on the way out."

"Sure. Give me their description and names. I'm not going to jump in a car with two strange men with accents."

Laughing, he said, "The oldest is Callaway and he's a big guy — really out of shape. The tall unattractive one is Patterson. But they're great cops. Be civil. And nice would be even better."

"Don't tell me what to do."

"Oh, Piper," He laughed. "You are going to love Louisiana. I can tell. You fit in with all the hot sauce."

98

Agent Piper Pierce ended the call and followed the signs to baggage claim, her high heels clicking. Twenty minutes later she exited the building to the pickup area pulling a rolling suitcase with a large garment bag.

She glanced at the long line of cars and texted Adam: What are they driving?

Detective Patterson got a text from Adam: Look for the gorgeous cranky woman in a suit. That's Piper.

Patterson looked out the front window. You couldn't miss her. Down the platform stood a tall, sexy woman in a black suit. Stunningly beautiful. With long brown hair, pink lips, sunglasses, and if her posture was any indication - attitude overflowing.

He laughed. Adam hadn't mentioned his cousin was female. Dripping hot. Now, why was that?

He told Callaway as he got out of the car, "Be right back. I'll get her."

"Her?"

He didn't answer and shut the door.

Piper saw the tall, delicious man in a suit get out of the blue SUV and walk toward her. Adam was too funny for his own good. The hunk detective had to be Patterson. He had one hot body under that charcoal gray suit. A smooth sexy gait. Longer than average blonde hair and a handsome face fighting a smile.

She wondered what description Adam gave them about her. They walked toward each other, noting, and filing away details for future contemplation. He stopped in front of her.

With blue eyes twinkling in humor, he said in a southern drawl, "I take it you're Piper. It seems Adam has a sense of humor."

She allowed a grin to twitch at the corner of her mouth and said, "Too much for his own good. I take it you're the unattractive Detective Patterson?"

He laughed. "At your service."

"So, what was his description of me?"

"Non-sexist that he is, he neglected to mention you were even female."

She laughed, taking off her sunglasses, shocking Patterson with her killer smile and blue eyes. She said, "He takes entirely too much leniency in the fact that we're cousins. It didn't help that he didn't have a sister to pick on. Somehow, I got the job."

"Well, I'm a good sport, Piper. Call me Maverick."

Giving him a direct gaze, she said, "Well, I'm not. I like to win. So, I'll get him back. And call me Agent Pierce, Detective Patterson. Now let's go. We have a killer to catch."

And she walked away, rolling her luggage to where a totally fit muscular guy opened the back hatch on the blue SUV. He smiled.

She said, "Hi Callaway, I'm Agent Pierce. And just to let you know, you owe Adam. He described you as a big guy, totally out of shape. You have my permission to knock his lights out."

Chapter 13

On the river, Adam and Raven gathered weapons while Dakota and Gabrielle had ran home to check on their house after the storm.

Raven looked at the impressive collection of weapons on the kitchen table:

Pistols: Five Glocks. Three 38 specials. Three Ruger's. Two Colts. Three Beretta's.

Long guns: Four shotguns.

Six hunting knives.

Two tasers.

Three blackjacks.

The drone.

Adam's bow and arrows.

And she couldn't help it. She giggled.

Adam said, "This is what you call overkill."

Callie walked out of the bedroom with her suitcase. She looked at the table and raised her eyebrows. Really? Raven shrugged with a grin.

Steel walked in the back door. After a long look at the table, he said, "I've got a few more at the barn if you're running short."

They laughed, and then the seriousness returned.

Raven hugged Callie. A long hug. And Adam and Steel walked outside to load the luggage.

Raven said, "I love you, Callie. If anything happens—"

"Stop."

"Listen to me, Callie. My parents are in Africa. You are all Lance has. If, and I say if, anything happens to me and Adam, I trust you and Steel to raise him. You are my beneficiary. Do what needs to be done. If something happens to me, and Adam survives, help him raise Lance."

"Raven, you know I will always be there for you and Lance. And Adam. Don't think about any of that. Just make sure Zack doesn't leave here alive. It's crazy that you have to go through this twice. But then again, maybe he drowned in Montana. Or a bear ate him. Or wolves. Or vultures."

Raven laughed. "Only survivors would think that is funny."

Callie said, "Or an aunt that loves you so much my heart hurts. I want Zack dead, Raven. Only you and I are the ones that know him. Know firsthand—"

"I know, Callie. But we've got this. Go. Call. Video chat. Just take care of my son for me. I'll see you in a few days."

***

Steel started his truck and looked at Callie. He touched her cheek and said, "How about we take a few minutes to spend some time together at my apartment before we leave for the ranch. You haven't seen it."

She smiled a yes, knowing what he wanted. She did too. When would she see him again? A minute later he parked in front of the barn and led her upstairs.

Slipping an arm around her waist, he opened the door and said, "Come check it out. It's a nice barn apartment. Great space. I love it."

The mud room was the foyer, which was appropriate for living above a barn. There was a closet nook with a hanging rack for jackets and rain gear. A rack for boots and shoes in a waterproof tray. A large sink with a spray handle. A slide window that looked over the stalls and barn below. Shelves. Supplies. Everything was neat and efficient.

Callie said, "What a smart room! I can't tell you how many times we've needed this kind of space at Raven's."

"Exactly. I do my best to keep the barn out of the living area."

And they walked into a large open area with three sections. She had expected something like a cabin, but it was all contemporary. Bright. No curtains. One area was the kitchen. The office and living room were combined. And a large, windowed workout area overlooked both houses and the river.

"This is amazing, Steel." Callie said. "I never dreamed you had all this room, and the layout is impressive. You even have a real gym. No wonder you look like you do."

Drawing her to face him, he said, "And how is that?"

Meeting his gaze, she said, "Strong. Sexy—"

And he lowered his lips to hers. In half a second, her feet left the floor as he drew her higher…tighter. And for the next several minutes they played with limited restraint.

He sat on the closest exercise machine and pulled her on his lap. He dropped his shirt on the floor and leaned back. She looked at his body beneath her and felt…everything.

Steel watched her as he grabbed the bar above him and pulled. He strained with the heavy weight. Metal clanked. And his hips rose beneath her. Her eyes met his. He did it again, groaning – and not because of the weights.

She flushed. Hot. And slid her hands up his ripped stomach and chest. Then glanced at him. Breathless.

He said, "You like this."

She "Steel…"

Kissing her, he said, "I know. We've got to get out of here, but when you come home—"

***

Detective Patterson turned off Highway 378 and headed down the road leading to the river. He glanced at Piper in the rearview mirror. She was texting.

Piper texted Sean in Montana: I'm hitching a ride with two detectives. They said we would be at Adam's in a few minutes. One, I'm in the middle of nowhere. Two, there is water everywhere. No wonder it floods here.

Sean: LOL. You're on the Gulf Coast.

Piper: Where is the blue water?

Sean: Not anywhere near the Mississippi River. You're near the mud dump into the Gulf after 2,340 miles through dirt from Minnesota. You know that.

Piper: Just making sure you knew. It's amazing here really. Great history. Rivers and swamps. And Raven and Adam live across from the state park, right?

Sean: Yeah. Right across the river. That's where the accomplice hid his boat. I hope you didn't bring all dress suits and heels.

Piper: I knew better. You three guys like it when I get dirty.

Sean: It's good for you. The world isn't all about prissy.

Piper: You can't say anything about prissy – I've seen Samantha in action. She could shoot someone in a party dress while putting on her lipstick.

Sean laughed: You are right about that. And strip too.

Piper: I can't wait to work with her.

Sean: Ugh.

Piper: Get over it.

Sean: Yeah. Yeah. You're going to find a man there, Piper. He's going to sweeten you up.

Piper: Shut up. And now I'm going to hang up. We're here. See you on video later. Boss.

***

Adam and Raven walked outside as Detective Patterson rolled to a stop and killed the engine. Piper was out of the car in a flash, group-hugging Adam, and Raven.

Piper said, "You are so gorgeous, Raven. I am crazy jealous. Why was I born with brown hair when your fabulous hair color was in the heaven gene pool?"

Raven laughed and said, "Honey, your gene pool is a work of art. It fits you – and all the men around you."

Adam smiled and said, "Well said, Raven. So, what do you think of the river, Piper?"

"All my fussing aside, it's amazing. A great wilderness right next door to the city. But…" She looked around the yard surrounded by woods, then down the river, and said, "It's nigh to impossible to know what is behind all these trees or around all the bends in the river."

Raven said, "True. But that's why I chose it. I wanted Lance and I to get in touch with our Native American side. And for my photography business. But then again, I didn't expect Hunter to be lurking in the woods or Zack to escape."

Piper looked at the gun holstered at Adam's side, and said, "Are you always packing out here?"

Adam motioned the detectives over to join them, and answered, "Most of the time. And we all do when we head in the woods."

Patterson shook hands with Adam and said, "Unattractive?"

Callaway said, "Big and out of shape?"

Adam laughed and said, "Look, you ought to thank me. I saved you from doing the - *my gun is bigger than your gun* competition between the FBI and the locals. After a good laugh we know who's in charge and move on."

Patterson said, "I see. Is this the method of governing you plan to implement when you are mayor?"

As everyone laughed, Dakota and Gabrielle drove up.

Reaching Gabrielle first, Piper touched her baby belly, and said, "You are such a beautiful momma. Your daughter is going to be gorgeous and strong like her parents."

Dakota said, "Of course she is! Now, where's my greeting?"

Piper laughed and disappeared in Dakota's bear hug.

He said, "It's good to see you. We've missed your calm demeanor and knockout smile."

She laughed and he motioned her away from Gabrielle and said, "Now show me what you've got."

Startling the detectives, Piper was out of her heels, and spun, kicking high. Dakota caught her ankle just before it hit the side of his head. Adam smiled - Piper was still quick. Gabrielle smiled at Raven. Tough women rule.

Piper said, "Come on, Dakota. You're turn. How long has it been since you've busted a move on someone?"

"Not often enough, but we'll spar later. The detectives look like they wish they had run a background check on all of us."

Thinking that very thing, Patterson said, "Guilty."

Chuckling Dakota said, "It's getting dark. Someone, help me get all this food out of the car. I'm starving and Gabrielle's eating for two."

Patterson and Callaway brought up the rear as they helped Dakota carry in Popeyes fried chicken, Wendy's salads, and Domino's pizza. Then the detectives stopped dead in their tracks at the sight of weapons covering the kitchen table.

Patterson counted thirty-three, and said, "Now would be a good time to explain what you have in mind here at the O.K. Corral."

Over dinner for eight and a half at the snack bar, Adam explained about hiding a few weapons in the house for Raven. And why. So, after the kitchen was cleaned up, Raven picked out five pistols, two knives, and one taser. She showed them where she wanted each weapon, and that's where they stayed. They put all the other weapons away, except the drone.

Callaway said, "I haven't seen a drone like that. Where did it come from?"

Adam said, "That's an interesting story. Our middle brother, Agent Sean Nash, is a technical genius. He built it. And his brilliant strategy during research and surveillance has made many an FBI case end swift and successful. But as for the drone, it's mine. And the most important thing about it is that Sean can man it from anywhere. He is linked into it."

Patterson said, "I'm speechless."

"Want to see Sean fly it?"

He laughed. "You don't even have to ask."

***

Adam texted Sean: Can you fly Eagle One for us?

Sean: Open the door.

***

Adam opened the back door. The drone powered up, rotated to the door, and zoomed out. They followed it outside. It made a few acrobatic loops and flew back to hover aggressively in front of Patterson.

Patterson said, "Stop it, Sean."

In Montana, Sean laughed.

In Louisiana, the drone wiggled in response, then spit a tracker on Patterson's neck. He yelled, "Hey!" grabbing his neck.

The others laughed and Adam said, "It's just a tracker. Go hide. He'll find you."

Patterson jogged around the house.

Sean watched the GPS signal travel in a half circle, then stop. He sent the drone after it. In three seconds, he hit the detective with a spotlight on the front porch in a rocker.

Sean asked through the drone speaker, "That the best you got, Detective?"

"It's wet. You wanted me to crawl in the mud?"

They both headed back toward the others while Sean laughed. That was totally true.

Demonstration over, back inside, Dakota, Piper, and Adam studied the layout of the first floor for the best place for the drone. They chose the backdoor coat rack and shelf where it was partially hidden by other items – but not penned in or blocked. It had a great visual of the front and back doors, den, kitchen, and stairs with the 360-degree lens.

Weapons in place, they headed upstairs to the office to bring the detectives up to date on the investigation.

A couple of minutes into it, Raven's phone rang. It was Lexi.

Raven grimaced and walked in the hall. She answered with an apology, "Oh, Lexi, I am so sorry. I was supposed to call you at three. I've had a lot going on and completely forgot."

Lexi said, "Don't worry about that. I'm just checking in to make sure you made it through the storm. I know it was your first and I haven't heard from Callie."

"The river covered the wharf and road but it's already back to normal. How about your place?"

"I live in a cottage that isn't close to the river, so I'm fine. I was just concerned about all the mouths you've got to feed over there and thought you might be running low on supplies. Do you still plan on me starting tomorrow?"

Raven thought about the case. Had Lexi seen the news? Was it even safe for her to be here?

She said, "Lexi, I'll be honest. We have a problem and I need to check with Adam to see if it is safe for you to come here."

"What do you mean, safe? Are you safe? Lance? The others?"

"Lexi—"

"I'll be there in fifteen minutes," and the line went dead.

***

Raven joined Adam in the office and said, "Lexi called. She's supposed to start work tomorrow but I explained it might not be safe for her to come right now. And that didn't go well."

"What do you mean?"

"She's on her way."

Smiling, he said, "Because she's like her dad."

"Yes. But I'm not comfortable with her being here. Maybe for a couple of days, but even Gabrielle shouldn't stay much longer."

Glancing at Gabrielle, she said concerned, "My baby isn't here either. I certainly wouldn't want yours here."

Dakota said, "I never intended you to stay, Gabrielle. You need to go to your parents' place by tomorrow night."

Adam said, "Raven, let Lexi work tomorrow and Friday. And then she'll be with her dad in the food truck Saturday for the grand opening - along with the public."

Piper asked, "What does Lexi do exactly?"

Raven said, "She's a chef. She helps her dad with his food truck, and she's a student at the cooking school at Sowela Technical Community College. She's impressive. Delicious food. Beautiful woman. Loyal with a capital L. She wants to build her professional resume and we are lucky to get her."

Patterson said, "I can have an officer escort her to and from home. But like you, after Quest grand opening on Saturday, it's best no one else is hanging around."

Piper said, "Speaking of Quest, Adam. What if you have a rescue job? Who are your employees?"

"I need to hire an airboat driver and plan to take applications and hire one Saturday. Then Quest would have Raven for medical, the driver, and myself. But I need to hire an assistant for Steel too. The yard, the houses, the equipment, the animals, and security are too much for one man now."

The dogs barked. Lexi was here. That was fast. Everyone headed downstairs.

Raven opened the back door on the first knock, and whatever Lexi had been about to say ended when she saw all the people inside. Her eyes locked on the three very intimidating people in suits.

Raven smiled at the beautiful blonde in jeans and a McNeese State University sweatshirt. She was petite but athletic. Long blonde ponytail. Lovely olive skin. Deep blue eyes. And full lips.

She said, "Come on in, Lexi. I'm sorry to seem so mysterious earlier."

Glancing at the others with a tiny frown, Lexi said, "I was worried."

Raven hugged her, and Adam said, "Lexi, by chance did you watch the news bulletin this morning about the fugitive in Montana?"

"I did see that."

That made it simple then, and Adam said, "He's missing. But if he's alive, he's coming here."

Her eyes widened and she looked at Raven in sudden understanding. She said, "So, the trial..."

Raven said, "I was the victim."

Pain for Raven flashed across Lexi's face, and she said, "I'm so sorry."

"Thank you, Lexi. You are too sweet. Now let me introduce the new faces."

Raven pointed to Piper and said, "Piper is Agent Pierce with the FBI. Adam and Dakota's cousin."

Piper smiled, and Lexi flashed a smile in return, plus dimples.

Raven continued, "And Patterson and Callaway are detectives." They nodded with a smile looking forward to the dimples. And got them.

Raven said, "Adam, why don't you take it from here?"

Adam said, "Lexi, the fugitive, if alive, could reach Louisiana by Saturday. So, after the grand opening on Saturday, you shouldn't be here until they are caught. And don't go anywhere alone on the property for now. So, for this week, how about working tomorrow and the next day?"

"Great! I would love to cook for all of you. Should I plan meals for this group of eight?"

Not knowing who all might be here, he said, "To keep it simple, yes."

Callaway said, "Since you will be brought to and from your house for the next two days, what are your hours?"

Lexi glanced at Raven and said, "Is seven in the morning to three in the afternoon, ok?"

Raven said, "It's perfect. Thank you. And are you sure your family will be ok with this?"

"It's my choice. But they trust you. They will be fine."

She paused and said, "So, Raven, you dance, then?"

"Not like I used to."

"I bet you are a beautiful dancer."

Raven smiled, touched. And for a moment, emotional.

Lexi said, "Should I check the kitchen to see if I need to shop before morning?"

"Sure. Whatever you need. And I have a card for shopping expenses."

Lexi headed to the kitchen. A few minutes later, Callaway escorted her off the river.

***

They were all upstairs working when Sean called on video.

Answering, Adam introduced the detectives.

Sean said, "Patterson and Callaway, I appreciate you staying abreast of the case and working with my family. Have you found out anything else on Hunter?"

Patterson said, "No. Just a few sporadic vehicle thefts on the way north. No hits on his fingerprints or DNA. Just a picture of him from Raven and an active warrant waiting on him if he comes back. Course, it looks like we'll have to get in line."

"Right." Sean said. "Everyone wants a piece of him. But anyway, now for updates. No bodies have been found in the lake or woods yet. Nothing yet on DNA. And this is the clearest image of both men in the white moving truck."

Raven walked closer to the screen and said, "If the passenger is Zack, I can't really tell. And the driver doesn't seem familiar at all. Even I would pass them by without recognition."

"That's their plan, I'm sure. And there have been no further pics since then. We don't know what they look like now. And they cover their tracks so well they vanish.

"The snowmobile for the escape was equipped with a GPS tracking device and amber lights for better visibility in snow. Zack drove his snowmobile right into the back of the truck. Unfortunately, it couldn't have been a cleaner plan. And then they simply exited the interstate, backtracked on a side road heading north to the lake, and crashed. Bled. And disappeared again."

Everyone was silent. What could you say?

Sean continued, "And we think there had to be two shooters. Zack shot the guards and the captain. But the doctor was killed on the road through his window. And he was dead longer than the guard. Now, the accomplice could have shot the doctor, but he would have needed inside information for that to play out.

"So, looking at inside information, it was the warden who made the medical emergency decision to send Zack to town when the doctor never showed up. And it turns out that Zack's family showered money for Zack's transfer from Minnesota to Montana. And on top of that, his family made it common knowledge money was available for whatever Zack needed. Including retribution in case he was harmed."

Piper said, "His family have that kind of pull?"

"They do. And the warden was concerned about retribution. So, he gave the order to the captain."

Dakota said, "Why didn't the captain cage Zack for the trip?"

"The prison bus wasn't equipped to handle a whiteout snowstorm. But the captain's Hummer was well-equipped to handle it with experience. Which strengthens the suspicion of inside information. I mean, the dominoes had to be in the right place - the warden saying go, the captain on duty with his Hummer, Zack sick, the doctor executed, and the accomplice preparing things with the snowmobile. There would have been no room for error."

Piper said, "But the only two in charge were the warden and the captain."

"Exactly. It could be either one of them or they worked in tandem. But the warden's not a tough guy. He's almost peed his pants ten times already. I'm leaning toward the captain who probably knew how to use the retribution angle to scare the warden into the decision."

Dakota said, "But what would have made it worth getting shot three times? How much money could someone pay you for those injuries?"

"A million bucks would make a few people I know think twice – but it doesn't mean they would do it."

Piper asked, "Weren't the captain's injuries critical? Wasn't he in ICU?"

"The wounds weren't critical. But blood loss and the weather almost did him in. Zack took his radio and phone, and he couldn't call for help. But the shots themselves could have been staged. Even the head wound was just a deep graze leaving a scar and a headache that won't go away."

"What's the captain saying?" Piper asked.

"Drama. Saying he'll never go back. It was too traumatic."

Dakota said, "He would know that would draw suspicion. How stable is his home life?"

"Finances in order. Thirty years on the job. Good marriage. Not a great retirement package but it would work for the life he lives. Good health. The only unusual financial activity was a hundred grand inheritance from his grandfather about the time he bought the Hummer. He used it all and didn't pay off his home which raises a red flag."

Piper said, "Maybe he decided he liked expensive things."

"Which is where we are on the investigation. They are about to get a warrant for his home."

Dakota said, "Did big amounts of money leave Zack's family?"

"The mother isn't cooperating. And the dad died about six months ago."

"Who's the beneficiary?"

"Zack and his mother."

"What's she like?"

"A pretty Tyrannosaurus rex."

Raven entered the conversation and asked, "What happens if they don't find the money or the money trail?"

Sean said, "They'll watch the captain, his wife, and the pretty T-Rex. It could be a long wait for them to slip up."

"And how long will they actively search for Zack?"

"Until he or his body is found." Sean said. "But we all know he didn't escape to run away to a tropical island or Mexico. If he's alive, he's coming here as fast as he can. He knows they'll track him somehow someway. He wants something before he dies."

Raven sighed. "That doesn't make me feel any better."

Adam said, "No. But it does give us time to prepare. Then I can kill him."

Piper said, "How is the investigation on Zack's family tree? Close friends? Yearbook? Social media back then? Even Ancestry DNA research if you have it."

"They're digging and interviewing."

Raven said, "He called his friend on the camping trip his blood brother."

Adam said, "That could be blood or close friend – a pact."

Dakota said, "Also have the team check local news on the family going back to high school. Gossip. Problems. Awards. And where did the family get their wealth?"

Patterson said, "In regard to the blood brother remark, I had some college buddies make a good bit of money as a sperm donor. I would check insemination banks for family and friends."

Sean said, "Great idea. It's added."

Piper looked at Patterson. Her gaze insinuated he had done it as well. He raised his eyebrows in challenge. She lowered her gaze to his pants. He smiled and hooked his thumb in his waistband. Bring it on.

Sean said, "Ok, everyone. Let's call it a night. I'll send updates as I get them. The Director wants them too. He said if the search for Zack moves south, we'll head that way. You won't face him alone. Until then, research, profile, be alert, and let me know if you think of anything else."

***

Dakota and Adam added a few things to the evidence wall.

Patterson glanced at Raven and said, "This is your dance studio. Do you plan to dance again?"

"Not publicly. I hope to teach my children one day."

Gabrielle said, "I can just see a red-haired daughter flying through the air."

Adam said, "You ought to see Raven flying through the air."

Glancing at Raven, Gabrielle said, "I would love to see you dance. Old pictures and videos are not the same as seeing it in person. Hint. Hint."

Adam said, "Dancing is her happy place. Raven, do you want to? We can move the tables out of the way."

"Maybe it will help clear my head."

"Then go change. I'll get it ready. What song?"

"I'll think about it…"

Chapter 14

Raven opened the white antique trunk in her bedroom. Shuffling under Lance's newborn toys, she found the zippered bag of competition costumes at the bottom. Pulling it to the top of the pile, she softly touched the embroidered bag, remembering all the beautiful dances. The grace. The expression. The feeling inside her at the connection of music and dance.

She removed a shiny gold one-piece full body leotard with a low back and slipped it on. She stretched and warmed up. Then after adding dramatic makeup, she pulled her hair in a ponytail and walked barefoot to the studio.

Adam heard her door close and glanced down the hall. Raven looked like liquid gold. Smooth. Sensual. Glitter around her eyes. He had never seen Raven the performer, and she was magnificent. She smiled at him and stepped into the room. The men quit talking but she was used to the hush before a performance. She glanced at Piper and Gabrielle and winked as they stared in open-mouthed awe.

Raven pulled up the song she was feeling and explained, "I love Jazz. The oldies. The soulful groove. And some of you might remember this song. *Ain't No Sunshine.*" And with a smile, she posed, and motioned for Adam to start the song. He hit play.

Gabrielle had never seen anything so sensual or beautiful. Raven's body could tell a story all on its own. Dramatic dance moves with rhythmic leaps, spins, splits, and jumps, she was spectacular from head to toe. Every move was graceful, powerful, body art.

Piper knew in a second Raven was extraordinary. That she would always draw people like a moth to a flame. And she knew she was seeing what Zack had seen. Touched. And wanted. Even to this day. But the beauty was, Raven only saw the expression of music. It wasn't sexual. She simply became the music. The message.

Dakota knew from the videos he had seen already; she would be a gorgeous dancer. And she was. Wow. And while he got what Zack dealt with, he hated him for trying to destroy something no one could take from her.

Patterson and Callaway shared one quick glance when she began dancing. Then nothing distracted them from watching her tell a story without a word.

And Adam…Adam watched his woman soar, realizing that every dance, every song, every day, her fire would flutter and change within her. She was a true flame. Powerful. And his. As the song faded, she spun and landed in his arms. He kissed her and then everyone tried to talk at once.

Afterwards, Gabrielle headed to bed. Dakota insisted.
Raven went to change.
Dakota and Adam joined Steel in the den.
Piper walked outside with the detectives. But Callaway was no fool and got out of the conversation and into the car.

***

Patterson leaned against the car, and said, "You have quite a family, Agent Pierce, from so many angles."

She smiled. "Right! And Raven fits right in." She paused. "I keep thinking of her dancing like that with Zack all those years. As a woman, she's extraordinary. As a performer, she is indescribable. I think the performer is who he fell in love with."

He nodded, and said, "Professional dancing is a whole other world to me. I've seen Dancing with the Stars. Watched entertainers. Seen TikTok videos. Everyone is dancing in some form or fashion these days, and it's drenched in sensuality. Some are just flat out vulgar. But Raven…turns into magic."

"She does. Do you dance, Detective Patterson?"

"I would like to dance with you. But that aside, don't you think after the intimate look you gave me upstairs, at least in a casual setting, you could call me Maverick."

She grinned and didn't answer.

He said, "I am not a sperm donor, Piper."

"I wasn't judging. Just teasing. Is it the act of donating, or the issue?"

"It's because I plan to raise any children I have."

She absorbed his answer. Impressed at the sincerity and integrity. She said, "That's the right reason, Maverick. I admire that stand. Though I understand medically the need for donors."

Gazing at her through the filtered porch light, he said, "Do you want to have—"

"Stop."

"You opened the door."

"And closed it too."

"Too late. We're into personal now. So, tell me, are you in a relationship?"

"You're the detective."

He said, "Ok. No ring on your finger. But I see interest in me. So, I say no relationship. Because even if you simply didn't put your ring on – no way I believe you'd play your man. Too much integrity. Too smart. That leaves me to think you like to play the game. So…come on Piper. Let's play."

She slipped her hands in her pockets, meeting his direct gaze, and said, "You are bold, Detective Patterson."

"Wait. What happened to Maverick?"

"I'm stopping you from thinking you'll get to kiss me."

"Come on, Piper. You will wonder what I taste like."

"Maybe. Maybe not."

He said softly, "Yes you will."

"Go home, Detective…my feet hurt."

She kicked off her heels. Slipped off her jacket and turned back to the house. He watched her go.

He called out, "Five-foot-seven. One hundred and fifteen pounds. Fabulous curves."

She reached the door and glanced back. He was still leaning on the car. Tall and sexy. Eyes locked on her.

She said, "You're brave too. You could have fumbled." She paused. "But you almost made a first down. Goodnight, Detective."

***

Raven was laid sideways across the bed dressed in LSU shorts and a purple work out top as she texted Callie.

> Raven: How's Lance?
>
> Callie: I'm sending you a video he made for you. He's having fun – but missing you.

Raven: Hug him for me.

Callie: I did. Kissed him too. Then tickled him.

Raven: Callie, I can't imagine life without you. Steel is going to take you, isn't he?

Callie: No. He's going to join me. I'm not going anywhere. He knows I don't come alone.

Raven: I'm happy for you. I love Steel already.

Callie: It's a good thing. I'll probably be on my honeymoon soon.

Raven: I figured. I never dreamed we'd get married at the same time. You're going to knock his socks off.

Callie: It's not his socks I'm thinking about.

Raven laughed: Yeah. Well, he isn't thinking about yours either.

Callie: Not hardly.

***

The bathroom door opened as Raven put her phone down. Adam looked at the long-legged beauty across the bed and glanced at the partially open door to the hall. He shut it. Raven smiled as she looked at him. Black shorts. Damp hair. And all that beautiful skin. He knelt in the bed, and she felt the fire in his eyes as he slid a hand up her leg, then laid next to her.

As he pulled her close, she whispered, "We're going to get into trouble."

"I want to kiss you. I'll open the door after that. Maybe."

"Our definition of kiss crosses into rated R with a healthy interest in X. You will not want to open the door. You know it."

He groaned and said into the air, "Siri, set an alarm for ten minutes, no, you better make it five. It's hot in here."

Siri said from his phone, "Your alarm is set."

Raven smiled as his lips covered hers.

When the alarm went off in what seemed like two seconds, Adam said a very unkind word to Siri as he opened the door.

A little later, Raven slept next to him as he sat propped on pillows checking messages. Piper passed by. She leaned against the doorframe and texted him so she wouldn't wake Raven.

Piper: I'm glad she let us watch her dance. It helped me understand Zack better.

Adam: Raven doesn't mind. She's lost in the song.

116

Piper: I saw the pictures. How is she with the scars?

Adam: He was vicious. But she's so beautiful you don't see them.

Piper: You are perfect for her.

Adam: And she's perfect for me. God loves me.

Piper smiled: He loves all of us.

Adam grinned: Not as much as me.

Piper glanced at him incredulously: Really? You think you've charmed God?

Adam: No. He charmed me. But on another note, your turn has come.

Piper: For what?

Adam: Love. Your man's here.

Piper: Mind your own business, hot stuff.

And with a roll of her eyes, she disappeared from the doorway. He smiled.

Chapter 15

At a rest area southeast of Denver, Colorado, an old man limped through slushy snow to the restroom. It was a few minutes before midnight. Pushing open the door, he stepped inside. Holding onto the wall he aimed for the handicap stall. Locking the door, he leaned down to look across the bottom of the stalls. He was alone.

Zack pulled off the gray wig and beard and rubbed his face. It itched. Then shaking out his own long hair, he massaged his scalp, then put it back in a ponytail. Changing into a clean flannel shirt he slid his fingers along the two scars across his chest. Then touched the scar at the base of his neck.

Raven had almost killed him.

His dream had gone all kinds of wrong that night.

But not this time.

Looking down at his ripped chest and abs, he smiled. Impressed. And thanks to the workouts in prison, he was now tough. Rugged. Evidently, her kind of sexy considering Beau and the new guy in Louisiana.

But regardless, he had a plan to make her *give* him what he wanted.

He said, "I'm coming, Raven. Can you feel me?"

Chapter 16

Raven screamed. Panicked. Fighting in the darkness.

Adam's heart lurched at the terror he heard and reached for her. Soothing her. "Raven, baby. It's just a dream. I've got you. You're safe. I promise."

Her heart pounded in her ears as she grabbed him, hanging on. Voice wobbly, she whispered, "It seemed so...real..."

Then Adam heard running footsteps. Piper ran through the door, gun in hand. Dakota behind her. They quickly realized what happened, and with a nod to Adam, they left.

Raven felt the remnants of the old nightmare crumble away. That's all it had been. Zack wasn't here. He really wasn't. Adam drew her trembling body down with him and pulled the covers up. Rubbing her back. Loving her. She fell asleep whispering his name.

He looked at the clock. Three a.m.

Then stared out the window.

Where was Zack?

***

The alarm went off at six the next morning. Adam silenced it, then kissed the top of Raven's head. She stirred against his chest. Purring like a cat. Stretching. Then snuggling. He pulled her against him, aching already, and groaned at the feel of her warm body.

She whispered huskily, "I agree. You feel way too good. But...the door is open."

"I can shut it faster than you can blink."

She giggled. "But it's only day seven."

He growled, caressing her, and tried to force his body to behave. He said, "I can act like I miscounted."

She laughed, and he smiled with an exaggerated sigh.

Raven brushed a finger over his lips and said, "I'm sorry about the scream. I haven't had that nightmare in a long time. And like all the nightmares, it seemed so real. I'm glad Lance and Callie weren't here."

"Did nightmares happen a lot after the attack?"

"Yes. Callie kept Lance in her room with a sound machine for about six months.

He said, "I know everything is triggering those memories. I'm so sorry. But today should be better since we have a lot to do. I plan to at least attempt to get back to normal as the FBI and U.S. Marshals do their job. And you need a break from all the research and discussions."

He kissed her softly and said, "I insist."

"No argument here. But…I do have to get out of bed. Lexi will be here soon."

"Me too. Unwillingly. But the contractor will be at my place at eight."

Getting up, he said, "We need to discuss house plans since we have two. And mine is almost move in ready."

Sliding out of bed, she said, "I do have something to run by you on that subject."

"Just say when, gorgeous. Just say when. See you downstairs."

***

Raven pulled on jeans, a sweatshirt, and flip flops. Brushing her hair, she thought about the nightmare. It was always the same. The rush of shock and confusion when she stepped out of the shower. Naked. And Zack was there with that crazed look of desire that terrified her.

And that was all it had taken. That first second of betrayal killed their friendship instantly. Poof. Gone like it had never been. And then came the violence. She touched her scars. They remained. Along with the hidden fear and anger when the memories were stirred.

Forcing it aside, she finished dressing and determined to enjoy her day. Hearing the others downstairs, she smiled and headed to the door. Then stopped. She looked at her lockbox. Zack might not have been here last night. But…

She holstered her Glock and jogged downstairs.

Raven smiled at the men as they drank coffee in the kitchen while watching the news across the room in the den. Gabrielle sat in the rocking chair with coffee and waved. Piper was outside in the yard on the phone.

Raven headed to the coffee pot.

A few minutes later a Sheriff's Department SUV drove up. Lexi got out. Callaway got out and helped her gather grocery bags. Steel headed out to help. And in short order, they were back inside. The dimpled chef smiled in delight at all the mouths to feed.

After everyone chatted for a minute, Callaway said, "I'm heading out. Lexi, someone will be here to bring you home at three p.m., or as close to three as possible."

She said, "Don't leave, Rex! I'll have pancakes ready in no time. At least let me feed you. Please don't say no."

Raven bit her lip to keep from smiling after she saw the look on Callaway's face. He wasn't going anywhere.

Raven said, "Make yourself comfortable, Callaway. Grab a cup of coffee and watch the news with us. It's early. Surely, you have a little extra time."

"Ok. Sounds good."

Lexi shooed the men out of the kitchen and got to work as efficiently as any chef Raven had ever seen. Pancake batter was poured into a hot iron skillet in no time while bacon baked in the oven.

Steel said, "I've never baked bacon."

Dakota said, "We do. They're evenly cooked. And no stained shirts from the splatter."

"Right." Adam said. "And bacon on the grill is great too."

Callaway said, "Bacon is great no matter how you cook it."

Raven said, "Stop, you're making my stomach growl."

Gabrielle said, "What stomach?" She patted her belly. "This is a stomach."

No one said anything as they tried not to look at each other. They remembered what she had done to Dakota over the watermelon comment.

Piper came inside and freshened her coffee. Leaning against the snack bar she noticed Callaway glance at Lexi. He caught her watching.

Enjoying the moment, Piper said, "Callaway, look at you, bringing our beautiful Lexie out here. Imagine that."

Callaway looked over the top of his coffee cup at her. Message clear. Zip it.

Piper smiled, thinking, not hardly. "Come on, Callaway. You know Patterson would have a comeback for me. Shoot."

He drawled, "Patterson's got a lot more than a comeback for you."

Everyone laughed as Patterson drove up.

They waved him in. He greeted everyone and took a lingering glance at Piper's hips and long legs in tight jeans. He met her gaze. He'd thought about her all night.

Piper pointed to the kitchen and said, "You look like a hungry man. Pancakes and bacon are on the way."

His look warned her as he said, "What if, what I'm hungry for isn't in the kitchen?"

Her whole demeanor changed. She smiled. Sultry. Promising. Stepping close, she touched his jacket and said, "Suck it up, handsome. I'm not on the menu."

Laughter exploded.

As soon as it quieted down, Lexi asked sweetly, "Anyone ready to eat?"

Random fits of laughter interfered as everyone served themselves. But the food was delicious. Lexi was queen of the kitchen.

***

Twenty minutes later, Adam left for his house. Callaway left for work. And Dakota, Piper, and Patterson met outside on the porch.

Piper said, "Raven needs a break. The nightmare last night confirmed it. Gabrielle and I plan to take her to Lake Charles. KPLC jumped at the chance to interview both Gabrielle and Raven. They are thrilled about the fugitive exclusive and descendant angle. But I noticed Raven's packing. Does she have a permit?"

Dakota said, "She does."

Patterson said, "And speaking of security, Callaway and I have been given the go-ahead to work surveillance out here till Zack is located. Tomorrow's already Friday. Things could snowball."

Piper said, "Appreciate it. Anything could go down in the next day or so."

Dakota said, "I agree. Connect with Adam. Steel has a great apartment above the barn he's not even using right now, and Adam's place is still unoccupied. Lexi will keep you fed. And on behalf of Adam and Raven, make yourself at home."

***

Raven and Gabrielle dressed for their interviews.

Raven chose a rich turquoise jumpsuit. Thick shiny silk with a fabulous belt. And of course, stilettos. Almost invisible since they matched her skin so

122

well. Dancer and descendant would be the point of the interview so, she aimed for eye catching but sophisticated. A victim fighting back. Confident. She would make Wolf proud.

Downstairs, Gabrielle sighed. Dressing was the one thing that was not fun at her stage of pregnancy. She decided to go for fall stylish in an ankle length deep orange sweater dress split to the knee. Dark brown boots with beaded ankle chains and buckles. Topped off with a brown bolero jacket.

Piper didn't care what she wore. She was just thinking about protecting the women as she chose a brown suit with gold flecks in the weave. Dressing quickly, she drew her hair back in a professional ponytail, holstered her gun, and walked out of the bedroom. Authority in place. Intense. She knew time would run out soon if Zack wasn't caught.

Adam and Dakota whistled when the women walked outside.
Slipping an arm around Raven, Adam said, "You look gorgeous. Are you good with this interview plan?"
"I'm nervous, but experienced hiding it. I'll be fine."
"You'll be amazing. Just stay in your comfort zone no matter what they do. And keep in mind that reporters like to throw in a few things for shock value. If I need to go back and knock someone out, just text. Dakota and I are taking out the airboat, but I'll have my phone on vibrate."
Smiling, Raven said, "My hero! But really, I'm looking forward to telling my own story. If it goes off script and I don't like it, I'll stop."
Piper said, "I'll stop anything that gets out of hand. No worries there."

***

Thirty minutes later, the women were in downtown Lake Charles. Less than a mile from the lake front Civic Center, north beach, fabulous Shell Beach Drive homes, and views of two massive bridges and waterfront casinos. Parks. Docks. Boats. Banks. And courthouses.
Gabrielle smiled at the history of what once was No Man's Land as she pulled into the Imperial Calcasieu Museum. Home of the now famous 375-year-old Sallier Oak, named for the street and homeplace where it stands.

Raven said, "I can't believe I haven't been here yet. Thank you for thinking of this Gabrielle. No telling what I will discover here today."

"I've only been here once, so there are still many things I haven't seen yet. We have thirty minutes or more before the news crew gets here. I'm sure the museum director is looking forward to meeting you. Come on…"

Piper stepped out of the car, looking around to make sure the coast was clear, and all three women went inside. And in a flash, they were transported years past. In amazement they walked through the front exhibits. The clothes. Furniture. Items from the past. Rooms set up like one would find many, many decades ago. Generations gone but not forgotten.

At the sound of fast footsteps, they turned to see a man and woman approaching them. All smiles. The older woman, Gabrielle knew, was Grace.

Grace shook hands, and said, "Hello Gabrielle, I didn't realize you were soon to be a mother. Congratulations! How exciting for you and Dakota! Oh. And please, let me introduce Lucas. He is our new director and a creative genius when it comes to history."

Lucas smiled, then shook Gabrielle's hand and said, "It is an honor to meet you. Of course, I have studied your ancestor's history and read of your connection. It's all amazing. We are looking forward to being a part of your event today - and meeting your friends."

Gabrielle motioned to Raven and said, "Lucas, please meet Raven. It was her grandfather, Wolf, an Atakapa native, that helped Jean Lafitte. And she is also soon to be my sister-in-law!"

Shaking her hand, he said, "Raven, congratulations! And, yes, I certainly remember reading of the connection. That is quite exciting. I am sure Wolf would be proud to know you are here now. And in fact, I have several items you might be interested in seeing."

"I look forward to it, Lucas. Anything you can share with me about my Atakapa ancestors would be greatly appreciated."

"My pleasure!"

He glanced at Piper, and Gabrielle said, "This is Special Agent Piper Pierce with the FBI. She is working on the fugitive case involving Raven. She is also Dakota's cousin."

Piper smiled at the impressed expression on his face. He and Grace glanced at each other as if to say, "FBI…do what?"

Formally, he said, "Agent Pierce, we are grateful the FBI is protecting one of our community members. Most grateful."

Piper smiled and said, "We all hope for a quick resolution. Will you let me know when KPLC arrives?"

"Why yes. Of course. Right away."

Then leading them down the hall, he said, "Come, please, Raven, Gabrielle, let me show you something you will want to see."

They followed him to an elegant seating area. There was a backdrop of antique black and white photographs of multiple sizes on easels showing groups of people from long ago. Huge wharfs. Ships. Wagons. Horses. People shopping. Talking. Men, women…and Indians.

Lucas pointed to the large photograph on the left easel and said, "Come closer, Gabrielle. See the man with the fancy jacket?"

"Yes. Is it—"

"It is! Jean Lafitte himself! And do you see the man next to him in the uniform jacket and large sideburns?"

"Yes. Who is that?"

"Sam Houston."

"Oh my gosh. They knew each other?"

"Yes."

Raven shared, "The Atakapa sang stories of my grandfather with Sam Houston – just like they sang stories about Lafitte."

Lucas said, "I am not surprised. Do you know that Sam Houston was raised with the Cherokee as a teenager?"

"No. I didn't."

Smiling now, he said, "So, then you don't know that Sam Houston's Cherokee name was Raven."

Raven gasped. And Gabrielle. Even Piper. Grace and Lucas clapped in delight.

Raven said, "I had no idea. What an intriguing idea that I could have been named after him. Are there any pictures of an Atakapa male with Lafitte or Houston?"

Lucas pointed to a photo on the right easel of six men standing on a wharf. A dark Indian with a mohawk style headpiece, much older, stood with them and faced the camera. Lafitte and Houston were behind him pointing at a ship.

And just like that, there he was. It was extraordinary for the museum to have that specific picture after all this time. A gift beyond time.

Raven said softly, "Grandfather..." And fighting tears, she said, "Is it possible to get a copy?"

Lucas said, "We can arrange it."

Grace's phone dinged. She glanced at Piper, and said, "KPLC is here."

***

Adam and Dakota were skimming across the river surface at close to 70 miles an hour in the airboat. They were in a secluded part of the river. No homes. Just inlets branching off into swamp areas. Cypress trees with knees dotted the shoreline. Patches of lily pads. Pine trees, various oak trees, and years of overgrown brush filled the riverbank. And the water was deep. Dark. Impenetrable to the naked eye.

Fish jumped as they passed, whether from the loud noise or natural habit. Alligator eyes watched from just above the water line. And birds and turtles scattered at the sudden roar zipping through their quiet domain.

Adam's maneuvers with the airboat were on point, confident, and thrilling as he gave the boat a workout. Then they switched positions and he let Dakota give it a shot. Adept at everything, Dakota did great for the first time driving an airboat. They high fived at the exhilaration.

An hour later, Adam pointed toward home and Dakota turned the boat around. Steel met them at the wharf and raised the boat out of the water. The Tahoe was already out of the barn and back in its dry dock. And the wharf was washed off and set back up. Steel had been busy. The guys headed uphill.

Adam's phone rang. Detective Patterson.

***

Adam said, "Hey Patterson. Any news on Hunter?"

"I wished. I'm calling about something else. Your airboat is ready for search and rescue, right?"

"Dakota and I just gave it a run and it's ready to go. Why?"

"Because I've got sad news. A deputy called from Cameron Parish and said that a father and son are missing. They went out in the marsh in a small airboat. I can't believe they did that after a storm surge, but it is what it is. If the search and rescue team doesn't find them today, another search and rescue mission will leave at dawn tomorrow."

"We'll be there if they don't find them. Can you text me the phone number of the search leader?"

"I just did. See you this evening. Callaway and I will be there sixish."

126

Back at the museum, the KPLC interview crew set up the camera and lights. Gabrielle sat in an antique chair near the easel with the picture of Jean Lafitte and Sam Houston. Raven sat in a matching chair next to the easel with the picture of the wharf showing Jean Lafitte, Sam Houston, and Wolf.

Krystal Tramonte, the reporter conducting the interview, sat in the middle of both women.

Everyone knew what had to come first.

Three. Two. One. The camera zoomed in on Krystal and Raven.

Krystal said, "Joining me today for an exclusive interview is Raven Macawi. She moved to Lake Charles four months ago from Minnesota. Why is this newsworthy you wonder? I'll explain."

"Just yesterday, a breaking news bulletin aired warning that armed and dangerous fugitive, Zack Dawton, escaped from Montana State Prison. A massive manhunt is underway by the FBI and U.S. Marshals.

"Zack had been imprisoned for life after the Deadly Dancer Trial in Minnesota where he was found guilty of attempted kidnapping, assault with a deadly weapon, and rape. And KPLC learned today, that Raven was Zack's victim...and competition dance partner."

Turning to Raven, Krystal said, "Raven, tell us why you came forward with this information."

Raven said, "Because it's projected that Zack's coming here to Lake Charles. So, while the FBI and the U.S. Marshals search for him, I want my community and those in his traveling path to be aware of the danger he brings with him."

Alarmed, Krystal said, "But what makes them think he's coming to Lake Charles?"

"Because I'm here. And FBI profilers have determined that he's not finished with me yet."

"Oh, no! That must be terrifying! It's crazy. But...Raven, please...help me and the viewing audience understand how something as beautiful as dance turned into such horrible violence."

"I know what you mean. That's a question that still haunts me. Along with my scars."

Snatching hold of the word, Krystal said, "Did you say scars?"

Piper took a step closer, and Krystal recognized the warning.

Raven glanced at Piper with the briefest nod, then answered, "I did. Zack broke into my home and attacked me. We fought. I ended up with many injuries including a Z carved on my body. And I left my knife in his neck."

Visibly shocked, Krystal said, "Oh, Raven, I am so sorry. It's hard to fathom—"

"Me too. We had been competition partners for years. He was one of my best friends. Around my family often. And I trusted him with my life. I never dreamed violence was in our future."

Krystal said, "But why did he—"

Raven shrugged and said, "Unrequited love. Frustration. He snapped. And I never saw the signs. Do I wish I had seen them? Of course, I do. But that wasn't how it played out."

Krystal had a thought and went for it… "Raven…if Zack hears this interview, is there anything you want to tell him?"

Piper stepped closer thinking, easy Raven…be wise.

Looking into the camera, Raven said, "Turn yourself in, Zack. At least you'll be alive. If you come here, you'll die. Everyone is looking for you. Just leave me alone. You can't make me love you."

Whoa, baby. Krystal couldn't believe she had all this on tape. This was the story reporters dreamt about. But all she said was, "Thank you, Raven. I hope Zack hears you – and listens."

Facing the camera, Krystal said, "Southwest Louisiana, be alert. It appears there are more storms on the horizon than tropical ones."

Then pausing dramatically, she smiled, and the camera view broadened to include Gabrielle and Raven with her.

She said, "And now for a treat Lake Charles! You should all recognize Gabrielle Sawyer Nash, descendant of Jean Lafitte, who is also with us today. Welcome Gabrielle! It is wonderful to see you again."

Gabrielle said, "Hello, Krystal. It's great to be here with Raven. It is important that everyone knows why Raven is in Louisiana."

Krystal said, "And we are thrilled to hear it! So, tell us why you and Raven are here together."

Gabrielle said, "Because our ancestral grandfathers were good friends. And we were finally able to meet…generations later of course. Over 200 years in fact."

Krystal said, "Two hundred years! What are you saying?"

"Do you recall, Wolf, the Atakapa native that helped Jean Lafitte from my news story?"

"Of course!"

"Well, Raven is Wolf's granddaughter. She came to Louisiana to start over in the land of her ancestors, then found me. She too is a Louisiana daughter by blood!"

Clapping, Krystal said, "That is unbelievable! History face to face. Wow. If that's not destiny, I don't know what is! Raven, this is intriguing news."

Raven said, "It is! Double intriguing, I might add. My grandfather was also friends with Sam Houston. And just a few minutes ago I found out that Sam Houston's Cherokee name was...Raven, if you can believe that."

Krystal said, "I had forgotten he lived with the Cherokee! So, you could be named after Sam Houston."

"I certainly could. Amazing, isn't it?"

Krystal turned back to the camera and said, "Yes, it is! And amazing is the perfect way to close the interview. Thank you, Gabrielle, and Raven for sharing your history. And thank you Raven for sharing the warning about Zack. Louisiana has got your back! You are home!"

And the camera stopped rolling.

***

In Deer Lodge, Montana, Sean walked with the FBI and U.S. Marshals into Captain Rollins' home. His wife was outside crying. Their son had just returned to college since his dad was out of danger – not knowing more problems were ahead. Sean knew this would be another bad day for the Rollins' family.

The captain was guilty...a participant in all of it. And it always amazed Sean that the perpetrators expected to get away with it. Some did for a long time. Some did for a while. But this wasn't even close.

Even if they didn't find the money, they'd get him. He'd lose his job. His home. Probably his wife. Certainly, he would lose respect from his family and the community. And in the end, he'd probably eat his gun to escape. Criminal thinking was always the devil's tool.

***

An hour later, they hadn't found anything in the house. Or her car. Or under the house. Or in the attic. Two agents headed to the garage. And it wasn't long before someone yelled, "Got it!"

Agents and marshals filed into the garage. A black bag sat in the middle of a canoe they removed from a wall rack. In the bag was a note that said, *"Why waste the money, Captain? You're already caught. Z."*

Sean could hear the prison door slam shut in his mind. Got you, Captain.

***

Back on the river, Adam watched the company install his Quest Search & Rescue sign on the hill in front of his house. It was gold, silver, white and black with a lime green neon stripe. It matched the airboat.

It also matched a magnetic sign he could slap on any vehicle door. The website and business cards were ready. Even their company shirts. He was fully legal with insurance, licenses, an accountant, and ready to go.

Steel walked up, wiping sweat. He had freshened up the barn stalls since Gabrielle's dad returned the horses.

Adam said, "Steel, I hope you find good employee candidates this Saturday. You need an assistant immediately. And a yard man. You choose their tasks and time."

"But I—"

"I insist. We're all busy with weddings around the corner. Honeymoons. And I need to move into my place. Besides the fact that Quest is on call seven days a week. With two houses and a barn apartment, there is always plenty to do. That's not counting Raven busy with her books and Lance.

"And I said all that to say, I'm determined that we get to enjoy our personal lives too. It will take extra people – with background checks. I want to know who's among us."

"Absolutely. Who's going to run the information table Saturday?"

"Gabrielle and Callie. Now come on, walk, and talk. I'm hungry. Let's see what Lexi has happening in the kitchen."

His phone rang. Raven. He answered as Dakota's phone rang too.

***

Adam said, "Hey. How was the interview?

Raven said, "About Zack, impactful, I think. It airs tonight at five.

"Did Piper have to step in?"

"It came close, but no."

"On what issues?"

"My scars. And her asking me what I wanted to say to Zack if he was listening."

130

He growled and said, "I figured she'd dig a little. Are you ok?"

"I am."

"Do you want to tell me what you said to Zack, or do you want me to watch it?"

"Just watch it. I want to tell you about my surprise."

"Tell me."

"I told you about my ancestor's songs of Wolf being friends with Lafitte and Sam Houston. But I saw a picture of them today."

"You have got to be kidding. All three of them?"

"Right! And this is the surprise. Sam Houston's Cherokee name was Raven."

Adam stopped walking. "No way. That can't be coincidence."

"I'm claiming destiny."

"I don't blame you! Wow. Very cool. When will you be home?"

"I'm here…"

The car rounded the corner and headed uphill.

***

After a delicious lunch from Lexi, Raven changed into jeans for target practice. Piper had insisted everyone be on their A-game. So, she holstered her gun. Then slid her knife in the scabbard. She slipped on boots and looked up as Adam stepped into the room. He shut the door. And if the door wasn't enough to tell her what was on his mind, the look on his face was.

She smiled. A sexy one, and said, "I see a man with—"

And his lips covered hers, his arms drawing her against him. Tight. He groaned as his hands slid down her hips. Thighs. His lips trailed down her neck. Her shoulder. His breath reaching her cleavage. At her sound of desire, he picked her up, kissing her as Raven locked her legs around him. She bit his shoulder.

In half a second, she was flat on her back in the bed - weapons, and all. On top of her, he paused, his mouth almost touching hers. He pressed against her.

She wet her lips. Squirmed. She said, "Adam…"

He said, "I have a question, baby."

"Now?"

His hot eyes drank in the sight of her under him, burning. Hungry for him. He said, "I love seeing you want me. You do, don't you, Raven?"

She arched. "Yes. The other night…"

He groaned remembering the same thing, and said, "Marry me tomorrow. No more waiting. Nine days was a bad idea."

With a breathless laugh, she said, "One day would have been a challenge at this point. You know a minister that can do it for us?"

"Hundreds."

She giggled.

He said, "A slight exaggeration, but I know enough of them, or I'll find one."

"What if we have to do the search and rescue tomorrow in Cameron Parish?"

"Afterwards then. I don't care what time or when. I love you, and you're going to be my wife by tomorrow night. And I'm going to take you all night long. And—"

Piper hollered up the stairs, "Don't make me come get you! It's time to practice!"

***

The detectives drove up about four-thirty that afternoon. They got off early.

Dakota and Piper were sparring. Karate. Adam was shooting bow and arrows at villainous hay bodies hanging from trees. They bled hay all over the ground. Raven and Steel were shooting at competition targets. And Gabrielle was throwing knives while wearing a sword.

Rex watched them for a second and said, "You don't see this every day."

Maverick said, "But then again, there is nothing average about this family."

"Excellent point."

Adam heard the dogs bark and turned to see the detectives getting out of their car.

He smiled as they got closer, and said, "Good timing, we're almost done. We need to catch the five o'clock news."

Maverick said, "Don't let us interrupt. We'll just watch."

Adam nodded, then pulled an arrow from his quiver and loaded the bow. He shot the villain. Once. Twice. Three times. He was flat out deadly.

Rex and Maverick walked toward Gabrielle.

She glanced and said, "Hey guys." She took a small knife from a pouch, then pointed to fence posts about thirty feet away, and said, "Pick a target."

Rex said, "The one by the magnolia tree."

And in a flick of Gabrielle's arm, the four-inch blade pierced the target.

Maverick said, "How long have you been throwing?"

"Since I survived my first serial killer in college."

First? They looked at the beautiful pregnant warrior, not quite sure how to answer. They had heard bits and pieces of her story but obviously missed that part.

Rex said, "And the second?"

"Was a group of them. They died."

She laid a hand on the priceless sword at her side and said, "That's where I got this."

And of course, they knew about the sword. She smiled, pulling it out and offering it.

Maverick brandished it first. He said, "Not everyone gets to hold history in their hand. A king held this. A pirate captain. How is this not great?"

She said, "It is. I'll never forget where it came from. Ever."

Rex took his turn and slid his hand along the underside of the long blade. He said, "This was a remarkable inheritance."

Then returning it to her, he said, "Can you show us a thing or two about fencing? I mean…nothing strenuous being pregnant…"

Smiling, she got into stance and showed them a few moves.

Dakota called, "Easy Gabrielle," as he and Piper headed toward them, wiping sweat. He kissed her on the cheek, and said, "No more practice for you. Let's get you inside. You've been on your feet long enough."

Then he picked her up and carried her.

Adam called to Raven and Steel, "Hey! Let's head in!"

***

Before long everyone had something cold to drink and was gathered around the television. The fugitive portion of the interview was spot on Adam thought. And while it would shock southwest Louisiana and the Lake Charles community, that was the point. Zack was dangerous.

And Raven's comment to Zack was direct and powerful…it was also personal and would be challenging to a man. Which meant, it wouldn't stop him. If anything, it would fuel his fire. Dakota and Adam glanced at each other. Agreed.

Adam's phone rang and he stepped outside to take the call.

In minutes, he was back inside but the interview was already over.

His face was concerned as he said, "They didn't find the missing father and son. So, Dakota and Raven, we need to leave here by four-thirty in the morning. We need to be in the water in Cameron Parish by dawn. Be prepared. Be armed. Expect the unexpected. The Louisiana marsh is going to be new for all of us.

"And though I'm pumped this is our first search and rescue mission, I think about the father and son. They may be hurt. Certainly scared. And I pray they are together and alive. That would make it a successful mission."

Everyone's phone dinged at the same time.

Sean texted from Montana: Video chat in five.
The group disappeared upstairs.

***

Hanging up a snow-dotted parka, Sean gave them a quick smile as he sat at his desk in Montana. He said, "Hey guys. I'll need to rush the chat. It's been busy here in the frozen state, but I do have several updates for you."

Dakota said, "Shoot."

"Searchers found part of a human arm in the woods. Not far from the lake. Male it looks like. We should have DNA on it by Monday at the latest. It would solve everyone's problems if it was Zack."

Piper said, "Anyone else missing from around there?"

"Possibly. We are still waiting for verification. A single guy from Colorado has a camp here and keeps a blue Jeep in his garage. A female friend has permission to use it. She went this morning to borrow it and the Jeep was gone. She tried to call him and couldn't reach him.

"Now that could mean he was using it, or it was stolen. But when she couldn't reach him, she went inside. That's when she called the police. Blood was everywhere, but there was no body. We don't know yet if it was the owner's blood or not."

Dakota said, "So you need DNA on the blood in the house and the arm you found. And hopefully a tie between the two to track the Jeep."

"Bingo."

Piper said, "So worst case scenario is Zack stole the Jeep, killed the man, and left body parts around the lake to sidetrack the investigation."

Sean said, "Yes."

Adam said, "How did the search go at the captain's house?"

"He was arrested. A duffle bag was found in a canoe in his garage. That was really bad news for him. The money bag was empty – except for a note

134

nailing him as an inside accomplice. He got himself shot three times for nothing."

Raven said, "Did you find out yet where Zack's family's wealth came from?"

Sean said, "Yes. And I have to say I was surprised. They own a string of sperm banks."

Raven was stunned. Zack had never mentioned that. But then again, she could see why.

Piper said, "Are they getting a warrant for donors related to Zack or his father?"

"Yes. And checking all the DNA registries. Good call, Maverick. I think this was bigger than you even imagined."

"It's unbelievable."

Then Adam said, "So, from the sperm accomplice perspective, there could be many possibilities."

Sean said, "If Zack, his dad, or other male family members donated, yes – if we are talking actual blood brothers."

Dakota said, "How many agents are doing interviews with his friends and family?"

"Six. Just let us know if you find anything interesting in Zack's social media information that we sent you. Especially you, Raven, if anything triggers a question for you, make a note and we'll check them out. Now, before I go, does anyone have anything for me? Anything happening besides the KPLC interview today? I had them send me a copy of the video."

Piper said, "No. Just that. Raven handled it well."

Sean said, "Yes, she did. Raven, interviews always have surprises, yet your responses were on point. Direct. But…you are aware Zack will take your personal message as a challenge?"

Raven said, "I don't care. He's going to come after me anyway. But at least my words will ring in his head for a change."

Chapter 17

North of Dallas, Zack stood on the bank of one of Lake Ray Roberts'
many wilderness inlets. It was a clear night. Cool, not cold, compared to
Montana. And the only sounds were insects and wildlife. There was a slight
breeze. He smelled a campfire somewhere. Smiling, he took a deep drag off
his cigarette, then blew smoke into the night air. He flicked the butt into the
water.

The darkness was his time. When he could remove the disguise and relax
with his Beretta tucked in his waistband as Kip slept. He thought about the
interview he'd seen with Raven today in Lake Charles. She'd been gorgeous.
Sexy. Hot silk.

But she had surprised him today by taking the offensive on air. She rarely
confronted directly. But then again, she knew he was coming. He wondered if
she was having nightmares like he'd heard about during the trial. Probably.
He'd had a few of his own.

He stretched, then laid his gun on the hood of the white SUV. He pulled
off his shirt and kicked off his boots. Unzipping his jeans, he slid them off,
feeling the cool air caress his naked skin. He thought of Raven's message to
him in the interview.

She was so wrong.

He could make her love him.

Even if she didn't want to.

Grabbing the soap, Zack made his way deeper and deeper into the lake.
Water lapped at his calves, thighs, hips, and chest…until he slid under the
surface and vanished.

Chapter 18

Quest Search & Rescue headed south to Cameron Parish before four-thirty the next morning. Cameron Parish's south border was the Gulf of Mexico, which meant that much of the land for miles inland was marsh. Salt water. Brackish water. And on any other day, it was great for fishing. Crabbing. Hunting. And sightseeing.

But not today. They were meeting Reggie, leader of the search and rescue company in charge. Cameron Parish Sheriff's Office and various other agencies were involved as well. Vince and Timmy Fontenot were the missing father and son. They had taken off in a small, two-seater camo airboat for an early morning ride after the tropical storm surge receded. That was twenty-two tormentingly long hours ago for their family.

Adam followed directions on the map. Before daylight, he instructed Dakota to turn west next to a flashing light mounted on a stake and they headed down a pot-holed shell road into the marsh. A line of other trucks towing boats led the way.

Five minutes later, the road opened into a small clearing at a large utility cabin on iron piers in the middle of the marsh. Complete with heliport. They unloaded their boat. In no time they were on board awaiting instructions.

Adam and Dakota were belted in on the higher driver's platform seats behind a small panel of directional implements and operational gears. Raven was belted in on a bench underneath them. All supplies were housed under a ten-inch lip that ran around the interior edges of the boat.

A helicopter flew over and landed on the heliport. The search leader handed out assignments to each boat team on the grid map. They were to follow that path as best they could, since debris, small land patches, or blocked waterways dotted the marsh after the storm. Every boat was required to have a flare gun and radio to communicate. Phone signal was not dependable. The helicopter would be the overhead eyes and assist as needed.

Reggie finished assignments and climbed aboard his boat. He yelled, "Let's go!"

And the noise was deafening as all airboats fired up their engines. Hopes were high as they roared off to find one man and a little boy in this wild world of marsh.

***

Adam checked his map and looked around. They had been advised the water was deeper in their area with patches of tall grass, ponds, and trenches. It would be a challenge to search and maneuver.

He motioned Dakota to stop and showed them the map.

He said, "We'll start here and go north and south in parallel passes. Use your binoculars. Dakota, keep it at a slow steady pace until we see something to investigate. Everybody needs to keep an eye out for anything attempting to get in the boat – snakes, bees, alligators, or anything else as we go through the overgrown areas.

"Raven, you take the low view. I'll climb up and take the high view. Dakota, you have the middle."

Raven unbuckled her seatbelt and knelt on the front deck steps. Adam unbuckled and stood, bracing against the fan screen. Dakota looked around for anything that shouldn't be in the marsh.

An hour into the search, Adam noticed a narrow water path through tall grass with an open body of water at the other end. He pointed it out to Dakota. It was a tight fit for the boat, but they could get through.

Sharp-edged grass slapped over the sides of the airboat for forty feet or more. Eventually they popped out of the grass into a large pool and couldn't help but notice the unusual something at the other end. It was certainly not natural.

Adam said, "That's metal. Let's go!"

Dakota sped up, moving closer.

A damaged airboat was wrapped around a steel beam with a metal grate high in the air. It was some type of hunter's perch or work area.

Raven said, "Someone is on top!"

As Dakota slowed, Adam said, "I see them. Watch for metal under the water, Dakota. Parts of the boat are not visible."

Adam fired the flare gun and called Reggie over the radio. Dakota edged closer to the platform for Raven to grab the short ladder hanging down. Adam boosted her up.

It was a man and boy. Undoubtedly, the ones they were searching for. Raven checked their pulse. They were alive, but the father was impaled in the thigh. Bloody. Unresponsive. The boy opened his eyes when she touched him.

He tried to talk but she couldn't hear over the engine. He was shivering. She removed her jacket and draped it over them.

She shouted to Adam, "I can't hear the boy. The boat's too loud."

Adam drew a line across his throat and Dakota killed the engine.

Raven startled when the boy panicked, trying to scream and talk at the same time. She got closer, and he croaked, "Shark!"

She spun, and a huge shark was about to ram the airboat. She screamed, "Shark! Hold on!"

Adam and Dakota turned in time to see a huge shark, mouth agape, attack the front corner of the boat. Adam grabbed the fan cage and hung on as the boat slammed into the mangled airboat next to them. Still buckled in the driver's seat, Dakota was slung sideways and hit his head on a spotlight. He went limp.

In disbelief, Adam watched the shark slide back into the water and disappear. He turned to check on Raven.

She said, "What's happening? No one said anything about sharks in the marsh!"

Adam said, "I have no idea! I've got to get to Dakota. Stay up there."

"It's coming back, shoot it!"

Adam braced himself on the driver's deck and shot into the shark's head and mouth until his gun was empty. It didn't stop it. The shark rammed the boat and dove again.

Raven checked on the boy. He was crying. She tucked him partially under his daddy's side and said, "Hold on tight. We are going to get you out of here."

Standing, she turned back toward Adam and pulled her gun. She watched for the shark as Adam checked Dakota's head gash. It was bleeding down the front of his shirt.

She asked, "Is it deep?"

"No, but he'll need—"

She saw the shark. "It's back! It's coming for Dakota's side of the boat!"

Unbuckling Dakota, Adam groaned, pulling him out of the seat. He wedged him next to the cage and reached for another magazine of ammo.

Raven yelled, "No time! Hang on - he's going to ram again!"

She shot continually as the shark tried to eat the boat. The metal was crumpling. A helicopter roared overhead. Low and loud. And the bleeding shark swam away.

Grabbing Dakota's gun, Adam shot the beast till it disappeared. Then he noticed the water in the boat. The shark was going to sink them. They reloaded.

Dakota woke as Raven yelled, "He's coming back! Look to your right."

Adam said, "Hang on, Dakota!"

The shark rammed them broadside, shoving them into the deck post. Raven dropped and covered the man and boy.

Adam shot till the shark disappeared and said, "This is crazy. How many bullets can one shark take? We've emptied almost fifty bullets in him."

Raven said, "Is that a great white?"

Dakota said, "Yes. An old one, at least a fourteen-footer. And he was injured before even getting shot."

The sound of the helicopter grew louder again. It was leading the airboats to them.

Raven yelled, "Here comes the shark! Broadside again! Hang on!"

Adam glanced at Dakota and said, "Get up there with them!"

"Forget it."

"Now, Dakota. Protect them."

Raven screamed, "No, Adam! Both of you get up here!"

Instead, Adam climbed down into the flooded area of the boat. He pulled his knife. The long blade glistened in the early morning light. The shark was about thirty feet away, moving slower, but still closing in on the boat.

Adam looked at Dakota. "Cover them."

Dakota climbed on top and braced himself over Raven. Neither of them noticed the helicopter overhead or the boats surrounding the pool. Their eyes were glued on Adam and the shark.

Adam crouched and braced. He gripped the handle tight and waited.

Open-mouthed, the shark hit the side of the boat at the same time Adam rammed the knife into its eye. The impact slung him over the shark, and he disappeared into the water.

Raven screamed.

Dakota dropped to the boat and yanked Adam aboard as he surfaced. The shark surfaced next, biting weakly at the water. Obviously dying but still deadly. Adam shot it in the other eye.

Then finally, they watched as it sank, mouth open, eyes blank, leaving a bloody trail behind.

And then the noise was deafening as the airboats neared and the helicopter lowered the rescue basket. Adam climbed to help Raven as they loaded the father and son. Injured, but alive.

Reggie's boat towed them back to the wharf. The tow truck was waiting and loaded the damaged airboat. Several other boats had towed the shark back after fishing the bottom with hooks. They strung the beast up for pictures. No way were they leaving the trophy behind.

Volunteers and law enforcement took pictures of everything. And the video taken from the helicopter was sent to KPLC for breaking news. Quest answered questions and told their story. And finally, they headed home. Victorious. And it wasn't even noon yet.

Once they got away from the marsh and traveled further inland, they had phone signal again. And then their phones blew up with messages.

Adam said, "I take it we've been on the news already."

Checking messages, Dakota said, "We have. Listen to this…

This is a KPLC Breaking News Bulletin. Deep in the marsh of Cameron Parish, a father and son had been missing since yesterday. Today, special search and rescue teams went out for a second day.

One of the teams, Quest Search & Rescue, came upon the father and son on a raised metal platform in the marsh. Their destroyed airboat was in the water below them. While Quest began the rescue, a fourteen-foot great white shark attacked their boat multiple times. A terrifying battle ensued between man, woman, and beast.

But in the end, the father and son were rescued. And the shark was dead. Shot over fifty times and stabbed in the head. (They played a live video taken from the helicopter.)

The Louisiana Department of Wildlife & Fisheries is retrieving the shark for research. It is presumed the shark was caught in Tropical Storm Mason's tidal surge earlier this week and due to disorientation or injury, became trapped in a deep pool in the marsh.

Quest Search & Rescue is owned by Adam Nash. He was assisted today by his fiancé, Raven Macawi, RN, and his brother, FBI Special Agent Sean Nash, the driver.

Thank you, volunteers, and professionals, for a job well done. The community is grateful for your service."

***

Forty minutes, and many calls later, Adam drove up the hill and parked in front of the barn where Steel waited.

***

Raven answered a video call from Callie and Lance as she got out of the truck.

Lance screamed excitedly, "Momma! You shot a big shark!"

Laughing, she said, "I did, sweetie. We all shot him."

"Why?"

"He tried to eat the boat."

"That was mean."

"Yes. He was not a nice shark."

"He was bleeding, and I saw Adam stick him in the eye."

Wincing, she said, "Adam was protecting us. The shark tried to hurt a lot of people."

"Yeah. Is the little boy, ok?"

"He is. His daddy too."

Getting bored with the conversation, he ran off. Callie's pale face filled the screen.

Raven said, "I know. It was dangerous. But who knew a shark was lurking in the marsh?"

Callie said, "I was so horrified I don't even know what to say. I'm just glad the thing is dead."

Smiling, Raven watched Gabrielle and Piper walk across the yard.

Steel walked by and she handed him her phone and said, "Callie, talk to Steel. I need to go. Love you."

***

Steel smiled at Callie and said, "Hey, sweetie. You, ok?"

"No. Yes. I don't know. I'm just in shock."

"They really are ok. The boat, not so much. So, don't worry. Now on another note…have you thought about exercising with me again? I think

142

about it all the time. I have all kinds of naked workout sessions planned for our honeymoon. Pushing. Straining—"

"Steel!" She gasped, blushing, because she had thought about it.

He winked, watching her. He knew.

She said, "You are shockingly direct."

"You have no idea how deliciously direct I can be. But you will, baby. You will."

***

Dakota hugged a frowning Gabrielle.

She said, "Let me see that cut. Look at all the blood on you."

"It's not so bad. The shark just slung me against a spotlight and knocked me out. I'm fine. You've seen me hurt worse."

"You need stitches."

"A few. Raven will do it. You know how much she liked stitching Adam after the deer attack."

They laughed.

***

Adam and Dakota met Piper's glare.

She said, "I trusted you with Raven. And what happens? All of you are almost human sushi. I couldn't believe I had to see it on the news."

Adam said, "Easy, Piper. We had no phone signal. And he scared all of us. A shark never crossed my mind – or anyone else's. Come on, give us a hug. You know you love us."

"Don't you touch me."

Dakota laughed; he couldn't help it. Then caught her fist just before she punched him.

Adam couldn't stop laughing.

***

Everyone headed back to the house. And while the Quest crew changed, Lexi dipped rich and creamy crawfish etouffee into wide shallow bowls. Then topped each bowl with a rounded scoop of white rice before setting the table. A wooden platter of toasted garlic bread sat in the center.

And for dessert, individual local pottery dishes were filled with Mississippi Mud Pie. A delicious concoction of pie crust with pecan bits, a layer of cream

143

cheese whipped with sugar, a layer of chocolate pudding, with a final layer of cool whip and chocolate shavings.

Glasses of homemade lemonade with sliced lemons and oranges came next. And just as everyone was getting seated around the table, Maverick and Rex knocked on the back door.

Adam waved them in. And for a while, no one talked. The only sounds were spoons hitting the bowl, the crunch of garlic toast, and the clink of ice in the glasses.

At least until Maverick asked, "I wonder what shark tastes like?"

Then howls of laughter and conversation joined the meal.

***

After lunch, Raven grabbed her medical kit and cleaned Dakota's cut.

She said, "Two stitches should do it. And it's just below the hairline, so I won't have to shave any hair."

"That'll work."

Gabrielle said, "Will it scar?"

Raven said, "Not so anyone would notice. Well, maybe you, but no one else."

Dakota said, "I'm not worried about a scar."

Adam said, "I guess not. That's a baby scar." Lifting his leg, he pulled up his jeans and said, "That's a scar."

No one could argue with that. Or Raven's scars for that matter.

Chapter 19

Early afternoon in Lake Charles, a blue van drove up to the entrance of a gated storage facility on Nelson Road. The driver's window slid down. Kip keyed in the security code and the gates opened. He drove through the complex until he reached a large door around the corner. Unit 409.

Getting out, he unlocked and raised the door. Inside sat a gunmetal gray Chevrolet Colorado pickup. Sporty. Masculine. And it maneuvered like a dream. Kip smiled. He loved his truck. He climbed in, backed it out, and drove the blue van inside. He knocked on the outside of the van as he closed the door.

Zack shoved the bags and blankets off him as the back hatch opened. Sliding out, he stood.

Kip grinned and said, "Welcome to Louisiana."

Stretching after being cramped for hours, Zack said, "How far is she?"

"Thirty or forty minutes, depending on traffic."

Zack smiled at his handsome half-brother. They were the same age. Twenty-eight. But Kip was shorter than him by two inches. Slimmer. Short brown hair. Laughing hazel eyes. A great smile. Fun. And he liked jewelry. When not in disguise, he always wore an earring and an engraved ring on his right hand.

Yielding to his brother's expertise in drama and costumes with his Bachelor of Arts degree and minor in theatre, he said, "What disguise will you wear?"

"I don't need one now. I'm not in any database and no one knows what I look like. Besides, my legal past is clear if anyone runs my name."

"Don't tell me I still have to dress as the old man."

"You better. Raven knows your body. Even though you're muscled up now, you still move the same. And you can't show blonde hair, even though it's long. Your voice, your coloring, and your movements are going to catch her attention if she sees you. You've spent years face to face with her. She will know. Wouldn't you recognize her?"

"In a heartbeat."

"There's your answer."

"Then add more disguise so I can get closer access to her."

Contemplating…Kip said, "Ok. It's warmer here so you won't need a coat. I say, wear blue jean overalls. A long sleeve shirt. Thicken your waist. Boots. Wear a thick but shorter gray beard and hair. Brown contacts. Use foam pads in your mouth to fill your cheeks. I have an age spot cream for your face, neck, and hands. And hunch over a bit to limp with the cane. With that, you should blend in with the elderly residents around here. But you can't talk to her. At all."

"Agreed. So, let's get what we need. How close will I be to her once we get to where we are staying?"

Kip said, "It's a surprise."

Zack said, "A good one, I hope. How many people are around her place?"

"Five live there. Then I saw contractors. Family and friends. And Adam's new business, Quest, that we saw on the news…which is having a grand opening tomorrow. Imagine that. Strangers everywhere. Anyone could slip in."

***

At two-thirty, Kip rolled up to the Sam Houston Jones State Park entrance with his window down.

A young woman slid open a glass partition and smiled at the handsome driver and an elderly man in the passenger seat. With a part southern, part Texan accent, she said, "Welcome! Are you here for the day or do you have a reservation?"

"Hi there! Thanks! I have a two-week reservation in cabin 11a beginning tonight." He handed her his driver's license.

She checked on the computer and said, "Sure. I have you right here. You are paid in full. Do you need to make any changes?"

"I may buy a canoe now that I'm in Louisiana. Is that a problem while I'm at the park?"

"Not at all. You'll see the boat ramp if you need it. Oh. And a boat without an engine won't even need to be registered with the state. So, enjoy yourself! And check out the rules for the Louisiana Department of Wildlife & Fisheries if you decide to fish."

"You're the best. Thanks."

"You are welcome! Let me print this out for you to sign."

"Sure."

He waited a minute while she worked, then said, "Is it safe here? Do you have security?"

"It is very safe, and yes, a minimum of two rangers are on duty at all times."

She finished printing out the paperwork. He signed it. She handed him the receipt, keys, and a card for his windshield.

She said, "Use the small key for the gate if you come and go after hours. And have a wonderful time! If you need anything at all, let us know."

He smiled, raising his window, and drove into the park.

Zack said, "You're kidding. That's it?"

"That's it. Wilderness galore. Freedom to roam. And a few park rangers to make sure the rules are followed."

"This is unbelievable."

"You've got that right. Wait till you see the trails."

"What trails?"

"The ones we're heading for now."

Chapter 20

On video feed upstairs in Raven's office, Sean said to the stunned faces, "Yes. That's what I said. Zack's deceased father has one hundred fifty sperm kids."

Raven said, "Is that even legal?"

"It is in the United States."

Dakota said, "Well, that just increased the suspect list exponentially."

Adam said, "Right. Now, tell me, was Zack's dad really all that? I mean don't the women choose per donor data?"

A picture of an attractive blonde man on horseback, mid 50s, popped up on the monitor, and Sean said, "Business owner, millionaire, healthy sexual appetite if we go by the gossip of all his affairs, healthy, and plenty charm and sperm to go around."

Piper said, "Well. There's that. But if he's so healthy, how did he die?"

"Get this. He fell."

Raven frowned. "You mean, like Beau?"

"To the letter – except for the camping trip. He was on a horse ride by himself. They figure the horse reared and he fell off a cliff."

Dakota said, "While Zack was in prison?"

"Yes. So, Hunter – if Hunter is the accomplice – could have, or most likely, did kill him. And until we know who Hunter is, we won't know his motive. That brings me to the next update."

The printer clicked and began to print.

Sean said, "Raven, I need you to look closely at the ten pictures I am faxing. We've gathered these from Zack's friends and schoolmates. I want you to see if there is anything familiar about any of the faces. And if so, from where?"

Piper lined the pictures in two rows of five across the table in front of Raven. Curious more than anything, Raven looked down at all the faces. Then she picked up picture number one and sat, studying the face. For all ten pictures. And apprehension spread through her.

She said, "I've seen most of these faces. Many times." Holding up number three with a blonde ponytail and glasses, she said, "He's a photographer. He was everywhere."

Then she held up number six with black hair, dark eyes, and a tattoo on his neck, and said, "This guy talked to Zack all the time."

And lastly, picking up number nine with brown hair, blue eyes, and serious expression, she said, "And he looks like a guy that moved into the apartment complex where Beau and I lived before we bought the house."

Adam said, "That doesn't sound good. Who did people say these guys were?"

Sean said, "Someone from Zack's past in Idaho. And our face scanner picks up similarities in each face. So, maybe one man."

Raven said, "That's creepy. So, he uses disguises?"

"It's possible." Sean agreed, then said, "Hey Maverick, can you get the lab to upload Hunter's DNA in the national database for me? We don't find it and I know he had to leave DNA everywhere in the hospital after the pig attack."

Maverick texted his buddy in the lab. "It's done and should be accessible in a few minutes."

"Thanks. The team is already checking out the 150 sperm kids. If Hunter is one of them, we'll find out who he is. Now for a few more updates."

Adam's phone rang. He said, "Hang on a minute, Sean, I need to take this call." He stepped into the hall.

A minute later he was back. He whispered to Raven, "The minister can meet us. We'll take the boat and leave in an hour."

She met his gaze. Only one more hour. Kissing her softly, he turned back to the others. But now Raven struggled to focus. The boat? How did she dress for that?

Sean continued, "Forensics is still working on DNA of the partial arm found. And the blue Jeep from the missing guy's camp has not been located. So, we've broadened the fugitive search to include vehicle thefts heading south out of Montana, Wyoming, and the Dakotas since Tuesday. We started with eight possible theft trails. We are down to six that have traced as far as Colorado, Kansas, and Missouri. Nothing to Louisiana yet. And with no bodies found, we'll be leaving Montana to follow those trails."

Adam said, "I've got plenty of room at my house if you get this far and want to set up base there. And there is plenty of room to land a helicopter. How many agents and marshals are on the travel team?"

"Five, maybe more. And your place sounds good. We'll plan on that if we make it that far before catching him. Just stay alert with extra security."

"We are already working on that. We moved Lance and Callie to Jimmy's ranch. Gabrielle will head there tonight. The rest of us, including Maverick and Rex will be here on the river. Angel and Jade are coming in for the grand opening tomorrow so they can help if we need anything.

"Then Raven and I plan to follow them back to New Orleans till Sunday night. She needs a break from all this, and they want us to look at a case they are investigating."

"Great idea. And good luck with the grand opening. Are you serving shark in the food truck?"

Grinning, he signed off as everyone laughed.

***

As the video ended, Adam drew Raven to his side, and said to the others, "Raven and I are leaving shortly for a date. We will be unavailable until Angel and Jade arrive around seven. This is not debatable. And Piper, you are not coming. She will not leave my side. So, everyone, take a break. Run errands. Do what you need to do. You don't know when your next break will be."

***

Adam walked Raven to her room. Kissing her softly, he said, "Does this count as eloping?"

"It certainly does."

His dark eyes simmered. "Dress for a windy boat ride, beautiful. And a husband at the end of it."

***

Kip and Zack wove through the woods in the park. It was hilly. Lush with pine trees. Hardwood trees. Vines. Magnolias. They ran across several hikers, women working off a few pounds. Others jogged. A few bikers. Bird watchers and photographers took pictures and stared into the trees. Many retirees strolled along unconcerned with the time at all.

But everyone was friendly. Chatty. And a complete waste of time, Zack thought. But to avoid drawing attention to themselves, they played the tourist game. Then once they were out of sight of prying eyes, Kip motioned east, and they jogged up a hill and disappeared.

It was more rugged away from the trail. Squirrels chattered and fussed as they ran up trees to escape the tall invaders. And deer scattered at the crunch of sticks as they traveled swiftly through the forest. Rabbits darted from one bush to another. And the sun's afternoon rays shot through the trees sunning lizards, insects, and the forest floor.

Before long, Zack heard boats on the river to the left. Distant voices. Laughter. And eventually, he could see the river through the trees. Kip turned toward the water and led him to a thick group of trees by the riverbank. He pointed.

Across the river was a large clearing on a hill. A Quest Search & Rescue sign and buildings were to the left. A couple of acres across, was a white Acadian style home. Certainly feminine. Raven.

The men looked at each other with the same thought. It begins.

Kip said, "Can you find your way back to the cabin?"

"Yeah."

"I'm going to get groceries and see what I can find out about the grand opening. Now, this is not a public area of the park so don't let anyone see you. If a ranger catches sight of you, act lost. You look like an old man after all."

"Just go."

And Kip was gone.

***

Across the river, Raven looked in her closet. How did she have nothing to wear with a closet full of clothes? Or maybe it didn't matter what she wore. She was just excited they were slipping out to get married. Adam would be her husband. To have and to hold…in minutes. The rush of anticipation kicked off a flutter in her stomach. She was so in love with Adam that it hurt in the most amazing way possible.

Pulling herself together, she slipped on a fancy blue jean skirt with white lace and rhinestone designs. Next, a white crop top turtleneck. Soft. Sexy. And last, white boots. She looked in the mirror. Adam would like this – and the wind wouldn't blow her skirt up.

Now her hair. She braided it loosely in case she needed to take it out when they got there. Otherwise, it would be wild on the ride. Then she touched up her makeup. And with pearl studs and perfume dotted in a few strategic spots, she was ready to go…to be Adam's wife from this day forward.

***

Adam could have cared less what was in his closet as he brushed his teeth, his hair, and put on her favorite cologne. All he thought about was loving Raven - in a million ways.

Making her his over and over knowing only he could hear her. Taste her. Listening to her breathe at night.

Watching her love Lance knowing more children would come.

Sharing kisses that were as sweet as honey but burned like fire.

Experiencing her heart as she gave even when the cost was high.

Admiring her bravery when fear wasn't far behind.

And looking forward to all the new things ahead of them. Because he already loved her for everything.

He zipped his jeans. Pulled on a blue sweater. Tied his boots. He didn't even look in the mirror. Picking up the marriage license, both wedding bands, and his phone, he was ready. Stepping out of his room, the house was quiet.

He went upstairs.

Raven heard his footsteps and met him in the hall. They were both beyond ready. She drank in the beautiful man before her and the look on his face. He touched her. Pulled her in his arms.

Voice husky, he said, "Let's go be one."

In minutes they parked his truck by the wharf. The ski boat was tied up and waiting for them. He jumped in and turned to lift her inside.

She said, "You can't get more romantic than this. A boat ride is crazy sexy to get married."

Leading her to the driver's seat, he grinned and said, "It is – but I have an ulterior motive. I can't hold you on my lap in the truck."

She laughed, as he sat with her in the captain's chair. And after a hard hot kiss, he cranked the engine. The 4.5-liter inboard engine rumbled, churning water like a beast ready to run. Adam backed the boat away from the dock getting further out in the river.

And for a quick second, Raven startled. She turned to glance across the river in the woods behind her. It was so much closer now. She felt...fear. Her skin crawled.

Then Adam said, "Hang on, baby," and hit the throttle. The beast under the boat roared and they flew across the water headed to downtown Lake Charles. Her fear was left behind in the wind.

***

Watching the boat with Adam and Raven fly across the water and disappear around the bend, Zack stepped from behind the tree. That was an unexpectedly wicked encounter. Very close. He slid one hand over his pistol fitted with a silencer inside the ugly overalls. Then lower. Aroused. He knew that Raven had felt him. But he wasn't surprised. You can't share what they had and not have a connection.

After the noise of the engine faded, it was still and quiet again. He continued his walk, hidden along the riverbank. He observed their buildings and property with binoculars. Scoped it out. Both houses were big, but Quest's layout was larger. Masculine. With a huge barn. Equipment.

He had heard horses earlier. And seen two dogs with the big guy getting the boat ready. The dogs had smelled him, staring across the river at exactly where he stood. The guy didn't notice the dogs though, and they didn't bark since he wasn't on their land. Zack knew they could be a real problem. He'd think of something – he sure would hate to kill fine dogs like that.

Once finished, he sat on the stump that placed him in the middle of both houses and watched, thinking about all he'd learned today. In large part thanks to the shark news bulletin this morning. Number one was that the guy in the boat was Raven's fiancé. He had searched Google on the guy.

He was handsome. Part Sioux. Athletic. Wealthy, even without the new search business. And respected – a missionary minister no less. And his two brothers were FBI agents. His two sisters-in-law had news bulletins under their belts too. One was related to a pirate. The other had been a prosecutor before going to the FBI Academy. They were all tough and smart.

Zack smiled. What an interesting game of chess this would turn out to be. Two kings. One queen. Raven.

Chapter 21

It was a beautiful afternoon to be on the river. Blue sky. High wispy clouds. Trees lining the river like soldiers brandishing swords as they sped between the banks in the fast red boat.

Raven leaned against Adam, his warm hand holding her bare waist, his lap under her. She touched his chest, sliding a hand to brush his neck, his jawline. He kissed her, then drew her closer, making sure the river miles passed swiftly.

When they rounded the next bend in the river by the rental cabins of the park, Adam slowed for the mandatory NO WAKE zone. Meaning no speeding. No waves. No roaring engines. The point was to provide safety and not interrupt nature for all the park guests. The cabins were busy with outdoor activity. Tourists on the bluffs grilled early dinners. Some rode bikes. Others sat around campfires laughing as kids played, fished, and ran up and down the hills.

Then came the boat launch, fishing deck, picnic tables, and a large pond. The tent campground was behind the road that passed behind it. Next was the boardwalk that followed the bank to the playground. And after that came the pavilion for parties, followed by a large, wooded area for picnics, with swings, slides, and a swamp pond on the other side of it that included alligator warnings.

As they neared the end of the main tourist areas, another trail began, and the speed limit was over. Adam sped up again. And for the remaining miles of river, the wilderness was dotted with large residential homes overlooking the river, camps on piers, and uninhabitable areas of marsh and swamp.

Then finally, they turned off the West Fork branch of the Calcasieu River and headed west to Lake Charles where two massive bridges and the downtown skyline were visible in the quickly dwindling distance.

Their eyes met.

Adam kissed Raven softly. "We're almost there."

Before long, they passed through the saltwater barrier gates and followed the banks of Westlake. Then drove under the 140-foot-tall Calcasieu River Bridge to enter the large lake for which Lake Charles was named.

To the left was the only white-sand inland beach from Texas to Florida. To the right was the Horseshoe Casino & Hotel, with thriving industries for miles inland. Straight ahead was downtown Lake Charles. Including the civic center surrounded by a seawall, parks, and marinas filled with boats. Adam aimed for the large area of steps in the seawall where the minister and photographer waited.

In a minute, he waved at two smiling men and pulled the boat alongside the deck. He tied off the boat and they touched up their appearance. They went ashore.

Adam hugged the older man holding the Bible, and said, "Hey Tom! Man, it's good to see you!"

Then drawing Raven forward, he said, "And this gorgeous woman is why we are here."

Raven smiled. "Hi Tom!"

Tom shook her hand and said, "Mercy. You're a beauty! No wonder Adam fell off a cliff to hurry home to a nurse like you."

They laughed and he continued, "I hear nothing but amazing things about you, Raven. It's nice to meet you in person and see for myself the love between you."

She smiled and said, "Thank you for officiating today. We're grateful."

Smiling to soften his words, Adam said, "Very. And in a hurry."

The photographer burst out laughing, and Adam shook his hand, "Hey Sid. I owe you for leaving a bar-b-que to come up here. I've seen your work. And since Raven is also a photographer, I knew we needed only the best. Except for hers of course."

"Of course! Hi Raven, Adam. And this is a treat. I haven't done wedding pictures on a boat. Very cool."

And shortly, they picked out a beautiful garden setting with the lake and boat in the background. And as Adam and Raven clasped hands and faced each other, the photographer hit play on background music and dropped it in his pocket. He picked up his camera and Reverend Tom began as strangers began to stop and watch.

"Today is your wedding celebration, Adam, and Raven. A beautiful moment in time in which your love and commitment forever unite you. It's not temporary. It's not casual. It's priceless beyond measure. And done before God and man, it reaches to the depths of your soul…searing you together. Always one from this day forward."

Tom nodded to Adam.

Adam smiled at Raven and said, "I promise to love, adore, and cherish you more than you ever imagined. You are the woman of my dreams. My wife. My future. The mother of our children. As a woman your beauty and your heart are exquisite. I receive all of you, Raven. Every glorious inch of you. And I give you all of me."

Raven touched his chest, and said, "I want all of you, Adam. Everything about you. Beyond your wild love and beauty, strength, and integrity, to the man that wants to touch the world and make a difference. I am in love with you in a way I never dreamed. I desire you. admire you. And with joy I yield all of me to you…giving you more than you even ask."

And following the ring exchange, Tom said, "By the power vested in me by the State of Louisiana, I now pronounce you husband and wife. Adam, you may kiss your bride."

Adam scooped her up in a kiss as her arms wrapped around his neck. He carried her all the way to the boat. Bystanders clapped and cheered at the eager couple. Once on board, Tom and Sid joined them so they could complete paperwork and take pictures.

The sun was falling fast in the western sky as the boat sped under the tall bridge headed home. Adam had one thing on his mind. Raven. And she had one thing on her mind. Adam. Their glances hungered.

Desire flared as they shared hot kisses as he tried to stay on his side of the river. And in between passing boats, and people on the banks, he discovered she didn't have anything on under her skirt. He groaned.

And after crossing the saltwater barrier, they finally reached an unoccupied portion of the river. Noticing a shaded inlet with trees to provide privacy, Adam turned sharply with an impressive water spray. He drove inside, pulling back on the throttle, and killed the engine.

He stood with Raven's legs already wrapped around him. Her skirt was rolled up. He unzipped. And a more thrilling boat ride began as the boat rocked.

Heated moments later, he held her as their breath and heartbeat slowed. Caressed her back. Kissed her head as her breath brushed his neck. Her hands still clutched him, and he felt the tremble in her legs. Their gazes met. Sweaty. Flushed. Totally intimate. Husband and wife forever.

He brushed hair away from her face and said, "We are so wild together, Raven. So wild. I've got to get us home before we start again."

They laughed as they straightened their clothing. He started the engine and drew her in the circle of his arms. They stood, facing the future, both holding the wheel as it should be. And headed home.

***

On the park side of the river, Zack heard the boat engine from a distance. It rounded the bend of the river just before the last light of dusk faded to dark. He raised the binoculars. They parked the boat in the bay next to the airboat and climbed on deck. Zack stared down the barrel of his pistol with Adam's head in the crosshairs thinking it would be so easy.

His phone vibrated with a text. Lowering the gun, he checked.

***

Kip: You came all this way just to shoot them?"
***

Zack chuckled and turned. Kip was standing about forty feet away with a bag. He motioned him over. They watched Adam and Raven leave the wharf and get in the truck. They drove uphill to the Quest house, and he carried her inside.

Kip waited a bit, and when Zack didn't say anything, he said, "Looks like they got married."

"It doesn't matter. It'll be a short honeymoon. Next one's mine."

***

Inside Raven's house, everyone received a text from Adam: *I'm turning my phone off. I have a gun. Don't knock or call.* Attached was a picture of a marriage license.

157

Dakota, Piper, Steel, and the detectives watched Adam stop his truck, then carry Raven over the threshold two acres away.

Piper said, "I'm terrific at reading people. But I did not see a secret wedding today."

Dakota said, "Adam's good. Very stealthy. He outdid Sean and Samantha."

Maverick said, "How's that?"

"Sean and Samantha planned an elopement out of the country. Texted us after the fact too. But this. This was good. Slid it right under our noses. I guess it's hard sleeping in her bed with the door open. Pun intended."

***

Across the yard, Adam pushed the door shut. Raven slid down; her eyes locked on his.

He kissed her. Deep. Sensual. Licking the fire he tasted, and said, "Come dance with me."

He led her to the fireplace he had prepared. Soft rug. Low lighting. Cozy. He lit the fire. And it was already crackling when the music started.

Raven watched Adam. The way he moved. The glances he gave her. His smile sexy. She loved the smooth sensual side of him. The depth. His intention palpable in the room – foreplay. She groaned as he neared her.

Adam smiled and drew her in his arms. Embracing. Caressing. Showing her that he loved the feel of her. The smell of her. They swayed. Tight. Intimate. The friction of the clothes between them arousing.

And he didn't kiss her till the second song. His lips started slow, coaxing, teasing, and quickly heated to hungry and possessive. He pulled her sweater over her head. Then his. And they danced shirtless. Embracing the sensations of her arousal and his.

As the next song began, he unsnapped her skirt, sliding it down to reveal beautiful hips and long legs. He stepped out of his pants. And then sensual turned to raging. And long before the song was over, he chased her upstairs. Both breathless. Both wild as sounds of love filled the house.

***

Later, they lay entwined in his king-size bed made up in luxurious Egyptian cotton.

Adam trailed his fingers across Raven's stomach, and said, "So, are we going to have two master bedrooms or move into one house?"

Rubbing her foot against his leg, she said, "Your place. Here. This is home now. I'd like to give my place to Callie. Lance would be at home in either, and certainly love running back and forth."

"I think that's a perfect idea. Especially, since I know Steel plans to marry her as soon as they can. And now that homes are decided, let's talk about our family."

He laid his palm on her stomach. "I can't wait to see our child growing in you."

"That would be soon then. I'm not on birth control. I've never taken it. Never needed to."

"How long did it take you to get pregnant with Lance?"

"Two months."

Smiling, he said, "You could be pregnant now."

"I could."

"How about showering with me to make sure?"

She kissed him and slid out of bed. Tossing her long red hair, she glanced back at him. He stood behind her. And it got steamy long before they ever entered the shower.

***

Across the river, Zack and Kip sat in the dark woods. But the moon was full. Bright like a spotlight on the stage they watched.

Zack ate the last slice of grilled steak Kip had brought, and downed one of the beers.

He said, "Man, that was a perfect steak. You could open a business and be a millionaire in no time."

Chuckling, Kip said, "I'm already a millionaire, especially adding what you paid me, and I don't have to pay taxes. Working under the table is much more profitable."

"I get that. But living two lives limits you."

"Some. But I'm good at it. Who knew after college, a door would open for me to work the dark side with acting and disguises? But it only works as long as I'm not in a DNA database – or caught of course. But enough about me. What about you? What's happening here? You have been tight lipped about it."

"I've got a plan that's coming together. But fill me in on what you found out about the grand opening tomorrow."

"First, I bought a canoe for you to cross the river if you want. An old man paddling shouldn't be a red flag to anyone day or night."

They fist bumped, and Zack said, "I will do that."

"As for the grand opening, welcome to the party. The public is invited. It will be on the radio. News. They'll be a food truck. Touring the Quest buildings. Checking out the search animals – very cool. Horses and dogs. Meeting the staff. Family. And get this, they are hiring three people. A yard man, an assistant for Adam's manager. And a driver for the Quest airboat. It doesn't get any better than that. So, I think I'm going to apply for the assistant position."

Zack said, "And then you'd be on staff. I could walk right in."

Kip nodded.

Zack smiled as his mind exploded with endless possibilities. He said, "Can my disguise pass a close encounter tomorrow?"

"Yes. I'll have to work the beard for a tighter fit in case it's windy. And you can't stuff your shirt with a pillow in case they touch you. Wrap sheets. Wear a thick undershirt to make your arms softer. Your arms and legs are not old. They're rock hard."

"They're not the only thing that's hard."

"And on that note, what are you going to do about Raven?"

"I'm going to see what plays out tomorrow. See if you get hired. Stay away from the cops and see if my plan will work. Once I decide, I'll move – hopefully, Sunday. I'll know by tomorrow after the event."

"Are you going to kill them?"

"Maybe. Depends on whether she obeys. Now, enough questions. Let's head back to the cabin. I know what I need to do now."

***

Westbound on Interstate 10 out of Lafayette, Louisiana, Angel's phone rang.

He hit the speaker and said, "Hey Dakota! Jade and I are only about an hour and a half out. Sorry we will arrive later than we thought."

Laughing, Dakota said, "No problem. I'm sure Adam will thank you."

Angel and Jade glanced at each other. What?

Angel said, "Come again."

"Well, Adam and Raven surprised us. They faked a date and took off in the boat to get married. They are now locked up at his place till y'all arrive. He warned us not to interrupt them."

Angel laughed.

Jade gasped. She said, "You mean they eloped and came back?"

"They did. I bet that was one wild boat ride."

Still chuckling, Angel said, "That's the truth! But it's great. They're spectacular together."

"Indeed, they are. But I called for a favor."

"Name it."

"Can you stop somewhere…anywhere for a cake and champagne? Steel has steaks marinating for the grill."

"Sure. Anything else?"

"Sympathy in case Adam is not himself. Can you imagine having seven guests for dinner on your honeymoon? Not several days later - but get out of bed honeymoon."

Angel grimaced in imagined pain as he looked at his bride to be in ten days. No way. He said, "That's a nightmare. A painful one."

"My thoughts exactly."

***

After the call, Jade said, "It's romantic. Doesn't a wild boat ride fit them?"

"It does."

Then sighing, she said, "But…a honeymoon with guests? And Quest's grand opening tomorrow? Not to mention a fugitive on the loose. It's unbelievable. That's what thriller movies are made of."

"That's why they're in a hurry, and what a fire-filled bed is made of. And that, Jade, is what I'm going to give you in a few days."

He laid his hand on her upper thigh. Very upper thigh. One finger brushing what wasn't her thigh. Jade slid her fingers between his. Half of her wanted his hand to push the issue. The other half held it back. Such was the battle of waiting till the wedding night. His other hand tightened on the steering wheel as he contemplated pulling off the interstate for a more thorough touch.

She smiled at her handsome Latino. Muscular. A tough former marine. He was very bold about his hunger for her. They'd started as friends. Then Salsa partners. And then business partners for over a year. The engagement was a few months ago. A hot, few months ago.

Angel glanced at Jade. Beautiful golden skin. Long dark hair. Latino and Russian. Dark brown eyes - exotic, with a bit of a slant to them. Voluptuous. Smart, inquisitive, and a great communicator. He loved everything about her…especially this part.

He said, "You want me to touch you."

161

"I do…but…?"

He sighed. "No. I can't take you in the car. Not your first time." He smiled. "Your second time, I'll take you anywhere."

***

Much later at the barndominium, Adam and Raven lay entwined on the sofa listening to music by the fireplace.

Adam said, "When do you want to tell Lance we're married?"

"After Zack is over. I don't want to go to the ranch and lead anyone to him. I messaged Callie, but she won't tell him. Maybe we can show him his room and tell him then."

"He's a gorgeous child, Raven. A beautiful spirit. I love him. You know that. He does too. And I don't want him to think I'm replacing Beau. I love him more than enough to honor his father too."

Raven's eyes watered. Her throat tightened.

He kissed her softly and said, "And he can call me whatever he wants. I don't want to coax him. I'll be his daddy no matter what he calls me."

She laid her forehead on his chest, still not able to talk. Her heart was exploding. When your man loved you was one thing. When your man loved the best part of you – your children – there were no words that came close.

A thought rose in her. Maybe that's how the universe was formed. God loved us so much his heart exploded over and over and over birthing galaxies. Over two trillion of them last she heard. Her soul whispered, thank you.

Adam waited, not rushing her. Some moments were like that. Love doesn't always have a word. You just feel it. The unspeakable gift. He smiled and kissed the top of her head.

Wiping tears off her face, she smiled and pulled his lips to hers.

Sometime later, they heard the dogs barking. Angel and Jade must have arrived. Raven tried to dress. Adam undressed her. He wasn't ready to leave.

And finally, they were late but satisfied enough for a pause. Lacing their fingers together, they headed outside. On the porch, Adam whistled. The dogs came running. And in the light of the moon, they strolled romantically across the yard to their guests.

***

Dakota made quick introductions for Angel and Jade. Then the women set the impromptu wedding cake on a stand while Angel put the champagne on ice. Dakota piled the marinated steaks on a platter while Angel and Steel prepared the patio and grill.

Maverick and Rex had just finished the last leg of a security pass around the property when everyone noticed Adam and Raven coming.

Cheers filled the cool night air.

Dakota reached them first, and hugging Raven, said, "Congratulations to both of you! Very stealthy, brother. I'm impressed you pulled this off. Sean called me a liar. He didn't believe you slipped in a wedding in the middle of all this."

Adam said "He's the last one that should be shocked. He eloped. But look at Raven…why is anyone surprised?"

"Oh. Don't get me wrong. Your method was the only shock. You've been chasing this beauty for months."

After all the hugs and congratulations, they cut the cake. French almond with raspberry filling. Champagne followed. And with close family and friends on video chat, they toasted the bride and groom. Then Steel put the steaks on the grill.

Over dinner they discussed the security plan for Quest's grand opening in the morning. Five a.m. would arrive quick.

Adam said, "Jax and Lexi will be here by six o'clock to set up the food truck. The radio van will be here by a little after seven. Gabrielle and Callie will be here around the same time. They will work the information table in the Quest house and make sure coffee, water, and donuts are ready.

"I expect guests to arrive by car and boat so there may be a lot of movement on the river and the road. Gabrielle and I will work downhill where the main flow of traffic will be. Her nursing station will be set up on the wharf near the airboat. I will greet incoming guests and watch for suspicious men focused on or lingering around her."

He motioned to Piper. Her turn.

Piper said, "I will shadow Gabrielle. That's my goal. No one will get to her without going through me. If I sense danger, I will intervene as the FBI. It's that simple. I'm not there to be friendly. And Maverick agreed to monitor around us in plain clothes."

She motioned to Dakota.

Dakota said, "I'll stay uphill by the house and barn monitoring guests as Steel handles the tours and job applicants. Rex will help me uphill. And everyone, keep in touch. We need to know if there's trouble."

Angel said, "I know we're extra hands, but just so you know, I plan to stay closer to Gabrielle while Jade mingles and watches. You need someone flexible. We've got your back and will be armed."

Raven said, "Thank you. All of you. This whole situation is unreal. Adam, don't you expect a good bit of law enforcement to show up? There will be more security than just us."

"Yes. Quite a few. And they would react at the first hint of trouble. But they don't know what to look for. And Raven, you more than anyone, need to check out every person you come near. You know Zack. And you've interacted with Hunter. If you see anything that makes you suspicious. Anything that looks off. An awkward feeling. A tingle up your spine. Someone watching you. Listen to your instincts and say something."

Raven said, "I will."

Dakota said, "Everybody, let's face the facts. If Zack and Hunter are alive, they could be in Louisiana. But they aren't going to walk in here looking like themselves. We all need to be suspicious. Especially of men their size."

***

Later, everyone moved to the patio and chilled with another glass of champagne.

As the conversation and laughter flowed, Adam watched Raven laugh. She was all that was on his mind. She was so beautiful. Tantalizing. And he loved the way she could spark into flame in an instant. And that reminded him that she hadn't been upstairs yet. Which meant, she was still naked under that skirt.

He checked the time. Ten o'clock. It had been a long day, but it was far from over. Standing, he caught Raven's eye. He nodded to the house. Her smile answered him.

Adam said, "Ok, everyone. We're calling it a night. See you bright and early. And it had better be a life-or-death situation if I hear from anyone."

As they reached the top of the stairs, Adam carried Raven, kissing her as he slid a hand under her skirt. Her sweet groan set him on fire as he stepped over the threshold. She slid down, and he turned to lock the door.

She stepped behind him and ran her hands around to his abdomen. And lower. He growled and pulled his shirt off. She unsnapped his jeans, licking his back. Adam groaned in anticipation as she slid his pants down.

She smiled at his hungry, "Raven…"

Chapter 22

Quest Search & Rescue

Long before dawn, Adam woke to the warmth of Raven's body partially under his. She was sound asleep on her stomach, his arm draped across her, his right leg over hers. He glanced at the time. Three-thirty. Kissing her shoulder, he rolled to his back. Memories of the night played in his mind.

Raven stirred, feeling cool air on her back, and rolled over. In the slivers of moonlight, her sleepy eyes met his.

Pulling her in his arms, he said, "Hey, beautiful."

She snuggled and said, "What time is it?"

"Thirty minutes before the alarm goes off."

She smiled. "I know you are thrilled about today."

"I am. But I'm more thrilled about yesterday and last night, Mrs. Nash."

She purred in remembrance. "Me too, baby, me too."

He kissed her and said, "Do you want to doze while I go start coffee? Or take a few extra minutes in the shower?"

"Extra time in the shower sounds perfect. I'll meet you downstairs. I know you have a million details to tend to."

"I do. It'll be busy today. Then we'll leave for New Orleans. But...I'm already looking forward to picking up where we left off a few hours ago."

Huskily she teased, "And where did we leave off?"

And in a flurry of covers, she squealed, as Adam flipped her face down, laying on her back. Intent obvious as he caressed her.

Moving her hair, he kissed her neck and whispered, "We were...right here."

"You're...going...to be late."

He groaned. "I disagree. I'm right...on time."

***

Later, Raven rushed as she heard everyone downstairs. It was…embarrassing to have company on their honeymoon. Not that she would have done anything any different. No way. But…she leaned over and stared in the bathroom mirror. She looked like she'd had a wild night of sex even after her shower. Her hair tangled in a bun. Swollen lips. Cheeks very pink from his whiskers. And love marks all over her fair skin. She groaned remembering every one of them.

Someone knocked on the door.

She called out, "Give me ten minutes!"

Piper said, "I'll give you fifteen. I just wanted to make sure he left you alive in there."

Raven laughed as Piper went downstairs, then reached for her jeans. Then boots. Quest hoodie. And after taming her hair, she pulled it into a ponytail. Then adding light makeup, lip gloss, and perfume, she was dressed. Opening the lockbox, she holstered her gun. Walking to the door, she stopped.

Now she had to face everybody again.

When she opened the door, Adam was there. And smiling, he picked her up for a quick kiss and escorted her downstairs. And of course…loyal friends and family that they were, everyone harassed her with cat calls and whistles as she entered the kitchen. Her face burned, even though she laughed.

Grinning, Adam kissed her.

Piper handed her a cup of coffee, and whispered, "You're a good sport. It had to be tough being in the same house with a crowd of people. But…you look beautiful and loved."

Raven said, "Thanks, Piper. But please, lie to me - tell me the guests won't notice today."

"Only someone looking closer than they should, will know. And they'll just be jealous."

"Ok. I'll go with that. I mean, I haven't even been a wife fourteen hours yet."

"Exactly. Soak it up honey, soak it up. You're just warming up."

"Oh, Piper. We passed warm when we met."

**

Outside, activity was underway on the cool November morning. Down by the river, the wharf was decorated with balloons and a large Quest Search & Rescue sign. Raven's medical display was ready for her to set up. The rescue airboat bobbed in the water ready for rides and demonstrations. Tables and chairs were set up in the grass along the riverbank. And the food truck was in place with canopies for shade.

Signs directed guests uphill to the Quest office in Adam's house for coffee and donuts. Inside, the information table was ready with job brochures, a small gift set, and job applications for the three positions. The barn and equipment building doors were open for tours.

Adam stood at the top of the hill and watched his vision for Quest come to pass. No one knew, like a victim, the importance and value of a rescue. He had suffered beyond anything he had ever comprehended on the floor of the Brazilian jungle. But for the rescuers that helped him, he would have died there. His leg bore witness with scars.

Reflecting, he knew he would have been a good FBI agent, but being good at something didn't mean it had to be his calling. The FBI handled criminal rescue. His passion was for wilderness rescue. Accidents. Injuries. Unforeseen weather and animal issues. Getting lost. His vision for Quest was to bring them home. Hopefully alive.

He heard voices and turned.

Raven, Piper, and Dakota were heading his way. They were undoubtedly giving Raven instructions. As FBI on duty, they were dressed in suits on purpose. One, as obvious security for Raven. Two, as a reminder to guests that a fugitive was still on the loose. And thirdly, to let Zack know he would be met with lethal force.

A horn blew. Gabrielle and Callie pulled up to the Quest office. Dakota waved at Adam, then took off to meet Gabrielle.

***

Piper continued instructions and said, "I need you to expect the unexpected, Raven. I need you to pause in awareness before warmly reaching out to anyone. You are a nurse, I get it. But don't let compassion blind you."

"I understand, Piper. I do. Not paying attention almost got me killed last time. I'd like to think I'm a little more cautious now. So, unless there's a medical need, I'll stop and look first. Okay?"

"I can live with that."

As they reached Adam, he said, "I decided to assign the German shepherd to Raven too. Everything about him should be a deterrent. And I will be watching of course."

Piper said, "Great. He's impressive. I love shepherds. Why don't you save me one of his male pups? Surely, you'll stud him out."

"I will. But I thought you didn't bring men home."

Maverick walked up in time to hear that comment.

Glancing at Piper, he said, "I've been to your place. So, does that mean—?"

"Easy, Detective, you helped me with the movers."

"But I have impressive skills you haven't even tapped into yet. And you want to. You really do."

Laughing, Adam and Raven left the couple flirt-sparring and followed Dakota to meet Gabrielle and Callie.

***

Dakota opened Gabrielle's car door, hiding concern at her movements. Her thin but athletic frame was dwarfed by the size of her belly as she turned to get out of the car. She smiled at her gorgeous, worried husband.

Knowing he was the luckiest man in the world, he cupped her face and kissed her. Softly. And helping her up, he whispered, "You are beautiful and strong, honey, but you need to be off your feet. Please. Be kind to your body. Let me help you. You are the one doing all the work for our baby girl. Let me do something."

Touching his face, she said, "Thank you. I won't argue. In all honesty, I am getting more tired by the day. I can't see her waiting to come for three weeks. I think our Christmas baby wants to be closer to Thanksgiving."

Serious, he said, "I think so too. Maybe we need to get you closer to Lake Charles. You are an hour away at the ranch."

"No. I'm fine. No contractions – just tired. After Zack is caught, we'll be back home, and I'll live the life of leisure as you serve me."

Chuckling as he carried her inside, he said, "Bring it on. I've got you, beautiful."

On the other side of the car, Steel took the large stack of donut boxes from Callie and kissed her.

Tasting his passion, Callie said, "I missed you too."

"Callie...baby."

"I know. Surely it won't be much longer till they catch him."

"They aren't even sure he's alive yet. But they are searching and ready to drop him like a stone."

"I hope so, Steel. He'll never leave her alone."

"Then dead works just fine."

***

Adam and Raven joined the couples inside the house.

Jade and Angel were already setting up refreshments. Angel poured coffee into carafes from the commercial Community Coffee machine, then joined Steel outside. Jade prepared a nice layout of donuts and coffee with Callie. Dakota carried a rocker in from the front porch and set Gabrielle up at the information table with a footstool. He stood hands on hips; still not sure she should be doing this.

Greeting Raven and Adam, Gabrielle said, "Please tell Dakota I'm fine. I can sit and get larger anywhere. At least working and visiting will keep my mind occupied."

Raven hugged her and said, "You are beautiful — all parts of you — and in a few weeks, you'll be running the trails again with Dakota in hot pursuit. This will all be a memory. And I'll babysit while you work on baby two."

Callie brought Gabrielle yogurt with granola, ice water, and coffee, and said, "They better hurry and pick a name for baby one first."

Adam said, "Are you still following grandmother's first-born tradition of a Native American name?"

Dakota said, "Yes. We've got it down to three."

Gabrielle said, "We've picked Aiyanna, Dyani, or Cheyenne."

Raven and Adam's eyes met. It wouldn't be long before they would be choosing a name. Not long at all.

Steel stuck his head inside and said, "Adam, the radio station is here."

***

By seven-thirty, the aroma of bar-b-que pork steak, chicken and sausage gumbo, and chili filled the air. Raven's stomach growled as she arranged her medical display on the wharf. The shepherd lay nearby, relaxed, but watchful. Piper was perched on a stool, her suit jacket tucked behind her weapon.

Maverick winked at Piper as he passed by the wharf. She pointed at her gun in warning. He laughed.

Raven noticed and grinned. She said, "I like Maverick for you."

170

Piper said, "Yeah. He likes him for me too."

"And?"

"I'm considering it."

"Consider faster."

"Maybe. But I recall you taking your time considering Adam."

"Not so long. I met him on July 4th weekend. It's almost Thanksgiving. He pursued me quickly like Maverick is doing you. So, if we compare time, you could be on your honeymoon in March, having swollen lips and whisker marks on your cheeks – among a few other places."

Piper felt the deep reaction inside at the thought of looking up at Maverick naked and sweaty. She stood to shake it off. Raven met her gaze, aware of the impact.

Piper said, "You really want your security distracted?"

Lexi joined them with a tray of tiny disposable dishes. "Anyone hungry? I have testers!"

The shepherd wagged his tail, licking his lips. Raven and Piper eagerly reached for the treat.

Accepting a small dish of chili and a saucer of steak, Raven said, "Lexie, you are the best!"

Smiling at the quickly emptied dog bowl on the ground, Lexi said, "I can't take all the credit. Dad grilled. I cooked chili. And we both cooked the gumbo. But the gumbo's not ready for testing yet."

Piper sighed. "This is delicious. You're beautiful and a chef. If you were a pole dancer, you'd be the perfect woman for any man."

Lexi laughed so hard she almost dropped the tray of food.

Raven laughed and said, "Really Piper. Where in the world did that come from? I never figured you for a sexist. Do you even cook or pole dance?"

Piper grinned and said, "Actually…I have a pole dance workout. It's fabulous. But no. I don't cook. I feel an itsy bit guilty about it though. I mean, I know men like food. They like naked women and food."

Lexi wiped tears from her eyes and said, "I did not expect this conversation. But I can give you cooking lessons if you promise to teach me pole dancing."

Only Raven saw Adam step close behind Lexi and Piper. He stopped dead in his tracks at Lexi's comment. His expression clearly said…what?

Looking at Raven, Adam said, "Who's teaching pole dancing?"

Lexi giggled. Raven pointed at Piper.

Maverick joined them in time to hear Adam ask, "When did you start pole dancing, Piper?"

Maverick dropped his saucer of steak as his gaze met Piper's. She could see his mind flip to an image of her on a pole. Naked. She winked teasingly as Lexi handed him another plate of food with a giggle.

He thanked Lexi, and said, "So, Piper, how come I didn't see the pole when the delivery guys unloaded your furniture yesterday? I would have noticed."

"It's on order."

"Let me know when the pole arrives. I'll…help you put it up."

"I just bet you would."

Rex joined the group, and said, "What pole?"

Dimples showing, Lexi handed him chili and said, "Piper is going to teach me how to pole dance."

With no hesitation at all, he said, "Do you have room for one more in the class?"

A deep rumble interrupted another round of laughter as a Harley-Davidson motorcycle rolled to a stop by the parking signs.

Adam said, "Here we go guys! Quest is open for business. Stay alert for Zack and Hunter."

***

Impressed with the motorcycle, Adam headed toward the tattooed man taking off his helmet. He hung it on the handlebar and ran his hand through early salt and pepper hair. He put keys in his pocket and turned at the sound of crunching gravel.

Adam held out his hand, and said, "Thanks for coming! You're my first guest. I'm Adam Nash."

Smiling, the guy gave a firm handshake. "Nice to meet you, Adam. I'm Jake. You sure have a fine place here – and a perfect place for search and rescue."

"Appreciate that, Jake. We think so too. Do you know much about search and rescue?"

"Only what I learned in the Navy for well over a decade. I moved here from New Orleans a few months ago."

"Thank you for your service."

"It was my honor. My family served. And speaking of family, I've seen yours mentioned in the news a couple of times recently."

"Which ones?"

"About the shark and fugitive. You seem to be the right man to have this business. How's the beautiful little lady with red hair?"

Adam pointed toward Raven and said, "She's amazing. And my wife as of yesterday."

Jake laughed and said, "You're more man than me working on your honeymoon."

Chuckling, Adam said, "It's just how it worked out. So, Jake. You want to look around? I can give you a personal tour until other guests arrive."

"Sounds great. In fact, you're the one I need to talk to."

"What's on your mind?"

"I'd like to apply for the job driving that airboat floating by the wharf. She's a nice rig and I can drive anything."

"I'm glad to hear it. Let's walk that way."

Adam had just introduced Jake to Raven and Piper when more vehicles pulled up. A car. Three trucks. Two deputy units. And a boat. He headed to the new guests.

Chapter 23

Across the river, Zack stood in the woods watching Raven. She was more beautiful than ever. He loved the sensual way she moved without any effort at all. Her graceful turns, the toss of her head, and her glorious mane of hair. And her body…well, she was just built for sex. And lots of it. His groin ached remembering the feel of her that night.

His phone vibrated with a text.

***

Kip: I'm almost there. When are you coming?

Zack: When there's enough people to blend in.

Kip: Isn't deception a trip?

Zack: Just hide that wound on your leg. That screams you're Hunter.

Kip: I will. I'll have to do a background check for the job too.

Zack: That takes time. By tomorrow or the next day, I'll be gone with her.

Kip: You mind if I take a woman for myself?

Zack: You touch Raven, you're dead.

Kip: There are plenty to pick from. I'll decide today. Gotta go. I'm here.

***

Kip smiled as he parked his truck down the road from Quest. He was stepping into his element. For him it was the thrill of deception, and the money Zack gave him. Basically, it was inheritance he couldn't legally access as a sperm kid. In return, he fed Zack's hunger for Raven any way he wanted it. It was as simple as that. Their two dark needs drove the relationship.

He'd found out about his sperm dad's business - and his participation in donating. It impressed him. The man had been smart. He bought the sperm bank and literally sold himself. The perfect donor. And success was rampant in his sperm. All you had to do was look at the name written across the top of the building - the donor request list - his picture on a stallion - his looks – and his money.

174

And Kip never blamed his mother for not providing an actual father. It was him she wanted. He admired her courage to raise a son alone. And she was successful herself. Not famous. But she worked steady modeling, acting, and finally landed an older wealthy fish. He was happy to pay for her looks and get a hot piece of her any time he wanted.

But the old fish didn't like him or the way his mother doted on him. So, to keep the peace, the old man paid for him to disappear. College. Trips. Anything. Just a life anywhere but with them. And it worked for him and his mom. They saw each other. Talked often. And he knew she suspected a side gig but didn't ask him. He knew she feared what he might tell her.

She wouldn't have liked his connection with his biological brother – among the many illegal things he enjoyed. But she loved him. Really loved him. And he loved her. The rest was…what it was.

He walked toward the celebration with a group of arriving people. Up ahead, he saw Adam shaking hands with a couple by the food truck.

He was an impressive man. Confidence, fire, and integrity were part of his stature. And for a second, Kip could easily imagine him dressed in buckskins astride a horse. Bow and arrows. A real Sioux warrior.

He passed a group of deputies chatting and smiled a greeting. Did anyone sense a wolf had arrived?

***

Adam couldn't keep up with all the people arriving. Angel had put on a Quest shirt and was helping him. They waved. Shook hands. And greeted who they could as they pointed the way to food and tours.

Noticing Dakota at the top of the hill, Adam raised a hand asking, is everything ok? Dakota gave him a thumbs up. All was well in the office and barn. Which meant, no Zack or Hunter.

Turning to Raven on the wharf, she was giving medical demonstrations and pointing out storage for her equipment on the airboat. He looked at Piper. She made a zero with her thumb and forefinger. No threats.

He smiled and glanced at the food truck. Lexi held up a Gatorade. He nodded and headed her way as a group of people walked up the road. Grabbing the Gatorade with a thank you, he shook hands with two deputies he'd met a few times at the Calcasieu Parish Sheriff's Office. Then watched Angel connect with a young family with four preteen boys who were thrilled to be there and wanted to see everything.

Adam shook hands next with an older couple while noticing several men close to Zack's age and height bringing up the rear. One was a slim cowboy with blonde hair. Another was heavier with black hair and a ball cap. And the third guy had short stylish brown hair with sunglasses. He waved at the three new guys. They smiled and waved back.

He watched them for a few seconds as they split up. One went uphill with a dozen people. One got in line at the food truck. And the other man walked toward the wharf and Raven.

***

Piper noticed the shepherd watching the crowd. He was no longer relaxed with all the strangers around. But Raven...she was loving every minute of her contact with the people. She was fabulous. Friendly. Gorgeous. Caring. Everyone was enchanted with her.

Most of the men tried to be respectful and not gape at her. But some saw beyond who she was – and contemplated what they'd rather do to her. All in all, Piper knew those were rarely the dangerous men. They were just appalling. But still, Piper stood close, alert, being a visual warning to anyone who might do more than think the thoughts in their filthy minds.

Raven smiled at Piper who looked like a secret service agent for the president. She whispered, "Stop it. You're scaring everyone."

"That's my job. You are like a neon light to these men."

"Not just me, I see them eyeing you too."

"Like I care."

"Some are cute."

"Who wants cute? If I want cute, I'll get a puppy or a kitten."

Raven laughed, drawing more attention.

An older man pointed to Piper and said, "Who are you? Why are you guarding her?"

Piper said, "I'm Special Agent Pierce with the FBI. A manhunt is underway for a fugitive that may be headed to Louisiana. You may have seen her interview on the news recently."

The guy's wife bumped his arm, and said, "I told you."

Everyone laughed softly at the cranky couple.

He snapped, "I can ask her if I want to."

Raven tried to distract them, and said, "Did you notice the shepherd? His name is Dragon. He's one of our search and rescue dogs. We have three. He helps with security too."

The man's wife said, "He's huge. Does he bite?"

"No. Only when attack instructions are given. Here, you can meet him." She called Dragon over. His tail wagged at the attention.

She continued, "The dogs are amazing searchers. They can smell a scent up to a quarter of a mile away. Many victims have been found by these animals. Horses can follow a scent for search and rescue as well, though they are typically used in large search areas with hundreds of acres."

Adam drew closer as he watched the man with blonde hair get closer to Raven as she spoke to the group on the wharf. Piper noticed Adam and met his gaze. He acted like he touched the brim of an invisible hat. Her eyes went directly to the man with blonde hair wearing a cowboy hat.

Automatically, she checked him for weapons, threatening posture, expressions, and compared descriptions of Zack or Hunter. Other than size, nothing was alarming. Adam saw her barely perceptible negative nod, but she still moved closer to Raven since the guy was next in line.

Stepping on the wharf, Adam made his way to Raven's side and nudged her hip, slipping an arm around her.

The blonde guy stepped up and removed his hat respectfully, and said, "It's a pleasure to meet you. I'm Tom. And I'm a nursing student at McNeese with a huge interest in your line of work. Have you had any rescues yet?"

As Adam and Piper relaxed, Raven said, "We have! A man was gored in the woods by a wild pig. And after the tropical storm a father and son were lost in the Cameron marsh. Their boat was damaged by a great white shark and the father was injured."

The guy said, "I remember the shark on the news! That had to be crazy."

Adam said, "It was a shock – you can't prepare for that. And as an update, we found out from the shark autopsy that his lateral lines were damaged and not working. That is the part of his anatomy which checks water pressure so he can escape to calmer water. That's how he got swept into the marsh.

***

Kip had purposely gotten in the food line to give himself time to get the lay of the land so-to-speak. Smiling, he watched Adam and the sexy female agent zero in on the blonde cowboy getting closer to Raven. It didn't take

177

long, and they scratched him off their radar. But eventually they'd lock onto him too. He was planning on that.

His phone vibrated with a text. Glancing downriver he saw the red canoe steadily heading to the party.

Then the little Louisiana hottie in the food truck said in her sweet accent, "Hi! May I help you?"

Kip smiled with intent to charm and said, "I'll take whatever you touch, beautiful."

She laughed showing the cutest dimples ever, and said, "How about you call me Lexi. Beautiful is a little formal as I melt in this hot truck."

He laughed, enjoying the banter, and said, "Well, hello, Lexi! I'm Kip. How about you choose me a drink and something beef. And it would be better if you could join me."

The Latino man in the truck with her said, "No can do, sweetie. We are too busy."

Lexi raised her hands, winked, and said, "Sorry, Kip. It wasn't meant to be."

Kip gave her a tip and a sexy grin, then carried his bowl of chili to one of the tables facing the river. He always preferred a front row seat.

***

Out of sight, Zack rowed across the river and slowly paddled toward Raven. He stayed about fourteen feet off the bank like he was just minding his own business and enjoying the ride. The wonderful smell of spicy chili, bar-b-que, and another aroma he wasn't familiar with wafted in the air. It made his stomach growl. Loud. He ignored it.

He just watched the distance between him, and Raven slowly disappear. Seventy feet. Sixty. Forty-five. Thirty. Then she saw him. She smiled a real smile and waved like she was thrilled to see him.

His gut twisted and his mind raced with a million thoughts. Some good. Some violent. But they were all hot. Sexual. He dismissed a fleeting remembrance of early love and waived hesitantly, like an old man might, and stepped into the role.

Raven was standing in the airboat when she noticed the old man in the canoe. She motioned him to the wharf and called over the noise, "Hi there! Welcome! Come join us!"

He quit paddling and let the canoe coast closer, watching her and glancing at the activity. He didn't answer.

When he got about ten feet away, Raven tried again and said, "We have great food today. Chili. Bar-b-que. And gumbo. Would you like to come ashore and eat?"

The old guy held up a cane with one hand and touched his throat with the other. He opened his mouth, but no sound came out. Raven's heart melted. He couldn't talk and obviously it would be difficult to get out of the canoe.

She said, "Would you like to tie up to the wharf and I can bring you a plate? I don't mind at all. Or would you like to come ashore? We can help you. Please. We'd love you to join us if you can."

He didn't respond for a second, then pointed to a sandy nook on the bank.

Raven said, "Piper, would you get Maverick to give us a hand? The guy can't do it by himself. He's disabled and mute."

"And you can't presume he's a sick old man just because he looks like one."

"But it will be easy enough to tell once he's close enough. I am not letting him pass without food. Look at him. Do it. Or I will."

"Stay behind us. We'll help him."

"Deal."

Zack paddled the boat into the shallow water by the bank. He watched Raven, the female agent, and a tall man position themselves to help him. They were all armed. The thought flashed that if they knew who he was, he'd already have bullet holes in him. But this way, Kip was right, it was thrilling to slide up into the midst of them.

Raven was the only one smiling. The agent wasn't pleased. And the tall guy wasn't either. He could feel the heat as their eyes bore into him, looking for deception. But unless they insisted on a more physical look, he was safe as a newborn baby – or a sick old man.

Piper and Maverick met the canoe as it slid ashore. Once it was stable, it took the old guy a bit to get up, but then he stood with the cane by his left side. Raven knew his opposite side was strongest and directed Maverick where to go to offer his arm.

Maverick met the old guy's gaze. Nothing about him looked like Zack, so he offered his forearm. The old man gripped it to balance and stepped out of the boat. He good-ole-boy patted Maverick on the shoulder as a thank you.

Raven smiled and said, "Awesome! Come on. I promise the food will be worth the trouble."

In several minutes he was seated at a picnic table while someone went for food. Zack glanced at Kip a few tables away. Then Raven sat across from him. And for the first time in years, she was close enough to touch. He knew he could grab her and make a run for it, but it would be a waste of time. She'd fight. They all would. And she'd get hurt and he'd be dead without ever accomplishing what he came for.

So, he let his eyes roam her casually like a stranger. Then he clenched his jaws at the obvious sexual activity. Puffy lips. Marks on her face and neck that her makeup almost hid. And of course, there was the sexual satisfaction in her eyes that a woman gets after being pleased over and over.

He growled silently. That's ok. He'd put that look there soon enough.

She said, "I'm Raven, the nurse for Quest. My husband, Adam, is the owner and rescuer extraordinaire."

She slid a pen and slip of paper to him, then checked his health appearance. He was a big guy. Much heavier than Zack. Late 60s or early 70s. She smelled a sweaty musty smell on him. He had brown eyes and lots of sunspots on his sun-darkened skin. Graying hair to his shoulder. And his beard and mustache hid his mouth. Even his eyebrows were bushy. But other than age, his hand was slow, but steady as he wrote. And he looked outdoors healthy, so he wasn't sedentary.

He pushed the paper toward her.

She read. "I'm Ben. Thanks."

She smiled and said, "Hi, Ben. You're welcome. And I need to get back to our guests in a minute but enjoy the food and tour if you want. We can get you a ride to the house where the office and search animals are located. The shepherd here is one of them."

She pointed to Piper, and said, "Agent Pierce stays with me, but we have plenty others to give you a hand."

He reached for the paper, and wrote, "Why?"

She read the question and said, "Why what?"

He pointed at Piper. Then saw a brief flash of anger, then fear, in Raven's eyes. He recognized it. He'd seen it the night they fought. But then again, there wasn't much about her he didn't know.

Raven said, "A fugitive is on the loose. He's after something he thinks belongs to him. She's here to make sure he knows he can't have it." Her inflection was obvious.

He pointed at her.

"Yes. But he's wrong. I never was his."

They were interrupted as his food was delivered.

180

Raven stood. Touching his hand, she said, "Eat up. It's delicious! We'll visit later if you like."

Zack's rage was pricked by Raven's remarks about him. He watched her walk back to the wharf. She'd pay for that. But his hand tingled from the soft touch of her hand. His crotch too. A shadow fell over him and he looked up at Agent Pierce. Stunningly beautiful. Sharp as a tack. Silently she made the point that she was watching him. He waved toward the seat across from him. She ignored his offer and wrote a few words on his slip of paper, then walked away.

He read, "People are rarely what they seem."

His humor returned. She didn't find anything truly suspicious, or he would be on the ground and cuffed – if not dead. But she wanted to warn him anyway. She was quite the adversary. Kip was going to want her. He'd bet another million on it.

***

Adam watched Raven and Piper leave the old man and return to the wharf. Then he glanced again at the guy in the sunglasses at a table further away. He'd lingered too long for a young man. Why was he here? Then like the man heard his thoughts, he cleaned off his table and walked to the wharf with a big smile on his face.

Adam followed him.

Raven and Piper both noticed the man with sunglasses. Not just because he was good looking and smiling, but because his size fit Hunter's profile. They'd seen him at the table and knew he had been hanging around for a while. Piper stepped in front of Raven and put out a hand to stop him from advancing.

At that move, several things happened. Adam appeared next to Piper, and a few seconds later, Maverick was on the wharf asking others to back away. Angel helped him. Dakota was jogging downhill. Even the shepherd growled at the alert in the air.

Kip held his hands up in surrender and said laughingly in a Texas drawl, "Whoa! Hold on! What's the problem? I just wanted to introduce myself—"

Piper said, "Well, introduce yourself to me first. And take off your glasses."

He removed his glasses, exposing gorgeous hazel eyes, and gave Piper an interested glance as he said, "I'm Trace. Trace Kirkpatrick. But everyone calls me Kip."

Ignoring his come-on, she said, "May I see your I.D.?"

"Sure. Just don't shoot me. I'm willing, beautiful. I'm willing."

He reached for his wallet, then handed her his license. Piper concluded that it was clearly him. Dakota joined them on deck.

Piper said, "Mr. Kirkpatrick, if you are up to date on national news, you are aware there's a national manhunt for a fugitive and his accomplice. I see that you live in Texas. What's your business here in Lake Charles?"

"I have financial freedom to travel and work interesting jobs. And since I'm good with animals, horses especially, I often take jobs on ranches. The flyers around town said Quest would be taking applications for a few positions today."

He chuckled good naturedly and said, "However, I didn't expect an interrogation to be part of the application process. No offense taken."

Adam shook his hand, and said, "No offense meant, Kip. You have the misfortune of having a similar appearance to the accomplice. That's what landed you in the spot you're in. My wife's safety is the priority. I'm sure you understand."

"Yes, Sir. Totally."

Adam motioned uphill and said, "And if you're still interested in the job, why don't you head to the office with Agent Nash. He can show you where to fill out paperwork. Afterwards, we'll talk and go from there. I appreciate you visiting today and your interest in being a part of the team."

Adam watched them walk away, then told the very interested guests, "Sorry for the commotion folks. The FBI is making sure there is no danger among us. Please, continue your meal and tours. We are honored to have you as guests."

***

Zack took his last two bites of chili. Impressed. They were being careful to protect Raven. But she wasn't in danger today. He had something else in mind. And when it was least expected, they'd be back, and she'd be gone.

He looked down for his cane. Black hiking boots came from behind him and stopped close to it. Looking up, he met Adam's dark eyes. Zack saw an alpha male ready to fight for his wife. His territory. But he also saw what he knew Raven loved. The hunter. Protector. Strength and wisdom. And he hated him instantly. Adam was everything he would never be. This man would kill a hundred dragons to keep her safe. Whereas he would kill a hundred dragons to own her. That meant Adam couldn't be around when he came for her. Pumped at that decision, Zack smiled at him.

Returning the smile, Adam handed him his cane and said, "My wife was worried about you. Thank you for coming ashore."

The guy reached for pen and paper, wrote, and slid it over.

Adam read, "She's quite a lady, and the food was delicious. Thank you."

"She is and you are welcome. Do you live on the river?"

Zack wrote again. "No. I hitched a ride with family. We're visiting with friends down the river."

"Sounds fun. It's a perfect day to be on the river. And just in case you want to hang around a bit and tour our place, I'll have a four-wheeler brought to you. No sense fighting to climb that hill. If you need anything at all, look for someone in a Quest shirt. Don't hesitate to ask."

Zack gave him a thumbs up, then pulled some steak he'd saved out of his pocket. He pointed to the shepherd. Adam left him feeding the dog and went to the wharf.

***

Raven looked up and met Adam's gaze through the few people on deck. She could tell what was on his mind. Smiling, she slid her hands down her hips. Offering. His eyes followed her hands and looked at her. Hungry. She wet her lips. Anticipating. He smiled. You're mine. She turned and glanced back over her shoulder. Teasing. He stepped up behind her.

By now Piper and others around them were noticing. There were several whistles. Encouragement yells. Even the radio station helped and played a sexy love song. Adam possessively held her left hip with one hand and slid the other around her – then spun her around. She laughed and posed. He kissed her. She danced a couple of steps. And he spun her over and over - arched and graceful - till he dipped and gave her another wedding kiss. The crowd loved it and cheered.

Laughing, Adam and Raven waved. Adam said, "She said yes! And we got married yesterday!"

***

Sitting amid the cheers, Zack felt like he'd been stabbed with a red-hot poker straight out of the fire. Of all the things he thought he might encounter today, watching Raven come on to Adam right in front of him wasn't one of them. He swallowed the growl in his throat. She made him want to kill.

He smiled. Oh, wait. He already had.

Rubbing the shepherd behind the ears, he whispered soothingly, "Good boy. We're friends now. I'll be back for her, don't you worry. No sirree. She better practice her *come on* because I'm going to work her over until she doesn't have anything left. And then I'll make her do it again. And again."

***

In the barn, Steel said, "The black stallion is Aladdin, the brown filly is Sable, and the white stallion is Baron."

Kip said, "They are beautiful and intelligent. You take good care of them."

"We all do. They are more than search or sport horses. They are family. Everyone here has Native American heritage, except for me. They ride these animals like they were born to it. Even Raven's son is learning."

"How old is he? I didn't see him."

"Three. And he's out of town for a while."

"Oh, right. With the manhunt, that's probably best."

"It is. Where do you live in Texas?"

"Huntsville. Off Fm road 980 out in the country. I'm not there much."

"No wife? Kids?"

"Not yet. But that may change…Louisiana has beautiful women."

"They do. Exceptional ones. Tough too. Keep that in mind. Weapons are not for display if you get my meaning."

"I get it."

Steel led the way upstairs and said, "Come check out my office/flat. It's impressive."

Kip followed him in and stopped, shocked at the layout, and said, "I've worked a lot of ranches. I've never seen this."

Motioning to the gym by the windows he said, "And now I see why you're all bowed up."

"I started working out in the army. I like the discipline."

"I would say you are disciplined. I do it to stay in shape."

"Better than nothing. A lot of people don't do that."

Steel got a text from Adam: I'm in the office.

He said, "Let's head inside. Adam is waiting for us."

Going downstairs, Kip rammed his injured calf against the handle of a rake protruding past the rail. He winced. It hit the stitches from the wild pig attack. Glancing down he saw a little blood seep through his jeans. The rest ran into his boots. That's just great. He kept following Steel knowing he might have to cut the visit short and get out of here.

Being the same size as the accomplice was one thing. Having the very same injury would land him behind bars or dead.

***

By the river, Zack saw the four-wheeler coming. He got up and headed slowly toward the road with his cane. A big guy was driving it downhill. Short hair. He looked military. Muscular. Tough.

The guy saluted and braked, then got off and said, "Hey. You must be Ben. I'm Rex. The signs direct you to the house and barn, but you are welcome to ride around the mowed area. Don't be alarmed if the dogs check you out. They like to follow the four-wheeler. Blow the horn if you need anything. Oh. One restroom is in the barn. Another in the house. Enjoy your ride."

Zack saluted back. He sat on the seat, then swung his good leg over the console purposely not using his left hip. Hearing a woman call out, Zack turned. A pretty, petite blonde jogged over with two soft drinks.

Smiling with dimples, she handed them both one. She said, "Hi! I'm Lexi. I thought you might want one for the ride."

Nodding, he rubbed his stomach and pointed at the food truck. She laughed and then glanced up at macho man. Even Zack saw the sparks between them. Waving bye, Zack revved the throttle and drove away. Little miss Lexie didn't know how lucky she was that Kip had his eye on Piper. He usually favored blondes sprawled out under him.

***

In the house, Adam looked over the paperwork in his office. He'd received eight job applications. But the top two were motorcycle-Jake for the airboat driver job, and sunglasses-Kip for Steel's assistant. Steel had already given clear approval for Kip. And Adam liked Jake for the airboat job - though he was way overqualified. Next came the background check and DNA clearance. That should be completed in a day or two.

185

In the den, Jake was talking to Dakota, Gabrielle, and Callie by the information table. Several others came through the entrance. A husband and wife, followed by an old man.

Gabrielle smiled at the couple, and said, "Welcome!"

The woman said, "Oh my goodness, you have to be close to your due date!"

Laughing, Gabrielle said, "Actually, I still have a few weeks to go...not sure if I will make that due date though."

The woman's husband said, "I'm not a betting man, but if I was...no. You won't." Then the man sniffed at the coffee, and they laughed.

Gabrielle said, "Please, help yourself to pastries and coffee. I'm jealous! I'm punished with healthy yogurt."

Callie smiled at the older man with a cane. She shook his hand and said, "Hi! Thank you for coming today."

Having seen him, Adam came out of his office and said, "Callie, this is Ben. We met earlier. He communicates in writing."

She offered a pad and pen as Adam said, "Did you want to come in to rest for a bit or look at the display?"

Zack wrote, "The restroom first, then a cup of coffee, please."

Adam showed him the way.

***

Zack locked the bathroom door and hung the cane on the doorknob. Leaning over the counter he looked in the mirror. He really did look like an old man. Weathered. Kip had spent a small fortune on the age spot cream, and it was waterproof as long as no one wiped it when it was wet. If they did, old skin vanished. So, no washing his hands today. He unzipped his pants and peed long and hard thinking about the beauties down the hall.

The pregnant woman about to pop was a stunner. Amber eyes and full lips. He knew all about Gabrielle. Pirate descendant. She was probably wild in bed. Hence, the belly. And Callie, Beau's aunt, was at least twenty years older, but one hot momma. He remembered her well from back in Minnesota. Flat stomach. Full butt. Voluptuous. Sexy.

But no one was like his Raven. And for the millionth time he remembered taking her— Then groaning in frustration at his arousal, he killed the thought and zipped up. Looking back in the mirror he smiled.

Soon enough, Raven. Soon enough.

186

Steel and Kip came inside to meet Adam.

Adam said, "What did you think about the horses?"

Kip said, "They're incredible. I would love to work with them. And Steel. I hope I make it to the top of your application stack."

Zack heard Kip's voice as he walked down the hall to join the others. Kip heard the cane and looked up. Their gazes met briefly. Talk about irony. With all Adam's security, the fugitive and accomplice stood right in front of them.

Then unexpectedly, the bloodhound came from Adam's office and sniffed Kip's wound. For a second, Kip froze. Zack tensed and headed toward the door, ignoring the coffee. It was time to get out of here. He felt the walls closing in on him.

Adam said, "Hey, Kip. Did you cut yourself? I see blood."

Steel glanced at Kip's calf.

Kip rubbed the dog's head affectionately, and said, "I just brushed against a splinter in the barn. No big deal. I'll probably get dozens if you hire me on. Who can avoid it?"

Steel laughed. "That's the truth. I get one every day."

Kip caught Zack's gaze as he stepped outside. And understood the clear warning. But it was too late, he had to play it out now. So, he followed Adam into his office. Besides, he decided not to rush off. He intended to get under Piper's skin again before he left. She was absolutely fire in a suit. Hot. And for him, it was all about the game.

***

Zack gritted his teeth as he stepped on the porch. There were cops everywhere. Visiting. Eating. Laughing. Touring. There had to be fifty guns between him and the canoe, including two marine units on the water. He felt cold sweat as he headed to the four-wheeler. He kept his head down. Just before he reached the machine, a woman called his name.

Callie. He growled and acted like he didn't hear her, then grabbed the handlebar with a sweaty palm. That was not good. The lotion would rub off. He had to remember not to wipe his face where sweat was beading. Then she called his name again. She was close.

He turned and faced her.

Smiling, she lifted a large to-go cup, and said, "You forgot your coffee. I added cream and sugar. I hope that's ok. I hate it black, so I always presume everyone does."

He forced himself to nod and give her a thumbs up. She waited till he climbed on and handed it to him. He took a sip and lifted the cup in salute. She waved and headed back inside.

He took a big swig. Super sweet. And the sugar rush was perfect. He turned the key and the rumble between his legs gave him added encouragement. Steering away from people, he rode downhill. Slow. Steady. Deceptive. He just wanted to look like an old man puttering along.

He reached the road and aimed for a low populated spot not far from the canoe. It would be a miracle if he could make it out of here without conversation or trouble. He wanted to run but couldn't look young and healthy. Sweat ran down his temple. His neck. His chest.

Parking a few minutes later, he swung his leg over and grabbed the handlebar to stand. He could see lotion smeared on the grip. There wasn't anything he could do about that now. Hopefully, it would just seem dirty to anyone that noticed it.

He headed toward the canoe glancing at Raven. She saw him and waved. And he knew what she was going to do. He clenched his fists. He was so close to losing control.

She jogged to meet him and said, "Ben, thank you so much for coming. Can I get you something to bring home?"

He shook his head, no, and pointed to the canoe.

Frowning she noticed the sweat. His tenseness. And understood that he was in a hurry. She said, "Are you ok? You don't look like you are well. Let me get you some water."

As she turned to walk away, he held her arm. At the question on her face, he closed his eyes, acting like he was nodding off to sleep.

She said, "You're tired. I'm so sorry. Let's get you in the canoe."

And for a split-second, Zack stared at her wanting to do all the things he couldn't. Drag her to the canoe. Shoot anyone trying to stop him. And laugh as they all ran for cover while he took her from right under their noses.

Instead, he swallowed the rage, almost choking on it. He hadn't realized how much being an old guy with a cane would draw attention. He glanced at the canoe and walked away. He heard her call out a couple of names and just focused on the boat. Get in the boat. Just get in the boat.

When he reached the small sandy nook by the boat, a muscle man in a Quest shirt jumped down and offered his arm. Zack just went with it, and grabbed his arm, climbing down. A beautiful exotic brunette he'd noticed several times jumped down on the other side of him. He was surrounded now. As the man and woman held the canoe steady, he faked a struggle getting in.

Then the little blonde cutie from the food truck ran down with a container and a drink. Raven and Piper watched from the bank. Zack motioned he was ready and the man with black hair shoved the canoe.

Floating backward into the river, Zack growled and paddled. Ignoring everyone but the river. He paddled. And paddled. Trying to release the energy about to blow. The voices began to fade. Eventually the music faded. Then blessed silence.

Rage covered his face. And he grabbed the cane and threw it as far as he could. He hadn't escaped from prison for this. The next time he was face to face with Raven, she'd know it was him.

Chapter 24

Two hours later, the airboat flew down the river. Adam smiled as Jake maneuvered the boat to perfection on his test run for the driving job. Raven, Jade, and Angel were buckled in on the deck bench below them. The women screamed, hair flying, with hands held high like they were on a roller coaster as Jake thrilled them with tricks he'd learned through the years. Angel laughed. But you could barely hear anything with the sound of the massive wind engine.

After a while, Adam checked his watch. It was already three in the afternoon, and they needed to get on the road to New Orleans soon. He motioned for Jake to head back.

By the time they returned home, the radio station van was driving off. The food truck was gone. And Steel was watching the rental company pick up tables, chairs, and trash cans. Piper and Dakota were on the wharf.

Piper said, "What time are you and Raven leaving, Adam?"

Adam glanced at Raven and asked, "How long will it take you to pack?"

"Thirty minutes. What activities do I plan for?"

"Casual. Evening wear. And it might be chilly in the marsh tomorrow. Maybe bring your Quest hoodie since we'll be on the job if anyone asks."

"Sure. I'll head up to the house now."

Piper said, "We've had strangers on the property all day. We need to clear all the buildings."

Dakota said, "Let's do it in one sweep. I'll take Steel and Rex with me to clear Adam's place."

Piper said, "We'll check Raven's."

***

Kip followed Dakota, Steel, and Rex up to the Quest buildings, picking up tour signs as he went. He thought about all he'd learned staying behind to help. Most importantly, that Adam and Raven were following the Latino couple to New Orleans within the hour.

As he threw the tour signs in the dumpster as instructed, Rex yelled across the yard, "All clear here!"

Kip smiled. That was the other surprise. Maverick and Rex were local detectives. Which meant, the FBI, U.S. Marshals, state police, and local law enforcement were on their tail. Everyone wanted a piece of them.

And yet…here he stood.

Steel motioned Kip to follow him to the barn. Smiling, Kip headed his way pumped about today. He got off being a wolf. A hunter. It didn't matter that he wasn't the alpha. Zack was born to be alpha of any pack.

***

Raven tapped her finger on her lips as she looked at three short evening dresses. One was a black satin halter. The material felt like silky skin. The second was a red strapless lace sheath with a high slit. Hot and feminine. And the last was a gold one shoulder number. Tight and classy. With a shrug she packed them all. Why decide?

Then she freshened up. Changed into jeans, designer boots, and a gorgeous boho top laced all the way down her back showing lots of skin. So, no bra. She had just finished braiding her hair when she heard Adam walk into the bedroom.

He said, "It's me, baby."

She said, "Hey…I'm almost ready."

He pulled off his shirt as he joined her in the bathroom. His jeans were already unsnapped, partially unzipped. Their gaze met in the mirror. Raven's eyes slid like hands down his chest, his waist, and lower…where his zipper waited to finish the journey. A hot sizzle raced down her legs. She looked at him. Lips parted. Wanting.

Adam smiled. Sexy. What man doesn't like knowing his woman likes what she sees? He pressed against her back then slid his hands around and unsnapped her jeans. Trailing his mouth down her neck, he slid her pants down.

***

Much later, Adam drove down Interstate 10 eastbound. They were near Lafayette, a beautiful college town with an intriguing history of its own. Looking at the GPS map, Raven knew next was the Atchafalaya Basin, then Baton Rouge, then southeast to New Orleans.

She said, "Which hotel did you choose?"

"I decided on a luxurious, but historic New Orleans atmosphere, and made suite reservations at Hotel Monteleone. And I know we'll only be there overnight, but the hotel is not far from the French Quarter, or Steamboat Natchez on the Mississippi River. We'll be in the middle of it all."

"That sounds wonderful! I can't wait to hear the music. New Orleans jazz is the best. I can imagine it already."

"They promised that we'd hear it everywhere. Especially, on the balcony."

"Our bedroom has a balcony?"

"Yes, the suite is impressive. There's a seating area with windows overlooking the balcony and courtyard. Canopy bed. And you'll love the bath and shower. They cleverly mixed historical with a touch of contemporary."

"I've never slept in a canopy bed."

He ran a hand in her hair and said, "And I'm not sure how much sleep you'll get in this one."

***

Back at the park, Zack stood against the wall in the cabin and watched as Kip unlocked the door and carried in beer. Tequila. Cigarettes. And a bag of groceries. Kip took one glance at Zack and knew he was wound tight enough to blow. He would have his work cut out for him and decided to start with the good news.

Kip said, "I found out a few things today while I was hanging with them." No answer.

He continued, "It seems that two of the men there today are local detectives. They are staying there. A tall blonde named Maverick who was sniffing around the female agent, Piper. And a military-looking dude called Rex, hungry for the dimpled blonde."

Zack said, "Did you recognize Callie?"

"Yeah. She still looks amazing. Isn't she almost fifty?"

"Close."

"I think she's the property of my new boss, Steel."

"I don't blame him."

"Me either. Oh, I also heard that she is keeping Lance offsite, away from Raven, at a fortress of sorts. Evidently, we'd need an army to get in there."

192

"Where is it?"

"North of Moss Bluff off Highway 190 somewhere. The owner is Gabrielle's parents. Her dad's retired army. Want me to find them?"

"I don't need Lance so it's no big deal. Did you decide to take Piper?"

"Yeah."

"I figured you would. Can you handle her?"

Kip laughed.

Walking out of the shadows without a disguise, Zack said, "So, what aren't you telling me? You remind me of a cat – antsy and ready to bolt."

Kip shrugged and said, "Adam took Raven to New Orleans overnight with the Latin couple. They'll be home tomorrow night. It'll only be a skeleton security crew there since she is gone."

"So, I can't take her tomorrow morning as planned."

"No. Monday will have to do."

"Then after dark we go to Lake Charles. I've got to get out of this cabin."

***

In the barn, Steel put the last of the grand opening supplies in the storage locker as Callie loved on all the horses.

She said, "So, what do you think about Kip being your assistant?"

Steel said, "He knows his way around a ranch and what needs to be done. He's good with animals, smart, and has a great sense of humor. I can't ask for more than that - other than a clear background check and DNA of course. Everyone must be cleared."

"How long will that take?"

"A day or two at most. Adam likes Jake too. That man can drive an airboat."

"Did anyone apply for the yard man position?"

"No. But Jake and Kip said they can handle it for the winter. We'll hire someone before spring."

"Sounds like you would have a good team."

Finished with work, he drew her in his arms and said, "I think so too. They are both single though, so I don't know how long they'll hang around. They might haul a Louisiana woman off into the sunset."

Touching his chest, she said softly, "I know you understand that."

He kissed her. "That's an understatement."

He sat her on top of the fence and while kissing her, ran his hands up her thighs. She knew he wanted to touch her where no man ever had. His hands kneaded her thighs. Her hips. He spread her legs.

Breathless, she said, "As soon as Zack is over—"

He finished for her, "We are having a wedding and honeymoon come hell or high water."

***

Messaging Steel that they were clearing the surrounding woods, Piper tried to ignore the hungry look on Maverick's face.

She attempted conversation. "Does anyone ever call you Mav?"

"They try."

"You don't want to be the star in Top Gun?"

"No."

"Mav was hot."

"I'm already hot, getting hotter."

She stopped and said, "Look, Maverick—"

He stepped closer.

She put a hand against his chest, and said, "You are not kissing me."

"Yes, I am. And you want me to."

"Not right now I don't."

"Liar."

"Get past it. I still need to clear the area and I've never been in these woods. If you weren't so focused on what's in your pants, you'd realize that."

"You are the one talking about what's in my pants. Why is that?"

Piper didn't answer him. They stared at each other, their eyes doing the talking. She did want his kiss. But she shouldn't. She still had way too much to think about. She'd have to hold him off. But he was onto her scent like a predator on the prowl.

She went for a dismissive tone, and said, "You don't even have to stay now that Raven is gone. I can handle it. And Steel's here."

He laughed. "I'm not going anywhere, and you know it."

"Then focus on the case and show me where Raven connected with Hunter out here. And one more thing, don't ever call me a liar...even if I did."

Turning, she leapt across a wide ditch, and slipped, falling backwards. Maverick jumped, wrapping around her to absorb the hard landing as they fell, rolling to a stop. He did not expect the humor in her eyes as he looked down at her.

She laughed. "You get an A+ for effort! That was a great save – and totally outplayed my snide remark. I'm impressed."

Her smile hit him in the gut. His gaze locked on her lips, then raised to her eyes. Raven's smile faded. Sexual awareness sparked between them. But her lips closed like Fort Knox.

Brushing his lips across her cheek, he whispered, "Open to me, Piper."

She ignored his words while feeling his body on hers. He felt so good – but she did her best to hide it from him. His slight grin told her she hadn't. He lowered his mouth to hers. Barely kissed her, then touched her lips with the tip of his tongue. He said, "Piper…"

He heard the sweet sound deep in her throat, yet still she fought it. So, he rolled, bringing her on top of him. "Then you kiss me. And hurry. You're killing me."

And she kissed him. Hot. He held her face to his, kissing her deep, and hungry as they discovered this thing between them. Bodies tight. Breathless. Then he softened the kiss. Sensual. Their gaze met.

He said, "I love the taste of you."

She blushed and that flash of vulnerability surprised him. But her abrupt words didn't as she said, "That is not your leg I feel," and rolled off him.

Groaning at the truth of that, he sat up.

She said, "We can't have this complication."

"Attraction is not a complication, Piper. And later will be perfect."

"What makes you think there will be a later?"

He stared at her. She didn't break the silence or the stare.

Pulling a few leaves from her hair, he said, "Will you let me know when the stripper pole comes in so I can help you?"

"I don't know. Will I, Detective?"

"I tasted your affirmative just a bit ago."

"We'll see how smart you are. We shall see."

***

South of Baton Rouge, Adam said, "You really don't mind Angel and Jade joining us at the hotel for dinner?"

"Not at all! They're terrific. We'll have fun."

"No doubt. Angel is a trip."

After giggling in agreement, she grew silent, then said, "Adam, I know they're thrilled for their wedding next weekend. Are you worried about being able to officiate with all this going on?"

"No. I wouldn't call it worried. I want to be there for them. I hope to. But if I can't, God will provide someone. They would understand that. You and Lance come first. It's as simple as that."

195

She said, "I know they would expect no less. It's just in the back of my mind. So is Lance. I miss him. I'm not used to being apart from him and it's already been four days. He's only three. Thank God for the video chats with him and Callie.

"And I know he'll be excited when he finds out we're married, but I hate that he missed being a part of the celebration. We need to do something, so he has a memory of us becoming a family. A specific point in time when things changed."

"I know, baby. I've been thinking about that."

"You have? What do you have in mind?"

"What if we have a formal reception after this is over? I checked and the Mezzanine room at the Lake Charles Civic Center is available mid-December. It's in a lovely central location on the second floor with a connected balcony and multiple staircases. I would love to see you walk down that staircase in your mother's dress. And maybe they could even come in from Africa."

She unbuckled and leaned across the console to hug him. "Adam…"

Slipping an arm around her, he said, "I take it you like the idea."

Kissing his cheek and lowering back in her seat, she said, "I love it! And I didn't know how much I wanted that till right now. And you make it sound perfect. Beautiful. But don't get me wrong, I wouldn't replace our boat ride for anything in the world – that was for us. But the reception would be a fabulous memory with pictures. Me in a wedding dress. You in a tux. And Lance."

"I want to see you in a wedding dress."

"And I want to see you in a tux."

He said, "Then let's make plans. You have about three weeks. And instead of waiting for an island honeymoon on Valentine's Day, let's go then. We can make it back for Christmas Day."

She nodded. Suddenly pensive.

He said, "What is it?"

"You do remember that I can't wear a bikini on a public beach with my chest scars."

"Honey…don't worry about that. There won't be anyone else on our island but us. In fact, go naked. Please."

Adam's phone dinged as she laughed.

It was a group text from Sean: Video chat in five.

Adam put his phone in the dash clip and pulled into a truck stop. By the time they parked, the phone rang.

196

Adam answered and his phone screen split into multiple views. Sean. Dakota. Piper. Maverick. Rex. And Steel.

Sean began, "I'm presuming there were no problems at the grand opening."

Adam answered, "No. There were dozens of strangers – many of them were cops. And several men fit the general description of Zack and Hunter but in the end, no problems. We chose two men from the job applications, but they won't start work until their background and DNA checks are completed. So, all went well."

"Good! Now for not so good news. Back in Montana, DNA concluded that the piece of arm found in the woods belonged to the owner of the missing blue Jeep. And that Jeep was discovered this morning at a truck stop in Wyoming off Interstate 25. Almost at the Colorado border. And while we still don't know if Zack and Hunter are alive, someone stole the Jeep and dumped it. We are going back through camera feed along the route, but the snowstorm makes vehicle and driver identification almost impossible.

"And then a few minutes ago, a female body was found buried in the snow at a rest area southeast of Denver. Animals got to her so it will take DNA identification to even know who she is, what she was driving, or estimate the time of her death.

"All of that leads me to this, we are down to investigating three vehicle theft trails from the original eight we started out with in Montana. Now we are moving the investigation to Dallas – hopefully to get ahead of them.

"By Monday at noon, we could be in Houston or Alexandria, Louisiana. And though the trail is narrowing, keep in mind, it's already been three days since the prison break."

Dakota said, "Meaning, they could be close."

"Or here." Piper said.

Sean agreed, "If they're alive."

Adam said, "Anything else on the sperm kids just in case?"

"Yes. So far, out of ninety-nine sperm kids, seventy males have been identified. I emailed each of you a list of names and pictures. We're not looking at the females at this point, but they are still working on identifying the remaining fifty-one names. And, Raven, as soon as you can, check the list for us. We need to know if anyone is a red flag for you."

Raven said, "No problem. I can do it while we're on the road. We still have about an hour before we get to New Orleans. I'll text when I'm done."

Sean said, "Thanks, sister-in-law. And all of you back on the river, don't take anyone or anything at face value while Adam and Raven are out of town. Be on alert. You are in the middle of nowhere. Strangers are not welcome."

***

Late afternoon as the light began to fade, the team of four on the river, Piper, Maverick, Rex, and Steel took a security pass around the property. Steel and Rex took the dogs through the woods. Piper and Maverick checked the tree line, road, and wharf.

When she was done, Piper stood on the wharf and looked across the river at the land the state owned. In her mind's eye she could see villains behind every tree. Every nook. With every sound. She sighed. Louisiana wilderness was only safe if you were prepared.

But how could she prepare for thousands of trees and a river deeper than a two-story house – and dark? Right now, the water looked like murky paint that was all mixed together for a brownish-black hue. Creepy. A perfect dwelling for things that needed darkness to hunt.

Hearing footsteps, she glanced down the road. Maverick had walked to the bend of the river to make sure it was clear. The property was alone down here. Vulnerable. How could Raven love this? Personally, Piper preferred the city jungle and a beautiful blue saltwater pool.

She walked down to the riverbank where the old man's canoe had landed today. He had been the only disabled person. And at day's end that stood out to her.

Maverick joined her at the water's edge and said, "What is it?"

"They could be here."

"I think they're coming. If they're here, why stall?"

"Maybe they found out Raven left for New Orleans."

"But she was accessible all day. All Zack had to do was snatch her and no one could touch him while he shot dozens of people."

"He has a plan. That wasn't it."

Something caught Piper's eye in the shallow water a few feet away. It was bumping against the cypress knees. Grabbing a stick, she pulled it over. It was the old man's cane.

***

Piper texted Sean: I'm by the wharf. Would you do a thermal scan with Adam's drone right now?

198

Sean: Sure. Open a door.

Piper: The land across the river is supposed to be uninhabited park land. Is anyone there?

Sean: We'll find out.

***

Piper saw Steel by the house and called him to open the door.

Maverick said, "What are you doing?"

"Getting Sean to thermal scan across the river for what shouldn't be there."

"Got it."

In the light of the porch, they watched the drone zip out the door headed toward the wharf. Piper pointed across the river, and it disappeared above the trees, virtually undetectable.

***

Sean knew something spooked Piper. He hovered high enough to scan a few acres and flew, searching for colored lights on his screen.

He knew the park had multiple trails. Some inland. Some along the river. Some short. Some quite a distance. He didn't see anything for a while, then about a mile from the wharf, he saw color and knew he was closer to the public area. The images were smaller than an adult though. Five of them. He lowered through the trees.

It wasn't long before he found kids playing on a trail. Chasing. Wrestling. He neared to get a visual. Boys. Eight to ten years old. Smoking. Cussing up a storm and enjoying themselves. Even taking videos. Sean grinned. If it had been Halloween, he would have sent them screaming for cover with a story for generations to come.

He noticed a few more images lighting up on his screen. Two people northeast. And further away, someone jogging at a good clip along the river. The two people were closest.

It turned out to be a man and woman walking in the moonlight. He spun toward the jogger. But by the time he caught up, whoever it was, had reached the cabin sites. Which meant colored images were everywhere.

On the way back to Piper, he scanned the woods around the houses. All clear. He flew toward the porch where they were waiting for him. Steel opened the door. Sean zipped the drone back inside and parked on the shelf.

Sean texted Piper: I didn't see anything across from you. I did see eight humans near the trails. Five kids. A couple. And a jogger that mixed in with the cabin crowd before I got to them. So, it looks clear.

Piper: Ok. Thanks.

Sean: What spooked you?

Piper: Elderly disabled guy came to the grand opening today. Raven's a nurse so she pampered him. Everyone did. And I just found his cane floating in the river. So, unless he drowned, he might not actually need one.

Sean: Shoot the next elderly disabled man that shows up.

Piper: LOL. Only I know that was a joke.

Sean: Right. But no more strangers on the hill. No mail man. UPS. FedEx. No one lost or bleeding. No one in a uniform. Even a cop. Call dispatch to confirm.

Chapter 25

New Orleans

Adam glanced periodically at Raven after they finished the video chat. She'd been quiet since she reviewed the pictures of the sperm kids. But she didn't offer to talk about her thoughts or discuss her findings.

She texted the team when she was done - including him – and said that none of the faces were familiar to her. And at that point, he realized she didn't want to talk. At all. He switched his phone to vibrate to give her quiet space. No music. No sound. No interruptions.

And then she simply stared at the countryside South of Gonzales as they headed into the lowlands and marsh. Then still, north of Laplace through the Maurepas Swamp Wildlife area. And even now, along the rim of Lake Pontchartrain that would take them into the suburbs of New Orleans.

Adam frowned. GPS indicated they would reach their hotel in thirty minutes. But another look at Raven's tense demeanor screamed she wasn't ready. With a silent sigh, he decided to give her a few more minutes before reaching out to her.

But a moment later, she shifted. Abruptly. And started tapping her finger on her leg. It was slow at first but increasing. And he sensed anger. But wasn't surprised. Why wouldn't she be mad? After all she'd been through, there was probably a deep well of fury mixed with a million other emotions hidden in her.

He needed to get off this bridge and find someplace private. A beach. A wharf. A park. An abandoned building. Something soon. She needed to vent before they reached anywhere public.

Raven felt the anger swirl inside her. The past mixed with the present, and it spun and burned like a whirlwind in her stomach. She tasted it as the rage rose. She swore if she looked at another face related to Zack with even a hint of resemblance...

201

If someone said his name again...
If she saw a man with blonde hair like his...
If she thought about him touching her...
If she felt his breath on her...
If she saw him...
And her neck tightened. Choking her as thoughts tumbled over themselves racing to get out. She grabbed Adam's hand. She was going to throw up. She gagged.

Adam had already crossed the levee, so he exited the interstate into Kenner, and said, "I'm stopping, baby...I just need a minute."

He whipped in and slid to a stop near a group of trees. She grabbed her mouth fumbling for the door handle. He snatched water and ran around as she threw up in the grass at a church. Holding her hair out of the way, he rubbed her back, talking softly – trying to bring some peace to her private storm. She threw up again.

Raven's hand trembled as she reached for the water. It spilled as she sipped. Then she rinsed and spit. Sipped again. Spit again. Adam wet some napkins and she wiped her mouth. Then enraged, she threw the bottle and the napkins, watching the paper flutter to the ground.

Adam knew it wasn't over. She looked at him. Desperate. And wild. He knew she had to release the torment.

He said, "Run with me. Let's run it out."

She kicked off her boots and they ran. And ran. Looping around the vacant churchyard until Raven didn't have any breath left. Sweating, they dropped to the ground. She was panting.

As soon as she found her voice, she said, "I hate Zack. I hate him. I wish I had shoved the knife a little more to the right that night and killed him. I can't get the mistake out of my head. If I had just—"

Adam stopped her, then looked around to make sure they didn't have an audience even though it was dark. He pulled out his knife and handed it to her. She was shocked. Then relief covered her face like an answer to a prayer.

And spreading her legs she stabbed the ground over and over and over till finally the anger bled into the ground...and she stopped.

Her arm throbbed and sweat dripped down her face. She looked at the knife buried in the grass. She pulled it out and handed it back to Adam. Appropriately, hilt first. He winked and wiped the dirty blade on his jeans.

He said, "You stabbed him fifty-seven times, wildcat. How do you feel?"

"Free. Powerful. I still wish he was dead."

"Me too. What do you want to do now?"

"Clean up and go on a date with you."

Standing, he offered his hand and said, "We might have to clean you up a little before we get to the hotel."

She laughed. And laughed.

***

At the hotel, Raven smiled at Adam in the mirror as she stood in black heels and panties putting on makeup. Red hair fanned across her back. Adam stepped into black slacks and zipped them just enough to hold them on his hips.

He said, "What are you wearing tonight? You have three dresses out."

"Pick one for me."

He touched them all and said, "The black one."

She smiled and leaned over to put on her favorite violet-red lipstick. He tucked in his white dress shirt while watching her. She rubbed her lips together and watched him zip his pants the rest of the way. She walked past him and took the black halter dress off the hanger, stepped into it, and clasped the neck hook. He slipped on his suit jacket.

They met at the bathroom counter. He brushed, then put his hair in a ponytail. She sprayed perfume. Then kissing her, he reached under her dress and left her panties in a lace puddle on the floor. She removed his ponytail, finger combing his hair. And with a private smile, they were ready to go.

***

When the elevator doors opened, they heard jazz music. Adam smiled at the look of bliss on Raven's face. Slipping an arm around her, they stepped into the lobby of Hotel Monteleone…or a palace would be a more fitting description. Glistening chandeliers. Creamy ivory walls and tile floors. Spacious foyer and seatings. Columns. Gorgeous windows overlooking the street. Lots of velvet.

Raven said, "This place makes me feel like royalty."

"You look like it too." Adam said. Meaning every word.

She was easily five feet ten in her black heels. The black silk dress stopped mid-thigh revealing her beautiful dancer legs. The halter bodice covered her chest but left her shoulders and back bare. And her red hair framed her gorgeous face. Adam heard the whispers around them.

Raven had seen the shock on women's faces as soon as Adam stepped off the elevator. Tall and sexy. A Native American dream come true in 21st century time. And drop dead gorgeous wearing a black suit and white shirt.

She leaned close and said, "I've seen three women drop things looking at you."

He laughed. Beautiful smile. Face like a dream.

She said, "Oops. Now four women."

Adam said, "I see a room full of men that don't know which part of you to look at first."

Teasing, she said, "Then it's a good thing they can't see under my dress."

Turning a hot gaze on her as they headed toward the Carousel Bar and Lounge, his hand lingered on her hip. He said, "There is nothing between your body and me but this little slippery piece of silk. I find that ravishingly erotic."

"Ahh. Yes. One would think this is a prelude to what comes later."

"And one would be right. All. Night. Long."

Angel's voice called down the corridor, "Come on! It's almost our turn to ride the carousel bar. We've been waiting almost an hour for our turn."

Joining him, Adam said, "I know you and Jade must be starving for dinner."

"Oh, no problem. What are friends for? We're on our eighth appetizer waiting on the honeymooners to finally *leave the bedroom*."

Laughing, they walked into the massive room. And Raven only had eyes for the golden carousel bar, rotating and lit up like a Las Vegas showroom. She didn't notice the heads swivel in their direction. One man's food fell off his fork with his mouth wide open as he stared at the red-haired beauty. But his wife didn't even care because she was looking at the man.

Adam smiled in admiration at Raven's lack of vanity as people around them watched every move they made. She smiled at some guests. Waved at others. And warmly greeted those in her path. There were always wolf leers, but she ignored them. Gracefully. Classy. A real lady in every sense of the word.

And of course, he saw, but ignored the women watching him. He was much less responsive to the public than Raven. He was kind but reserved. No lingering. And he barely gave a passing glance to the women predators. To him, their behavior made them ugly no matter what they looked like.

The first table along the windows was a family of four. A middle-aged couple and two older daughters. One daughter was outgoing and beautiful.

Blonde like mom. The other was clearly shy, a brunette - wearing glasses and clothes to help her disappear into the crowd. Obviously, she felt out of place.

Raven met her gaze and smiled, laying a gentle touch on her shoulder. The young lady responded with a timid smile – that turned to shock as she met Adam's gorgeous gaze behind Raven.

He saw the blush as shyness overwhelmed her. And nervously she knocked her phone off the table. Ignoring her beautiful sister's *clumsy as usual* remark, she swiveled to pick up the phone.

Adam, compassionate, already had it and handed it to her. He said, "Here you go. No harm done. We all drop things."

He glanced at Raven, and she dropped her purse, with an "Oh!"

Smiling at the young woman, Adam winked and said, "See!" then picked up Raven's purse as they moved on.

Jade, beautifully dressed in black as well, had watched it all from a couple of tables away. She hugged Raven, then Adam, and said, "That was beautiful. Thank you for that. I was an ugly duckling and ridicule is painful. That young lady will measure all men by that encounter, Adam. I hope she finds someone like you." And reaching for Angel's hand, she said, "I did."

Angel said, "I don't think so. I'm hotter than Adam."

Laughing, they sat at the table just as the bar messaged it was their turn to get on the carousel.

In moments they were part of a rotating party - a literal bar ride. And not far away, a band played jazz on a stage with windows facing Royal Street. Delighted, Raven and Jade ordered red wine and talked about weddings and receptions. Adam and Angel ordered a tequila shot and pulled their stools further back and talked work behind the women.

After their allotted time at the bar, they were back at a table by the windows again. For a minute.

Then Jade watched Adam escort Raven to the tiny dance floor. She smiled at the beauty of their romance. They were such a spectacular couple - by character and looks. Their inner beauty made the outer beauty shine that much brighter. She was so happy for them.

Angel said, "That will be us next Saturday. Married, baby. And we'll be wild in bed."

"Will we make it to the bed?"

"The bed is a metaphor. If I could take you in your wedding dress in the limo, I would. No greater love does a husband have than to make his wife wild with passion."

Touching his cheek, she said, "That's not exactly how that scripture goes, Angel."

Kissing her softly, he said, "My Jesus has a bride. He knows what I mean."

"I love you."

"Baby, I love you. And I want this to be the happiest week of your life. But I have a question."

"What?"

Serious now, he said, "Adam and Raven are in the middle of this fugitive hunt. We need to get another officiant. He's got his hands full, and she hasn't even seen her son in days. Coming to New Orleans was as much to get her away from Lake Charles as it was to help us on the case tomorrow."

"I agree. He'll argue but it's the right thing to do. My heart hurts for Raven. And I know it sounds terrible, but I hope Zack is already cold in a watery grave. He killed her husband. Her son's father. And attacked her viciously. I can't fathom him coming after her again. I just can't imagine the fear she hides."

Slipping an arm around her, he said, "Easy, baby. I didn't mean to upset you. Just look at them now. Love makes a way…"

***

Adam loved the way Raven moved to the music. Fluid smooth without any effort at all. He could feel the professional roll of her hips as she stepped with him. The perfect yield as she moved where he led. He could tell she needed to cut loose.

He whispered, "Why don't I do what I normally do, and you do your thing. Your dress is snug, no one will know there is more to see. Have fun. Wow the room even more."

She smiled. "Wowing you is all I need."

"I'm already wowed."

"Then I'll just…play a little."

The song changed and Adam was fascinated at the transformation in her. She smiled, teased, and spun. He didn't have time to look at the crowd but the look of admiration on the faces of the band told him what he already knew. It was like Dancing with the Stars right here. Right now.

Raven loved it and the band picked up the tempo more and more. She swiveled, spun, and moved faster and faster. Red hair flying. Feet fast. Cheers loud. When the third song ended, she stopped dramatically in his arms and kissed him. And everyone clapped. Even the band.

***

It was late by the time they left the lounge and ordered dinner at the Criollo Restaurant in the hotel. It was fine dining at its best. The women ordered first.

Raven chose a Shrimp, Crab & Avocado Stack with a dessert of Butterscotch Bread Pudding with sea salt gelato and whiskey sauce.

Jade chose Lobster Mac & Cheese and French Market Style Beignets with praline sauce and strawberries for her dessert.

Adam and Angel both ordered the same thing. Duck gumbo. Wagyu tenderloin with veggies, butter, and sauce. And the Butterscotch Bread Pudding.

As they waited, Adam said, "Jade, do you have all your plans in place for the wedding? Seven days from today you'll be saying your vows."

She said, "We're ready. My plans snowballed at first and threatened to turn the wedding into a huge event with tons of work, but we toned it down. That made it more personal and less of a distraction from what really matters."

Angel spoke up. "Which is the honeymoon."

Everyone laughed as he expected. He winked at Jade.

She said, "But we all know you're not joking."

He kissed her hand and said, "You know me well. And you're going to know me better."

She slapped his leg in exasperation.

He said "Jade, in truth, consummation of a marriage is the conclusion of the vows. The wedding isn't over until—"

She said, "Don't you even say it."

Acting shocked, he said, "I would never—"

They laughed. He certainly would.

***

It was almost midnight and Adam was ready for the meal to be over. Pushing his plate back, he dropped his hand to Raven's thigh. She met his gaze, then covered his hand with hers. They both thought about her panties lying on the floor upstairs. He slipped his hand under the black satin as he

207

glanced across the table. Angel and Jade were occupied. He slid his hand higher, watching Raven's face. Her lips parted as he touched her.

He whispered, "We're leaving."

**

Adam and Angel took care of the ticket and waited for the women to return from the bathroom.

Angel said, "Listen, I have something to lay out there, Adam. No argument. Just take officiating the wedding next weekend off your plate. You and Raven don't need another thing to think about."

Adam said, "You know——"

"Yes, I know. But it is what it is. If it turns out you're free, come to the wedding – just to celebrate with us. If not, we'll connect for your reception later in December. You would do the same thing if it was us. You know you would."

"I would. It's just unbelievable. If someone had told me a fugitive would target Raven, we would marry, fit in a honeymoon, and have a business grand opening all in a week, I'd never have believed them. You just can't prepare for some things."

"My point exactly. Enjoy your honeymoon and make sure you kill Zack."

They fist bumped as the women returned. Then made plans to meet at six a.m. and said goodbyes.

**

Adam led Raven through the lobby. Neither of them noticed the glances their way. And after subtle caresses in the back of the crowded elevator, they finally reached their door. Adam kissed her as the latch unlocked and they slipped inside.

He shrugged out of his jacket as she set her purse down. Sliding his hands up her satin covered body, he cupped her face, and said, "You've been hit with a lot of emotions this week. Big stuff. Even a few hours ago.

"And while we could go up in flames in a second, I think…" He kissed her. "I need to give you time. You lead where you want us to go now. Do whatever you want. Any way you want it. Any speed. It's all about you."

Raven pulled his lips to hers and was lost in the taste of sugared whiskey on his tongue. The smell of him. The feel of his restrained power. Running her hands down his chest, she unbuttoned his shirt. He pulled it off and tossed it, never taking his eyes off her. She glanced at the balcony where the sound of jazz filtered through the windows.

At that, he knew she needed the music. He led her to the glass doors. She stepped onto the balcony and Adam stood close behind her, holding her, facing the city. Waiting and loving her. Raven closed her eyes and they swayed softly to the soulful jazz. His lips brushed her hair. And before long, she felt the ashes of today float away on the breeze.

For one song.

Two.

And on the third song, she pushed Adam's hands down her stomach. And lower. Inviting. And fire burned as he touched her, pulling her back against him. He groaned at the sensual rotation of her hips against him as she mixed passion with dance. He moved in time with her, stoking the fire.

Until she reached back and slipped her hand in his pants. Then growling, he reached for the doorknob, bringing her with him into the room.

Once inside, she reached for his zipper. He pulled her dress off and pressed her against the wall. And then it was hard. Fast. And wild.

***

In Lake Charles at the Blue Martini Lounge in the Golden Nugget Hotel & Casino, Zack watched a brunette with long curly hair. He could imagine it spread out on the pillow as she smiled at him – and he wanted that. Which surprised him. His intention tonight had been rough sex. Paid sex. Or rape. Something raging and vicious like he deserved.

But now, he wanted something else. A forgotten dream. With her. There was just something about her. She was beautiful but not blatantly sexual. She was feminine. Interesting. Wearing jeans and a yellow shirt with an open back. But she had a do not approach air about her.

She had been sitting alone watching the crowd and checking her phone. She had maybe two glasses of wine. He wondered why she was here. Lonely? Passing through Lake Charles?

It was time to find out and he stood. It was midnight and he needed to make his move. Kip had already been upstairs in his room with a blonde for an hour.

Tonight, Zack had shoulder length brown hair, blue contacts, and a few fake tattoos around his wrists. Even one on his neck. He was dressed in jeans, expensive sandals, and a tight pale blue pullover. He knew he smelled and looked good. Wealthy. He headed her way.

He came up behind her and leaned against the post. He glanced at her phone. She was checking the weather. He waited. Before long, she smelled his cologne and glanced over her shoulder.

She looked the handsome man over and said, "I don't mean to be rude, I'm just not in the mood for small talk tonight."

"Which means, random is boring to you. I get that."

"Well, that's a better line than most."

"That's because it's not a line. It's an accurate speculation. Right?"

"Pretty much."

"Why come to a crowded place to be alone?"

"Good question."

"And?"

"I don't feel alone. I like my own company."

Intrigued, he said, "I like your style."

Interest flickered in her eyes, and he waited.

She said, "Ok. I'll bite. What's your name?"

"I can't tell you and I'd rather not lie to you."

"That's certainly not a line either."

"No."

"Why would you admit that?"

"If we're going to talk, may I sit?"

She pointed to the other side of the booth.

As he sat, he said, "Call me Zee. What's your name?"

"Gigi."

"Is that a nickname? Ginger?"

"Yes. Why did you choose me tonight, Zee? There are a lot of eager women in here."

"I need something and only you have it."

"Really. So, what do I have?"

"Class. Grace. Peace."

Gigi watched him silently for a moment. Something warned her he was trouble, but she liked his style too. She decided to play the game a little longer. It wasn't boring.

She said, "You realize you have an air of danger about you?"

"Yes. I'm sorry to be clandestine. It's unavoidable I'm afraid."

And this is where Gigi knew she should shut it down. But she loved mysteries. And he was one gorgeous mystery. She was hooked. But she didn't do this type of thing. Ever.

She asked, "Am I safe with you?"

He loved her question and knew she would believe his answer. And suddenly that meant everything to him. He said, "I would never hurt you."

"Are you a criminal?"

He stuck with honesty, and said, "Yes."

She closed her eyes.

When she opened them warily, he said, "I'm sorry."

"Tell me what you need, Zee."

"I'll be dead in two days. And I want to spend the night in the arms of a woman who wants to be with me. I could pay any amount you want. But...I would rather you give yourself to me so I can give myself to you. I want to see pleasure on your face."

The intimate blow was quick and hard. Never in a million years had Gigi expected any of that. Tears pooled. Zack saw her lip tremble as she grappled with her emotions. When the wave passed, she looked at him. Deeply. And that's when he knew she was seriously considering it.

He said, "I would love us to share a night that we'll never forget."

"I've lost my mind."

"Just for a single night."

"Can I trust you?"

"Yes."

"Why two days—"

"Let's not go there. This is about us. Tonight."

Her mind spun. It was such a wild concept.

He said softly, "Will you spend the night with me, Gigi?"

"I can't believe I am saying yes."

He smiled.

She said, "Where?"

"Do you have a room here?"

"Yes."

He texted Kip and stood. He didn't want to use the room by Kip. He didn't want Kip anywhere near her.

***

Gigi was nervous as they reached her hotel room. Her hand shook a bit with the key card, and she looked at the gorgeous guy she was about to let in her bed. In her body. He took the card and unlocked the door.

And the Zack that Raven would never know, was kissing Gigi by the time it locked. He gave her over and over the little bit of love that hadn't been warped. And he got to be what he always should have been.

211

Well before dawn, Gigi watched him put the wig back on. And the contacts.

He sat beside her on the bed and said, "That was the most beautiful gift anyone has ever given me."

"Zee—"

"Call me Zack."

She smiled. "Zack."

He said, "Birth control didn't come up last night. If you're pregnant after tonight, please, call my mother."

He keyed the number in her phone contacts under his name, then said, "You would give her a miracle beyond all miracles."

"I'm a little embarrassed I didn't think of it. I'm not on birth control."

He touched her face and said, "I bet you would be a wonderful mother."

"My husband divorced me because he didn't want children."

"Idiot."

She smiled.

Kissing her softly, he said, "Thank you."

He stood. She pulled back the covers to get out of bed.

"Don't get up." Zack said. "This is the hard part. And don't be sad. You got more love from me than any woman on this earth."

Covering her back up, he said, "And I hope your future is as spectacular as you."

And in ten steps, the door opened and closed. He was gone.

***

Before dawn at Sam Houston Jones State Park, Zack and Kip returned to their cabin unseen. It would be a long day before Raven returned home.

***

Right at five a.m. at Hotel Monteleone in New Orleans, Adam opened the door for room service. He wheeled the cart near the bed. Then added cream and sugar to Raven's coffee and turned on the shower for her.

At the sound of water, she stirred under the covers and a long slender leg slid out trying to encourage the rest of her to follow.

Adam chuckled.

She flopped the blanket off and Adam almost got back in bed. She grinned at the debate on his face and sat up, reaching for her coffee.

He said, "Raven…"

"We'll be late. Again. So, don't come any closer."

He laughed. And two sweet sips of coffee later, she jumped in the shower to rinse off and dress.

Thirty minutes later, the valet brought their truck, and they headed southeast to Southern Investigative Services, Inc., the business and home for Angel and Jade. In the spring they had bought a three-story Victorian home to remodel while they lived in it to save paying two rents.

Originally, the plans were for the first floor to be the business. The second floor to be Angel's flat and the top floor to be Jade's. But after their engagement, construction plans for the living quarters had changed and been completed a few weeks ago.

Pulling up to the porch, Adam parked. Angel met them outside and said, "Come on in. Jade is almost dressed. I have fresh coffee if you want some."

Following Angel inside, Adam said, "Show us around if we have a few minutes."

Angel motioned to the large desk and work area on the left side of the room. Computer and office machines. Files. Maps.

He said, "This part of the office is administration. Jade handles incoming communication. We both share all forms of schedules and investigations. I handle investigation equipment. Tracking. Weapons. And rentals as needed."

Pointing to the massive Louisiana wall map, Angel said, "The map is marked with our active case locations. Visual is always helpful, and as you can see, the pins are color coded. The last thing I want to do is dig through a file when I can glance at a map. And we use case boards like law enforcement as well.

Adam looked in the equipment room. "You have impressive toys in here. What jobs do you usually take?"

"We get a lot of domestic cases. And as everyone knows, they can be explosive and dangerous, but clients need help with information for their legal cases. We do what we must. We also get some intense stalking cases, online harassment cases, and theft."

Raven asked, "Do you find surveillance uncomfortable?"

Angel said, "At times. I make myself look beyond the peeping tom aspect and use what I learned from Sean – to focus on the good it will do."

"What is the most interesting job?" Adam said.

"You're kidding right? Interesting is shooting a shark then stabbing it in the head with a knife. My work is boring compared to yours."

They heard laughter as Jade jogged downstairs to join them. She said, "I second that, but I'm ok with it. I don't want anything to do with a creature that has that many teeth. Being eaten alive is a nightmare."

Angel said, "Come on, baby. I'll save you from the monsters."

"You better, if you want to see me in my wedding dress."

***

After refilling coffee cups for the road, Adam and Raven grabbed their Quest backpacks and rode with Angel and Jade. In minutes they were heading down Highway 90 out of New Orleans toward Madere Marsh Boardwalk in Bayou Sauvage National Wildlife Refuge. And you have to take a breath just to say that mouthful.

Angel explained, "Three people have gone missing after visiting the boardwalk. Their abandoned vehicles were found in the parking area with no sign of a struggle. No evidence. No video cameras. No photos. No witnesses. They simply vanished in the middle of nowhere. And seriously, there is only marsh as far as the eye can see."

Adam said, "I'm sure you have the same kind of wildlife there as we do back home."

"Yes. Nothing friendly. So, I find it incomprehensible that anyone would go into the marsh. They certainly wouldn't survive any length of time. I've been there several times and wouldn't want to get off the boardwalk. So, why would a young woman, a middle-aged woman, and a teenage boy?"

The question didn't require an answer.

Jade said, "The family of the young woman contacted us to investigate but there is nowhere to hide for surveillance, and we don't have permission to post cameras on government property.

"It's scary to fathom what it would take to get the officials interested in a case like that. There just isn't any evidence - much less evidence of foul play."

***

An hour later, they parked at the boardwalk. There wasn't a soul in sight. Just miles of marsh and a boardwalk that looked like it led to nowhere. This took the idea of investigation to a whole new level. Everyone brainstormed as they toured the land area about the size of a baseball field.

Jade said, "Why would a woman come out here alone? No help. No protection. No bathroom."

Angel checked his phone and said, "And signal is sporadic at best."

"Maybe they were meeting someone. Online dating, that kind of thing." Adam said.

Raven said, "Online has issues all by itself. You couldn't pay me to come here."

"So, how would someone lure a stranger to the middle of nowhere?" Angel asked thoughtfully.

Raven asked, "Were any of them photographers or nature buffs?"

Jade jotted the questions down. Every thought might help with the puzzle.

Adam said, "Surely, park employees were questioned."

"One would think so, but they aren't going to share that information with us." Angel responded.

Then walking to the boardwalk, he continued as if talking to himself, "This could be an opportunist killer running across someone randomly, or a pattern killer choosing their victims."

Jade couldn't write fast enough.

Angel said, "Come on. Let's follow it out into the marsh and see if anything looks suspicious."

Raven said, "I don't know. The last marsh I was in had a shark. And we don't have a boat."

Angel laughed for quite a while.

The boardwalk by appearance was a wooden deck trail on piers about three feet above the marsh. No rails. No seats. No way of knowing how deep the water was below them.

They were able to see open pools of water, grass, mud, and scattered brush with small trees. Wildlife paths were evident everywhere.

They reached the lookout wharf at the end and climbed up to gaze across the landscape.

Jade said, "Who in their right mind decides to walk around out there? Do you see all those alligators?"

Raven said, "That is a lot of teeth."

The guys looked through binoculars.

Adam said, "Surely that's an unusual alligator population. I wonder if tourists are feeding them. That's not a good thing for them to associate people with food."

After a few moments of silence, Angel said, "What if missing people were forced to go out there?"

Adam said, "That's wicked. You mean execution style?"

"Or entertainment."

Raven and Jade looked at each other, horrified. Goosebumps ran up Raven's back.

And solemn at the thought, everyone filed off the lookout wharf.

Jade was several steps ahead of Angel, and looking back, said, "Maybe we can—"

And she tripped. Off balance for a second, she teetered on the edge. She gasped and Angel reached for her. But shockingly, an alligator jumped out of the water clamping down on the hem of her jeans. And without time to scream, Jade was pulled into the water.

Raven screamed in horror.

Angel and Adam followed Jade in. And a second later the gator rolled, slinging Jade in the air. She gasped for air, and it rolled again. Angel straddled the gator and fought to keep it still with its jaws above water. Adam fought to hold Jade up and cut her pants free from the teeth. It wasn't working.

Adam yelled, "Get out of your jeans!" and the gator rolled with her again.

When Adam pulled her back up, she kicked free of her jeans, gagging and gulping air. Adam slung her on the deck by Raven.

Jade was in shock. Half-naked. Filthy. Shivering from head to toe with terror and cold. Raven quickly pulled the wet sweatshirt off her, then wrapped her jacket around her.

She turned to check on the men just as Adam blew a hole in the alligator's skull. And then crazed motion in the marsh drew Raven's attention. Alligators!

She screamed, "Get out! Hurry! Alligators are coming!"

The men jumped and pulled themselves up just in time to see the boiling mass of reptiles tearing into the dead one.

Angel went to Jade. She shivered uncontrollably as Raven checked her for injuries. Angel and Adam shucked their partially wet jackets to help cover her. Then Adam ran to the SUV for their Quest backpacks.

Raven said, "Angel, I need your shirt."

He whipped it off and she used it to clean Jade's face. Other than mud, Raven saw scrapes. Claw marks. Nothing deep. Only minor blood.

She handed the shirt back to Angel and said, "Wipe her back and check for injuries."

And once they were able to confirm she didn't have life threatening injuries, they tucked jackets around her. She panted. Wide-eyed. Too scared to cry.

Raven talked softly and said, "He didn't bite you. Just cuts and scrapes. You are going to be ok. Tell me…did you swallow any of the water?"

Jade nodded, gagged, and threw it all up. Angel lifted her long filthy hair out of the way and stared in shock at what he saw. It couldn't be…

Adam returned and Angel waved him over, then motioned for silence. He pointed to Jade's hair.

Adam knelt and froze. A partial human hand was tangled in her hair. His stomach churned and he looked at Raven.

Seeing the look on their faces, she said, "Wha—"

He pointed at Jade shaking his head.

Angel hurriedly took pictures on his phone for evidence, and using knives they removed the hand from her hair. Then wrapped it in a bag from the backpack and hid it.

Angel wrapped her hair in a towel and pulled her on his lap. And in his arms, she was finally able to cry.

Adam walked away and called 911. Angel and Jade had real evidence now. The case had just blown wide open.

Before long, the police arrived. First responders. Park rangers. The coroner. The Sheriff's Office marine division in airboats. Even the Louisiana Department of Wildlife and Fisheries. Followed by helicopters and reporters.

Once they wheeled Jade off the boardwalk, she sat on the stretcher while the paramedics wrapped her in heated blankets and did their own check for injuries.

The young paramedic said, "You are in good shape considering what you endured. Like your nurse friend said, nothing's broken. No stitches needed. Just get to the ER if you have trouble breathing. And make sure to shower with antibacterial soap."

Jade nodded, then asked Angel, "What's with all the law enforcement commotion for an accident?"

He glanced at Raven, hesitant to answer Jade.

Jade said curtly, "What aren't you telling me?"

"We found evidence on the case. Adam called them."

"What evidence?"

"I'll tell you later. Let's get you home and cleaned up."

She felt horror creeping in. She clutched his shirt and said, "Tell me!"

He knew she wouldn't let it go, and said, "We found human remains. A hand."

She gasped. "But I didn't see it. Where did you find it?"

"Baby—"

Why wouldn't he tell her? Heart pounding with fear, she said "Tell me!"

"In your hair."

She screamed. A scream of terror none of them would ever forget. She jumped off the stretcher and her hair fell all around her. Turning. Spinning. Screaming, as she tried to keep it from touching her.

She yelled, "Cut it off! Cut it off!"

They couldn't calm her down. The paramedics wanted to drug her.

Raven snapped at them, "No drugs! Give me your scissors! Now!"

They obeyed.

Angel held Jade's face and said, "Focus, Jade. Look at me. You have got to be still so Raven can cut your hair."

She nodded. Over and over. Eyes wild.

Raven said, "How much do I cut, Angel?"

"Half. Stop at her bra line."

Raven cut it. Officers bagged the hair and took it for evidence. Paramedics wrapped Jade in a sheet and twisted the rest of her hair in a plastic bag.

Then Angel and Adam had to change out of their wet clothes into paper scrubs. Forensics needed to check everything they wore in the marsh for human remains.

Adam joined Raven as she watched Angel carry Jade to the truck. He slipped his arm around her. Grateful, she leaned into him.

He said, "You are calm and impressive tending to patients. Your mind clicks into gear, and you know what needs to be done. No matter how shocking. You soothe with compassion and treat with confidence. Watching you today, reminded me of returning from Brazil. You had every answer I needed. You're amazing."

She said, "Thank you. But look at you. Instinctively brave and protective. You and Angel jumped in and fought the beast for Jade. She wouldn't have survived long, Adam. You know that."

She glanced across the marsh and said, "And what if we hadn't come with them today?"

"But we did, honey. We were where we were meant to be. And it was great teamwork. They did their job investigating – and in the end found the evidence. And we did ours by rescuing. We are all in the right line of work."

And that reminded her. She said, "Let me see your hands. Do you have any cuts?"

"The paramedics checked Angel and I when we changed. We both have a few cuts and scrapes from teeth and claws. Nothing serious. They doused us with antibacterial gel that burned like lava and told us to shower good when we got home. I promise."

His phone rang. Piper.

***

He answered, "Where were you when I was wrestling an alligator?"

Piper said, "Adam. Really? The FBI field office just called me from New Orleans. What did you and Raven stumble into over there? Is Raven, ok? Jade? All of you for that matter."

"Stumble is a good word for what happened. Jade tripped on the boardwalk and the gator jumped out of the water and latched onto her jeans. He pulled her into the marsh. Angel and I followed. Saved her. Killed it. And got out before we were lunch for the million other gators that showed up for a snack."

"Please tell me Raven was not in the marsh."

"No. She was the hero nurse."

"I heard about the hand in Jade's hair. That's a nightmare."

"It was bad, Piper. I still have cold chills from her scream."

Chills ran up Piper's neck just imagining. She said, "How is Raven? She needed a break – not this."

Watching Raven's solemn look as she watched the Medical Examiner leave with the hand, he said, "I know. When we get Angel and Jade settled at home, I'm going to play tourist with her for a while. I can't have her go home with this on her mind."

"Good idea."

"How are things at the house?"

"Quiet today. I did find an old man's cane floating in the river before dark last night when we were making rounds. I called Sean to use your drone and check across the river. No one was lurking around."

Adam's mind flashed to the old man at the grand opening. He said, "Maybe he didn't need it because he wasn't old."

"I know. But we're watching."

219

Adam said, "Good idea about the drone. I need to remember to use it."

"Or just open the door and let Sean use it."

"Point taken."

She said, "In fact, why don't we have Sean change the voice activation code of Eagle One so any voice can turn it on – not just you or him. At least until this is over."

"You are a smart agent. Tell Sean to do it. And, thanks, Piper."

"Anytime. And be sure Raven laughs a lot this afternoon or you answer to me."

***

Back at Angel and Jade's place, both men went to shower with antibacterial soap while Raven helped Jade in the shower. She was beginning to limp after all the twisting and turning with the alligator. They washed her hair a half dozen times. And bathed her in steaming hot water with a bath brush.

After she dressed, they checked all the wounds again. Raven was bandaging the last cut when she caught Jade's frown in the mirror.

Raven said, "What is it?"

"I hate alligators."

"I get that. I hate Zack."

"Oh, gosh. He betrayed you. That's the worst."

"Yeah. At least your alligator was just hungry."

Jade giggled. Raven winked. And they burst out laughing.

Unintentionally catching the conversation in the hall, Angel and Adam looked at each other. Fist bumped. The women they loved were going to be just fine.

Chapter 26

It was dark on the river as the team made a security check around the property. Adam and Raven would be home around ten o'clock.

Piper walked along the road. Watching for danger. Listening for trouble. But other than that, she was finally getting used to the sounds of river wilderness. And while it still had a strong element of mystery for her, she was learning to appreciate the wild wet beauty and the delicious food it provided.

Steel had boiled crawfish for lunch on a huge burner in the yard. He had bought two sacks of hundreds of little angry lobster-looking critters from rice farmers east of Iowa. He poured salt on them, and they spit bubbles forever. He called it purging, which sounded appalling.

But the aroma from the red seasoning he poured in the giant pot of boiling water was scrumptious. Then he added large jars of chopped garlic. Chopped lemons. Red potatoes. Corn on the cob. And lots of real butter.

Maverick mixed up a bowl of dipping sauce that she would dip anything in. Steak. Fried chicken. Baked fish. Even her finger. It was delicious. And Rex picked up a dessert from Lexi who insisted they needed caramel apple toffee dip to go with fresh apple slices. Piper groaned in delight with every mouthful.

But when it came time to eat the main dish, trying to peel the hot crawfish was hard work. Rip your fingernails hard work. So, charmingly, the men peeled them for her, laughing as she drowned the crawfish, potatoes, and corn in sauce. Then promptly guzzled water to cool off the seasoning setting her lips on fire. It had been wonderful, and she was still full after the feast.

Stopping on the front of the wharf, she looked across the river. It wasn't a totally full moon. Almost. And it lit enough to see the difference between pitch black in the woods and shadowy darkness everywhere else.

She heard Maverick's footsteps drawing closer.

He stepped beside her and said, "Everything ok?"

"I don't like it. It's like the calm before the storm."

221

"I hope not. Raven has had enough."

"But Zack didn't just vanish in Montana."

"A bear could have eaten him if he survived whatever happened in that truck."

"No. It was staged. We just can't prove it."

"That's why we're on alert."

Maverick turned to face her in the moonlight. She ignored him and stared across the river.

He whispered, "One kiss."

"No."

"Two."

"Really? Double no."

He stepped closer, and whispered, "It'll be worth it."

She felt the brush of his breath against her neck. Sizzles traveled up her body. He was killer sexy. She wanted to yield.

Instead, she warned, "I have a gun if you don't stop."

He slid his arm around her and said, "I feel that. Which makes this so, so, hot. Don't you think?"

Staring across the river trying to focus, Piper suddenly saw a tiny flash of light. Just for an instant.

Turning to face Maverick, she said, "Someone's watching us from the park. They lit a cigarette."

He shifted so he was between her and the watcher as they walked away. She texted Sean. Maverick called Steel to open the door.

***

Zack ran. He'd lit the cigarette without thinking about the light. He was sure Piper had seen it when they walked away on their phones. He moved fast along the riverbank knowing he could make it back to the cabin in a few minutes with the moon lighting the way.

***

It took Steel two minutes to run from the woods to the house. The drone was waiting for him when he opened the door and zoomed out.

Sean flew high above the park looking for heat sources on his monitor. He saw five figures that were a long way from the cluster of people by the cabins.

The closest was a large figure standing motionless a good distance into the woods. Not by the river.

In a minute, Sean hovered above an older man having video sex with a young blonde that was probably not his wife. His wedding ring sparkled in the moonlight.

Moving on to a fast-moving figure, he chuckled. An older guy jogged off the trail with a headlamp. Knee socks with green stripes. Sweatbands. Shorts pulled way too high with a yellow shirt marked with reflection tape. He must have been afraid of heavy traffic out here.

Then he turned the drone west toward what ended up being two figures working on becoming one. The fire they were lighting was not a cigarette.

And the last figure was almost to the cabins and running fast. Sean remembered the same scenario yesterday. Maybe it was the same guy. So, he flew toward the river. From a distance he could tell the figure was tall. A big guy. And he was heading for the crowd. Sean sped up.

But missed him. The figure disappeared around a building into a crowd of people partying by a campfire. Cars were moving around. People going in and out of cabins.

Sean landed the drone on the roof of a corner cabin. He would watch for a few minutes to see if he recognized anyone.

***

Zack shut the door behind him, breathing hard. Sweating.

Kip was in the kitchen pan-searing steaks since that's all Zack wanted after being in prison. Steak, eggs, bacon, ice-cream, coke, beer, and Raven.

Kip turned off the fire and said, "We have trouble? Did they see you by Raven's?"

"They knew I was there. That's all. I lit a cigarette without thinking. Piper and the tall detective were on the wharf."

"Zack—"

"Shut up. I don't want to hear it. I've waited as patiently as I can. Get over it."

"Getting caught will defeat your purpose."

"Running your mouth will defeat yours."

"Is Raven back yet?"

223

"No, but they were doing a security check around the property, so they are probably on their way home."

"Well, there you go. She'll be home for you in the morning. When are you going to tell me the plan?"

"When it's time for you to know. Just be ready to leave at three a.m. And we won't return to the cabin, so pack."

**

Sean flew back to the wharf where Piper and Maverick waited.

He landed the drone and spoke through the speaker, "Five people were closer to here than they should have been, but not threatening. A cheating husband. A 70s jogger. A couple on top of each other. And a runner. I think he might be the one I saw last night. Big guy – and fast. I didn't catch him again. I sat on a roof and watched the crowd for a while. Nothing caught my eye."

Piper said, "I'll call the park ranger and see if he can check out the area across from here. I know Hunter used a spot near there too. And I'll see if I can get a list of cabin guests. Is a state park even notified of fugitives?"

"Just by the news, like the community. And I seriously doubt they identify all their guests or have criminal printouts. They are a public place with constantly changing visitors. They probably only get identification on the one paying for the reservation."

Maverick offered, "Ranger Dubois helped us with Hunter. I can call him. I have his number."

Piper said, "Great. Thanks."

Sean said, "Let me know how it goes. And remember, our team arrives in Alexandria, Louisiana tomorrow. We hope to have the last of the DNA and sperm kid results by then also. Let's plan on a video meeting with the director before noon."

"Got it. Oh, I see headlights, that must be Adam and Raven. Do you want to talk to them?"

"Tell them we'll talk in the morning. I've got to go."

**

Piper climbed in the truck with Adam and Raven and headed uphill. Maverick stayed behind and called Ranger Dubois.

**

The Ranger answered, "Hey, Detective. How's it going?"

"We've been busy keeping an eye on Raven because of the fugitive. That's why I'm calling."

"What do you need?"

"We think there might be a watcher on your side of the river straight across from the wharf. Wondered if you might check it out at first light – but be careful. Our drone catches a runner but that's it."

"I hate to hear that. Hopefully, it's just a jogger enthusiast. They rarely stay on the trails. But I'll check and get back with you."

"One more thing, can I get a list of overnight residents at the park?"

"I'll verify to make sure I can give you that information, but even so, we'll only have the one who paid. And possibly a general count of the number in their group. We don't monitor."

"Let me know if you need a warrant. No problem."

"Sure. I'll give you a call when I get to the riverbank in the morning. You can ride over if you want."

"Sounds like a plan. See you in the morning."

***

Maverick walked inside and gave Piper a thumbs up. She nodded. Adam was telling the story about Jade and the alligator.

***

Thirty minutes later, Adam climbed the stairs. Raven was getting in bed when he walked in.

He smiled and pulled off his shirt. "I'm going to take a quick shower. I won't be long."

She said, "You better hurry...I won't be awake long." And laying on his pillow, she smiled. She smelled him in the linen.

A few minutes later, Adam turned off the bathroom light as he walked to the bed. Raven was sound asleep. He scooped her in his arms as he slid into bed.

Her eyelids fluttered. She whispered, "I tried...to wait..."

Kissing her softly, he said, "Sleep, baby. You need the rest," and with a smile, she was out again.

225

He listened to her breathe. Held her. Loved her. Prayed for her. And then his eyes closed.

***

Well after midnight at the park, Zack couldn't sleep. He was roaming the hills and trails. He watched Raven's house for a while. Thinking. Fine tuning his plan. There were a whole lot of moving pieces that had to fall into place in a few hours. All for Raven.

Suddenly, the sound of footsteps and cracking branches carried through the trees. Zack hid and watched a flashlight shine a path almost straight at him. When he saw the uniform, he knew it was a ranger.

Ranger Dubois walked through the woods shoving an occasional cigarette butt with the toe of his boot. He stared across the river and knew there was a watcher in the park. Again. Frowning, he picked up his phone. Zack hit him across the head, and he dropped like a stone.

Slinging him over his shoulder, Zack carried him to the cabin.

When he stepped inside with the ranger, Kip threw up his hands and said, "Can you make this any more difficult?"

Zack said, "Get tape. It's almost time to go."

"Where was he?"

"Looking for me. Piper probably called him. I saw him first."

"Do we kill him?"

"Tape him to a chair. Tape his mouth but cut a slit so I know he can breathe."

"Why do you care if he lives?"

"When I was disguised as an old man, he was nice. Considerate. This is my way of thanking him. The cleaning lady will find him when we vanish, and he'll end up being a hero with a great story to tell."

***

At six a.m., Adam's Quest line rang. He answered, "Quest Search & Rescue."

A distraught man said, "Adam Nash, please! Help! I can't find them!"

Sitting up and reaching for pen and paper, Adam said, "What happened and where are you?"

226

"My boys snuck out last night to go camping. They're lost. Scared. They texted me but their battery must have died. I tried to find them but can't. I called a deputy but he's late because of a bad wreck. I saw you on television. Can you come? Don't you have dogs?"

Getting his pants on, Adam said, "I'm coming. How old are they?"

"Eight and ten."

"Where are you?"

"Off Baggett Rd. northwest of Mittie. Six miles from LA-26 on your left. Red house."

"Where do you think the boys are?"

"West of here. They headed to Whiskey Chitto Creek and got turned around in the dark."

"What's your name? Theirs?"

"I'm John Baggett. They are Liam and Brian. How long will it take you to get here?"

"A little over an hour. Keep me updated."

"Hurry, Mr. Nash. I'm scared for my boys."

"I'm coming, John. We'll find them."

***

The line went dead. Adam pulled on his boots and turned to Raven. She was almost dressed.

He said, "They aren't hurt. Just lost. I wish you would stay here with the others. I'll call Dakota to go with me."

"But what if—"

"You and the girls have plans today. Good plans. I want to know that you are having a good time at Scarborough's. You need a spa day. Rescues will be a part of our lives forever."

She followed him out. Everyone was up. Steel ran to get the dogs ready. Maverick and Rex made a security pass around the property.

***

Adam called Dakota.

Dakota answered, "What's wrong."

"I need you to come with me to track two lost boys an hour north of here in the woods close to Whiskey Chitto Creek. Ages eight and ten. We'll bring the dogs. The Sheriff's Office is tied up with a wreck."

"I'm up. I'll be ready when you get here. Is Raven going?"

227

"No. I refuse to mess up their spa day. Piper, Maverick, Rex, and Steel will be here till they leave for the spa. And we'll be back before they're home again."

***

Raven watched Adam's truck race down the road and all she could think about were the two little boys alone in the woods. She tried not to think about the dark they had endured. Animals. Snakes. The fast-moving creek. And predators on two legs.

Piper said, "Let's go back inside. We only have an hour to drink coffee and get ready ourselves. Our appointment is at eight. We need to leave by seven-thirty."

"At least we don't have to dress up or wear makeup."

"Hallelujah!"

They had just fixed their first cup of coffee when Steel came in. Then Maverick. And last was Rex. In moments, they were all around the table.

Maverick got a text and frowned. He said, "You're kidding me."

Piper said, "What's wrong?"

"I've got to be at a deposition by seven-forty-five. Which means, I've got to leave early. It was scheduled for Wednesday but got moved up. What time are you ladies leaving?"

Raven said, "Gabrielle plans to be here before seven-thirty to get us."

Rex said, "Go Maverick. Piper, Steel, and I are here. And I'll follow them out and then head to the office."

***

Wearing jeans, flip flops and ponytails, Piper and Raven watched from the porch as Maverick left and Gabrielle arrived early. They groaned as she got out of the SUV. She looked ready to deliver any second.

Gabrielle said, "Stop looking at me like that. And forget watermelon, I feel like a walrus. I can barely fit behind the steering wheel. And the only thing that makes me feel better is knowing I will be pampered and massaged all day. And going to the bathroom of course. My bladder is the size of a pea. Pun intended."

Rex said, "Why don't you stay there. We can all leave now and save you a trip inside."

With a sigh, she said, "We can't. I've got to pee."

228

Rex carried her inside. Steel kept watch outside.

After a flush and the sound of her washing her hands, Gabrielle returned and said, "We better hurry. I'm living in the bathroom today."

Rex said, "If you don't mind," and he scooped her up again and carried her to the passenger side of her SUV. He said, "You do not need to be driving."

She gave him a soft touch on the cheek. "Thank you, Rex. Dakota thanks you too."

He smiled and headed to his car. He backed up and waited for the women to pull out. Steel watched as he walked to the barn. As the women drove away, then Rex, Steel waved. Once they were out of sight, he headed to the back of the barn. Whistling. The horses danced, eager for his attention.

***

Raven smiled, glancing across the river as she followed the winding road out. It was a beautiful day. Sunshine flashed through the trees. A boat passed. And two squirrels played chase around the base of a pine tree on the passenger side of the road.

Gabrielle said, "Oh, no."

Raven said, "What?"

"You aren't going to believe this."

"You have to pee."

Her groan was agreement and Raven braked, then backed into a trail and turned around. She came alongside Rex's car and they both stopped, lowering their windows.

Rex said, "What's wrong?"

"We're heading back to the bathroom."

"I'll follow."

"Go on. We're fine. Piper's here. And Steel. It's just taking a while with little momma this morning."

His brow creased and he glanced at Piper. She saluted him. He nodded. Raven smiled and headed back to the house.

***

Rex watched them in his rearview mirror. Then rolled down his passenger window and looked in the woods. Thick. A million places to hide. He backed towards the house, watching the woods. Uneasy. He rested his hand on his gun.

Just before he reached the bend in the road, a flash by a tree caught his eye. He braked. And too late he saw the gun. Without a sound, his head flopped sideways. Blood sprayed. And his foot slipped off the brake. The car rolled in reverse.

As the road turned, it rolled onto the grass. Then off the bank into the river where slowly, it sank.

***

Back at the house, Raven parked.

Gabrielle said, "What's wrong with me?"

Raven said, "Have you had any pain at all? Bleeding?"

"No."

"Then the baby is taking up all the room in your abdomen. You are tiny. I think you need to plan on being a mom very soon."

"I believe you."

All three women went in the house leaving keys and purses in the car.

***

In the back of the barn, Steel hung up with Callie and dropped the phone in his shirt pocket. He looped the horse gear around his neck, then bent over, straining, and lifted the new saddle for the stallion. He heard a noise, and turned, arms full.

Two men stood there. Kip shot him three times in the chest. Blood flew, then pooled under him as he landed in the dirt on his back. There wasn't even a sound to startle the horses.

***

Zack and Kip ran across the yard parallel with Raven's garage where there were no windows. Reaching the side of her house, they ducked below the porch and headed for the back door. Looking through the windows, Zack saw Raven in the hall. And Piper was between him and Raven. He didn't see Gabrielle.

Zack pulled his gun and glanced at Kip. He said, "This is my party. Got it?"

Kip nodded.

230

Zack ran up the steps and kicked the door open. Wood cracked. Glass flew. Women screamed. And by the time Piper shielded Raven and spun with her weapon, Zack's gun was in her face. And Kip, the new employee, was a few steps behind him, gun drawn. Her nostrils flared with fury.

Zack said, "Give me the gun, hotshot. You have no options."

Hearing Raven's ragged breathing behind her, Piper squeezed her hand. Meaning, easy…be smart. Then she let her gun dangle from two fingers and lowered it to the floor. Zack kicked it toward the kitchen, and she heard it ding against the aluminum trashcan.

Looking at Raven, Zack shoved Piper to the den and said, "Keep her covered, Kip. I'm busy."

Raven stared at Zack's transformation. The man she had known before the attack had been strong but slimmer, debonair, fair, and handsome with short blonde hair and smiling green eyes. But the Zack before her now was ruggedly handsome, tanned, with long blonde hair and powerful muscles. And he was no longer deceptively dangerous. It was obvious. His green eyes slid over her.

She refused to show fear at the look on his face. He looked like he could eat her alive. His gaze met hers and she recognized the message. She wanted to throw up, kill him, and run all at the same time. Terror and anger warred within her.

He smiled and tucked the gun in his back waistband. He said, "Come here."

Anger won. She spit on the floor in front of him.

He growled with desire at her passion. Walking toward her, he said, "I have missed you, Raven."

She backed up, and snapped, "What? No girlfriend in prison?"

He charged and caught her before she had taken two steps. She screamed and fought. He laughed and carried her toward the kitchen.

He put her down once he was back where he could see Piper. Pinning her struggling body against the wall, he said, "Stop it. You're wasting—"

Raven swung and hit him in the face. He crushed her against the wall, grinding his body against hers as he kissed her hot enough to catch the house on fire.

Kip watched. Aroused at the scene. He ripped Piper's shirt down the front. Caressing one breast, he trailed the tip of the gun down her stomach with the other hand.

231

Piper interrupted his mauling with a quiet comment. "I guess you're the mysterious Hunter. Creep and accomplice."

Kip ran the gun between her legs and said, "Too bad you didn't know who we were at the grand opening. Some security, Agent Pierce."

Zack said, "Shut up, Kip."

Piper glanced at Zack. He had been the old man. No doubt about it.

Irritated at Zack's interference, Kip reached for Piper's pants.

Piper's mind raced to all the facts about Hunter in the investigation – and latched onto the pig attack. His right leg was injured. It would still be raw after only a week. And deciding to save her karate skills for later, she kicked him in the calf.

He yelled and backhanded her. She hit the floor. Eyebrow cut. Lip bleeding.

Furious at the continued interruptions, Zack pulled Raven behind him and in three steps nailed Kip in the chest. Hard. Kip stumbled back. Gasping for air, blood running down his leg.

Zack snarled, "Keep it in your pants for one hour or it'll never get hard again. Do you understand?"

Kip saw his fury and sucked it up. He didn't say a word but glanced at Piper. She knew he would make her pay.

Zack said, "Tape Piper's wrists to the staircase railing. Over her head. Tight. Let Ms. Agent enjoy being a prisoner for a while. And both of you, KEEP YOUR MOUTH SHUT."

Kip motioned Piper with the gun, his eyes bright with rage. She walked to the staircase and raised her arms, back to the stairs. He pulled them high and tight. By the time he finished, her heels didn't even touch the floor. She was on her toes. And it hurt.

Sweat dripped down Piper's neck. She glanced at the clock. Seven forty-five. It had only been ten minutes but at least they were still alive. But she didn't have a good feeling about Steel at all.

Zack turned back to Raven. He touched her lips and said, "No more fighting. Not this time. What I am here for, you're going to give me."

"Then why waste a trip? Didn't you hear me on the news? You can't make me love you. Or want you."

He drew her face close. His lips trailed over hers. He licked her, and said, "Oh…but I can."

She turned her face away in disgust, and said, "That's impossible."

He pulled her face back and said, "Not at all. I've thought long and hard about this. We're going to do what we always did. Dance together…perfectly. Only this time, I'm the judge of the competition. You've got to make me believe what your body promises. That the dance is real."

Her mind spun. "We haven't danced together in years! How—"

"You can do it. You better. Because I will shoot Piper with every mistake you make."

In shock, she glanced at Piper. Piper smiled with gritted teeth, blood dripping, and gave her a thumbs up above her taped wrists.

Raven turned to Zack and said, "No…I can't dance under that pressure. Who could?"

"Listen Raven. I will not fight you. And you *will* give me what I want. Piper is your incentive. And remember, there is always Gabrielle."

Heart racing, she had hoped he didn't know about Gabrielle, and said, "Zack—"

He yelled, "Come on out, Gabrielle. You're missing the party."

Raven begged, "No, Zack, please—"

The bathroom door opened, and Gabrielle walked out. Pale. Slow. Determined.

Zack said, "Impressive, Gabrielle. No whining. Crying. The true descendant of a pirate."

"I wish I had my sword."

He laughed and pointed to the den. Make yourself comfortable, and I mean that. You look…pained."

She chose a recliner close to a bookcase near Piper. She hoped Raven and Piper remembered what was hidden there. Moaning, she lowered herself to the chair and closed her eyes. She already needed to pee again.

Zack held Raven by the arm as he looked at Gabrielle and Piper. He had his captives. It was time.

Gabrielle interrupted and held up her hand with a question. She said, "Zack…"

Zack sighed. "What?"

"I have been going to the bathroom all day. I can't hold it."

"Pee in the chair. Wait…are you in labor?"

"Not that I know of," and that said, her water broke. It flooded the chair and the floor. Her eyes widened.

Raven said, "She is now."

"How long does she have?"

"Guessing, a few hours. You need to let me tend to her. Get her comfortable."

He smiled with real humor, and said, "Cute. Good try, but you have more pressing things to tend to...like keeping them alive."

Looking at Gabrielle, he said, "Tough it out for an hour, Gabrielle. It's going to hurt no matter where you are. And be quiet. Raven will be tending to me."

Gabrielle nodded and felt the first contraction.

Dragging Raven with him, Zack headed upstairs, and said, "Gather what you need for the dance. Do it fast. You have five minutes or I'm going to think you want an appetizer of me now."

"I'll hurry. What song do I plan for?"

"What's the last dance routine you've done?"

"I...I just started dancing again. I have a solo routine to *Fallin'* by Alicia Keys."

Intrigued, he said, "Ok. Then we'll do your routine. I can improvise. Now, which bedroom is yours?"

She hesitated. "Zack..."

"Raven. I want you like you can't imagine. Hurry up and get your stuff or I'll take you right now."

Digging in her hope chest, she found the type of costume he liked. Makeup. Dance heels. She knew him. Knew what he liked. What moved him. She could do this. She just didn't know what came after the dance.

Breathless, she turned and ran into him. Startled, she stepped back, and was surprised to see pain cross his face for just an instant. And she thought about meeting him at eighteen. Young. Innocent. Good friends. Totally unaware of what would lie ahead for them. And for a second, they both remembered.

She said, "I never knew you loved me. I never meant to hurt you."

He brushed her cheek. Gently. "I knew that."

"Then why—"

"Because you should have known. I showed you a million ways."

"But we weren't— Dance wasn't love—"

"You didn't even try! But...turn on the music and you let me dance like a lover roaming your body all day long. You came on to me easy enough then, didn't you?"

She winced at his harsh perception of a dance partner routine. It sounded so nasty. But that wasn't the only ugly truth between them by far.

She said, "And violence? Ambushing me in my shower, raping and almost killing me was your definition of love?"

"I waited too long. And you pulled the knife first. Now let's go…it's time to dance."

***

Downstairs, Gabrielle clenched her teeth as Zack and Raven argued upstairs. There was no mistaking the pain now. Her lower back and abdomen were aching. Throbbing. Burning. But more than that was going on. She glanced at Piper. With Zack upstairs, Kip was back for more.

Piper saw the look on Kip's face as he reached her, smiling at her exposed chest. He pushed up her bra and licked her. She ignored him. Then he pressed against her and pushed the pistol barrel between her legs again.

She knew he was making up for not being able to do it himself, and said, "I think your intelligence is overrated. If Zack sees you hot and bothered again, you'll pay for messing up his party."

"I had enough brains to roam the grand opening and get the job."

"So. I still didn't like you. And Zack is still going to rip your head off if he finds you here."

"We're brothers. He'll get over it."

And there it was. The link. They were sperm brothers. She said, "Obviously you came from the frozen stuff. Zack's the real deal."

Enraged, he bit her breast. Pain radiated across her chest, and in karate reflex, Piper kneed him. As he doubled over and stepped back, she kicked him in the head. And while her wrists screamed from holding her full weight, the satisfaction was worth it. He stumbled to one knee.

He looked at her with pain, clenched jaws, and a promise of death after a whole lot of naked activity.

Zack frowned from the top of the stairs and said, "She's bound, and still whipped you."

Knowing he deserved the ribbing, Kip got up, wiping blood off his cheek. It stung.

Curious as he stepped off the stairs, Zack said, "I've never seen you without discipline. Always the cool customer. Do we have a serious problem here, Kip?"

Walking away, aching, Kip said, "I was just having a little fun while you were upstairs. No problem. No problem at all."

"Don't let there be a next time."

The brothers stared at each other. Kip turned away first and looked out the window. But all he saw was Piper.

Pointing at the hall bathroom, Zack said, "Go change into costume, Raven. I'm going to download the song and change."

And ignoring Gabrielle and Piper as Raven left, Zack grabbed his backpack and pulled out a pair of black slacks, socks, and dress shoes. He stripped and tossed his jeans, boots, and backpack aside.

He was naked and in no hurry to dress. Piper and Gabrielle glanced at each other before glancing back at him. Raven was going to flip out.

Raven walked out of the bathroom and said, "Do you prefer—" and in shock at his nakedness, dropped the bag she was holding. Makeup rolled across the floor.

Zack stepped into black slacks and leaving them unzipped walked over to help her pick up the makeup. She wouldn't look at him.

Smiling, he said, "I'm more your type of man now. I figured it out. Rugged makes you hot. In fact, I think Adam and I are close to the same—"

Her look was furious as she said, "Hardly. Now, back off. Do you want my head in the dance or not?"

He didn't want to fight. He was too close to his goal. "Ok. I'll give you that. What was your question?"

"Do you want dramatic makeup?"

"Yes. Get dressed and come out here. I'll do it."

***

Raven stared at herself in the mirror. 60s hot pants. Crop top. Fringe and sequins. Multicolor. And dance heels that made her legs long and sexy. Zack loved this outfit. But scars were visible now. She swallowed as her stomach swirled. She was running out of time. She thought of Adam. He would be crazy upset. Raging. Grabbing the makeup box, she stepped out of the bathroom. Winging it.

Zack looked up and it was like years fell away as Raven walked toward him in costume. He held out his hand to take the makeup from her and she knew what was coming next.

He spun and lifted her, then molded her against him before bending her backwards. Her hair brushed the floor. It was the introduction they used for all their competitions.

Then he pulled her back up and motioned her to sit. He sat legs spread in front of her. He pulled her closer, glancing at the scars her costume didn't hide. He touched the ones on his bare chest. Their gazes met without comment. Then he worked on her face like so many times before.

Except intimacy made things different for them now. They knew things about each other they hadn't known before. Awareness was now their reality. Would it affect their performance Raven wondered? Everything depended on the dance. Piper. Gabrielle. And her.

A few minutes later, movement by the windows caught Raven's attention. Kip's anger was mounting as he watched Zack with her. He clearly resented having to wait. That made her more than a little nervous since Zack was already upset with him. And angry dynamics between villains was like a ticking time bomb for everyone.

***

Kip glanced at Piper. And with a quick middle finger aimed at Zack's back, he climbed the steps to sit behind her. She tried to move away from him. He grabbed her waistband and shoved his hand down the back of her pants. Raven jumped as Piper slammed her butt against the rail - smashing his hand. Piper screamed as Kip dug fingernails into her tender backside.

Zack cussed, snatched his gun, and headed to Kip.
Piper yelled, "Eagle One," which meant nothing to anyone in the heat of the moment.
The drone activated.
Kip jumped up and yelled at Zack, "You are taking forever! I want Piper and I don't want to wait for your dance. Besides, Gabrielle is more than enough incentive for Raven. Now leave us alone."

Piper knew it was now or never to get rid of one of them. She remembered the speculation the investigation had brought up and went for it.

She said, "Zack, why don't you ask Kip why he killed your father. Did he get tired of waiting on something from him too?"

The look Zack laid on Kip said everything. He said incredulously, "You killed him? Why? I was providing you inheritance."

Kip shrugged. "He refused to acknowledge me as his son."

Zack said, "Along with the other one-hundred-forty-nine of you. Big surprise."

"Well, you were in prison, and I thought he might take a shot at getting to know me."

Zack said, "I'll take a shot," and blew Kip's face off.

Piper had seen it coming and closed her eyes as the blood hit her. Raven and Gabrielle screamed.

Zack turned to Piper covered in blood splatter.

He stepped close and said menacingly, "Is that what you had in mind, Agent Pierce? One bad guy down?"

She didn't answer. She didn't need to.

He continued, "And now that he can't bother you, there shouldn't be a single reason for you to open your mouth again." It wasn't a question. "And what will happen if I hear your voice?"

She glanced at what was left of Kip.

"Then we understand each other completely."

He glanced at Gabrielle in the recliner. She was sweating. Panting. And had thrown up on the floor. And still she hung in there.

He turned to Raven. She gritted her teeth determined not to throw up at the blood on him. And on the death dripping down her walls.

Zack said, "I'm going to clean up. Don't you dare get out of that chair. We will pick up where we left off when I get back. Hit play on my phone and get in the mood."

She hit play as he walked down the hall - but looked at Piper, ignoring the music.

Piper mouthed, "Run!"

Raven shook her head no, glancing at the open bathroom door where he was. At Gabrielle. And back to Piper.

Piper mouthed, "Drone," and looked at the shelf by the back door.

Raven followed her gaze and saw the green light on the drone. It was activated. The FBI knows. She nodded. And began to listen to the music, thinking. Zack would want to practice maybe five minutes. The dance would be less than four. Normal dance delays would give her a little more time.

She glanced at the clock. How fast could the FBI get here? And what would she have to do to buy more time? She thought about Adam and Lance. She would do whatever she had to.

The blood was gone when Zack returned. He sat in the chair to finish Raven's makeup and met her gaze. The music filling the room was sensual. He felt the pull of it. He smiled, knowing she did too. He added glitter around her eyes, cheeks, and neck. He handed her the mascara and red lipstick, watching her put it on.

He said, "Glitter me."

She stood, tilting his face as he sat, and added the exotic touch of glitter around his green eyes like she used to. She ran her hands through his hair for the wild sexual look he liked. He looked at her lips. And hungry, he pulled her close, running his hands up the inside of her thighs.

She backed away from him.

He stood.

Raven faced Zack. Overwhelmed for a moment as she stared at him. He walked closer. It was down to the wire.

Gabrielle watched in silent pain. She looked at Piper. Fear flickered for a second. How could Raven possibly do what he wanted?

Piper's body hurt and she tried not to think of Kip's blood all over her. She nodded to encourage Gabrielle with a confident stare, that was partially real.

Handsome and deadly, Zack smiled at the tension in the room and said, "Dance, Raven. Their lives depend on it. You better make me believe you love me."

239

Chapter 27

Sean frowned as he read FBI Director Washington's message from the search back in Montana:

Divers found a large plastic container from a blood bank wedged under a log in the lake. The blood matches the blood in the prison escape truck. Which means, the truck scene was indeed a setup like we figured. They are not dead. Get to Lake Charles and find them, Sean. Yesterday.

Dropping the phone on the seat, Sean looked out the helicopter window. A headache started. How had Zack evaded them? Rarely does one simply vanish in the current day of technology. There was always a trail to follow by someone who saw something, security cameras, or video fanatics wanting to become the next TikTok sensation. Everyone was a reporter now.

His phone rang.

***

His buddy in the lab said, "Hey, we finally got a DNA match on the accomplice in the fugitive case for you."

"Who is it?"

"Remember the missing guy, Hunter, from the Lake Charles hospital? It turns out he's the prison escape accomplice. And get this, he's one of the sperm kids - Trace Kirkpatrick. Nickname, Kip. I'm sending you his picture and info."

"Send the information to intel asap. They need to run his driver's license and credit cards. Find him!"

***

A few minutes later, the helicopter landed in Alexandria. Sean climbed out and his phone alarm went off. The drone was active at Raven's house. He clicked connect.

And then nothing else mattered as the camera opened and he watched Zack shoot a man in the face. Was that Kip? Stunned, he saw Piper bound. Injured. He saw Gabrielle throwing up and Raven screaming.

This was a home invasion in progress.

Where were Adam and Dakota?

Yelling for his team, they climbed back into the helicopter.

***

Adam hit the brakes and Dakota grabbed the dash. The dogs slipped in the back of the truck and slid into the cab.

Adam said, "I can't find the house. Has the father answered any of your calls yet?"

Dakota said, "No. And I have phone signal."

"Maybe he doesn't. I'll ask a neighbor while you call the Sheriff's Office."

Adam floored it to the white house in the distance.

Sliding to a stop, he jumped out of the truck as Dakota explained to the dispatcher about the search for the missing boys. An older man came out of the garage wiping greasy hands on a rag.

Adam said, "Sorry to be abrupt, but I'm looking for John Baggett. He has a red house about six miles from the main road. His two boys are missing. I'm Adam Nash with Quest Search & Rescue in Lake Charles."

The man frowned and said, "There isn't a red house on this road. And I don't know a man named John Baggett. I've lived here all my life. You sure you have the right road?"

Horror ricocheted through Adam's brain. No. It wasn't real.

Dakota yelled, "Adam, there's no search—"

And Adam's phone rang. It was Sean.

***

Motioning to Dakota to join him, he answered on speaker, "Sean—"

Sean said, "Just listen to me. Is Dakota with you?"

"Yes. What—"

"They are alive, but Zack has Raven, Gabrielle, and Piper captive. Where are you so I can come get you?"

Adam said, "Northwest of Oberlin off LA-26 on a fake Quest call."

Dakota activated his GPS watch and said, "Follow my GPS signal."

Sean said, "Got it. We've left Alexandria and are headed your way. Be there any minute. Is there a place to land?"

Adam said, "Yes—"

"Just leave your truck there and we'll be back on the river in fifteen minutes. Watch for us. And Adam… the drone was activated. Connect to the link – and prepare yourselves."

Adam connected to the drone…and ignoring the fear and rage, they watched…

***

Zack said, "Dance. Their lives depend on it. You better make me believe you love me."

And he shoved furniture to the edges of the room creating a dance floor. He pointed to the center.

Raven walked out and posed. One thought repeated in her mind. I can do this. I can do this. And her eyes closed.

Zack hit play.

Locked in her role, Raven opened her eyes and looked at Zack. Intentionally dramatic. Sensual. Her body undulated to the rhythm all the way to the floor and up, sliding her hands along her skin.

Zack felt the sensual burn climb his spine. He responded…mirroring her movements perfectly. She smiled and spun, leapt, and landed on all fours. Wild. And that's when Zack saw the difference in her. The power. It was unbelievable.

He said, "Show me more."

And Zack watched the solo dance she created. Amazed. It was more sensual than anything they had ever danced, and he couldn't take his eyes off her. She teased him. Touched herself. And fanned the flames for the battle at hand. A few minutes later she landed face down, hair spread around her. And Zack knew it was the perfect last dance.

He said, "You're better than I ever dreamed. Spectacular. Are you ready to dance it with me?"

Flipping hair out of her face she stood, meeting his gaze, and said, "Are you sure you can handle me? I'm not who I was."

"I see that. But neither am I."

She shifted her position. Confident. Daring. Aflame.

Zack looked her over and said, "I came a long way for this."

Bold now, she narrowed her eyes and said, "And you've done a lot of things you shouldn't have. Like killing my husband."

He smiled. "I wondered if you would mention that."

Fury crossed her face. "You made sure I knew. Wasn't that what the package in the mailbox was for? Although the note about him not falling was unnecessary."

He said, "What do you mean?"

"The necklace told me."

"How's that?"

"He never took it off."

"Ah. That explains why he purposely gave it to me. You might also like to know he tried to pull me with him over the cliff."

She glanced at his gun lying on the table. He pointed to Gabrielle and Piper in warning.

She said, "You sick coward."

He yanked her close, and snapped, "But one that you are about to prove undying love for. Right? You owe me. Pay up."

Raven slapped him. He kissed her. Hard. Ravaging. Then stepped back and looked at the clock. He had to hurry.

She wiped blood off her lip and said sarcastically, "Too bad your dance finesse doesn't extend to sex—"

He jerked her off her feet. "Shut up, Raven. And dance."

"And after?"

"You know what's after."

She did now.

In a minute, they were posed in the center of the floor. He was behind her. Hands on her hips. Intimate. Intentionally sexual.

Zack said, "Hit play, Gabrielle."

And Zack and Raven moved with the music. Professionals. They undulated together to the floor and up as his hands followed hers over her body. He moved in perfect synch with her. Watching and feeling her beauty shine, he moved in and out of the dance while she declared her love for him. Her hunger. With every touch. Every expression. And every connection of their bodies.

He wasn't thinking about anything but her now. She lured him, with a kiss here. A lick there. And he couldn't help but touch what he wanted. And with a smile, she touched him with eyes that promised everything he craved.

Beyond them, Gabrielle reached into the bookcase and slid a knife into her chair. She glanced at Piper and hung the blade along the side. Watching Zack, Piper raised her right foot close to the knife. In a second it was between her toes.

Raven noticed the weapon exchange. And keeping Zack's back to the women, she jumped, wrapping arms and legs around him as she drenched him in heat. Her mouth. Her body. Her whispers for more.

Piper kicked her leg above her head and grabbed the knife with her fingers. The burn of cuts was inevitable. Blood dripped but didn't matter. She began to cut the tape.

***

A mile away, Maverick ran through the woods. Fast. The trees were a blur. FBI, U.S. Marshals, and Swat followed him as Sean barked orders in their earpiece: Get in place. Do not engage. Repeat. Get in place. Do not engage. We are five minutes out.

Maverick's phone had been blowing up with calls when he got out of the deposition. No one could reach Rex. Then Adam called and everything became a nightmare. Now they were running to get there in time.

Slowing down, he crept toward the edge of the woods. Law enforcement fanned the perimeter. A few men followed him to the barn. All he could hear was the shuffle of horses and the sound of music from the house. And they all knew what that meant. The dance wasn't over yet.

He tried not to think of Raven's deadly mission in the arms of a fugitive. Or Piper's injuries. Or Gabrielle's pain. Much less the level of their fear.

Rounding the back of the barn he saw Steel on the ground. The men cleared the barn as he hit his knees by Steel. He was silent in a puddle of blood under a massive saddle. Pale. Eyes closed. No movement. Maverick touched his neck. A faint pulse.

He radioed: Steel's down. Barely alive. Multiple shots. Then they hid alongside Adam's house and watched where the music played.

In the helicopter, Adam and Dakota stared at the scene playing in the video.

And Sean's gaze was glued to the monitor in his lap where he waited for a chance to make a move with the drone. He walked it to the edge of the shelf in the house knowing time was short. Zack was quickly losing control. And there was no doubt danger was imminent.

Sean glanced at his brothers for just a second. They looked up. They all knew. A million scenarios were possible but only one would play out.

Adam could taste the fear peppered with rage. But he was almost home. All he could think was, stay alive, Raven. Whatever you've got to do. Just stay alive. I'm coming and Zack's a dead man.

The agents in the helicopter prepared him for action.

***

Raven knew the song was almost over. And she had done well since Zack was locked on her. He licked her. Kissed her. Touched her. Very hungry. Obviously aroused from intense contact and lots of grinding. They were all but having sex through their clothes.

Then she glanced over his shoulder at Piper. She was still bound - cutting the tape - but not free yet. What did she do now?

Zack pulled her mouth back to his and she raked nails down his back, rotating her hips. He hit his knees with her. Raven laughed sensually and bit his neck. Thinking…she had to get him out of the house. Away from the guns and the women.

Surely Adam was almost here.

But the song faded.

Time was up.

Zack rasped, "Raven…"

"I know, I've got what you want."

He reached for her fringed shorts.

She held his hands, and said, "No audience. Just us."

In a second, he was pulling her toward the stairs.

She yanked her hand away, and said, "I'm not climbing over him."

245

Zack had totally forgotten about Kip and turned to the hall.

"No," she said, and growling, he looked at her. Losing it. All he could think about was ripping off her pants and diving into her.

She knew. They all knew. It was obvious.

Licking her lips, she said, "Take me outside. Away from all this. Hurry, Zack…"

And since the back door was in pieces with broken glass and wood, she ran for the front. Playfully. Dancing. Touching. Luring him.

She opened the door. And he kissed her, carrying her outside on the porch.

But behind him Raven saw movement. The drone was coming. She broke off the kiss and said, "Let me kick off my heels."

She stepped to the side and flipped them off. He smiled and unsnapped his pants.

The drone slammed into the side of his head. Hard. He stumbled onto the rail and went over. He hit the ground, blood on his head.

And as the roar of the helicopter rounded the bend in the river, Raven ran toward the wharf. Hair and fringe streaming, she screamed for Adam who was standing in the open door of the helicopter.

Zack roared in rage and staggered after her.

Sean radioed, "Take the house from the rear! Do not engage the fugitive! I repeat. Do not engage. Do not shoot! There is no clear shot!"

The helicopter moved to intercept Raven at the wharf. Adam dropped out of the open door attached to a cable.

Raven reached the bottom of the hill and crossed the road headed to the wharf. Zack was screaming and gaining. Raven never slowed.

Adam opened his arms and screamed, "Jump, Raven! Jump!"

She went airborne in a flash of fringe and sequins, reaching for Adam. He caught her. Then unexpectedly, Zack jumped. And all three hung from the cable. Fighting.

Raven was slipping.

Dakota and Sean climbed out, held by other agents, and grabbed her arms. She swung free, screaming as Zack still tried to grab her.

Adam pulled his knife, and grabbing Zack's hair, he yanked his head back, and growled, "Get your hands off my wife!"

And buried his knife in Zack's chest. Zack blinked once and let go. His body fell. Bounced off the edge of the wharf and landed facedown with a splash in the river. Blood turned the water red.

Adam reached for Raven as they pulled him up.

Sean radioed, "Fugitive down. I repeat, fugitive is dead in the water. Get first responders to the house and barn asap!"

***

Maverick entered the back door followed by law enforcement who filled the house. Gabrielle wasn't bound so he headed to Piper - pulling off his shirt. He wrapped it around her exposed chest as officers on the stairs finished severing the tape that held her.

Piper dropped on legs that buckled. Maverick caught her. She groaned in pain as her arms fell to her sides. Useless.

She said, "Tell me we have Raven."

"We've got her. Zack's dead."

***

The helicopter landed in between both houses as first responders were pulling up to the barn and the house. Dakota and Sean hit the ground running for the house. Agents followed.

Adam kissed Raven, still breathing hard, and said, "I don't want to let you go, but I've got to check on Steel. He's been shot. Are you ok?"

"Yes! Go, hurry…" and she ran to the house while he ran to the barn.

Quest was working now.

Dakota ran over the broken glass and met Gabrielle's eyes across the room. She panted in labor. Her lips quivered as he scooped her out of the chair.

"Gabrielle…"

Paramedics wheeled in stretchers, and he turned to one.

She said, "No. Get me in the shower. I'm not having our baby filthy like this."

Dakota headed for the hall bathroom.

247

An officer carried Raven over the glass, and she ran to Piper, Sean, and Maverick.

Piper said, "No Sean…I'm fine. Check on Gabrielle."

Sean said, "You are not fine. Get her on a stretcher."

Maverick motioned to a paramedic, and in seconds laid her on the sheet. Her body was beginning to tremble.

Trying not to panic as her body fell apart, Piper looked at Raven as the paramedics began taking vitals. She said, "My arms don't work. My wrists…"

Raven asked, "Can you move your fingers?"

Piper wiggled them.

Raven continued, "The muscles and tendons were heavily strained. They'll x-ray you. Probably stitch some of your finger cuts. Don't fight the trembling. Your body needs to release the pressure it's been under."

Pained to ask, Sean said, "Piper, do you have any other injuries?"

She knew what he meant and said, "No rape. Not yet. He slapped me around. Bit me. Cut me with his fingernails."

"Which he?"

"Kip. Hunter. The man dripping down the wall."

Maverick said "I saw the bite. I didn't see claw marks."

"Down the back of my pants."

Maverick didn't say what he wanted to, but Piper saw it in his eyes. And the look he gave the man with no face, killed him again.

Raven said, "Where's Rex?"

"No one can find him," Maverick said.

Raven and Piper frowned. Piper said, "But we left him less than a mile from here on the road when we came back for the bathroom. We told him to leave."

"How long after you left him was the attack?"

"Maybe ten minutes." Raven said.

Piper met Maverick's glance. Pain crossed his face.

Piper whispered, "Rex saw them."

And still without a shirt, Maverick ran out the door yelling for help. His screams of officer down…officer down…faded in the distance.

***

In the barn, Adam joined the medical group kneeling around Steel. He said, "Why is he still on the ground?"

The older paramedic said, "I think the saddle has compressed his blood flow which kept him alive. If we take it off now, he'll bleed out."

Looking at the puddle of blood already on the ground, Adam said, "Then let's take him with the saddle. Now! Move!"

They grabbed a board to slide under him.

***

Raven knocked on the bathroom door and said, "Gabrielle."

Dakota yelled, "Come in!"

Shutting the door behind her, Raven saw Gabrielle in the shower as Dakota helped her strip, holding her up.

Raven said, "How fast are your contractions?"

"Ten minutes…and steady. And my water only broke, what, thirty or forty minutes ago?"

"But I think you've been in labor. We need to get you in the ambulance. We don't know how far you've dilated. You need to rinse off and get out of there. I'm running to grab you something to wear."

***

At the bend in the road, Maverick saw the hood of Rex's car under the water. He swam out and pulled him out of the car. Both windows were down, and it was obvious he had been dead before the car ever left the road.

Somber officers and agents helped carry him to the grass. Someone covered him with a sheet. Someone else handed Maverick a sweatshirt. He was wet and shivering as he called his sergeant, the medical examiner, and a tow truck. He wasn't ready to call Rex's family yet.

Then he sat next to his partner on the riverbank. He wasn't leaving him alone until he was in official hands.

And all law enforcement there honored their fallen comrade. The only fatality besides the criminals. If Steel survived.

***

Adam ran to check on Raven as they loaded Steel in the ambulance. And then returning, he jumped in with him to ride to the hospital.

The second ambulance with Gabrielle followed the first. Dakota called her parents and the doctor as he rode with her.

249

The third ambulance held Piper. Raven climbed in with her and watched the door shut. Now she had to call Callie.

***

Callie answered on the first ring, "Hey Raven, I thought y'all were having a spa day. Did you change your mind?"

"Callie. Something came up. Is Lance with you?"

"No. He's outside playing with the twins. I'm upstairs folding clothes."

And the pause that followed scared Callie. Heart pounding, she said, "What happened?"

Raven knew there was no way to soften the blow, and said, "Zack and the new employee, Kip, attacked us. Steel was shot and he's on his way to the hospital. Adam is with him."

Callie gasped, and tears poured, like they had been poised waiting for the floodgates to open. Voice ragged with pain, she said, "Is it bad?"

"Yes, but he's alive and that's all that matters."

Callie bit back the sob and said, "Are you hurt, Raven? Don't lie to me. I know what Zack did last time. And what about the others?"

"I'm going to be fine. But they killed Rex. And held me, Gabrielle, and Piper captive. Piper is injured. And Gabrielle is in labor."

Callie sank to her knees, sobbing.

Raven said, "You need to ride with Gabrielle's parents to the hospital. Her grandparents will keep the kids. We'll all be at the hospital. And I'm so sorry, Callie. Just hurry…and remember that God still does miracles. Every single day."

***

Chapter 28

In trauma room three at Lake Charles Memorial Hospital, a team of doctors and nurses surrounded Steel under the huge saddle. A nurse added a second bag of fluid as they watched his vitals improve. They had to build up his blood pressure before they removed the saddle since he'd already lost a lot of blood. They watched the clock. Ten minutes was their go time to remove it.

Raven glanced worriedly at Adam and texted Callie. What if they didn't make it before the procedure? But the quick text response said…we're here. She took a deep breath of relief.

Adam hugged Raven again, the image of her terror as she jumped through the air still ripping his heart to shreds. And he was concerned because she refused to get checked out by a doctor. She insisted she was fine. But he saw the ugly bruises darkening on her skin, the busted lip, and several scrapes and cuts. And that's only what he could see.

Callie came through the trauma doors with a nurse. Tear tracks on her face. Fear fighting an obvious battle within her. She saw them first, grabbing their hands. Then wobbled weakly at the sight of the saddle on top of Steel and all the machines and medical staff around him.

She looked at the nearest person in scrubs and said, "Let me talk to him. Please."

The doctor motioned her up and said, "You have two minutes."

Callie hurried to the head of the bed and didn't notice the moan she made when she saw his condition firsthand. Blood splatter. Huge bloody gauze pads. An oxygen mask, and needles and wires everywhere.

Slipping her hand in his, she kissed his forehead. With quivering lips, she said, "Steel…I'm here, baby. I'm here. We're all here."

Shocking those close by, his eyelids flickered but didn't open. But his response was good news.

Callie said, "Fight, Steel. Fight hard and I'll get our marriage license when you wake up. We'll get married tomorrow if you want."

His feet moved and the medical staff smiled. But his heart rate increased.

The doctor said, "I think we better take it from here. You were better medicine than anything we could give him. Now…out ladies. Adam, stay and help the orderlies with the saddle."

Then pointing at a nurse, the doctor said, "Get the orderlies and gurney in here asap!"

They lined the two gurneys side by side. Four men, including Adam grabbed the saddle and prepared to lift at the doctor's command.

With a glance at the clock, the doctor said, "Now!"

And groans filled the room as the men lifted and moved. The saddle dropped loudly on the gurney and medical staff pushed it away and surrounded Steel. Alarms went off everywhere as blood dripped on the floor and vitals plummeted.

Adam joined Callie and Raven in the hall and held them as the medical team worked to save Steel's life. They prayed. And finally, the alarms stopped. An x-ray machine was rushed into the room. A few minutes later the team shoved the gurney with Steel through the doors and ran down the hall to surgery. The rest of the team walked out peeling off masks and dropping bloody gloves in the trash.

The doctor that spoke earlier looked at Callie, and said, "We don't see miracles often. But we saw one today. One bullet went through the thickest part of the saddle, then hit his phone, then hit the horse's bit that was wrapped around his neck, and somehow passed between the heart and spine – missing both.

"Bullet two went through the shoulder. Bullet three is lodged in the upper part of his chest with what looks like a metal stud from the saddle and a piece of the phone. So, I said all that to say, once the debris and ammo is removed – without complications mind you – you might be able to get that marriage license soon."

Callie burst into tears.

It wasn't over yet, but the miracle was getting them there.

***

Gabrielle was moved to labor and delivery. She was having contractions every five minutes.

Piper was in radiology having x-rays of her wrists, arms, and hands.

Sean had ridden with Maverick to the same hospital. They were headed to Rex's father's room. Delivering bad news was always hard. Crazy hard when it's one of your own.

And just before Maverick knocked on the door, a man said, "One second, Maverick."

Sean knew that voice and smiled, grateful his director joined them.

With a nod to Sean, the Director offered his hand to Maverick, and said, "I'm Director Washington with the FBI. I hope you don't mind if I go in with you and Sean."

"Not at all, Sir. It's an honor to meet you. And I know Rex would appreciate you doing this for his family."

"Then, whenever you're ready, let's do what none of us ever want to do."

Maverick knocked and opened the door.

***

Gabrielle panted. Sweating. Dakota wiped her face with a cool rag. She'd struggled hard all morning. Now he was straining with her.

After a knock on the door, Dakota called out, "Who is it?"

Gabrielle's parents walked in.

Gabrielle said, "Mom…"

Wiping Gabrielle's tears, Serena kissed her and said, "Hey, baby, it's almost time. You'll get to hold her, and you'll forget all the other stuff about today. Even the pain. I promise."

Gabrielle said, "Dad…"

Jimmy said, "Hey, beautiful. I'm so proud of you."

"For what?"

"For giving us another beautiful you. And for being a warrior in the worst of circumstances."

"I wish I could have fought."

"You did. You saved your daughter. Sometimes the right fight is surrendering."

The nurse came in and said, "I need to check you, Gabrielle."

"I don't feel like it."

Jimmy walked out before he laughed. Dakota grinned. He could only imagine how irritated he would be after all Gabrielle had been through today.

Winking at the nurse, Serena said, "I don't blame you, sweetie. We all know she probably dipped her hands in ice, but it might help to know when your daughter is coming."

Gabrielle glared at the nurse who took it all in stride. It came with the territory. Dakota glanced at Serena. He saw how she did that. Very smooth. Serena smiled and walked out.

***

Piper was wheeled from radiology back to ER. The Director, Sean, and Maverick were waiting in her cubicle. She winced, awkwardly getting out of the wheelchair, only to realize she couldn't shake his hand.

The Director looked at his injured agent and hid the fury. And at the same time was unapologetically satisfied that Zack and Kip were dead.

He said, "Excellent work today, Agent Pierce. And although an ambush is never the chosen battle, it has a way of revealing the depth of one's skills and strengths. Which in your case, are impressive considering you took out Kip without a weapon. Or should I say your mind was the weapon?"

"Thank you, Sir. But impressive was watching Raven and Gabrielle. The video will only show part of it, but I will include it in my report. Every bit of it."

"Noted. We all look forward to the details. But now, tell me about your injuries."

"I have no broken bones." She held up deep purple wrists and said, "These are bruised only. And my arms are sore but uninjured. I will need a few stitches on my left hand where I cut myself trying to cut the tape."

"The bite?"

Not surprised that he knew about the breast injury, she said, "It didn't break the skin and my tetanus shot is up to date."

"The fingernail gouges?"

Acting like they weren't talking about her butt cheeks, she said "Sore, but shallow. Home care only. They will dismiss me shortly."

"How long before the doctor releases you for work?"

"Two to three weeks."

He smiled and said, "Terrific. We'll talk about your choice of assignments later."

What assignment? She asked, "Sir?"

"New Orleans, Denver, or Atlanta. Think about it and we'll talk later."

***

Callie looked up every time the surgery doors opened. And sighed every time it wasn't news on Steel.

Raven said, "No news is good news…right?"

"I know that in my head." Callie said. "But my heart doesn't care what my head knows."

Raven nodded with a glance at Adam. He drew her closer. Amen to that.

A couple of minutes later, Sean, Piper, and Maverick joined them in the surgery waiting room.

Callie hugged Piper. Gently, while groaning at the injuries on such a beautiful powerful woman.

Piper said, "I'm sorry about Steel. Have you heard anything from surgery yet?"

"No. Hopefully, they'll send someone out with an update soon. How are you? It looks painful."

"I'm fine, actually getting better by the minute. I'm just glad that the men that shot Rex are dead."

"Do we know which one shot him?"

"Not yet. But I think it was Kip. Zack was focused on Raven."

"Well, I heard you took care of Kip."

"I just encouraged Zack to do it for me."

The surgery doors opened, and the doctor walked out. Callie jumped to her feet. They all stood.

The doctor smiled and said, "I heard you have a wedding planned."

Callie smiled with a sob of relief, tears rolling down her cheeks. "Yes, Sir."

"He's doing fine in recovery. Better than he should be doing. We took out the bullets and debris. Cleaned him up and stitched him.

"And the small incisions on the outside don't tell the real story of what he went through. He has a lot of chest and back bruising which means - no lifting anything over five pounds for two weeks. Even on the honeymoon. It's not debatable. Unless he wants to return here."

She said, "No problem."

"Big strong men like your fiancé don't listen well."

"But I will have the marriage license."

Everyone laughed.

The doctor said, "He'll stay in ICU overnight for observation. We were close to his heart, and he lost a lot of blood. You can see him later. And give him two days. He'll be home the day before Thanksgiving. How's that for a wedding day?"

**

Everyone headed to the labor and delivery waiting room. After tears and hugs with everyone for the trauma of the day, Jimmy and Serena anxiously watched the busy delivery door that kept opening with new babies.

Sean and Adam sighed knowing Dakota must be wild by now.

Raven smiled, remembering when Lance was born and what a life-changing moment it had been. She touched her stomach and glanced at Adam. He put his arm around her and kissed her forehead. Yes, to lots of babies.

Sitting next to Piper, Maverick watched her lean her head back against the wall. He knew she had to be exhausted. Hurting.

He opened his arm and whispered, "Let me…please. We've both been through hell and back today."

And at the compassionate look in his eyes, she leaned into his arms. He held her close. Gentle. And for a moment, Piper rested and closed her eyes.

Sean noticed and looked at Adam. Adam smiled. But Maverick wasn't looking at them. He was just holding the woman that rocked him to his core…beyond grateful that she was alive.

The delivery doors swung open.

Dakota walked out with a pink bundle and a huge smile on his face. He said, "Everyone, meet Cheyenne Skye Nash!"

After the brief celebration, Sean texted the video announcement at the same time the breaking news bulletin aired about the fugitive.

**

Gigi listened to the news as she packed to leave the Golden Nugget Hotel. She was heading to her new meteorologist job at a Dallas television station. A breathless female reporter caught her attention on TV talking about a home invasion on the West Fork of the Calcasieu River. She turned to watch…

She said, *"This morning at approximately seven thirty, fugitive, Zack Dawton, and his accomplice, Trace Kirkpatrick, came here to the home of Raven Nash, newlywed of Quest Search & Rescue owner, Adam Nash.*

"They killed Detective Rex Calloway whose body was found shot in a submerged vehicle in the river. They shot and critically wounded the Quest property manager. And they took captive three women.

"The target was Raven Nash. With her was an expectant mother, Gabrielle Nash – wife of FBI Special Agent Dakota Nash. As well as, FBI Special Agent Piper Pierce, cousin of the Nash's who was assigned to Raven's case.

"KPLC recently learned in an interview with Raven that her and Zack had been competition dance partners that had gone terribly wrong. Zack had been sentenced to life in prison after they both almost died after a violent encounter. But today, the fugitive somehow, someway, found her. Took her. And from what we heard, forced her to dance with him to save the lives of the other two women.

"The only other fact we have at this time, is amazingly, the following video captured by a lone fisherman. He recorded the victim escaping from the house chased by the fugitive. The FBI intercepted at the wharf. Watch…"

Gigi watched Zack. Her one-night stand stranger of barely two days ago. Beautiful. Sexy. Passionate. Loving and gentle. But today he screamed viciously and chased a beautiful red-haired woman in a sparkly costume down a hill to a wharf…where a helicopter stopped. Where he died. And where he floated in the river.

She threw up. Twice. Then thought about what he said about dying in two days. And she also thought about the beautiful encounter with him. Wiping tears away, she finished packing, checked out, loaded the car, and headed to a new life in Texas.

Crossing the massive Interstate 210 bridge, she looked at Lake Charles. And at that point, decided to take the beautiful memory of Zack with her…including any child. The rest could stay forgotten on the river.

***

Raven laid Cheyenne back in Gabrielle's arms, and then smiled at Dakota.

With his heart in his eyes, Dakota said, "What you did today was incredibly brave, Raven. I know of few people who could have pulled that off."

"I didn't think of it as bravery, Dakota, love was just stronger than fear."

"And that's even better, sister-in-law."

Raven turned to Adam and softly touched his chest. "I'm ready to go home."

Without a word, he scooped her up and carried her to the car. Sean, Piper, and Maverick followed. Maverick chauffeured them since no one had vehicles.

***

They dropped Sean at the airport to fly home to Virginia.

Adam walked him to the door and said, "I haven't thanked you, Sean. If you hadn't already been in Louisiana... If you hadn't been in a helicopter..."

"But I was. And a rush plan, became the perfect plan for the rescue of a lifetime."

"Thank God."

"I do. Often. We can't do what we do and think we do it alone."

Adam nodded, then said, "Will you and Samantha be back for Angel and Jade's wedding this weekend?"

"We'll fly into Lake Charles Thanksgiving morning. Samantha insists on seeing all of you for herself. Then we'll drive to New Orleans Friday. And after the wedding Saturday, I've got to hurry and get her back to the academy. Which reminds me, I've got to hurry before I miss my flight."

***

Adam, Raven, and Piper were quiet as Maverick drove along the river bringing them home. Adam glanced at the time. It was only three p.m. How was that possible? It felt like three days in one.

Raven thought about all the blood on the stairs. The broken door. How long would it take to remove the graveyard from the house? The wharf? Maybe Callie wouldn't want to live there now.

Piper looked at Maverick. Concerned. She knew they were getting close to the place where he found Rex in the river. That would be tough. All of this would be tough for them. It's not simple to dust off trauma and step into life again. Scars and all.

Maverick stared at the road trying not to look at the river. But he still saw the dark water in his mind. And the car. He pushed the thoughts away knowing this was the hardest part for all of them.

But a few moments later they saw cars. Trucks. People. And Maverick rolled to a stop at the spot where Rex's body had laid. He swallowed hard as his eyes burned. Someone had planted a magnolia tree in the same spot.

Adam got out of the car. So did Raven and Piper. Then Maverick. And people were everywhere. The wharf was freshly cleaned and decorated with new tropical plants. There were yellow ribbons on the mailbox.

And up the hill there were trucks and men working in the barn. Women coming out of Adam's house. At Raven's place there were carpenter trucks. A glass company. A crime scene cleanup crew. And in the middle of it all sat Jax's food truck and picnic tables.

Raven burst into tears. Happy ones. Grateful ones. Someone rescued them. Adam smiled and took her hand. They walked uphill. Maverick and Piper followed. Hearts lighter because people cared. It truly made all the difference in the world.

From the food truck Lexi saw them coming. She stepped out. Watching them. Fighting tears for them and Rex. And then she just ran to meet them. Others saw them coming too. And in no time, everyone welcomed them home.

***

Raven was amazed when she walked on her porch. They were just hanging a new door in place. Prettier than the old one. And all the shattered glass and wood on the floor was gone. And the furniture was back in place. A new chair sat where Gabrielle had been. A nice rocker for the new momma with a pretty, pink balloon that said congratulations. What a thoughtful touch.

Raven and Piper walked to the staircase. The crime scene cleanup crew had just finished. The floor had been steam cleaned. Rugs thrown out. Special cleaners stripped organic material from everywhere. The walls all around the stairs would need to be repainted because of the cleansers, but even that wasn't strikingly obvious.

Piper touched the railing where the knife had cut into the wood.

Raven said, "That can stay there. If anyone doubts that you're tough, tell them I have proof."

Piper hugged her. "We're all tough."

Then Raven headed to the front porch where the final act had begun. But there was no blood. No cracked railing. No trampled flower beds. No broken drone. Just a new rug and pretty flowers.

But then she thought about the chase to the wharf. The costume. And the reason for it all. She headed to the kitchen.

Piper said, "What's wrong?"

"Can you get someone to light the fire pit for me?"

Piper called Adam at the barn.

Raven grabbed a trash bag and ran upstairs. She opened the hope chest and pulled out all the dance costumes, heels, and workout gear from the past. Anything from her time with Zack went in the bag. She checked her closet too.

Adam came into the bedroom. Trying to grasp what was happening, he said, "Raven? Why do you need the fire pit?"

His question didn't even register. She just said, "Is there anything left in my office relating to Zack or the case?"

He checked. "A few things. The FBI took most of it along with the guns."

She went to her office studio. Several things were still taped on the mirror wall. A few stacks of things on the table. Unread faxes in the machine.

She started shoving it in the trash bag. Getting the point, Adam helped her. And in a few minutes, her office looked like it did before.

He hauled the extra tables and chairs outside. She gathered all the theatrical makeup out of the kitchen and added it to the trash. She checked the hall bath. A bag of dance makeup was there. It went in the trash. And the clothes her and Gabrielle had on when Zack broke in went in the trash.

Back in the den she looked around. Anything Zack used went in the trash. Even the chair he sat on went out the new door. And finally, she was done. She headed to the fire pit with the chair and bulging trash bag.

Adam tried to help but she shook her head no. Piper and Maverick watched the mission she was on. Volunteers stopped to watch her drag the items to the fire.

But Adam knew what she was doing. Go for it, baby.

The fire was roaring when Raven reached it. She threw the chair in. Sparks flew. And piece by piece she erased Zack from her life. The silver fringe costume. The green silk. The red siren one. The black. The purple. And lots more. All of them sizzled in the fire. Sparkling. Burning. Melting. Disappearing like the wicked witch in the Wizard of Oz.

Then the shoes. The makeup. The investigation papers. And when there was nothing left, she threw the trash bag in too. Chest heaving, she watched it burn. And then it was just the fire. Zack was gone.

Raven glanced at Adam.

He began to clap. And everyone else began to clap.

Smiling, she ran and jumped. He caught her again. He always would.

***

An hour later, all the volunteers were gone. Adam and Raven waved as Maverick drove Piper home to an apartment she hadn't even slept in yet.

***

Adam said, "Is there anything else you want to do? Anything at all."

Raven was quiet for a second, and without looking at him, said, "You watched me dance with Zack."

He expected this conversation, and said, "I did."

"It wasn't real."

"I know."

Facing him, she said, "Give me words, Adam. You watched what I did. How did you know?"

He tilted her face to his. "It was easy. One, because you are a rescuer by heart - saving is what you do – especially with those you love. Two, because I've seen pictures of the damage you can inflict when you are free to defend yourself.

But mostly, Raven, mostly, because I know you. And I know you would do anything to come home to me and Lance…just like I prayed you would. That was all that mattered."

She felt relief hearing it - not just knowing it, and whispered, "Ok. Now…before we go get Lance, I need one more thing, Adam. Something big."

"Anything."

"Ride me on your stallion."

He knew what she meant, and the image flashed across his mind. Touching her cut lip softly, he said, "I would love to…but…are you sure you are ready for that? Today was—"

"No. Listen to me…" She grabbed his shirt and said, "I need you to burn him off me, Adam. His smell. His touch. His kiss. His passion. You are my fire pit. Burn me."

Kissing her, he carried her to the barn. Glancing at the sky, he knew they had an hour of dusk. He pulled out the eager stallion. Raven stripped naked. And all he could see was her beauty through the bruises.

He kissed her. Wild. Hot. He lifted her to the blanket. No saddle. And leaving his clothes behind, he mounted behind her, pulling her against him. Tight. Intimate already. The stallion ran toward the trees as Adam let the burn take them. And in the late afternoon shadows, he made sure Raven knew there was no other touch but his. Ever.

***

At her flat in downtown Lake Charles, Piper sat at a large wooden snack bar with a cup of coffee that had long grown cold. In silence, dressed in thin baggy low-rise warmups and a crop top, she filled out her crime report while it was fresh in her mind. Details meant everything.

She was glad almost half of the attack was on video. Except for the part where she was half naked and sexually assaulted for the world to see. Thinking about it made her shoulders tight and she already hurt.

Walking to the windows, she watched cars pass. Heard laughter. And could see the lake in the distance. Even the tall Interstate 10 bridge. It was amazing how life absorbs things like today and moves on with barely a hiccup. Poof. Next scene.

She looked at the stacks of boxes still packed. Why unpack them just to move again?

Someone knocked.

It had to be Maverick. No one else knew where she lived. Heck. No one else even knew her. She walked barefoot to the door aware that they had gone from sexual attraction to…something else…in one vicious morning.

Another knock.

Maverick said, "It's me."

Smiling a little, she opened the door. He looked tired but gorgeous. Blonde hair falling in his blue eyes. Shadow beard. Perfect lips.

She said, "Luckily I know who me is."

He smiled back, noticing how beautiful she was. Her face. Her body. He said, "I'm glad you know me too. Do you mind a little company? I'm wound so tight my string's about to pop."

"Sure. Come in. I am too." She headed to the kitchen. "You want coffee?"

Following her, he said, "No. I brought wine."

262

"You don't look like a wine guy."

"I'm not."

"Then why did you bring it?"

"Because I figured frozen margaritas would melt."

She laughed and realized she needed that.

He noticed the forms on the counter and said, "That won't help you unwind."

She shrugged. He saw the weariness, mixed with beauty, with an unhealthy dose of cuts and bruises.

He said, "You missed your spa day. Let me help. I need to do something besides feel guilty I left y'all behind."

"Maverick—"

"Don't give me all the reasons I shouldn't feel guilty. You would too."

"I know. I do. But we can't change it."

He pointed to the green velvet sofa that didn't look like it had ever been sat on, and said, "I would offer to rub your shoulders but that might hurt. How about letting me rub your feet?"

"That will make you feel better?"

"Serving you will make me feel better."

She walked toward the sofa and said, "Tell you what, if you rub my shoulders for a while…very softly, I'll go with you for a margarita if I'm still awake."

He smiled and followed her. She pointed. He sat. She sat on the floor between his legs and leaned back.

His warm hands touched her shoulders and he said, "Tell me if I hurt you."

"You'll know if I hurt you back."

He laughed and felt better already.

They didn't talk as he softly slid his hands up and down her neck. Across her shoulders. And down her arms. She began to relax as much from his presence as the gentle rhythmic motion. So did he. Then she began to nod. Then doze. She fought it.

He said, "Lay down. Please. Give me your feet."

And in minutes, she was on the sofa, feet in his lap, sound asleep. Twenty minutes later, he laid his head back and was out.

***

On the river, Raven bathed Lance while Adam went outside to meet the men returning the truck and dogs. She had just finished dressing him when she heard Adam shut the door. The dog's toenails clicking on the floor and woofs of joy at being home sent Lance screaming out of the bathroom.

He met them on the stairs where they were sniffing frantically and whining. It might be clean, but they knew death had been there. Adam glanced at Raven. They knew the crazy moments would stop at some point. Life was already beautiful again.

Adam said, "Lance, do you want to watch a movie?"

"PAW Patrol! PAW Patrol!" was the thrilled response.

As Adam got the movie ready, Raven threw pillows and blankets on the floor. Screaming in delight, Lance dove in. Simba joined him as the bigger dogs settled close by. Adam laid by Raven. Lance slid in the middle of them.

Raven said, "You tell him."

Adam smoothed Lance's hair out of his flushed face, and said, "We have a surprise for you."

"A pony?"

Chuckling, Adam said, "Not tonight. It's something else."

"A bike?"

Adam looked at Raven and said, "We know where we fit in the totem pole of value."

She laughed. Kid truth.

Adam said, "Mommy and I got married."

"What's married?"

They showed him their rings. Adam said, "We are a family now. A mommy and a—"

Lance knew what came next and eyes wide, he whispered, "A daddy."

Raven's throat locked with emotion. Her heart hurt.

Adam said, "Yes."

"My daddy?"

Adam's eyes burned as he pulled him into a hug and said, "Forever and ever. I love you very much."

Lance touched his face and said, "I love you, Daddy. What about Mommy?"

"Oh, I love Mommy very much."

"Is she both of ours?"

Raven smiled as Adam said, "She is."

"So, can I have a pony now? And twin sisters instead of a bike?"

264

Adam smiled and said, "We're working on it. How about the movie for now?"

His agreement was scrambling over them to curl up with Simba. Adam pulled Raven against him. And before long, they were all asleep.

Chapter 29

Thanksgiving

Three days later, Lexi was directing the men as they carried in heated serving dishes to Raven. The new kitchen at Adam's place was quickly filling up with a Thanksgiving feast on a warm Louisiana day. A wearing shorts warm day.

But the heat wouldn't stop any of them from enjoying the roast turkey and gravy. Beef roast with au jus gravy. Cornbread dressing. Rice dressing. Candied yams. Green bean casserole. Sweet corn cooked with butter, bacon, and onions. Along with cranberry salad, plus traditional pies, and melt in your mouth yeast rolls. Nothing was considered healthy or low calorie. But it was considered delicious and worth every bite for a day or two. Or three depending on the level of leftovers.

Dakota, Gabrielle, and baby Skye were there. Piper too. And Maverick. Sean and Samantha had made it in from Virginia. Even the new Quest airboat driver, Jake, was there – already a part of the family. Lance ran up and down the new stairs.

And Steel was there, handsome in silver gray pinstripe slacks and a black dress shirt. He looked strong and healthy after being dismissed from the hospital late yesterday – still arguing over his ridiculous lifting limitations.

But Raven professionally explained that he had a lot of stitches in his chest along with the massive bruising. And Callie promised him she would reward him. Today. And he wanted that reward like he'd never wanted anything. He glanced at the hall. She was getting dressed for their after-lunch wedding.

A few minutes later Steel heard a door open and close, then the click of heels. Callie rounded the corner, and there was no one else in the room for Steel. She was gorgeous in a backless white dress that hit above her knees with a fluttery skirt. His eyes roamed long golden legs that ended in very high heels strapped at the ankles.

Callie's pale green eyes sparkled like tinted crystal as she neared him, raising red lips to his. He took what she offered as wolf-whistles and catcalls filled the room.

And unconcerned that they were the focus of everyone, Steel said softly, "Marry me now, Callie. Right now. I don't want to wait another minute."

Callie smiled, glancing at Raven and Adam.

Raven said, "Oh, gosh, yes! Right, Adam?"

Adam was already heading for his Bible. And in minutes, Adam officiated the ceremony.

And after brief congratulations, the couple left for the barn apartment. The keys for the house they didn't know they owned were in the pile of unopened gifts.

Piper watched them from the window. She was thrilled for Steel and Callie. It had been such a close call for them.

She said, "It's a shame she didn't get to wear her dress very long."

Dakota snorted and laughed. Gabrielle elbowed him, giggling.

Shocked, Raven said, "Piper..."

Turning, Piper said, "I'm not being crude. She was gorgeous. I'm just making a casual observation. I mean, she had the dress on for what? Sixteen minutes?"

Sean and Samantha were still locked in silent laughter after the first comment.

Laughing, Adam said, "Raven...personally, I think Steel would appreciate the comment."

Raven said, "But in a minute he's going to realize he can't carry her over the threshold!"

"And then the dress will come off faster, and you know it."

Samantha fell over on the sofa still laughing, wheezing now.

The new employee, Jake, walked out on the porch trying not to laugh and get fired. Steel was his boss.

Maverick asked conversationally, "Are all your family holidays like this?"

***

At the barn, Steel turned off the engine, kissed Callie, and said, "Wait right there."

She hurriedly slid out anyway and walked to meet him. Surprised she hadn't waited, he instinctively reached down to pick her up. And at that point realized he couldn't carry her up the steps or over the threshold.

Callie had prepared for this challenge and kissed him. She slid her fingers inside his waistband and said, "I have something for you. Watch…"

She climbed a couple of steps and spun, letting her skirt fly up. No panties. Steel went up in flames and joined her on the stairs, hands reaching under her skirt. She gasped as he…encouraged her up the stairs…one hot step at a time.

They were both breathless by the time they reached the door. Her heels landed somewhere in the hay below. Her dress was on the stairs. His zipper dropped. His pants. And he backed her toward the nearest furniture. A reclining piece of exercise equipment. He sat, guiding her to his lap, and Callie gave him what she had never given anyone.

***

Back at the house, Adam said the blessing, and everyone dipped their plates way too full. Laughter, conversation, and stories rounded the table for a good while. They all had a lot to be grateful for.

Later, the men headed outside – staying well away from the barn. The women stayed inside. They all wanted to talk about the attack but not in front of each other.

Samantha understood what being a victim was like. That's why she was an FBI agent in training at Quantico. But she had been unable to talk with them or be a part of the investigation, so she asked questions from their point of view. And in no time was impressed at the strength and calculating wisdom they applied under the circumstances.

Thinking about the burning of all the dance costumes, Samantha said, "Raven, if you don't mind me asking, do you think you will be able to dance again? I know it means…"

"Yes. Though not in competition or exhibition dance. And I know I will never dance to that Alicia Keys song again. Or listen to it. And that…really…just…" and not finding another word that fit, said, "Pisses me off since I loved that song."

With a laugh they high fived. Who doesn't love *Fallin'*.

Then Samantha said, "The academy is supposed to let the cadets watch the drone video for training purposes next week. Are you good with that?"

Piper answered first. "I'm not thrilled about them studying it in slow motion with me half naked, but it flashed on the national news anyway with blocked out portions. And cadets have got to learn how to improvise and use what they have as a weapon. It is what it is."

Gabrielle said, "I've already peed and made a mess on national television, why not."

They laughed for a while.

Then it was Raven's turn. She grimaced and said, "I know…I know it's important, Samantha. But then I will meet them at your graduation in the spring. I wonder how many will wonder if I was acting during the dance?"

Samantha said, "Honestly, a few will see your smoking hot beauty and think about the dance. But then they'll see Adam and remember how it ended – and keep their mouth shut."

Raven smiled. That worked.

Gabrielle said, "Ok, let's lighten up. It's time to talk about handsome men. Heroes. Passion. And lots of yummy things. You know, like Dakota."

Samantha said, "You wish. It's Sean."

Raven said, "In your dreams. It's Adam."

Piper drawled and said, "Well… it sounds like all the hot men are taken. I guess we need to change the subject."

Raven said, "You're the only single one left. That leads us to Maverick. Talk."

"Thank you for the insult. And no."

Samantha said, "Oh, come on, he wants to pour whip cream on you and have dessert."

Laughing, Piper said, "What is wrong with you? I'm nowhere near ready for that."

"Oh, chill out. It's called stirring the pot."

"Well, *get out* of the kitchen."

They laughed. And then waited as Piper quieted and grew thoughtful. She said, "What started as a spicy chemistry with Maverick…is now in the aftermath of Monday. It's suddenly a different kind of something. We're getting beyond what happened and now there's respect. Trust. A closeness. But…you know I'm moving…somewhere. And I haven't decided anything about anything."

Gabrielle responded softly as she rocked Skye, "You know, I met Dakota right after college graduation. Then wasn't the time for us. But we connected again later. Now look at us." She touched her daughter's nose, point made.

Piper remembered those connections, and said, "Tell me again, Gabrielle, how many killers were after you?"

"Six. But who's counting?"

Boom. Mic drop.

***

Outside, most of the men headed to the wharf. Jake took the dogs for a run on the four-wheeler.

Adam said, "I have a proposition Dakota and Sean. And don't stress, Maverick. It's not private."

Maverick said, "I'll still take a walk."

Dakota said, "Sit."

As Maverick sat on a deck chair, Adam said, "I bought an island. Raven and I are going there for our honeymoon mid-December."

Dakota fist pumped. "Yes!"

Sean calmly asked, "What kind of island?"

Maverick interrupted and said, "Is no one, but me, shocked that he bought an island? Who buys an island?"

Dakota said, "People that can afford them."

Adam laughed.

Sean said, "Quit laughing at Maverick and answer my question."

Adam pulled up pictures on his phone and passed it around. "It's in the Bahamas. One hundred forty-four acres of secluded, partially developed forests, hills, and white sand beaches. There's a small runway. A large beach house and several cottages."

Sean said, "What did it cost you?"

"Eighteen mil."

"Million?" Maverick asked incredulously.

Dakota said, "We aren't weapons dealers, Maverick. Our family is wealthy."

"That isn't wealthy. That's rich."

"A play on words. Continue, Adam."

"So…are y'all interested in a family partnership? I won't be there often enough to make the improvements that would be impressive. I'd rather it be used. Enjoyed. We can schedule to use it privately or share it for group vacations."

270

Sean said, "I'm in. But I've got to pay a third, otherwise, I'll feel beholden, and I hate that."

Maverick said, "It'll only cost you six mil to get rid of those beholden feelings."

Laughing, Dakota said, "Me too. I'm in with six mil…even though I'm not feeling beholden."

Without humor Maverick looked at the Nash brothers having a good laugh at his financially limited expense. Then something occurred to him. He said with a casual warning, "If the FBI ever looks up my checking and savings account balances and I find out, the fight is on."

Adam said, "I wouldn't."

"I believe that. But Dakota and Sean would. Look at them. They probably already have."

Dakota tried to look insulted. Sean went for the innocent look. Though of course he'd already run the background checks. Financial included. Piper was family.

Chapter 30

Reception

Adam zipped his tuxedo pants. They were black. Perfectly snug. He smiled as Raven watched him in the mirror. He glanced at her long bare legs in heels as she leaned closer to put on lipstick. This was his favorite part of getting dressed.

Raven finished the last coat of lipstick. Deep red. And rotated her hips like a belly dancer to capture his attention. His gaze quickly returned to hers as he buttoned his silk shirt.

He said, "What can I say? You are beautiful from your head to your toe. Off the chart sexy."

Turning to face him, her red hair entwined in a fancy braid with a tiny ribbon of flowers, she smiled and said, "Then we must be on the same chart."

He invaded her space, inhaling her scent, and felt the familiar rush of love and desire. He said, "I know the limousine will be here soon, but I have something for you before you dress. I'll be right back."

He returned with a white satin box with a black bow. Very elegant. He said, "I wanted you to have this for tonight."

Raven could tell it was jewelry. Glancing at him with a smile, she opened it. And gasped. Emeralds. Lots of them. Made into a fabulous choker and matching earrings.

She whispered, "Adam…it's—"

He said, "Not nearly as gorgeous as you. Let me put it on for you."

Awed at the beauty of it, she watched him clasp the choker. Then she slipped on the earrings. Posing in delight, then kissing him, she said, "I love it, really love it. Surely, I can wear an emerald choker every day?"

He chuckled, then watched her open a vanity drawer. She handed him a small gift box. No bow. Just white velvet. He opened it. And it was empty.

Raven touched her belly.

Adam whispered, "Raven…" and drew her face to his and kissed her. Sweeter than honey. Softer than silk. He slid his hand over her belly. And then excitement took over as they laughed, and he swung her around.

Someone knocked on the door.

Callie said, "Sorry to intrude, just letting you know that the limo is here."

Raven said, "Thank you! We won't be long."

Adam said, "I haven't seen your dress. Where is it?"

"Look in the back left corner of my closet, please. It's the long black bag."

He hooked the bag over the edge of the door. She unzipped it, sliding the dress off the hanger, and held it in front of her.

It was a one shouldered white chiffon gown covered in sparkling raised flowers. Different colors. Ethereal. Like something a fairy queen would wear.

Adam touched it. "Baby…it's beautiful. I've never seen anything like it. Your mom wore this?"

"Yes. Dad had it made for her in Ireland."

He held the dress as she unzipped, then stepped into it. He zipped it up.

She turned around, flaring the train, and smiled at him. And just like that, emotion slammed Adam. His heart hurt. He swallowed, loving her too much to speak a single word.

Wrapping her arms around him, she said, "And that, Adam, is the compliment of a lifetime. I'll never forget."

***

Downstairs, Steel, Callie, Lance, and Raven's parents waited. They heard them coming and looked up as they reached the staircase.

Raven's parents stared at the shine of their daughter's beauty. Her Dad saw the Native American shape and features of his wife, with her quiet depth and stunning strength. Her mom saw the Irish coloring of her husband, complete with his passion and integrity. They grabbed hands. Their daughter was a magnificent woman. Admired. Honorable. And loved and adored by her husband.

A few feet away, Callie smiled at the spectacular couple she loved and felt happy tears escape. Steel squeezed her. Totally healed now. His strength restored.

And Lance gasped, in the beautiful wonder of a child as he ran upstairs. "Mommy, are you a Disney princess?"

Adam picked him up, and Raven said, "Tonight I am, sweetie. Just for you and Daddy."

Adam said, "And we have a surprise for you."

"A pony?"

Raven laughed, and said, "How about a brother or sister?"

And they heard the thrilled gasps below.

Lance said, "Why can't I have both?"

Raven said, "Well..."

"Where do you get the babies?"

Adam said, "God gives them to us."

Smiling, Lance said, "Oh! Can you just tell him I need two?"

***

They reached the Lake Charles Civic Center at five p.m.

Brightly lit Christmas decorations were everywhere. The building. The grounds. The park. And even along Shell Beach Drive that bordered the lake. Lake Charles at its most beautiful.

Adam escorted Raven inside.

On the second floor, the Mezzanine, a central area accessed by multiple staircases from the balcony, was awash with snow flocked Christmas trees and white lights. A flash of winter with snow scenes. Massive chandeliers glittered from above. Round tables were strategically placed around the room. Cozy. Creative. And a dance floor filled the center.

Adam and Raven looked over the balcony at their family and friends below.

Dakota and Gabrielle were here with her parents.

Adam's parents had flown in yesterday and spent the night with Dakota and Gabrielle to see their new granddaughter.

Sean and Samantha were in from Quantico, but they had to return tomorrow.

Angel and Jade made it. They had just returned from their honeymoon.

Piper arrived with Maverick.

Lexi, chef extraordinaire, rode with Jake, the new driver.

Steel and Callie watched Lance in the kiddie winter wonderland just for him.

FBI Director Washington came. Maverick and Rex's captain too. The helicopter pilot came with a few FBI agents and U.S. Marshals. The mayor

274

and sheriff came. A few neighbors. And Park Ranger Dubois who had recovered with only a scar.

Smiling, Raven said, "Thank you for this, Adam. It's perfect."

Tilting her chin, he kissed her softly. "It's simply your backdrop, Raven. You're the star."

"You spoil me."

"I've barely begun."

"Speaking of...when are you going to tell me about the island?"

"I'm not. I'm going to show you."

"When will we get there?"

"After midnight. It'll be late. But we have fifteen days...and fourteen nights...to explore and dive as deep as we want. Any way we want."

She whispered, "I don't think the ocean is on your mind at all."

"It's not."

They heard Lance's laughter ring out.

Smiling at their son, Adam said, "That's our cue."

He texted Gabrielle's dad – their favorite singer - who headed to the microphone. Then they walked to the top of the staircase and paused.

The romantic lyrics of *Amazed* began.

Standing, everyone turned to the only staircase wrapped in lights. Awe filled gasps echoed through the room at the shockingly beautiful couple descending to join them. Fair and dark. Vibrant and sensual. Wildly in love.

Smiling at each other, Adam and Raven knew that some moments in life were beautiful flashes. Some become cherished memories. Some left passionate imprints. And some were intricately etched in time with the chisel of love. Like now.

As they reached the last stair, Adam led her to the dance floor, where in each other's arms, the love song played.

Then cheers erupted, and the wedding reception began. The couple greeted their guests. Took pictures. Cut the cake. Then the caterer served an assortment of Louisiana specialties. Crawfish Etouffee. Steak with creamy Cajun shrimp sauce. A trio of fried seafood: catfish, shrimp, and oysters. Along with boiled shrimp and dipping sauce.

After dinner, love songs filled the air, and it was time for dancing.

Dakota dipped Gabrielle on the dance floor, then pulled her back in his arms. He said, "Have I mentioned that you look fabulous in that gold dress?"

Raising her lips for a kiss, she said, "A few times. Thank you. I'm just glad our bodies fit together again now that Skye—"

He groaned, pulling her hips closer. "Don't remind me. I want to fit together like you can't imagine."

She whispered, "But I can…"

"How much longer do we have to abstain?"

She laughed. "There's no way you've forgotten."

"Smart woman. Three long weeks."

"And yet…think how creative you've already been."

He smiled. She was right about that.

***

Piper caught Maverick's gaze on her. Again. He looked incredible tonight in his suit. Dark blue with turquoise pinstripes. Silk shirt fitting his body. No tie. But it was the hungry look that set it off.

Maverick knew Piper was attracted to him. Deeply. But she wasn't giving him anything romantic beyond that…except for spectacular companionship. Verbal sparring. Intensity. Working out at the gym. Meals together. Along with arguments and debates. They were great together. But not even a single kiss since the attack.

But looking at her tonight in red velvet was gut wrenching. Healed and whole now, her beauty was on display. And the barely latched lid on his passion - began to hiss and sputter threatening to boil over. He pulled his chair closer, and her knee touched the inside of his thigh.

Piper wasn't surprised at his move, but played it off, and said, "Do you want to sit in my lap?"

"I'd rather you sit in mine. But for now, let's dance."

Their gazes met.

In answer, Maverick stood, looking down at her. He touched her neck. And even though Piper knew there would be repercussions to being in his arms any night – much less a romantic night like this - she joined him.

And in a few steps, he slid arms around her on the dance floor, guiding her closer. Knowing his intention, she stopped, leaving a tiny bit of space between them. His sexy grin flashed. He wasn't having any of that and pulled her against him.

Piper felt the delicious heat of their bodies touching, and said, "We shouldn't—"

"We should. We are long past should. Give me this dance, Piper. You know I'm moving tomorrow, and I miss you already. And you are going to miss me even though you won't say it."

She knew she would and slid her arms around his neck. Touching his hair. Inhaling his cologne. And heard him groan as her chest pressed against his, completing the embrace. Maverick's hand spread across her lower back as he kissed her ear, whispering her name. Squeezing her. Piper felt his hunger. And the sensation of his hot breath felt so good. She turned her lips toward his neck and brushed them against his skin.

And his mouth covered hers.

Before the song ended, he said, "Stay in touch with me, Piper. Don't ghost me. This thing between us is not over."

***

Sean danced sensually with Samantha. She loved it. He held her hip with one hand, an obvious intimacy indicator. And his other hand, held the back of her neck, fingers in her hair. Possessive. And he led with his body. It made her knees weak every single time they danced slow.

He said, "I miss us not being at home alone for the weekends."

"I know. Me too. Having to share you for two weekends in one month is hard."

His breath brushed her ear. "Exactly."

The sizzle climbed her legs. "Sean…"

"I feel you. But we won't be apart much longer. In a couple of months, you'll graduate. And we'll finally be together like newlyweds should. Then we'll get assigned and move. A steady diet of wildfire passion and the FBI. Our new life."

***

Adam and Raven visited each table of guests. Danced. And spent time watching Lance play in his winter wonderland. But it was getting late.

Callie said, "Raven, why don't Steel and I leave a little early and take him home? He's played hard and will be asleep before we leave the parking lot."

"Thanks, Callie. And are you sure Lance isn't too much to handle for ten days? We won't be back till Christmas Eve."

"I had a classroom full of first graders for years. I've got this! Besides, your parents will be there. And Lexie will be staying overnight till you return. And Jake is there to help with anything we need. Go enjoy your honeymoon. We will keep in touch."

Adam walked up carrying Lance, and said, "Raven, maybe we should make our announcement before he's too tired. He is going to sleep good tonight."

***

The music faded to silence, and the guests watched the young family walk to the center of the dance floor.

Adam said, "Raven and I wanted to thank all of you for coming tonight to celebrate with us. It's hard to believe that just a little over three weeks ago, in the middle of a firestorm of events, this gorgeous woman took a wild boat ride to the Civic Center to marry me. No bouquet. No wedding dress. No decorations. Just us and a fast boat."

Everyone laughed. But Adam and Raven smiled at each other. That had been an incredible boat ride.

Continuing, he said, "The wonder that her and Lance have brought into my life has been more than I could ask or imagine. And she is my dream come true. Beyond beautiful. She's intelligent. Brave. And lest we forget - the hottest dancer around."

The guests laughed as Raven groaned and covered her face. Cheeks bright pink.

Adam kissed her and said, "And on that perfect segue, we have an announcement to share before the last dance."

Raven handed a microphone to Lance, who was delighted - breathing, blowing, and making all sorts of exciting sounds in it.

Adam said, "Lance."

Excited, Lance said, "Daddy! Look what Momma gave me to play with."

"I see that. Now, would you tell everyone what you want God to bring you?"

"Twins! And a pony!

There was no last dance. Just congratulations.

***

Less than an hour later, Adam and Raven were in the limo headed to the airport. They had a nine-thirty flight to Nassau. Gone was their wedding attire. Now they were dressed as tropical honeymooners.

278

Adam texted the pilot they were on the way while Raven called Callie with one last instruction for Lance. But Raven's call clearly lasted too long based on the unmistakable look in Adam's eyes. She winked, and looked him over appreciatively, as she listened to Callie.

His tall, dark, and handsomeness was sexy in white linen pants and a thin button up top. Soft. Airy. Leather sandals and a gold bracelet. Where had this Adam come from?

Adam looked at Raven in a floral sundress. Short. Enticing. And she still wore the emerald choker. Her red hair draped around her. Roman sandals laced up her calves. She slid a hand on his thigh.

He met her gaze.

She whispered, "One minute…"

He smiled and pulled her on his lap. No minutes. Taking the phone, he said, "Bye Callie…" and Raven's mouth disappeared under his hungry one.

In no time they were at the airport.

Chapter 31

The Island

Raven stared at the plane as they got out of the limo. "I can't believe you hired a private jet."

Adam smiled as he escorted her to the steps. "Baby, I want you to myself. I bought an island. I hired a plane. And though I may still get a pilot's license in the future, tonight my hands are free. And you're going to be very glad about that."

She laughed as he hurried her on board.

The captain met them as they entered. "Welcome aboard, Mr. Nash. Everything is prepared as you requested."

Adam shook his hand and said, "Thank you, Captain. Call me Adam. And this is my wife, Raven. And please, informal is fine. How long until we reach Nassau?"

The captain smiled at Raven and said, "Evening, ma'am." Glancing at Adam, he said, "We should arrive at one a.m. eastern time. Your air taxi will be waiting to fly you to your destination."

"Thanks again, Captain."

"Yes, Sir. And it's a beautiful night for a flight to the Bahamas. If you need anything at all, let us know. My co-pilot assists as a flight assistant. Other than that, you won't be disturbed except for departure and arrival announcements."

Adam gave Raven a tour of the plane as the luggage was loaded.

There were multiple cream-colored leather chairs. Roomy recliners with cup holders, chargeable phone holders, and attached, mahogany adjustable tables. Two small sofas. Designer carpet that made you feel like you were walking on art. And the restroom was three times the size of a commercial airliner with a shower. Vanity. And luxury robes. Next door was a changing room.

They heard the plane door close and latch.

By the time they reached the main cabin, the captain had disappeared into the cockpit. A large television came on with all the available options for their viewing pleasure. Their luggage was stacked neatly in a closet rack. And a mini kitchen was stocked with catering trays.

Adam pointed to the chairs and said, "We might want to get settled for takeoff. It won't take them long."

A few minutes later, PLEASE BUCKLE UP appeared on the television.

The captain announced, "We will be taxiing to the runway in ten minutes. Please buckle up and enjoy your flight."

Once they were ready for takeoff, Adam said, "Do you like to travel?"

"I do! The furthest has been Ireland. But packing up to move to Louisiana was by far my biggest adventure. I wouldn't call myself a traveler by any means…but you sure look like one."

"I love traveling. Survivalist hikes and mission trips were most of it. But I was free to roam the world. I don't usually travel in a private jet though. Usually, first class on commercial airliners was my norm. At least until I reached a jungle, desert, safari, mountain range, or mission field. Then it became sweating or freezing without luxury."

"It sounds exciting and wild. And it's so easy to imagine you doing it. I mean, since your Brazilian accident, I've seen you face to face with a shark. Fighting an alligator. Speeding in boats. Shooting bow and arrows. And dangling from a helicopter."

"Says the woman with a whole different set of skills, and a body to kill for."

Gasping, she said, "You did not say that!"

"Baby let's face it; we are an adventure. Both of us. You're breaking free from the past filled with a fabulous fire. The competition dance gave you an outlet, but you outgrew it even more powerful than before. Then we met. And we burn like a raging inferno. Then what about the warrior in you? Instinct? Everything about you is wild and magnificent."

She thanked him with a kiss, then said, "Is there anything else I don't know about you? You know everything about me."

"I am what you see. I've been to different locations. Had different experiences. That's all. Our world has been small since we've been together, but that's over. The island is just the beginning. We're going to make love in all kinds of destinations. And raise children of adventure – in between rescuing people back home."

The jet engines revved up.

A second later the plane screamed down the runway. And in a flash, they were climbing into the starry night sky over the Gulf of Mexico…headed to paradise.

***

After one a.m., the captain announced they would be descending into Nassau.

Adam helped Raven put her sandals back on. Licked her leg. Kissed her swollen lips. And they both knew their passion was hot enough to melt steel. Adam moaned when he sat. Adjusted himself. Their gazes met.

They were about to light their island up.

They landed in the Bahamas. The air taxi was waiting, ready for the one-hour flight. Adam and the much less formal retired marine pilot, with the nickname Killer, loaded the bags into the much smaller six-seater plane.

Raven glanced at Adam. Killer? Really?

Killer said, "Adam, I heard about you wanting a pilot license. Sit up here with me for a free lesson. And Raven, make yourself comfortable. If you sit in the middle, you can pretty much see what we see. Not that you'll see much in the dark, but come morning, you are going to be tripping at the beauty of your island."

Adam said, "What kind of landing lights are on the island?"

"Solar with battery backup. If one doesn't work, the other will. And the groundskeeper and housekeeper will be at the landing strip ready to return with me. I understand they have the house and property ready for you. Do you need them to tour with you before I leave?"

"No, thanks. I have a video of the house and property. And a Jeep will be there for us. I just need you there to pick us up at eight p.m. on December 23."

"Will do."

Adam said, "So, why do they call you Killer?"

Killer laughed. "It's kind of late for that question. And you better buckle up. This ain't the big jet."

About an hour later, Adam and Raven watched through the darkness the row of runway lights that Killer pointed to up ahead.

He said, "It's a great place. Well kept. Beautiful beaches. Amazing fishing and diving. Trails. Lagoons. Forests. There are tons of things to do. But I'm sure you know that since you bought it. And remember, when you need supplies, message me on the satellite phone. It'll cost you, but I'll come."

Adam said, "I appreciate that. I'll pay a marine any day for help."

Killer gave him a thumbs up.

Raven said, "What animals might be on the island?"

"Big stuff, probably iguanas and pigs. Small stuff, maybe parrots, flamingoes, racoons, snakes, spiders including tarantulas, and frogs. Insects. Keep repellant. And anything and everything swims in the ocean from sea horses to whales."

Adam and Raven smiled at each other. Their island. And they watched the landing strip get closer and closer till the wheels touched down quietly on the dirt lane. And it was a fairly smooth landing considering they were on a dot in the Atlantic Ocean.

They could see water to the right, and trees to the left, as Killer rolled to a stop by a wooden building. A man and woman waited next to a Jeep with the headlights on.

The man who had obviously been in lots of sun opened the door. Smiling, Adam jumped down and shook his hand, then helped Raven down.

After quick greetings, Adam helped load their luggage in the Jeep while Raven thanked everyone. And in a few minutes the plane headed back down the runway and disappeared into the darkness.

***

It was windy as Adam and Raven faced each other. The sound of ocean waves was loud. Exciting. The smell of salt and tropical plants was heady. Romantic. And they smiled – finally alone.

He picked her up, spinning her around as they laughed. Kissed. And it quickly got hotter. Flaming. And just that fast…they were right back where they had been on the big jet…melting steel.

Climbing in the Jeep, they headed for the house lights shining through the trees.

Raven watched Adam drive. Wind whipping his long hair. He was in his element. Wild and sexy, with adventure in his blood. Beautiful.

Smiling at her, he pulled his shirt over his head. The wind took it. And the look he gave her was thrilling. She groaned, aching.

A few moments later, he parked at the side of the house closest to the beach. He grabbed the large duffel bag and led her to a lovely veranda that was lit with tiny white lights.

He smiled, as Raven gasped when they rounded the corner. It was magical. An open bedroom faced the ocean. Glass walls. White billowy drapes and bed linen fluttered in the breeze.

She spun around, arms opened wide, and said, "Adam…"

Smiling, he pulled her in his arms, and said, "It is the perfect backdrop for you. And while we will explore every inch of this island tomorrow, tonight, I have other plans for us. A surprise."

He kissed her, and said, "And I don't want you to see anything yet. So, will you close your eyes and let me get you ready?"

"I'll do anything you want."

His kiss was hot in response, and her eyes closed.

She listened. The duffel bag unzipped, and things rustled. Then Adam kissed her shoulder and lowered the straps of her dress. It pooled at her feet. The breeze embraced every inch of her skin. He groaned and kissed her neck. Their bare chests touched.

Trailing his lips down, he knelt and untied her sandals and tossed them aside. Then ran his fingers along the rim of her panties. His hot breath touched her stomach as he slowly slid them off.

Raven whispered, "Adam…"

"I know, baby. It won't be long. Hold my shoulders and step into the bottoms."

He pulled up a short skirt of sorts. Soft. And it had a lot of moving parts. Fringe? But there was nothing underneath it. And no top. His kiss found her then. Hot.

Once. Twice. Three times.

Voice tight with passion, he said, "I'll be dressed in a second."

She heard his sandals hit the floor. His pants.

After a little rustling, Adam said, "I'm going to carry you outside but keep your eyes closed. I promise, you'll know when to look."

In a second, she was in his arms. She felt the duffel bag on his shoulder and heard his soft footsteps as he walked barefoot through the house. He opened a sliding door and stepped outside.

It smelled different as he walked. Smoke. Then she heard it. Fire. She opened her eyes and met his. He lowered her.

She looked at him dressed in nothing but a fringed leather loincloth, and a look hotter than the fire. And she could imagine him hundreds of years ago just like this. She touched his hard stomach. Then the edge of his loincloth. His nostrils flared.

She looked down at herself, naked except for a matching loincloth. He touched her breast. Slid his hand down her stomach to tease at the top of her loincloth. He wedged a knee between her legs. Proclaiming she was his without words.

And Raven felt the beat begin deep inside her. Generations old. The fire. The warrior. The drum. The dance.

Adam reached into the duffel bag and held out her drum. Surprised, she reached for it. She hadn't played since the day she reached Louisiana. Dakota and Sean had danced that day with Lance. But Adam had been in Brazil. She had never played for him. Till now.

Sitting on a stool with the drum between her knees, she watched him near the fire. She began to play, and the native beat filled the night. She kept her eyes on him as he danced for her. He stomped in perfect rhythm. Spun. Jumped. And mimicked the battle around the flames.

And before long, his beautiful body glistened as his eyes watched hers over the fire. His passion was raging. Black hair flying. His muscles hard, his warrior movements bold and direct. And then he began to encircle her with each pass around the fire. He touched her. Brushed his loincloth against her, leaving sweat and fire behind. He licked her.

Raven tried to keep playing for him, but her body ached. Throbbed. And before long, she threw the drum aside and jumped up. Wild. Adam met her blazing gaze and smiled. That was the look he wanted.

He reached for his phone in the bag. And glancing at her, he hit play. The sound of her drumbeats continued to play. He had recorded her. Motioning her to the fire, he began to dance again, and she danced alongside him. Two warriors. Two lovers. Around the fire.

She matched his dance movements for a while. Red hair flying. Gorgeous. Powerful. Till her own dance came through. More sensual. Feminine. Alluring. Working her hips faster and faster as she backed away.

With a growl, Adam reached for her. But she darted around the fire. He smiled and darted to catch her, but she bolted in the opposite direction. Their gazes locked. He dropped his loincloth. She dropped hers.

And without warning, he ran. And jumped the fire. She stared, shocked at the magnificent image of him over the flames.

He landed in front of her, hungry like a wolf. She jumped. He caught her…and took her…as their cries of pleasure echoed across the island.

Across the ocean.

To the stars.

The End

Other books
by Patti Corbello Archer

Debut Novel

Double Target

Louisiana Secrets: Series

Bloodline - Book One

Obsession – Book Two

Killer Dance – Book Three

Book Four pending fall 2024

About the Author

Patti was born and raised in Lake Charles, Louisiana, surrounded by lakes, rivers, and bayous. Only thirty miles from the Gulf of Mexico and thirty-five miles to Texas. Which means, she loves the Cajun culture and cuisine, seafood, and steak!

Her days include family, faith, research, and writing. Including relaxing in the pool, taking road trips, and imagining and plotting stories. She loves holiday activities, nature, movies, oldies music and dreams of living in the mountains.

In addition to writing, Patti also creates all her book covers and marketing videos. And does book signings at several local markets for face-to-face time with her readers.

Her debut novel was published in June 2022 and her fifth novel is pending publication in fall 2024.

You can follow her blog at PattiArcher.com.
Her author page is at amazon.com/author/patticorbelloarcher.cajunlady.
And you can find her on most social media.

If you enjoyed the story and encourage others to read it, please leave a review on Amazon. Simply go on Amazon – search Patti Corbello Archer – and all her published books will populate. If you click on the book you have read, then scroll to the bottom, there is a place for you to enter your review.

She would love to know! Thank you!

www.ingramcontent.com/pod-product-compliance
Lightning Source LLC
Chambersburg PA
CBHW030958260626
47169CB00002B/590